T0208596

Bread of Shame

Bread of Shame

Marjorie Meyerle

iUniverse books may be ordered through booksellers or by contacting:

iUniverse
1663 Liberty Drive
Bloomington, IN 47403
www.iuniverse.com
1-800-Authors (1-800-288-4677)

ISBN: 978-1-4401-4957-3 (sc)
ISBN: 978-1-4401-4956-6 (e)

Print information available on the last page.

iUniverse rev. date: 08/26/2015

To Michael and the other men in my life, Jon, Jerry and Jim

Prologue

He awoke to blackness so complete he couldn't see his hands stretched out before him. The walls held his stifled sobs. The taste of bile rose in his throat — bitter and terrible — yet he refused to allow the sensation to control his thoughts. His face was hot, his mouth dry and scorched. His head echoed the violent hammering in his chest. An intelligent man, he might have thought he was having a heart attack or stroke, if it weren't for the certainty of what he'd done. A man of many lapses, he realized that this could be the one that killed him. He'd always known the day would come when memory yielded to that dark remnant of his past which he could never rectify and which now sounded through clenched lips — banal and terrible even to him. He'd known it would come to this, but he'd persisted living the lie till it swallowed him up and left him for dead. He'd been finished for a long time, he realized, in a paroxysm of fear and regret.

He pulled himself up on all fours and like an animal unsure of the territory, tentatively moved in what he hoped was a path to somewhere – the bathroom perhaps or a place with light. He didn't know where he was, just that he was very sick, possibly dying.

He thought of Ann, their son, his work — all the responsibilities left undone; and with that honest acknowledgement, the purest grief passed through him. How had his life come down to this, and to what purpose? Did the past so irrevocably claim one's destiny, or could he have evolved beyond his dark center with someone's help and his own submission to a truth, any truth that would free him? After all, he'd spent his whole life in the search for truth. Couldn't he be ransomed for that reason alone? No, he decided, life was not that simple, even if some felt it was.

Beyond him (down a hall or across a room?) there was a shaft of light as if from beneath a closed door. Still on all fours, he heaved his unwilling body toward it. He felt small rocks, debris, pieces of food under his open palms. The stench of toxic substances hovered on the cold, unventilated air. His esophagus swelled and retched the unsettled contents of his stomach and liver. Dizzy and weak limbed, he doggedly tracked his body through it. There were sounds coming from behind a door at the end of the hall where a dim light stretched in a thin, unearthly glow. Trudging forward, he saw a patch of carpet then a closed door. With enormous effort, he pulled himself up and leaned against the wood, turning the knob. He pushed the door open into a vortex of hard rock music blaring from a television in the corner.

Beside a rumpled, dirty bed, a woman lay sprawled on worn gray carpeting. A nightlight in a socket near the floor affixed its pallid gleam upon a collection of drug paraphernalia. The woman's eyes were closed, black dreadlocks covering her face.

He staggered toward the light. "Yvonne?" he cried. "Oh, God!"

He patted the side of her face, felt the coolness of her forehead. He leaned down and listened to her chest. He could feel her breath on his face, hear the faint churning of her heart. He smelled the odor of unwashed hair, the reek of garlic and sweat. The miasma of similar memories washed over him in a tide of self-recrimination. What was the use? After all his efforts to make a difference in the world, it had come down to this. He lay back on the woman's stomach and gazed at the cracked ceiling, at the spiders lodged in the grimy corners, the water stains leaching through lead paint. He had never felt so alone. He reminded himself that he'd always been alone, would always be. For some there was the sweet justice of human companionship and love; for him it was not to be. Aloneness was his lot, the legacy of all those who fled self-knowledge and grace.

Sick as he was, he knew now was not the time for self-pity.

Something wet seeped down his face. He touched his nose, bringing back a wash of warm blood. It had turned his vision of the meager light crimson. He felt the slithery essence spill from his eyes, his lips and over his chin. He choked as some retreated down his throat and gagged him. Gasping for breath, he sat up and watched in horror as it spurted out of him in a huge, scarlet arc, spraying the yellowed sheets.

This is it, he thought: what man lives and dies for.

He closed his eyes and lay down to sleep, opening his arms around his knees, strangely stoic, while his curiosity drew him onward into the biggest mystery of all.

From far away, in quite another dream, he saw a woman, her arms reaching out to him, her eyes closed in prayer. She stood on a hill before a whited sepulcher. As if summoning a flock of wayward sheep, she drew him and others across a vast plain into a fire-lit circle of something beyond yesterday and now. He concentrated hard on her words moving mysteriously through his altered consciousness and then added to those — so eloquent, so wise — his own ignorant mutterings, as if his heart-felt plea could possibly arouse mercy from any entity out there.

Remember me...

Chapter One

The night was cold. The fire had gone out. Around the room, shadows moved in tandem with the brittle branches blowing against the house. From the west, bursts of icy rain blasted the roof. Jack could feel the storm's fury thump in his heart as he watched the cascade snake down the driveway to the road below. Karen had died in the deep chill of such an autumn. Bundled in the bed upstairs, they'd listened to the same cacophony of ice and water as the rain turned to snow, and her time ran out. She'd left the place to him, imprisoning him as surely as his ex-wives had before her. Broke, he'd had no place to go. So he'd stayed on in the little house. Stayed on in the boring town of perpetual snow and limited people. Another of his mistakes, he admitted now. Miranda would have called it a failure of courage. But what did Miranda know?

When he'd first seen Leadville — the white on white of snow and ice and silly Victorian homes in pink and blue and yellow — he'd thought it a nice place for anyone else but him. Yet he'd remained, cellophaned by Karen's generosity of spirit, her rousy laugh that teased him out of his brooding. She'd been gone a year, and he still dreaded the nights. Nights that tasted like the ash that blew from the fireplace insert. Ash flew on the drafts from the gaping casements. It burst from flames smothered in the cold flue, barely able to breathe in the creosoted chimney

He stared at the computer screen. It bothered him to think that had Karen lived, she'd have seen him for what he was: a washed up author with nothing to write about but sad memories and dead relationships. They had talked about his writing an uplifting book, a sort of Clyde Edgerton, user-friendly novel about the simple life.

Such was love, when you wrote to please... He could not have written her kind of book because unlike her he was not positive; instead his was a wary vision. Besides, these days he had nothing to say. His one consolation was that through the ordeal of her dying, he'd somehow kept her love. It had been a miracle and not one he was likely to minimize, whatever the future held. There had been a time when Karen's steady eyes on him aroused a purity of purpose of which he would not have thought himself capable. He now realized it was unconditional love, something he had never experienced before Karen. Acknowledging that gift of hers only made him more miserable. He wasn't naive enough to believe love could happen to him again, not with his track record. Had Karen lived, she might have found him unacceptable, like the others.

The rain fell harder. It splashed the windows like someone angry. It pounded the roof in a deafening roar. From the gutters huge, glistening streams spilled onto the battered hedges. Jack shut down the computer and walked to the front window. Below, the road was invisible beneath the heavy canopy of trees and the impenetrable darkness.

He had never felt so alone.

It was autumn. The time of year he most hated, that early grave of a season when the leaves fell and the dreams dried up. When it was cold but not cold enough. There was no moon tonight, just a fury of breaking clouds and lashing wind. He couldn't write with this compounding of the elements, so why try?

As his eyes finally engaged the darkness in the canyon below, he could make out the uprooted pines, flung in disarray against the hillside. He couldn't see the hairpin turns, but he could feel the house shudder. Shadows shifted against the living room wall like fighters in the ring, incongruously throwing their vast weights against each other. Lightening split the sky. Trees bent into the rock and dirt. He couldn't hear himself think in the chaos. He'd thought he could write tonight. He'd felt that momentary surge of inspiration he hadn't experienced since Karen died, since... To his surprise he was crying. He brushed away the stream and cursed himself for his sentimentality. He was getting old when memory yielded to womanish feeling.

He walked into the kitchen and poured himself a Jim Beam. He drank it straight and felt its burning warmth in his mouth and throat. He imagined what he must look like to any one of his four ex-wives. In a flash, he realized the futility of his vocation. He might have used his imagination to make his real life work rather than dwell in fantastic worlds of his own creation. He wondered if other writers felt thus diminished by such a misplaced emphasis

When he finished his drink, he started up the fire again and waited till it caught. He brought in more wood from the porch and turned on the copper lamp in the corner. It was still dark in the house, but now the shadows seemed endowed with a beneficence he could accept — all part of the somber and confusing yet somehow consoling past. He could imagine Karen's body beside him, the smell of her cooking and the curious way she splayed her feet when she walked. Hardly a beauty but solid and indomitable, or at least, so he thought till the lump in her breast leached her sassiness, her humor and her childlike curiosity. He was surprised how much he missed her. He thought he'd tire of her like he did the rest, or she of him. But then again, maybe she simply died before one of them decided to leave. He wasn't sure what it had all been about now. Untimely deaths obscured the truth, he decided, feeling vaguely disloyal.

Another thunderclap shook the house and then an eerie brightness bathed the living room before extinguishing the copper light and throwing the house into a blackness so complete he could see nothing for several seconds. He could hear his breathing over the pounding rain, an anxious sound like cloth tearing. Then beyond the terrible clamor of the elements, as if from another planet, he heard the sound of a car motor. He turned to the window and stared down into the blackness.

A white SUV moved inexorably up the hill, its lights on high beam, sweeping the dark terrain in a yellow blaze. As he watched, it lurched, slowed, bounded forward, stopped, and then erratically proceeded up the steep road, around the turns, up and up to the lonely driveway in the thick mantle of trees below the house.

The car stopped, and a person climbed out. The figure struggled with a large umbrella and peered upward at the house against the hillside, where Jack watched back from the anonymity of the unlit window. The person might see a shadow, but probably whoever it was saw nothing. He wondered who it could be.

He heard feet stamping up the flagstones by the side of the house, the unceasing roar of the wind and rain. Fists pounded his door. Pounded and pounded, insistent. He waited then opened the door.

A figure in a voluminous cloak stepped backward into the rain-splattered darkness beyond the porch covering. The wind howled from deep in the trees, blowing the black cloak flat against a slender body. Jack stepped forward, taking the visitor's hand and pulling her into the room. As he did so, she collapsed the umbrella and threw it aside. It rested in the corner by the door, spilling a river of water across the pine flooring.

"Jack?"

He barely recognized the woman's voice. It had been a long time. She peeled back the black hood and her white mane of tangled hair leapt out at him. She looked like a ghost with her pale face and wide eyes, the grizzled, electrified hair.

"Miranda?"

She stepped out of the shadows, and he saw her clearly — the familiar whited complexion, the strange, pale eyes of an albino, the colorless hair that stood out from her face in a thick frizz – chaotic, full, wild – like the damaged trees and disordered air of the outside landscape. Over them the thunder rolled, the rain poured. He could hardly hear her gasp his name.

She untied the cloak and the rain ran down her legs and pooled around her feet. She tried to smile, but her extraordinary eyes were confused and frightened. He was reminded of her sermons in the tiny Texas town revivals, the ineffable call to action her words invariably summoned. He'd been cowed by her rhetoric, by her sheer presence, whether on stage or in his arms. She'd been too much; he couldn't deal with the enormity of her personality. Now he found himself curiously protective of her, as if for once her strength had been quelled.

He reached out to comfort her, as one would a frightened child. But she flashed before him in the glare of a lightning strike. She seemed to loom over him in the distance between them, her shoulders straight, the wan face clenched with purpose. Her eyes reflected the light — eerie and intense as she had always been.

"I tried to phone, but there was no listing. Even Information—" She sounded angry.

"I let the phone go. It didn't seem important."

"You don't make things easy."

"It's not like I was expecting you," he said, feeling his irritation rise. The set of her face in the meager light recalled the superiority always implicit in her manner. "Why are you here, anyway?"

"You don't have to get mad." She dismissed his annoyance as one would the actions of a spoiled child. "I'm here to ask a favor. Something you must do for me. For both of us, actually." She had not moved. Her eyes remained riveted on him — accusatory, dominant.

"Do you realize what time it is?"

"Yes," she said wearily. "I've been on the road for days. All those dreary Texas towns."

It crossed Jack's mind that Miranda had finally gone over the edge. High strung from time to time, she now seemed borderline crazy. Their mutual friends had thought her at the least eccentric, possibly mad. There'd always been stories and Jack knew how capable of bizarre behavior she truly was. But then she was a poet, so it was natural that she would be unusual. He hadn't considered her pathological, just weird and quite interesting. Sometimes fascinating, actually. And despite her coloring, Miranda was beautiful in an exotic, ethereal way. Somehow her strange features congealed into an alluring, complex presence that had never ceased to arouse his imagination.

"How's the writing coming?" she asked.

"The same. Blocked lately, but I've been there before."

"No freelance?"

"Not at the moment." He looked down, feeling the familiar sense of failure any discussion of his writing presented.

"You know you can write well. You did it once. You can do it again."

"You may be the only person who doesn't think that first book was a fluke. After all, I haven't exactly torn up the pea patch since."

She gazed at him as she had in years past – a searching, astute glance that seemed to pierce his defenses. "Your book was magnificent, and you know it."

She leaned against the doorframe and looked around. Even in the darkness her presence moved him. She was so utterly feminine in the gauzy reflection of her skin and slender body against the pressing, shadowy dearth of light. He thought of peace marches, late nights of passing pipes on the Arizona desert, the bangle earrings and absence of makeup that defined the times then. Such a long time ago. Such an idealistic time. She'd been a faith healer; he presumed she still was. She'd been good at it, too.

"If my book was so terrific, why is it out of print?" he pressed.

"Shit happens. That doesn't mean you give up." She rummaged in her skirt pocket and drew out a pack of cigarettes. Still standing before the doorframe, she lit her cigarette with a butane lighter. She inhaled then blew a ghostly cloud into the air. "I've told you, you keep running from yourself," she murmured. "Closing doors. Using your writing as a shield against living... Writing about things that don't matter. You need to write about something important."

"As if I don't try." His feelings of attraction were giving way to annoyance. Her supercilious air had always irritated him. He resented the ease with which she composed her poetry. For him writing was always hard.

She leaned toward him. "When was the last time you felt anything, I mean really *felt*?" She tapped her heart area in a clichéd effort to make her point.

"You think I'm shallow? You know better than that."

"On the contrary, perhaps your depth keeps you from tackling the tough subjects."

"Meaning?"

"Fear," she said. "I mean you've always avoided difficult relationships, you know, the *real* challenges."

Suddenly he wished she would leave. Miranda surely knew he hadn't married her precisely because she was too complicated. At least she couldn't say he didn't know himself. Yet watching her laser eyes penetrate his own defenses, he struggled, as he had so many times before in her presence, to justify his life. Behind her the copper light flickered and went out. As he started toward the kitchen, it came back on. "So you're saying I've made the same mistakes in my writing I did in my life?" he asked.

"How can you write with passion when you avoid emotion?" To his amazement her eyes brimmed, and a compassionate smile softened her face.

"As a matter of fact, I sort of broke down this evening. So I must feel strongly about some things. Don't we all?" he muttered, impatient with her and his own inability to communicate without self-pity. "Anyway, what do you know? You have this predictable life, enough money to live on. Stability."

"You've always underestimated the challenges of my situation," she said quietly. "If you weren't so self-absorbed, you'd realize others have problems, some more paralyzing than yours." She looked over her cigarette at the pale sheen from the copper light. "It's just that some of us have learned how to balance the various aspects of our lives."

He didn't know what to say. She invariably outsmarted him. It bothered him how words came so easily for her. He begrudged her seeming effortless grasp of the timeless verities. More than that, he envied her apparent ability to live by them. Women, it seemed, were able to indulge an intuitive leaning that cleared them of the necessity to be rational. For him, such a manner of living would be dangerous.

He guarded his emotions, for to give them free rein had been the cause of past mistakes. Or so he reasoned.

"So why did you cry?" she asked.

"What difference does it make? I don't see where emotional expression is a condition for good writing."

"You wouldn't," she said, in a contemptuous tone.

They stood in silence, she breathing in and exhaling talons of smoke, he looking down into the splintered flooring as if it lodged a solution to his indescribable yearning for order and justice. Perhaps Miranda was right, but he was who he was and he probably couldn't change, even if he wanted to.

"It's a cocoon of your own making, you know?" She glanced around the room at the spare furnishings, the absence of material objects, the bare, worn floorboards. Her eyes came to rest on the computer in the shadows. "A sort of denial."

She had on a magenta top. It folded loosely over her small breasts that rose and fell in the darkness. She had always exuded a heightened sensuality, but at the moment he was more curious than sexual, too depressed to extend himself. "I did cry," he said, embarrassed but moved in the direction of truth. "For Karen, I think." He was surprised to feel the stream slide down his face again, but he refused to wipe it away.

"Good," she said. "Then maybe you're ready at last."

"You think?" he said, in spite of himself. He knew what she meant.

The familiar, knowing smile greeted him like a long, lost friend. He relaxed into it, feeling an intense gratitude. He found himself smiling back.

Miranda's guarded eyes softened. "I need a place to stay tonight." She touched him softly on the shoulder.

He felt himself warm under this vague sense of support or familiarity or whatever it was. He nodded. "Of course."

She walked past him into the little kitchen and turned on the water. They both watched as she doused her cigarette and tossed it in the garbage. "I'm going to give this up," she said, grimacing. "But first I need to get some sleep." She kissed him on the cheek. He felt the tears well up again and turned away from her.

"We'll talk later," she said, starting up the stairs.

"Why later?" he asked. "Why not now?" He was baffled. Their last meeting had been unpleasant, and she had left angry. He hadn't expected to see her again, but then Miranda had a way of popping up in his life when he least expected it. Either she was passing through, or he was curious about her and called. He'd phoned more than once in the final months of Karen's illness. While they seemed to infuriate each other, they patched up their differences and went on, not seeing each other for years, and then suddenly they were in touch. Like two estranged siblings, they maintained a tenuous relationship.

"You risked your life driving up here in this storm. What's it all about?" he pressed. He saw the dark places under her eyes, her unsteady, tentative step on the stair, and yet he had to know what had brought her here. Miranda was not one to act on whims.

The light was dim, but he could see her eyes darken to an opaque blandness. He'd seen her this way before, and it unnerved him, but he told himself to wait. He felt a sense of urgency, as if time were fast-forwarding, and he needed to chase down something important before everything disappeared. He gripped the railing and waited while his heart pounded over the rain and the wind howling in the canyons below.

"I'm just so tired," she said, turning to look him full in the face. "It seemed important I get here right away, and now I'm too exhausted to talk. There's a lot to say, and I need to do it right." She looked frightened and confused, as she had when she stepped away from him on the front porch into the pouring rain. Once again, he felt protective of her; he didn't want to make things worse. Jack knew from experience that Miranda didn't ask for favors. She didn't resort to ploys. Whatever had prompted the visit was important or she wouldn't have risked her safety. Moreover, after their last disastrous reunion, she would not have wanted to lose face with Jack, who alone could arouse her old insecurities.

"My head's throbbing," she said, looking around her as if in an unfamiliar place. Her clouded eyes surveyed the walls and outside landscape without focus.

"Stop it!" he said. "Look at me."

"I am," she said. "Only I can't see you." She drew back as if she expected to be slapped.

"What are you talking about?" he said. "What do you mean you can't see me? I'm right here, Miranda. Right next to you. *Earth-to-Miranda....?*" He chanted as he had in times past when her weirdness overwhelmed him.

"I can only see *him*," she said, looking down.

"Who?"

"Professor Theodore Hudson. The reason I'm here."

"Okay, that does it. You either tell me what this is all about or I take you into town and put you up in a hotel." Jack told himself this was not going to be one of those times when Miranda jacked him around. He was going to know straight up what the visit was all about. That way, he reasoned, she wouldn't trick him into doing something that was not in his best interests, as she had on many occasions in the past. He could so easily be duped, he knew. But not this time.

"Give me a couple of hours," she said faintly. "Then I'll tell you everything. I'm just so tired."

"All right, it's a deal. You go on up to the extra room, and I'll wake you in two hours." He left her at the base of the stairway, annoyed for the thousandth time in their relationship. Whether she meant it or not, things usually ended up on her terms. These days he wasn't in the mood for one of Miranda's hare brained schemes. He'd had plenty of opportunity for that kind of thing since Karen's death. These days he had a sense of his own mortality, and only the essentials mattered. They were no longer kids chasing chimeras, enfolding themselves in a sixties time warp, oblivious to a world that went on without them, leaving them behind in their self-imposed prisons. He'd lived long enough to regret those years.

"You aren't going to bed?"

"I'll have a drink, watch television. Then we'll talk."

"Still don't trust me?" she asked.

He thought for a moment. He didn't know what to say. On the one hand he trusted her above anyone he knew, but then again, he didn't trust himself in relation to her. She could get him going, and he wasn't sure he could allow himself that indulgence right now. He had no money, no prospects, just a dreary stretch of Leadville cold, plenty of stacked wood for the winter, and the hope that his talent would not forsake him. He told himself he needed solitude to write and uncomplicated emotions, something impossible with Miranda in the picture. She was a genius at arousing him from lethargy, but after she disappeared from his life once more, he would be left with the same sense of failure and regret. He needed to write, and that was all he needed. He could not allow her to intrude on his imagination.

"I trust you," he said sincerely. He sighed. There wasn't anything else he could say. He tried to see beyond her blank stare to the essence of the woman, but he couldn't find her. "Sometimes I know you, sometimes I don't," he said.

"I understand." She paused for a moment then started up the stairs. He watched her slowly mount the steep staircase. He noted her heavy step, the sense of utter weariness and immediately regretted his own impatience.

"Gosh, Miranda, I'm sorry," he said in spite of himself.

"Don't worry, Jack. I know what you're thinking, but you'll understand when I get my chance to explain." Her voice was heavy and dull, so unlike her except when she was in the grip of an obsession, one that confused her but that she was powerless to resist. He'd been there before. He understood that she needed time to get herself together, but he resented the temerity that prompted her presence in his house in the first place. She seemed to have no fear of consequences.

He walked back into the living room. Around him the shadows formed a cozy presence. He poured himself a drink and turned on the television. Below him the wind still howled and the canyon had begun to fill up with snow. He threw more wood on the fire and sat down in the sofa. The woman was crazy, he told himself. He would humor her and then she would leave, reasoned out of her dubious mission and set straight.

He couldn't help but wonder what scheme she had in mind this time.

Chapter Two

He didn't hear her come down the stairs. The wind had died down. The flickering television brightness blended with the moonlight and pale sheen of the outside landscape. The snow had stopped and settled into a thick blanket deep in the canyon and across the mountainsides. He shivered. The room was cold and the ice in his drink had melted, leaving an amber inch or two of booze. He reached for the glass just as Miranda walked into the room.

She had on his bathrobe, and her feet were bare on the cold floorboards. For a moment he was annoyed at her audacity to have sought out his robe, but then he remembered he'd left it in the guest room, having used that shower recently after hanging his wet jeans to dry in his own. Miranda's proprietarial tendencies aside, he would have resented her going into the room he'd shared with Karen. He sighed deeply, finishing off the last of the whiskey. He hadn't always felt that way; in the past he'd been amused by Miranda's boldness, her seeming unawareness of personal boundaries, but now he found it distasteful and vulgar for one her age to be so presumptuous. Time had taught him not to take anything for granted, and he resented those who operated with a sense of entitlement.

"Do you do that often?" she asked with a concerned expression.

"Do I do what?" he asked, looking up at Miranda. Her hair was wet, her face very pale without her customary makeup, the violet eyes receding into the shiny glow of her unlined complexion. He had to admit that time had been kind to her or perhaps it had been her life choices that preserved the spirit of the face he still recalled with nostalgia. She had always been so unusual and in their time together then, she'd defined the times with a spontaneity he'd never experienced in a woman since. He realized much of this had to do with the fact that he left her; had she left him he might have felt the bitterness he still reserved for his ex-wives, all of which had turned on him when he needed them the most.

"You sighed so deeply just now," she said, frowning. "I did that when I was depressed."

"*You* depressed?" he asked. "You're always so *up*. Since when were you depressed?"

"*My* secret." She laughed and tossed her wet hair. He felt water drops alight on his face and arms. Standing over him, she appeared much taller than she really was. Larger than life, like she seemed when she preached before the crowds of the lonely and confused that were her clientele in the shabby west Texas church. Poor wounded birds, the disenfranchised, the tremulous, the fearful… They warmed to her voice, the sense of confidence she exuded, even her openness to the other side, which so many others in her position ignored. She was a seeker, and in her unique capacity as guide, surrogate mother, sister, daughter or whatever, was admired by the ragtag parishioners she cultivated. She was their miracle, their own discovery, a quaint and eccentric angel.

Jack knew this from experience. He'd marveled at the hold her words seemed to have on them yet she'd appeared oblivious of her unique powers. "It's just the *Word* itself that inspires them," she'd say when he'd remark on the rare blend of magnetism and intellectuality her sermons expressed. He never told her that in his judgment she spoke in the self-assured voice of a prophet nor did he mention that there were times she frightened him with her understanding. On occasion, he'd felt his flesh move as the layers of her insight constructed for all of them in the rapt congregation a pyramid that was both epiphany and dead-end. Such was the nature of an elusive mind, but one capable of much beyond ordinary reasoning. She scared him. Yes, she did.

"Nevertheless, I can't imagine you without a certain buoyancy, an *élan vital*. You depressed? I don't believe it."

She sat down beside him on the old worn sofa and leaned her head on his shoulder, like the old times – not a romantic gesture, but a cherished one, borne of a million memories. He could smell the citrus scent of Karen's shampoo, and his stomach involuntarily tightened against the remembered intimacy. He moved his arm to rest above Miranda's shoulders, grateful for her trust and affection. In the scheme of things, she was his oldest, and now that Karen was gone, perhaps his dearest friend.

"It happened after you left," she said, not looking up at him. For the moment, her voice sounded flat, and then he could imagine her depressed, although this was the first time he'd experienced any sign of it.

He thought for a moment. Surely her depression hadn't been because of him, he reasoned. He'd left because their relationship didn't seem to be going anywhere. She'd been as discontented as he. They'd talked about the inevitable dampening of emotion all long-term relationships entailed. Both had been at loose ends, he wanting to be alone to write, she ready to explore the "mysteries" he debunked in his ongoing battle of trying to impart a sense of rationality to his loopy lover. In those days, she'd been his definition of a flake: albeit an intelligent one, but still one of those women who attuned themselves to the emotional and invisible worlds more than examining what he considered to be the real world. It made a difference to him which reality she embraced because at that time he felt he needed someone solid and stable. He laughed to remember that. Then along came Felicia. Concrete, yes. *Solid and stable?* Hardly. Married to Felicia, he'd missed the unpredictability, the vast creativity of the mind that was Miranda's. Still, as the years went on, he'd made peace with the fact that theirs would have been a disastrous marriage. They simply weren't suited to be anything more than friends.

"What happened?" he asked.

"I can't explain it well," she said, holding the flap of the robe close to her neck. Her hands against the washed-out velour were nearly as gray, her face bloodless and uncertain. "It wasn't like I wanted us to stay together, but the break was hard nevertheless. A part of me was lost, and I didn't know what to do."

"You could have fooled me," he said, staring into her eyes to see if she was being straight with him. In his mind, she'd been tired of him. It had seemed she was always on his case. He still suspected it was her discontent that drove him into Felicia's arms.

As if reading his mind – she had always done that – she said, "I was a good sport, that's for sure. What else could I have done? You loved Felicia. I wanted you to be happy, Jack."

"You and Felicia were friends. I thought you approved."

"I suppose I did because that's what you wanted."

Jack felt a dull ache in his chest. To think he left Miranda when perhaps she'd still cared for him. It hadn't seemed that way at all in those times of ephemeral relationships, but had they merely postponed the breakup, he was certain he could have weathered the years with

Miranda. Now, however, he mused that too much water had passed under the bridge. They had gone their separate ways and grown into different people from the young idealists they'd been then. For some reason, he thought of Karen's withered breast, the sad shading of the truth there. You can't go home again, he reminded himself, as he had so many times before. And besides, there was no point in looking back. The present slid by so fast; it was best to forget the past and its many regrets. "If I hurt you..."

"Don't apologize," she murmured, not looking at him. "Our breaking up was for the best, I know that now."

"Not for me, it wasn't," he said, squelching a laugh. "You know yourself what a balls breaker Felicia was!"

Miranda's face relaxed into a smile. She'd always been beautiful when she smiled, as if she opened herself up entirely to the vast and beneficent universe. She used to remind him of a heroine in an existential novel, the antithesis of Camus' tortured protagonist: caring, emotional and possessed of an ardent innocence. As she had with Jack, she was capable of arousing one to his life's purpose. It was she who'd inspired his novel, she who'd first recognized his talent. Yet it was Miranda's scorn that finally drove him away. Her imperious observations had made him feel inadequate. He'd enjoyed feeling important that one time in his life when the world seemed to be his oyster, when he was published, rich, handsome, well spoken. Those were the qualities Felicia admired, and they were the goals he sought then. He shuddered to recall that at the time, he'd felt he was growing beyond Miranda. That her girlish ways lacked the sophistication of others with whom he associated, members of Felicia's circle – all rich, entitled, attractive... Even Miranda's wholesomeness had seemed common and somehow suspect. He realized now the absurdity of that attitude.

"I wasn't easy to be around in those days," she admitted. "You a rising star and me just coasting. Along for the ride..."

"We were all along for the ride in those days," he countered. "I got derailed, that's all."

She looked at him quizzically. "How so?"

"I was too full of myself. You were right to give me a bad time. I let my success go to my head."

"Yeah," she agreed, bowing her head into his shoulder again and looking out at the frosted hills against the illuminated sky. A silver circle of light showed through the precipitation. "Full moon."

He nodded, remembering how they'd made a celebration of that moon every 24 days, if it were visible. The skies in Arizona were the clearest he'd ever seen till Leadville. "We were just kids in those days. Kids make a lot of mistakes."

"We expected so much of each other."

"Speak for yourself," he said. "I thought you were great just the way you were."

"Maybe it was about my possessiveness," she said, "but you were moving in fast circles, away from me."

"I was foolish to let you go," he said, still looking out the window at the moon over the trees.

"We could have been quite the team. I wouldn't have let you give up on yourself."

"What makes you think I have?" he asked.

"What you've said over the years, that's all."

"I write all the time," he reminded her. "I just haven't locked on the perfect vehicle, that's all. Don't give up on me, I may just surprise you."

"Well," she said, standing, towering over his body sprawled on the low sofa. She seemed to melt into the vast outside whiteness. "That's why I'm here!" Across the valley the trees weighted with snow stood like obedient soldiers against the hillside.

"With some new scheme, no doubt," he said, almost laughing in spite of himself.

"Be serious," she said. "I have a great idea. It suits your talents and your uh…uh… superior grasp of human nature, not to mention your appreciation for those of our, shall we say, unique generation?"

"Boomers," he said. "Such a simplistic label for a diverse group."

"You got that one right. Remember Don Parrish?"

"That pothead? Always lurking around, waiting for me to leave so he could have you to himself. Dead by now would be my guess. He went to Nam, didn't he?"

"He heads up Merton."

"The oil company in Dallas?"

She nodded. "We're friends," she said quietly.

Jack felt himself flinch. "Not close, I hope. He was a creep then; I'm sure he's a creep now." Jack felt like punching the guy who'd freeloaded off them for a year before going to Viet Nam." One night he was simply gone, their old air mattress cleared off and settled squarely against the dining room wall. He'd left a note for Miranda, which come to think of it, she'd never shared with Jack.

"How long has that been going on?"

"Since you left," she said, utterly surprising him. In all those years she'd never mentioned Don Parrish. Jack and she had been in touch. She'd called; he'd called. There had been her fantastic proposals, and in all that time she never mentioned the guy. Jack felt betrayed but didn't know why. It was her life, her choices so why the clutch deep in his stomach? He sipped the empty glass of Jim Beam.

"So why did you come?" he asked, hearing the coldness in his voice. She could rile him faster than anyone. "What's your plan this time?" He knew he sounded rude, but he didn't care. Damned woman. Her haughty manner annoyed him, her tendency to put him off guard and deliver the quick, silent blow to his self-esteem. She held power over him, and she knew it. It always came down to this: his needing to gain her approval and her cold, hard terms.

"I just wanted you to know about him," she said softly, clearly wounded. "He lost an arm, you know. I admire him."

"For what?" Jack exploded. "Because he lost an arm in an inane war? The very war he denounced. Why the hell did he go in the first place? His daddy was rich. He had a law degree."

"Some things you just never understood," she said, still leaning against the window, absorbed in the silent scene below.

"Yeah, right," Jack said. "Like talking out of both sides of your mouth! The guy led the peace marches, for Christ's sake!"

"And then he changed," Miranda said, turning from the window, her ghostly pallor part of the strange nocturnal landscape. Her eyes caught the light from the window as she stared in his direction.

Jack wanted to get up and go to bed, but he forced himself to remain rooted to the sofa. *Let her tell her story*, he thought, remembering a conversation he'd had with Don Parrish weeks before he'd left. Don had said Jack took Miranda for granted. That had angered Jack so much he'd refused to speak to the jerk. He recalled the awkward silences in the evenings after that. Then Parrish left, and Jack had been glad. He'd never thought of the guy since.

"He's very good to me," she said. "I love him for his decency, his honor, his honesty." Even in the darkness Jack could see a flush spread across her throat, like it used to when she had to speak before a large group. He was reminded of her defense of Don Parrish even then, and it annoyed him.

"I'm glad for you, Miranda," he said. "That you have a decent, honest, predictable man who appreciates you."

"He is," she said. "And he does." There was sarcasm in her voice, too, he realized, and for a moment he hated her more than Don Parrish.

"So what's he up to these days besides making money? I thought he wanted to help the poor, that he wasn't interested in possessions. That his fancy Ivy League education was intended to right the injustices of an imperialistic society? Isn't that what he said then? Geesh, Miranda. What a hypocrite!"

"People change," she said. "He did Nam. He came back a different person."

"So how could war change you that way?"

"Maybe he forgot what he was before. Maybe he realized that in the end there's no one else but yourself. Maybe he just wanted to take care of his family. I don't know," she said. "I don't really care. He's good and kind and responsible, and that's what I want at this point in my life."

"And what you've secretly wanted for years, it seems," Jack said, petulantly.

"He was married for a long time," she said. "We've only been together a while now."

Well, good for you," Jack said sourly. "Now can we get to the purpose of this visit?

"Please, Jack, try to understand. He isn't a loser, and I want you two to be friends."

"Don't hold your breath," Jack snapped. "Because it ain't going to happen. "I don't like people who speak with forked tongues."

He thought for a minute, remembering vague telephone conversations, a certain wariness on her part. "So I suppose you had a long affair while the man was still married?" Jack said, feeling his anger rise from deep in the pit of his stomach. He was unexpectedly very hungry and started toward the kitchen.

"I did," she admitted. "That's why you never knew — I couldn't tell you — but now he's divorced, and we plan a life together. In Dallas."

Suddenly it seemed too much. Miranda in Dallas, schmoozing with the social set. He imagined she could pull it off, but he resented her betrayal of the values he thought they still shared. He thought of Felicia; he knew the kind of people who'd occupy Miranda's sphere in Dallas. People beneath her in terms of substance. People who would hurt her. Who wouldn't appreciate her depth. He felt abandoned again. She had this effect on Jack, and he didn't know why. After all these years, how could she possibly wield such an influence over him?

"You'll be alone," he blurted. "The deepest, darkest, most terrible kind of alone."

"That's absurd," she said. "I'll have Don. Our life together. New friends."

"What about your followers? Your church? Your healing? For Christ sake, Miranda, you have a *gift*."

"Ha," she said. "You used to laugh at my *gift*!"

"Me, laugh? I never did. I was amazed at your talent," he said truthfully. "I thought you knew that."

"Maybe I did. I don't remember. Anyway, I'm ready to move on. To venture into new territories." She let out a nervous giggle. "Besides, there have been some dicey moments lately. Things that scared me. I think I'm ready to give it all up and lead a more conventional and predictable life," she confided. She looked away from him and made a show of crossing her legs and sitting up very straight. He had the impression of a teacher justifying an unpopular rule to a classroom of angry students.

"But you can't just give up on all those people," he persisted. "They've supported you for years and years. Abandoning them now would be wrong. Why, you've just completed the new church. That was a big sacrifice for most of them."

"I know that," she said evenly, "but don't I deserve to have a life of my own? Without the constant responsibility of others? You have no idea how restricted my life has been all these years. Sure, I did it for them, for *humanity*, but now I'd like to spread my wings and indulge myself. Is that so bad?"

"Like all the other boomers?" he teased. "Like your friend Don Parrish, who does as he likes, without the encumbrances of personal responsibility!"

"That's nasty," she said. "And unfair. Don takes good care of his ex-wife and family, and he works hard for his company and his community. Who are you to criticize, anyway? It seems your only obligation in life is to write, write, write… Others see their responsibility as requiring a more comprehensive involvement."

"Such as?" he asked, his wry sense of justice assuaged by her defensiveness. Her face was a livid pink, so unusual for her that he almost felt like laughing except that her criticism stung and he didn't like being compared, even peripherally, with the likes of Don Parrish.

"You need to get outside of your imagination and write about some of the things that really matter in our lives today." When he said nothing, she added, "Maybe you should explain how our generation lost itself. How we—"

"—Turned away from social activism to pad our pockets?" Jack finished. He thought of Parrish. "Your precious Parrish is the archetype of our generation, wouldn't you say? Our great journey from idealism to narcissism? Or was it from anti-materialism to gross materialism?"

When it was Miranda's turn to remain silent, he goaded her with, "All that oil money must have really assuaged his conscience, all right!"

Clearly wounded, she shot back, "Well, at least he was a productive member of society and didn't sit around harboring hostility toward those who were successful. At least he didn't keep marrying to improve his finances so he could merely write. At least he did something besides hide behind his imagination!"

"You think I hid behind my imagination, you who write poetry?" he said, a flush rising over his face, making him feel hot and humiliated like he did as a boy when the teacher returned his geometry papers, mutilated by a thousand red marks.

"Yes," she said, her body adopting a ramrod defiance. "You've spent a lot of time hiding behind your imagination. You've lost touch with the real world. You don't live. You merely exist." She looked down at the floor. Her shoulders slumped. The wind seemed to have gone out of her. She had a pained look on her face, as if she recognized the hurt she'd inflicted. "I don't mean to be cruel, but you need to get a grip," she finished.

Jack felt the familiar doubt assert itself. She could so easily diminish him. He hadn't expected her ire. He hadn't meant to argue with her, but here they were, locked in their familiar style of combat. At times like this he felt helpless.

"Look," she went on, avoiding his eyes, while the little room held her voice as crisply as if they were alone in a closet after a hurricane. "We both know the world is a mess. There's war, there's greed, there's poverty, there's injustice. With our talents we should be focusing on the human condition. We should further the agents of peace through our writing!"

"And how are you going to do that as a poet, or have you decided to switch genres and become a journalist?"

"I would if I had the talent, but you know I could never write non-fiction." She paused and fiddled with a strand of her hair. It had gone completely dry, he noticed, and stuck out all over her head like a big mop. "Besides," she looked down at her long, thin hands resting in her lap, "I don't know enough about the concrete world, the physical, the *scientific*," she finished.

"You can say that again," he laughed with her. "But what has that to do with it? You'd take one step at a time, and I bet you could do it. You could make the transition. Why not?" He felt the anger ease out of him, like air leaving a deflated balloon. It felt good to let it go, he thought.

"You know I couldn't do that kind of writing. It would take a discipline I don't have, not to mention a background I also don't have."

"You graduated from Northwestern with a philosophy degree. Don't tell me you don't have a comprehensive education. I know you do."

"I avoided the sciences."

"So? What's that got to do with writing about the big issues that face us as people today? I'm not following you, Miranda. Moreover, I'm really tired and feel like going to bed. We aren't having the discussion you promised, remember?"

"I haven't forgotten," she said. "I'm just working up my courage. It's your fault we got off subject."

"Well, okay," he admitted. "But now let's get down to business. Why are you here?"

She still stood before the open window, just another shadow in the room, her eyes turned toward the hills – white shades in the opaque landscape. "Have you heard of Theodore Hudson?"

"The Nobel Prize winning immunologist? Hasn't everybody?"

"His story is huge," she said. When he said nothing, she repeated *"huge."*

He waited. She said nothing. The cold house was silent and the world outside mute as well. In the strange light, it was as if the world had ended and two minds reached out to grasp something beyond words, something inexplicable perhaps. He made a show of listening but to what he could not explain.

"All right," Jack said. "I'll promise this. I'll let you try the idea on me in the morning. Right now I'm too tired to make a decision or even listen long on the subject. I wanted to hear about it tonight," he said, touching his forehead. "Right now you've got me so riled up, I have a murderous headache, but I'll take the idea into consideration." When she rolled her eyes, he rushed to reassure her although he wasn't sure why. "No, I mean it, Miranda, I will think about it." His mind was already weighing the idea on some level. He'd majored in Molecular Biology. The subject interested him. Theodore Hudson was a man worthy of biography although Jack wasn't certain that was a good use of his own talents. Still, it beat short freelance pieces that paid poorly.

"Let's get some sleep," he said, taking his empty glass into the kitchen.

"Please don't let Don be a problem," she said as she followed him up the stairs.

"I learned long ago there's no accounting for what some women see in men," he said.

"Or vice-versa, don't you think?" she said, slyly looking him up and down as they stood at the top of the landing.

He awoke early and sat in the dark living room till the sun came up. He hadn't slept well after getting the spare room ready for Miranda. Perhaps that was because since Karen died, he'd slept there himself, reluctant to disturb the dead in the room where she'd slept alone before she took him in. He laughed to recall that she'd adopted him as one would a stray dog, and he'd complied, obviously needing nurturing that no one else was eager to provide. In those days he might have hated women, so dark had seemed his previous experience with the fairer sex. His anger at both Felicia and Miranda would flare at odd moments of tormented memory. Karen seemed to understand that, although he had never detected anger at the past in her nature. Her generosity had been astounding, he now realized in his abject grief. Few accepted people for what they were; no other woman he'd known had been willing to see his own good buried under layers of resentment.

He'd watched Karen's robust color and plumpness dissipate into a gray mass of skin and cartilage. Each night had been the same – for months and months. The fire crackled downstairs; the fir trees leaned against the house, whispering frantically. Inside the tiny upstairs bedroom, aromatherapy candles burned in soldered sockets on the window sills. He could still feel her grip at twilight when the wolves howled in the ravines below. She hadn't been able to eat, and he, too depressed by her need and his own helplessness, had adjusted his belt for weeks before buying a new suit to bury her in. It was several sizes smaller than he'd been for decades. At the time, everyone seemed to worry that he'd follow her to the grave soon, but he hadn't.

The smell of coffee filled the place. He sat and watched the darkness yield to a pink sky with violet clouds then switched on the computer and stared for moments at the blank screen. After awhile he began writing. He didn't expect Miranda to awaken early. He wrote a few pages, but his heart wasn't in it, and after awhile, he gave up and wandered out onto the deck and sat down with his coffee. He couldn't shake a sense of gloom. Miranda's presence simply reminded him of unfulfilled dreams, the sense of a shackled imagination and his own diminishment.

He lit a cigarette and gazed out at the brooding mass of trees across the way. Below the road was muddy, and branches had fallen across the way and down the embankments. He'd have to get the driveway graded again, but he didn't have the money right now. Karen had left him the house, but neither had ever owned much. What little they had bought luxuries that final year: steak or lobster, music she liked, a larger television. And all the Jim Beam a man could drink, he thought bitterly. She liked the smell on him, she said. It helped him sleep, but he always woke deep in the night, hearing the trees and the night wind and feeling incredibly alone. When at last he had gotten used to her wretched presence in the bedroom with the constantly burning candles, she died.

He thought of Miranda sleeping upstairs, tucked into the down comforter, her colorless hair spread waywardly over the pillows, her pallid skin blending into the white. He could recall how she'd slept when he knew her – always on her back, like a child afraid of the darkness, alert at a moment's notice, her slender arms at her side or across her stomach. Thinking of her made him want to go upstairs and make love to her, but he didn't. Instead he sifted through the pile of C.D.'s and found Mendelsohn and put it on and sat back on the sofa and listened to the sound of the violin rise in the little room – so sweet, such a pure sorrow, he thought. Outside the aspen moved in the wind, protected by the ponderosa, and the hot morning sun gleamed in pools of water in the damp meadow grass. He got up and went into the kitchen. He put a can of orange juice concentrate in water to defrost and waited for Miranda.

Chapter Three

He heard her behind him and turned to see his terry robe loosely tied around her slim waist. Her wet hair was tied back in a tight knot and she smelled like soap. In the sunlight her skin was luminescent. He had always thought her beautiful and ageless, but now staring at her, he noticed the gray flesh under her eyes, the small mouth that had started to droop and the tiny lines that fled upward from faintly parted lips. Age would be kind to her, he knew, but its subtle mark on her lovely face was evident.

"I hope you don't mind," she said, holding out her arms in the voluminous robe. "It was cold in the bathroom."

"No problem," he said. "Coffee?"

She nodded and glanced outside. "It's gorgeous here. I can see why you stayed."

"I didn't plan to," he said, handing her the coffee mug.

"I thought you wanted to get away from the city, its hubbub and disarray. You always said you needed quiet." She laughed. "Well, I guess you have it now."

"A strange alliance," he said. "Just me and the trees…and the wildlife…"

"The colors." She stared out into the meadow at the flushes of bright yellow revealed by the melting snow. "I love aspen."

"I always told you there were places better than Texas."

"Right!" she said, rolling her eyes. "You said I'd love New York City, remember?"

"I thought you would," he said, still hurt she hadn't. "Small town girls always love the Big Apple."

"Not Yours Truly." She glanced at him sharply. "You should have known that."

"I guess," he admitted. "Well, you had your … *profession*."

"Friends, the dry, hot earth, straight, empty landscapes, big sky, few people. It was what *I* wanted, but you had different notions." She sighed. "I'm not the kind of person you can make over." The teasing lilt of her voice had gone hollow, he noticed. He had an insight finally borne of his chaotic past. He supposed he'd had unrealistic expectations of her in those days. Now he had none. No illusions either, he reminded himself.

"I made my peace with Texas." She had a faraway look in her eyes, that dreamy ineluctable light of awareness he recognized from their long time together. Its familiarity smote him with conflicted loyalties. Ah, the past....

"So," she said, "What did the Big Apple do for you except cultivate an arrogance that wasn't justified?"

"You got that one right." He thought of Felicia, the fast and empty crowd he'd been all too happy to cultivate after his novel was published. The world had seemed to open before him like a rare landscape – exciting, lush, nuanced, till what his companions had all taken for granted in their privilege and sense of entitlement came to seem as banal to him as it did to them. New Year's Eve he and Felicia agreed to divorce. His second marriage, it seemed nothing to let her go. It had never been hard to let any of them go. His seventeen-year-old bride, Felicia, Amanda after her. Nor Linda whom he'd married in the throes of middle age. Not until Karen did he feel like sticking around.

He shrugged. "I did learn some things, though."

"Right," Miranda said with a hint of mockery. Today she seemed endowed with a rare strength. He had the sneaking suspicion that she was thinking how grateful she was he had dumped her when at the time it had been terrible for her, he knew. She'd never married, never had children.

"Why didn't you marry?" he asked, emboldened by her open, frank face, the pale eyes taking in the bright light from the kitchen. Now the truth mattered when before their relationship had been about something else.

"No eligible man wanted me." Her words rang false in the quiet room. Miranda knew her value.

"You're wrong," he surprised himself by saying. "There were years we could have been together."

She searched his face, as if she thought his earnest confession cavalier and unworthy. "You know that wouldn't have worked." And now he could tell for sure she counted herself lucky they hadn't remained together, and the thought made him sad. Why had she come, anyway?

"Time to talk business," she said. Her shoulders squared and she quickly withdrew from the kitchen. He heard her bare feet move along the floorboards and up the creaking stairs, a drawer open and her quick descent. How light she was compared to Karen, he mused. For a moment he wished he'd stayed in that meager West Texas town full of the rednecks of his youth.

She spread a sheaf of newspaper clippings on the pitted pine table in the kitchen.

He glanced from one article to the next. Several had pictures of a distinguished appearing man with a refined face and silver hair. *Nobel Prize Winning Scientist Dead at 62*...A molecular biologist at Yale, he'd been the leading authority on auto-immunity. His death had been unexpected, its circumstances under investigation although there was no reason to suspect foul play, the police chief in New Haven had stated. The professor was survived by a wife and son.

"So?" he asked. "What's this got to do with me?"

Her eyes fastened on him. He had the impression she was leading him on some esoteric journey, but then he'd felt that in the years of their love as well. She was enigmatic; he had never known what she expected of him.

"Remember those strange dreams I used to have?"

"Boy, do I," he said. "You were a piece of work in those days. Still taking mescaline?"

"Of course not. I haven't done drugs since I was twenty. You know that."

"Do I?" he said. "What do I know?"

"Not a lot," she said, the faint sense of contempt rising in her clear contralto voice.

"You used to scare me, you know." He thought of the weird visions she often had, the seeming pre-cognitive dreams. The bizarre imagery and sequences seemed to defy the rational. They were so elliptical she had finally consulted a Jungian analyst. Jack didn't know what had become of that, since he'd married Felicia around that time and lost touch with Miranda for awhile.

"I scared myself," she said quietly. Her eyes were glassy as she looked away from him. He recalled the dream she'd had of a man hanging from the ceiling of the butcher shop in Sweetwater. A week later a woman was dead and the whole sorry story of her relationship with the butcher unfolded in a nasty follow-up that resulted in the butcher's suicide.

"So why the professor? What does he have to do with you? With me?"

"I don't know." She had detached herself from the moment when just seconds ago she'd possessed the same passionate urgency he'd associated with her all those years since their wild days in Texas and Arizona. That passion scared him then; it scared him now.

"Hell, Miranda, don't tell me this is about one of your weird visions. I can't deal with that stuff anymore. It's just plain irrational, and you know it. You came all the way from Texas to tell me about a dream?" He swallowed some of his cold coffee and slammed the mug down on the table. The liquid slopped over the rim. A brown stain formed on one of the articles.

Miranda turned her back to him and looked out over the yellow and green landscape. Her narrow shoulders rose and fell for several moments. He was afraid she was crying, but he was so angry he couldn't take her in his arms or walk around and face her. The two stood in silence with the Mendlesohn playing in the living room and the bright sun shining on her silvery hair.

"I don't want to get mixed up in your weirdness," he said quietly. "I'm too old, too tired."

"I know," she said, leaning her head into her hands. He heard her sniff. "But someone has to listen. They just have to."

"Why?" he asked.

"Someone has to tell his story," she said, turning around. A smearing sallow stream washed her cheeks. "*Because the truth does matter.*"

"Of course, it always does, but what has he got to do with you?"

"*He was about truth,*" she said, almost inaudibly. Jack would have asked her to speak up, to repeat what she said, but she seemed so vulnerable and unsure of herself that he didn't want to press her. "He was a noble man, a great man. His story must be told," she repeated.

"There are lots of noble men out there. Reread the biographies of Lincoln, of Ghandi, of Martin Luther King. It's not hard to get ones fix of nobility if he knows history and wants to revisit it for courage or edification or whatever." Jack could hear the impatience in his voice. Miranda, the consummate idealist. He was once one himself, he thought sadly. Nowadays he considered himself a cynic, a skeptic, an infidel. Jack didn't believe in hope; he didn't want the complications and irrational premises of religion. *"When I was a child, I thought as a child, but when I became a man I put away childish things..."* In his present frame of mind would he even consider Saint Paul a great and noble man? He wasn't sure. An idealist, certainly. Foolish? Maybe. Duped? Possibly.

"He came to me."

Jack relaxed a little. So she knew the man. "You mean he attended one of your healing services? Was he ill?"

She shook her head sadly. "No, it wasn't like that. I never actually met him."

He stared at her, incredulous. "So we really are talking about one of your loony dreams?" He felt the anger rising in him, the bitter memory of all their unpleasant moments together, those horrible defining occasions of confusion and hurt he'd experienced with her so many times before. He would never understand her. It struck him that one of the reasons he could so readily leave his women was that Miranda had taught him how mysterious they really were. How you could be constantly confused and frustrated by this alien breed and the more you tried to understand, the deeper you fell into a pit of need and indecision. "I won't do it," he said. "You can just count me out on this whole project."

"You haven't changed a bit."

"You don't know who I am. We never really knew each other."

"I know that you would never do anything that wasn't *your* idea. You were always so stubborn. Obviously you still are!"

"I did plenty you wanted me to, and you know it."

"You want to write, then write his story," she said, summoning a strength he would not have thought possible under the circumstances.

"Why would I write *his* story?" Jack asked.

"You'll learn something. You'll enrich humanity. You'll get outside yourself and your grief.... and your...*narcissistic preoccupations*! It'll do you good," she said emphatically.

"Always the teacher. Why don't you find someone else to mentor?" His sarcasm was seething. He realized this could get ugly and reminded himself she had traveled a long distance to see him. That alone showed she cared for him.

"You're the only person for this particular job." Her face was so serious that the light seemed to have gone out of her. It was the kind of weirdness he always associated with her. She could disappear right before his eyes, a strange vanishing act he was helpless to explain.

He resisted the impulse to laugh. Here she was again, Miranda, the drama queen. He had to admit she was strangely mesmerizing in this role as in others.

"He was a great man, and you'll learn something about yourself — as we all do studying noble men. His story must be told." She had her arms out wide; he had the impression of an angel – the wings, the unnatural whiteness of her complexion, eyes that shone with sunlight. *"The truth must out!"* she said in a desperate tone, her face still streaming. "Jack, you have to do this," she said. "You will, won't you?"

Her physical fragility, her passionate vitality, the puffy eyes, the somber mouth – all the varied movements of her expressive nature summoned his sense of purpose. She had always had that effect on him, he realized. Perhaps he had spent all these years escaping her implacable will that he'd feared might seduce him into mysterious and threatening terrains from which he might never emerge intact.

"Why should I? What's in it for me?"

"Perhaps you need a change," she said, glancing around the room. Outside the sun shone brightly in the aspen grove. "You don't really belong here," she said quietly. He followed her eyes deep into the yellow thicket and the melting snow.

He tried to think. Well, what did he have to lose these days? After all, it was she who had inspired that first book. She whose support he'd thrived on when everyone else seemed to scorn his efforts.

He thought for a few minutes, staring into her serious face, thinking of Karen. He thought of the dark nights alone, languishing in his sense of failure. Of his feeble yearnings to get it all right, for once. Of Karen's blind faith in him. Yes, he had let all his wives down. He had disappointed Karen, even. But worse than all that, he had let himself down. Miranda was more right than she knew. Countless sordid memories of his cowardice rose up to spite him.

"All right," he said, wearily. The effort entailed was nothing compared to the supreme energy required to suppress the demons from within, he thought in a sudden flash of understanding. He could do this. And maybe Miranda was right. Maybe he could resurrect something in himself – a flicker of greatness that the years had subdued and contained. He wasn't entirely washed up if she could summon his own dreams out of the darkness and the shame.

"We can start tomorrow?" Her face was radiant from the sun and her own boundless enthusiasm. He guessed he missed that in a woman.

"Tomorrow," he agreed.

"You don't really want to understand," Miranda was saying that evening. "Dark things always upset you, remember?"

She was right, of course. He supposed he was one of those people who demanded others follow along, never wanting to deal with dissent. He'd always hated argumentative people, especially when they were women. In his mind women should always be pleasant. They should try to please. Beyond that, he disliked the gray areas – those places of uncertainty and confusion when one's perception was challenged and there were no rules.

"I don't try to know those dark things either," she said, frowning, "but they intrude anyway." She placed her hands in her lap and looked around her. She had applied makeup, tracing kohl-colored lines around her eyes, blush that colored her pale skin, faint lipstick that flattered a full mouth. For the thousandth time he thought her beautiful. He liked the way she moved, her voice that trembled in the dark – a kind of esoteric music in its own right. Her face possessed character, unlike Felicia's, for instance, whose sculpted beauty was enviable but ordinary. He had always been attracted to unusual women. Studying her face now, as he had so many times in the past, he still found it inscrutable and strangely ethereal. He knew few people were as honest as Miranda, but even she was helpless to explain the imaginative leaps her intellect experienced as a matter of course. It wouldn't have surprised Jack if her essence suddenly took flight and floated off into the hills. She caught him looking at her too closely and turned away. Not one who yielded to scrutiny, she had always had her secrets, and he respected that.

"So the professor *just came to you?*" he asked. "That simple?" He laughed despite his resolve to give the impression he took everything she said seriously.

To his surprise, she laughed, too, and they both let loose for several moments. She laughed so hard her eyes brimmed and spilled over, tears flowing down her cheeks. "I know it sounds crazy," she said at last, still holding her chest dramatically. He was reminded of all the good laughs they used to have so many years ago, usually after smoking weed with the smell of sagebrush in the air and the cool desert breeze blowing their hair. "Remember how frustrated you used to get when I had these…*moments?*" How you said I was the most irrational woman you'd ever met?"

"Do I ever," he said. "I almost killed you."

"But you're older now. And wiser."

"I guess," he admitted, thinking about the times he still felt Karen's presence. Such things couldn't be rationally explained, but that didn't mean they didn't have some kind of validity. He guessed he'd learned, however obliquely, that one true thing from Miranda. "So in the scheme of things, the professor was that important?"

"Quite extraordinary. He was a world renowned scientist, an advocate for the family, one of the most important men of the twentieth century. It was terrible that he died when he could have accomplished so much more. They say he was on the brink of an AIDS breakthrough."

"Why not the subject of Einstein or Hawkings? An important statesman? Or a famous writer? Someone who does something I understand?"

"I don't know," she said quietly. "He insists his story must be told."

"Plenty will write his story. Scientists who understand his contribution. People who worked with him. Why me?"

She shook her head. The set of her shoulders, her pursed lips, a sudden hardness that swept over her, told him to stop his questioning. She glanced behind them through the doorway to the kitchen. "The dinner smells ready."

He followed her into the kitchen and opened the oven. He had fixed a roast with potatoes and carrots. He took out the heavy pot and placed it on the table. "I'll make a salad," he said, pulling out lettuce and tomatoes from the fridge. "You pour the wine." He pointed at the opened bottle of Chianti. She'd always liked red wine.

"This is nice," she said as they sat down to the table. They sat before the fire in the living room. Snow had started falling again in giant flakes, and the valley had a spectral appearance out the front window. He watched her sip the Chianti, the sensual press of her lips to the glass, the joyful gleam of her eyes at the sensation. He was reminded of how he'd loved to please her way back when they were young. When she'd had all the power, and all he wanted was to hold onto this rare creature whose moods and imaginative flights of fancy dictated their otherwise prosaic existence. It seemed now that had he stayed with her, they might have made a meaningful life together. One could certainly do a lot worse than Miranda.

"Delicious," she said. "You always were a good cook."

"You're so different from Karen," he blurted then felt ashamed. Any man knew you didn't make comparisons of that nature.

She paused, looking at him with what seemed infinite pity. He'd never thought back about how empathic Miranda really was. It was a fact he had let go of somewhere along the way. "You want to tell me about her?" she asked. "It would do you good."

He thought for a moment then got up and went over to the little table in the corner and turned on the faint copper light. He walked into the kitchen and brought out the bottle of wine, turning off the light in there. Now the living room seemed right, the shadows moving on the walls, the snow swirling downward, the silence of it all.

"She liked things simple," he began. "And that was fine with me. No demands. She was down to earth; she had a great sense of humor. She could tease the sadness right out of me."

"Quite a task, as I recall," Miranda said.

He wondered at that, too. Had he really been such a burden? Was he still? The horrible thought occurred to him that Karen had left out of sheer frustration. Maybe she couldn't take it anymore and had simply shed her mortal coil as a final act of desperation. Maybe that's all cancer was, a giving up. God knew he'd wished his own death many times.

He closed his eyes, imagining her. He could see her laugh, her teasing eyes, the wild sense of humor she directed at him when he was in one of his moods. No, she'd really loved him, he decided, as he always did, deep in the dark moments of his own self-doubt. "I stayed," he said, just realizing it himself for the first time, "because I really liked being around her."

"She was a lot of fun," Miranda said. "You needed that. You've always taken yourself so seriously. As a matter of fact, I could have used it too. She held up the wine glass, studied its rosy glow in the firelight. "We were so damned serious in those days, weren't we?"

"Me and my writing, you and your visions."

"Mine was about helping people," she said. "Connecting, healing, spirituality, while yours was about being famous."

"You're right," he admitted, but he still wondered if it was so wrong to want to be recognized for talent, the hard won accomplishment of honesty and hard work. He hadn't written something banal. He'd had standards. He hadn't compromised. Surely he deserved some credit for that.

"I'm sorry," she said, studying his face. She had wounded him again, and she knew it. Her judgment had always mattered to him. "I didn't mean to suggest you weren't a true artist. Your aspirations weren't *all* about ego."

"I wanted to write something good for her," he said, feeling his eyes spill over. Thank God it was dark in the room. "She deserved that. But she got sick, and I couldn't do it."

"A lot of water has passed under the bridge," Miranda said, standing up. She had her empty plate in her hand, and her elongated form before the front window seemed to be just one more shadow in the room. She paused to look down the sloping terrain from where he had watched her car edge its way upward last night. How long ago it now seemed.

"Why did you come?" he asked softly.

"I never gave up on your talent," she said, her back to him, her eyes peering down into the darkness of the ravines below. "Don't you see, the snow keeps falling, so gently, so relentlessly, covering everything up, obscuring it all?" She turned around, her pale face in the darkness reminding him of something he couldn't name but which at the moment was more important than any idea he'd ever had. It crossed his mind that he could turn on the computer right now, and the words would fly from his fingertips as he simply regarded the shadow before the window, the faint suggestion of light from the gently falling white curtain of snow.

"What is it the snow covers?" he asked, trying to follow her elliptical observations. This was the process that once frustrated him beyond words; now it seemed necessary.

"All the tracks," she said. "The reasons. The huffery and the puffery." Then as if exhausted, she returned to the table and sank down opposite him. It was as if she folded, like the huge umbrella she threw to the floor last night.

He got up from the table and guided her to the sofa. He put his arm behind her on the back of the sofa and drew her closer till her head rested in the crook of his shoulder. He could feel her trembling from the effort to make him see something, but he wasn't sure even she knew what the truth was. They sat, stilled by a tacit understanding, listening to the fire crackle and each other's subdued breathing. It was a self-conscious moment, Jack realized, when both experienced a strange communion, more intuitive than informative. An illusory sort of thing that the years had bought back, but which for the life of him, he would not be able to put into words – to her or anyone else.

"It must be terrible," he said at last, "To have a grasp of something that you can't explain."

"I think you're beginning to understand what this is all about," she said. "I think you're beginning to *feel* it." She placed her hands on her lap, at once childlike and patient, too. She stared down at her hands, the faintly glowing ruby on her ring finger, then up at him. Her presence moved him beyond words. He had the urge to devour her and by so doing to metabolize a power he not only would never understand, but that would transform him from the helpless man he was these days to the man he'd once been, driven by the authority of his own convictions, as she still was. She placed her hand in his. "Obviously, that's why I need you. To put it all into *words*."

"To render your vision," he said, not at all annoyed for once. "To make sense of what you cannot?"

"Something like that," she said quietly.

They sat for a long time before the fire. Jack had the desire to claim some intimacy in the moment – her presence drew him irresistibly in that direction – but he held himself in check in memory of Karen and in the desire to preserve an integrity to the whole experience stretching before them, binding them as they had not been since their teens. He did not want to spoil something good. Perhaps this was the most enduring sort of closeness he could ever achieve with Miranda now that so much water had indeed passed under the bridge.

At some point he must have drifted off to sleep with the fire crackling and sputtering, the soft music from the stereo playing quietly and the snow falling in a thicker and thicker haze. He awoke shivering. The fire had gone out and the room was cold. Miranda's head was locked beneath his, her face trusting in the pale light. The faded afghan draped her body, and her mascara-ed lashes fluttered from her dreaming. He didn't want to wake her, so he sat in the cold. He could feel the grit in the air from the fireplace insert and trace its silty shadow across the floor. From far below came the plaintive cries of the wolves and then as had happened so often before at around this time of night, he could smell the aromatherapy candles, their jasmine scent, as if Karen were still there upstairs waiting for him. He sighed heavily, almost expecting her fingers to dig into his arms, almost feeling again her nameless fears. He'd always thought that if he'd been she, dying and knowing it, a good person to the last, he'd have gone to his maker unafraid, but she had been very much afraid, as it turned out. He knew there'd been some consolation in his presence during those last terrible months.

"Jack?" Miranda's eyes fluttered open then closed again.

"Yes?" he said, stealing his arm underneath the afghan and drawing her closer. He could smell shampoo in the stream of her hair on his shoulder.

"You can do this," she said. "And it will be so good." She had a bemused expression on her sleeping face. Was she still dreaming?

"Shhh," he whispered, moving some of her hair away from his chin.

She moved closer to him, and the afghan parted and her warm breasts pressed against his arm. He felt the hot blush of desire. Careful not to yield to it, he let it wash over him nevertheless, reminding him of what it had been to be young and filled with longing. To recall what it had been to hold a beautiful woman in his arms. What it had been like to live in the moment — unwary, without apology, without ambition or obsession. Just the pulse and throb of expectation, a sense that the moment itself had meaning, and beyond that perhaps nothing else that mattered.

Ah, Miranda, he thought. For one sweet glimpse into the human heart, he had spent all these years writing, and yet in the final analysis, the ultimate insights had eluded him. For the moment there was just one truth, and it was embodied in the woman lying oblivious in his arms. He studied her face and traced in his mind's eye its balance and proportion. Then he gently lifted her, encased in the afghan, and walked up the creaking stairs and set her down on the bed in the guestroom. He pulled off her shoes and carefully rearranged the covers over her. She barely moved except for her arms that stretched across her stomach and lay still.

He walked down the hall and fell into Karen's bed, wrapping the heavy blankets around him. The house struck him as unusually quiet. Then the wolves started up again, their plaintive cries echoing through the canyons. For once the sound consoled him. He watched the moon for awhile and fell asleep.

Chapter Four

The sun awoke him. He thought right away of Miranda sleeping down the hall. He showered quickly and put on a clean shirt and jeans. He made the bed then walked down the hall and knocked on Miranda's door.

"I'm taking you out for breakfast," he said through the door. He was tired of the house, the sense of confinement. It seemed he hardly left the place anymore.

All right," she said. "I'll be right down." Moments later he heard the water going in the bathroom upstairs.

He glanced out the front window. Several more inches of snow had accumulated on the road. The sun was bright, already warming the mountainside. Miranda's Blazer stood at the top of the hill below the driveway, its windshield buried by snow. He backed the Jeep out of the garage and left the motor going then shoveled the driveway.

The sky was a clear blue above the snow-covered, rocky landscape of Leadville. Around the hills the thick trees, mantled by the glistening blanket quivered in the rising sun. Later on it would be one of those warm Colorado days when you peeled off your parka and walked around in shirtsleeves, squinting into the blinding sun. A broken tree sprawled across the first turn in the road. Leaving the car running, he walked down and pushed its narrow trunk over the edge into a thicket far below.

He had to hand it to Miranda. Not just any woman would have driven up that perilous road late at night in a storm. She had always had a lot of courage, or perhaps, an inability to anticipate the consequences of her impulsive actions. At any rate, she had always been more daring than he. Whereas he weighed the cost to himself of any action, she merely plowed forward, sometimes into disaster, from which she inevitably emerged intact. Her Blazer moving steadfastly forward up the steep road the other night was merely a metaphor for the woman herself. Yeah, she was something all right. Karen had exhibited a similar courage and the same enviable independence. He counted himself lucky that such women found anything redeeming in him.

He turned off the ignition and walked up the flagstones and around to the front of the house. The red enamel door was faded from the sun, the iron pot beside it full of debris and dead chrysanthemums. He pushed open the door and stamped his boots on the splintered flooring. Miranda stood before the window, peering downward, with a steaming mug of coffee in her hands. She had on a long wool skirt and a loosely knit sweater over a black top. Untamed curls flew around her face, softening her features and trailing into a braid fastened with a magenta ribbon. She reminded him of a Midwestern woman on a Christmas card from the thirties.

"You look ravishing," he said as he closed the door. She ignored him, staring off into space over the rim of the coffee mug. Her face was serious and intelligent. He was reminded of those times decades ago when he had wanted to know what she was thinking. He had given up asking; she rarely shared her reflections and then only when it was her idea to share.

"I made coffee. I hope it isn't too strong for you."

He walked into the kitchen and poured himself some. When he returned, she was sitting on the sofa, seemingly lost in thought. He lowered himself into the rickety rocker by the fireplace and remained silent. The water continued to trickle down from the eaves, and the bright sunlight filled the house. He swallowed the coffee, stronger than he usually made it, and glanced around the room. The papers on his computer table needed straightening. There were books lying around and a few magazines. He set his coffee mug on the floor and ordered the papers and restacked the books where they belonged then picked up the magazines and took them into the kitchen and threw them in the sack beneath the sink. When he returned and took up his coffee, Miranda had a knowing look on her face.

"You always were a neat freak."

"Compared to you, yes," he said, laughing to recall that for some reason Miranda simply could not be orderly. Totally right brained, she led her life as a distributor of objects. Her place was a crowded mélange of details – tiny Victorian figures, faded tapestries, cards, bric-a-brac, paintings, even a portrait of the Moonie leader on a chair in her bedroom. Jack didn't know if she cleaned the place although it never appeared dirty – just impervious to a dust rag. Books, magazines, whatever, stretched like abandoned toys across the cluttered landscape of her home. The rooms smelled of incense and potpourri and old books. Being there, surrounded by her eccentric collection of stuff, was like visiting a museum and for him it always conjured up visions of the past and suggested a disordered imagination. Even as a young man and certainly later, he'd never been able to envision coming home to a house Miranda kept.

"So, a penny for your thoughts?" he said, expecting the usual dismissive gesture. He sat down in the rocker and took a swallow of the coffee she'd made. "Nice and strong," he said, raising the cup in a mock tribute.

Her eyes held the glassy expression he had always associated with her mulling over something important to her. "What was I thinking just now?" she murmured. "What was it?" she repeated, as if she herself did not know.

He waited. It suddenly occurred to him that she might have had one of her weird visions. He had never been able to figure out if they were paranormal, as she claimed, or hallucinations stemming from a disordered mind. He often suspected the latter, so he didn't want to hear about them. Since their earliest times together they'd had a tacit understanding that she would avoid discussing them. "I thought you might be thinking of your professor. I still can't imagine how the idea came to you. Why you want me, of all people, to do it."

"Hush," she said, putting down her cup and bringing her expressive hands to her face. "It will all be clear, I suppose, as time goes on." She stood and smoothed out the folds of her skirt. "It's not like everything has to have a reason, you know. Sometimes you discover purpose through doing, don't you think?"

"Whatever," he said. "I'm just along for the ride, remember that."

"No expectations?"

"No. And no illusions."

"Good," she said. "That way you can't lose."

"That's the idea," he said, finishing his coffee.

"Ready for breakfast?" he said, standing.

"Just sit here for awhile, will you, Jack?" Beyond the wistful, dreamy expression, he thought he saw a flicker of insight pass across her face. She rose and went into the kitchen. He could hear her pour another cup of coffee and imagined her gazing into the grove of aspen, her nimble mind working over something.

He leaned back in the chair and thought about Karen. She'd loved the aspen, too – the bright days, the blue sky, the simple Colorado life. It had suited her to walk the property, working out the nits in her own brain. Sometimes she'd disappeared for an hour or two, and he presumed she'd walked way down the road or up onto the rocky ledges to gaze out over the winding road below. She'd had a simple, childlike love of nature, and he loved her for that as much as anything.

Slowly he was realizing why he remained in the town he thought he had never liked.

"Jack?" Miranda was settling herself back on the sofa. Her booted foot trailed a circle in the air. She held the mug close to her face, and the ruby on her finger caught the sun. "I wish... I wish..." Her voice sounded hollow, as if some nameless grief had asserted itself in her memory, but she went on, looking over his shoulder at the stone hearth. "I never have been able to explain things like I want. I... I..."

"Miranda, don't get yourself so worked up. It doesn't matter." He could sense the misery in her effort, and he didn't know what else to say – he who was glib by nature, although less so with her than nameless others. So he waited, fumbling himself for words that escaped him in the clutches. Miranda had that effect on him, he realized, whereas with Karen he was never at a loss for words. It had always seemed to him that when Miranda doubted herself, she was the most lost and vulnerable. Yet it was Miranda, who when filled with conviction, could unloose a rhetoric so powerful that it moved both the doubtful and the assured to action. In those moments her vocabulary, her ideas, her emotion would flow together into a force that astounded him. She was unstoppable then, possessed of remarkable and inexplicable powers. And frightening, too, he admitted to himself. Beyond the fascination the woman evoked had always been something that aroused a faint sense of uneasiness in Jack.

"I don't know where it comes from," she said, raising her mug to her lips and looking down into the cavity. "But I know when I get like this that it's something important. It pulls at me." She sat the cup down on the table and covered her face with both hands. "I know it's crazy, but I see something that simply must be clarified, and I don't even know for sure what it is." She removed her hands from her face, and he could see the tears in her eyes and the absolute confusion in her features. Her hands trembled as she stared through her tears at the hearthstone, as if searching for the truth behind the slabs. For once, he could feel the pain she experienced; she had somehow made him feel it this time. However inarticulate she was in moments like that, this time it was her gestures, her countenance, her tremulous anticipation of his response that aroused his empathy.

He walked over and sat down beside her. He took her shoulders in his arms and kissed her wet cheeks. "There now," he said. "You don't have to explain. We'll discover together what you mean, what you see. I promise to be patient this time."

"You're always so logical," she said. "I just can't be that way."

"Some things you just have to take on faith," he said, squeezing her shoulders. "So, for once, I'll just believe in your weird visions."

"You'll trust me?" she said, astonished.

"Isn't that what friends are for?"

"I'll get my things," she said, walking upstairs. He listened to her move around in the bedroom then went into the kitchen and turned off the coffee pot. He drank some of the strong coffee and thought about writing. Suddenly he felt there were things he had to say when it was the right time.

"You never explained why you didn't marry," Jack said. Around them the quiet murmurings of separate conversations blended with the kitchen sounds. A large crowd had gathered for breakfast, but the tone of the café was subdued. People shuffled in and out with clumps of snow trailing them to their tables. A fire burned in the old stone fireplace in the corner.

"I think that when I was young, marriage seemed the inevitable fate." She glanced around her through the bright windows to the outside street where cars slogged slowly on the plowed surface. "You and I said we'd marry someday. I always looked to you for decisions, so I accepted that as my future. Didn't all girls in those days, especially in small Texas towns?"

"I guess we were all pretty conventional."

"After you married, I felt myself change. I didn't think about marriage anymore, just about living."

"I still can't believe I married Felicia, as if the mistake with Myrna wasn't enough. "He thought of the seventeen year old he'd married, whom he thought he'd gotten pregnant. That was stupid, all right, but marrying Felicia was beyond the pale. "What was I thinking? We were totally different beings. As a result I wasted four years of my life – and hers."

"I was surprised," Miranda said, "but you always were unpredictable, and Felicia was beautiful." She turned her face to the window so he couldn't see her expression. "For that matter, so were Amanda and Linda. I suppose Karen was as well."

"Hardly," Jack said, "but she had other virtues."

"You always went for the beauties, as I recall." Jack could detect a bitterness in her voice, but it was more the implication that he was shallow that bothered him. What man didn't prefer beautiful women?

"You were more beautiful than all of them, but I think I was afraid of you."

"Come on, afraid of *me?*" Her face was open and laughing, without reserve. He hadn't seen her like this in a long time.

"Yeah, you were so deep, so complex. I guess I knew I wasn't equipped to deal with such a complicated woman."

Miranda laughed again. "You were the complicated one! Seriously, I think I was relieved when it all ended. I realized we could never have been happy together. Maybe we were too much alike."

Her words had the ring of truth. He did wonder, however, if she found him half as interesting as he had her all these years. He recalled how he'd sought her out right after he decided to end it with Felicia and before that, Myrna. How after the others, one by one, he'd run to her to regroup. If was as if he could not let her go entirely.

"Did you ever miss the security of a really close relationship?" he asked. When she looked confused by his question, he clarified, "You know, the kind with a deep commitment?" When she didn't respond, he added uncomfortably, "You know, a more conventional relationship?"

She smiled. "What makes you think I needed that?"

Jack felt himself knot in the stomach. She had always been able to hurt him this way. That was another reason why it was lucky they hadn't worked out as a couple. He would have always been beholden to her, continuously baffled by her take on things, the impulsive way she reacted, rarely attempting to please, as he guessed he expected of a woman. He was the conventional one, when you thought about it.

She went on. "Just because I don't choose to be trapped by marriage doesn't mean I don't value being heart to heart. Body to body. You're right, we never did understand each other. Not really."

"Maybe too much emphasis is placed on understanding. Maybe it's enough to simply react and see where being together will go," Jack said, thinking of Karen. Had either of them really tried to understand the other? Or had they simply lived the life they shared while somehow time worked it out between them? He was inclined to think that then he merely stumbled on in life, but the familiarity and the lack of complexity had aided the situation. He stayed because there were no demands. It was easy to remain with a woman who expected little. The thought made him sad, though. Just what did she get out of it? He glanced at the waiter bringing their plates, at the chrome clock moving through the hours, at the blue embers in the fireplace and felt for once in all these months that life was not only hard, but its lessons unfathomable.

"That's how I feel," Miranda said. "If you can get to that point, where nothing seems necessary and everything possible, you can just live in the moment, and that feels good."

"Sounds like psychobabble to me."

"Maybe we could all use a little therapy," she said pointedly.

"Maybe we should read more books, watch good movies."

Miranda's violet eyes fastened on his. A shadow crossed them as another, more complex insight presented itself. Just watching her face was like studying an intricate geologic formation. "It's more about *writing* the book," she said, taking a bite of her omelet. "*Like creating in the ultimate sense…like making your life work for you.*"

As usual, Jack had no clue what she meant. More weirdness, he presumed.

Chapter Five

Evening shadows drew the unlit house at the top of the hill into a compact black box above the trees – forlorn and uninviting. As Jack's Jeep sputtered up the steep road, the structure, with its dark siding and uninspired architecture, reminded him of a headstone in a neglected cemetery. At least it wasn't one of the countless Victorian cottages one saw in town, Jack reflected. Karen's tastes, like everything about her, had been practical and simple. Her home with its straight lines and barely pitched roofline took the elemental batterings well, standing humble and exposed above the ragged landscape.

As they neared the topmost hill below the driveway, the snow began again. It seemed to Jack that the snow never stopped falling these past years in Leadville, as if the dreary city invited the harshest conditions. He was tired of it all.

"Home just in time," Jack said, pressing the garage door button and peering through the murky landscape. "A couple of hours later and we'd have had a dangerous climb up here."

"Ever been snowed in?" Miranda asked.

"Once," Jack said, remembering an evening five years ago when he'd first met Karen. He'd come to read a story he'd written and ended up staying the night.

"You can't go down the mountain in this weather," she'd said. So he'd remained – reluctantly – and then somehow had stayed on, like a stray dog that senses an earnest benefactor. One couldn't say he'd stayed for sex: it had been weeks before they'd ventured into that. It hadn't been about money either, although he was broke at the time. He'd have gotten a job or simply borrowed, as he'd done before when he was down and out. She'd made it easy for him to stay – so natural, like eating a meal or swallowing a drink. Weeks later he was dumbfounded to realize he was still there. Women usually annoyed him after long stretches amidst their scents, their orderly and confining ways, their dreary observations.

After the snow melted, Karen had simply come and gone, satisfying her own needs for routine and sustenance. Her unaffected manner implied he was welcome to enjoy her hospitality indefinitely. She didn't lock the place so that on the couple of occasions when he'd left for town with all his stuff, he'd been able to return. She didn't talk on the phone or play distracting music. She had no television then. After a week, he brought his computer there and set it up on the dining room table she never used. Beneath the sad visages of her dead relatives in beveled glass and somber frames, he wrote, unblocked for the first time in years. The sun slanting over his shoulder in the morning, trees blowing against the siding, the bend of the sturdy home in the unceasing wind, drew him on into his own imagination, now unfettered by responsibility and domestic details.

He wrote a novel, but it hadn't sold. Then Karen became ill, and his enthusiasm for the book waned along with his appetite and his hope. The days had progressed dully, like the pages of a pedantic piece of literature, one by one and without variation, till the day she mercifully stopped suffering. He thought he'd seen the worst of it then, but the monotony of his life after that was even more unbearable. The sleepless nights, the confusion, the howling wind were all part of a terrible malaise from which he was now receiving a brief respite in the person of Miranda, brought back from the past, invigorating him with her own need and the remembrance of what it was like to have a sense of purpose, to be clothed in meaning, as only Miranda was able to make him feel.

He told Miranda the story. It still felt good to recall Karen. Each time he talked about her he brought her back to life.

"I am surprised," she said after listening intently to his rambling memories, the retreating impressions he'd recaptured for the moment. "You were always so afraid of being, what did you call it? *Engulfed?*"

"How did you know that?" he asked, feeling sheepish.

"It was the message you conveyed after every breakup, every divorce. Same old, same old...," she said wearily.

"Am I really such a boor?" He drove into the narrow garage and turned off the ignition, waiting for her reply. When it didn't come, he stepped out of the Jeep. Outside the snow fell silently, relentlessly into the anonymity of the vast landscape. He shivered. It had to be twenty or more below zero.

Miranda shrugged her shoulders and opened the car door. She stepped down from the truck. "All I can say is that you weren't easy yourself, and yet you had all these expectations of women." She grabbed her bag from the floor of the car. "You didn't understand how little you offered."

"Come on, I was a nice guy. I still am. You know I get along with all my ex-wives."

"That's because they don't have to live with you. It's the same with me. You're an adorable friend sometimes, but..."

He decided to let that go, as he did most such remarks on the part of women. What was the point: To get into a spirited argument about his own lack of sensitivity? Hadn't he been through enough of those senseless quarrels? Everyone had faults, and certainly his women had had their own share of imperfection and downright selfishness. Women were simply more verbal about their complaints, but that didn't make them right. Men, too, had issues; they just didn't jaw about them till they drove you away with your tail between your legs. He'd had enough tongue-lashings for one lifetime, thank you.

Miranda remained silent. Her profile as he turned the key into the door was marbled and smooth in the incandescent, snowy light. He waited for her to say something, anything, but her silence filled the dark stairway till they reached the main floor and looked out over the whitening pine below. Still she said nothing. He opened the door, and she took off her gloves and threw them and her knit cap onto the sofa. He heard her sigh as she moved listlessly away from him.

"A drink?" he said heavily. He wondered if she heard the hollowness in his voice. Would she consider it an admission of complicity in the myriad of failures his life represented?

"No thanks," she said, wandering toward the stairway, her feet as heavy as his own voice.

"You can't just go to bed like that," he said angrily, surprising himself with a bluntness unusual for him. It was not his style to be so direct, but her superior tone had always annoyed him. Just what right did she have to set herself up in judgment of him, she whose life was as sorry and unfulfilled as his own?

"What's the point?" she said, sighing that deep unmitigated expulsion of negativity, whose source, he knew, must be her low opinion of him.

"What do you mean, *What's the point?*"

"You refuse to listen," she said. "You've heard it all before. You just don't choose to admit it so it makes no sense to have the discussion again. Good night!" Her little black boots stamped the stairway in irritation.

"Look," he said, grabbing her arm and pulling her back from the stairs. "If we're going to work together, we are damned well going to get some things straight!"

The light went out of her eyes. She appeared incredibly bored. He wanted to shake her like a rag doll or punch her as he had the weighted boxing bag his parents bought him when he was a child. "To get out your aggressions," his mother had said.

"You could always hit me," Miranda said sarcastically.

"Just what is that supposed to mean?" he said, grabbing her by the wrists.

"It's the same," she said in a monotone. "Physical abuse, emotional abuse."

"What?" he said, trembling. He dropped her wrists and looked into her face which now struck him as dead. The pale countenance with its perfect symmetry and lack of expression reminded him of a cadaver. This was the eerie side of her from which he normally recoiled, but now he stood his ground.

"You expect so much of your women, but you give very little in return."

He looked down at the face, at the eyes which were regaining their gleam, at the skin growing rosier by the moment, the smooth, beautiful mouth parting in indignation and contempt. He still wanted to slap her, but he felt also a need to understand something, but what that was he wasn't certain. He seemed to feel Karen's presence on the landing above and to sense her approval. That fortified him against the hungry dog that had tormented him all his life.

"You have so little respect—" She turned away from him.

He felt the life go out of him, too. Karen's presence on the landing disappeared, its warm comfort diffusing into the dark, leaving him shaky and uncertain. "I don't know what you want," he said, helpless. "What do you expect of me?"

Her face held an expression of ineffable pity. The harshness of its lines a moment ago dissolved and in their place appeared a stoicism he found repugnant. He saw it as woman superiority, the same expression he'd seen on the faces of his mother and sister all the years he'd grown up in that lifeless West Texas town, amidst the sanctimonious ravings of all the women then. The teachers, the aunts, the crazy grandmothers. All the sick kin whose genes he harbored and for whose legacies he still atoned.

"I don't expect *anything* of you," she said wearily. "I just get tired of being disappointed."

"By what? Why?" he said, fumbling for the analytical tools to deal with her remarks. He wanted to understand something here. It was important, but he clung tenaciously to his own hard won independence.

"You'll understand when you get there," she said, turning away again. She raised a foot to the stair and looked back over her shoulder.

Suddenly it was as if every woman who had ever slighted him stood there, turning her back on him. He could no longer stand still. He tore after her, his body summoned by her confident, dogged ascent up the stairs.

He stopped at the landing and looked down at the front door. His heart was racing, all the nameless moments of humiliation and defeat rising up in a phantasmagoria of half-remembered images. "God help me," he thought, in a sudden moment of understanding. "I must get a grip."

He held onto the railing as Miranda quietly disappeared behind the guest room door and the sounds of the trees whispering outside slowly lulled him back to rationality and a studied calm. He walked into his room and looked out over the blanketed hills below then up into the hazy blur of falling snow. The moon's yellow light suffused the descending cover with an unnatural sheen and the thumping of weighted branches against the house soothed his anger. What was it Miranda said about the things snow covered? *The hurly burley?* What was it all about, anyway? What did these disagreements mean or really matter in the scheme of things? Who ever said Miranda had all the answers? He'd wait. He'd learn. He'd understand, but meanwhile he would not allow any woman to play mind games with him.

Chapter Six

Jack awakened to the rattling of the casement window. For a moment he thought of Karen near the end when the cold seemed to seep into her bones. She couldn't stop shivering, even when he held her and chafed her shoulders, or when, for old time's sake, they made love. He'd pile on goose-down comforters and make tea to warm her, but it took a lot of coaxing to get her to sit up in the bed with the damp chill in the room and the windows glazed with ice. Sometimes he'd go on downstairs and light the fire, and as the heat rose up to the little bedroom, her face would flush with gratitude. He'd play Mendlesohn and they'd drink their tea together. She liked the way he served her tea – with fresh ginger and a splash of cream. Even at the end when no amount of sweet-talk would entice her to eat a meal, she'd drink the tea with one of his cookies. That last year he'd made every conceivable kind: molasses crinkles, chocolate chip, lemon bars, Swedish butter cookies, peanut butter ones with soft middles, shortbread – anything that would give her body something to work with. Before her illness, she'd loved all kinds of pastries. She made her own pies, slapdashedly concocted every conceivable pasta dish. She liked to say it was her Italian heritage that made her plump; to love heavy food was in her genes.

Just recalling her meals made him hungry. He'd never met such a good cook. Jack wondered if the culinary gift had something to do with the touch of the food itself. Karen took her time with the preparation, seemingly playing with the food, rubbing, slicing, cajoling until, like richest alchemy, her sauces transformed the cheapest cuts into succulent dishes. She never needed a recipe.

Her dinners were a far cry from the hummus and raw vegetables Miranda served. Although Miranda made her own yogurt and granola and cultivated herb and vegetable gardens, nothing she prepared ever seemed tasty. She thickened her few cooked dishes with tofu, never ate red meat, avoided white flour. He presumed she existed on less than a thousand calories a day. When asked about her eating habits, she smiled ironically. "I eat to survive. Do you think our ancestors lingered over every bite?" She'd given him a bad time about his weight gain after his second marriage, suggested a diet following his divorce from Myrna. An older woman, she still had the figure of a teenager. Yoga and a measured asceticism had allowed her to turn back the clock.

The snow had stopped falling, but there was a sense of its resuming at any moment. No birds flew across the sky; there were no visible clouds, just an opaqueness so dense it oppressed him. *A Leadville horizon,* he thought. It seemed he had awakened to this sterile scene forever. This past year the Chinooks had been few, the bright mornings rare, or had it merely seemed that way, he wondered, recalling yesterday's sun. He didn't know anymore. All he knew was he needed a change. He had to leave the place with all its memories, at least for a while.

He stood up and looked around the room, noting the layer of dust on the dark furniture. His books lying on the table beside the bed reminded him that it had been months since he read anything other than non-fiction, as if incapable under the circumstances, of a willing suspension of disbelief, required of fiction. It occurred to him that he might remain unable to appreciate fiction indefinitely, but he dismissed the possibility. Such things took time. *Grieving took time...* He recalled that after he and Amanda separated he hadn't read for a year or longer. Such events rendered one helpless and flat, like a tire after the unforeseen occasion of a nail piercing it.

The vapor of his breath diffused into the air. His lips felt chapped. He pulled the comforter off the bed and draped it over him and trudged to the bathroom. There in the mirror he regarded his pallid features – light blue eyes crowded by folds of skin, a sagging chin barely concealed by a thinning beard that at the moment appeared unkempt. His spare brows arched over what some might call harsh eyes, raptor eyes. In the mirror's dim light, they were vigilant, perhaps fearful. He peered at them, trying to discern the man Miranda saw. *The man who offered little and expected so much.* He had to admit there was a glint in them one might interpret as ruthless, but he didn't see himself that way. "Actions always speak louder than words," Miranda repeatedly reminded him, but he had never viewed his actions in the same way she did. Now, weighed down by the misery of his aloneness, he wasn't sure what to think. He wanted to believe he'd been good to Karen, that somehow those last months in particular had partially ransomed him from his past. But then again, perhaps she was just too accepting and he hadn't really grown at all.

He took out the barber shears and trimmed the tattered beard then quickly shaved. His hands trembled from the cold. He needed to get a fire going before Miranda awakened.

He turned on the shower and waited till the room steamed up, then, shivering violently, stepped out from under the comforter and into the shower. The hot water felt good on his body. He lathered and watched the soap slide away from his skin, lost in thought. Just days ago he was wondering what he would do with his life. Then Miranda came, and now he had an engrossing project that might get his mind off Karen and still allow his imagination some release. Yet the idea of petty conflicts with Miranda was not inviting. He knew from experience that failing to maintain harmony with her brought its own share of misery. How could it be so good when they got along and so terrible when they did not? He knew part of the answer was that it mattered to Jack how Miranda felt about him. When he sensed she was indifferent, something of his that was fundamental and precious died, as if a limb or other important appendage were severed.

He thought of her lying in the guestroom upstairs, staring at the etchings of old Leadville scenes Karen bought years ago. Miranda's poetic imagination had probably linked the subjects' grim expressions with the Colorado mountain climate, the austerity of the frozen hills, men's fatuous dreams of gold and glory. For Miranda there was a story in every detail. Her poetry had an odd resonance – something beyond the words and tone, even the implicit wisdom – a characteristic, he supposed, of all good poetry. He imagined she had published many poems in the years since they'd been close, although she'd never mentioned it. He wished he'd been privy to the process. It had always seemed to Jack that her method of writing was like the mysterious process of a player piano – music without the benefit of human hands. As if the musician or poet were plugged into some cosmic wavelength. Miranda often didn't know what she'd written and then couldn't remember it later, ascribing her creations to a sort of automatic process beyond her conscious effort. Nor would she revise her work, at least, in any fundamental sense. Her refusal to edit was incomprehensible to Jack, who labored over every word and then revised the piece a hundred times over.

He stepped out of the shower and began toweling off. Already his skin prickled with goose bumps. He pulled on his warmest sweater, a thick, fishnet wool. Outside small tufts of moisture, like a baby's breath, hovered over the steely landscape. As he walked downstairs, the smell of creosote and aging banana rose on the stagnant air. He threw the bananas into the sack below the sink and made coffee. Then he brought in wood from the deck and set the fire. It wasn't easy to get it to start in the cold flue, but he kept after it until the flames finally sparked and worked their way upward, tentative tongues at first till he blew steadily for a while, and they rose higher and merged into each other as the shaft slowly warmed.

He listened for sounds from the guest room, but there was only the crackling of the fire. He drank cup after cup of coffee, peering down into the icy landscape below and wondering when the snow would start up again and how deep it would get this time.

At last he heard the guest bed creak and knew Miranda was up. Watching the fire burst into bright flames that sputtered in the silence, he suddenly had an idea. He turned on the computer and wrote several paragraphs then closed it down, furtive in his desire for secrecy. He wasn't even sure what he'd written; he'd examine it later. Just as he was rising from the table, he heard the soft lull of her step on the creaking wood floor behind him. He turned to see her eyeing him with curiosity. The devil was in the details, and Miranda knew it, her watchful eyes scanning the scene: his stooped posture, the sudden movement to shut down the machine, his evasive eyes, looking out into the grayness rather than face her uncanny insight.

"A little inspiration?" she said, turning into the kitchen. Sheepishly, he followed her as she poured the last of the coffee and searched the fridge for milk. "It's all gone," she said, her voice unexpectedly quavering.

He started to explain that he needed to get groceries, but was stopped by the sudden appearance of tears in her eyes. She quickly looked away out over the gray meadow, her face somber, chastened by the dull landscape.

"What is it?" he said, alarmed.

"Nothing."

"No, what? Tell me!"

"So little..." she said in her oblique way. She offered nothing more, just a sense of melancholy she rarely exhibited. She walked into the living room and sat down by the fire. He heard her move back into the sofa, the groan of the drying wood frame and a deep sigh that filled the room, over the snapping of the fire.

He made another pot of coffee, measuring extra to satisfy her tastes then walked back into the living room and sat down in the rocker. Already he felt tired, and he didn't know why. He had the sense she pitied him for his poverty and lost opportunity and failure; always there was the failure. It spoke to a visitor in the austerity of the place, the lack of materiality, the aged, crumbling structure itself.

She attempted a bright smile, but they both knew she was acting. He didn't know what to say, but he sensed that pressing her would simply reveal thoughts he didn't want to understand.

"I'll make you breakfast," she said, getting up. She swallowed the coffee and moved toward the kitchen.

"No, stay by the fire for a moment," he said. "Breakfast can wait." He watched her sit back down then went into the kitchen. He brought out the coffee pot and poured her another cup. He could see that her eyes were now dry and clear.

"So are you going with me to New Haven?" he asked. "Or do you expect me to do this alone?"

"Right now I have to get back to Texas," she said. "I'll join you as soon as I take care of a few matters."

"How long before you can get there?"

She thought for a minute, her lovely eyes nervously surveying the grim outdoors. Across the vivid landscape of her features, there flickered a thousand thoughts. He wondered what they were and marveled at how many could flash in succession. It was like watching an old ticker-tape silent movie. "I can't come right away," she said.

"Fine. I'll do my research, meet the professor's wife. Whatever." It would be good to be out there alone, he decided. He'd size up the situation without her. After that, maybe the two of them could piece it all together. By then whatever they were doing would begin to fall into place. The project would indeed be a collaborative effort. He felt a flutter of anticipation. It had the potential for adventure, the imminent possibility of discovery. The idea of it all made him feel young, as if for a moment the empty past melted away and before him stretched new and limitless horizons, like those days so long ago when the two of them sat up all night on the cool desert sands, staring at the stars and dreaming – he of his books and she of poetry and human suffering.

"I've never been to New Haven," she said, frowning. "What if I don't like it?"

Jack thought of the place. It had been years since he'd set foot in the city, but he did recall a corroding infrastructure, houses choked by excess undergrowth, and a hideous downtown. He hadn't much liked it himself, accustomed then to the equally unaesthetic Texas. And compared to New York City, even with its piles of garbage and the relentless rats, New Haven had seemed ugly and lifeless.

"It's not your kind of place," he said.

"So why am I doing this?" Miranda asked herself, sighing. "I must be crazy."

"That's what I like about you," Jack said, smiling at her. To his delight, she smiled back. Their quarrel was over, the tension of yesterday dissolving into the spirit that had always defined them when they were together: a curiosity borne of wayward imaginations and unfulfilled yearnings.

"Let me make you breakfast," she said, grinning down at him. The room seemed to light up as her mood expanded to include him. Then he wondered what she'd serve and how he would feign appreciation.

You couldn't ruin an egg, could you?

Chapter Seven

He watched Miranda's Blazer drive down the hill and around the hairpin turns. During the night, several more inches of snow had accumulated. He knew from experience how slippery the road was. She drove slowly, her pale hair in the meager light full and electrified, as if illustrative of a heightened sense of purpose on her part. He didn't have to be there to see in his mind's eye the firm set of her mouth and chin as she met her fate headlong, expertly maneuvering the car over the treacherous terrain.

He wondered what it was that demanded her attention in Texas and felt a stab of jealousy. He no longer knew what her life there was like. For her part, she was more secretive than she'd been in the past. There had been a time when she told him everything without his asking. She'd been one of those open women who have no secrets and talk as a way of including others in their sphere. He'd always found her mind fascinating, her lack of boundaries welcoming. A natural storyteller, she never ceased to amuse him, revealing an outgoing, eclectic nature. She was an adventuress, an existentialist in the truest sense. To keep up with her, he'd been forced to stretch, to nose out of his cocoon. She'd accused him of being a voyeur whenever he spent too much time writing or reading. Compared to her, he was, preferring the contemplative life to one led in the arena.

He smiled to recall some of the wild things they'd done under her influence. He supposed all of that was well worth remembering now since it afforded him some solace from his self-doubts, but it also made him realize that he no longer knew the woman, not really. Particularly lamentable was the fact that his lost sense of her had been a recent phenomenon, probably occurring during Karen's decline when he'd been too depressed to contact anyone. The realization too closely tied to his bereavement simply felt like one more terrible loss. He didn't want to think of Miranda that way. And yet they'd known each other so long; he supposed they both felt an irrational sense of ownership when it came to each other. It was silly to be jealous of the intervening years of which he knew virtually nothing about her romantic life. He reminded himself that once she was away from him, he'd forget her. She held him in thrall only by her charismatic and demanding presence. Once on his own, he'd revert to his reclusive self and be content with a life that lacked complications. He wanted things simple again.

He found his traveling bag and started loading it. In the back of the closet was his blue blazer. He took it off the hanger and applied a wet rag to remove the coating of dust along the shoulders. It was of a good quality and hadn't been worn much. He tried it on and was pleased to note that it fitted fine. A few years back it had been tight and he'd meant to have it altered but hadn't. He threw in all the underwear he owned, all the white shirts and the few ties he'd had for years. He didn't expect to be wearing his usual fare but he'd take along a pair of jeans and a sweater or two for the times he would be on his own. He stuffed the rarely worn black loafers into the bag.

Standing there in the bedroom with untidy piles of clothing surrounding him, he considered how out of his element he would be interviewing the wife of a world famous scientist and intellectual. Well, he was what he was. There was no need to represent himself as otherwise. If she refused to see him, he would at least have met his obligation to Miranda. It was quite possible the venture would prove a disaster. Nevertheless he felt like chancing it. He had spent his whole life focused on his writing. Now faced with past failures, he realized how little he had risked and how fearful he had always been. This once he would spit into the wind. What did he have to lose? The thought made him laugh. He had no money. It was possible he'd have to borrow from Miranda; it wouldn't be the first time. He thought of the old Kristofferson line: *"Freedom's just another word for nothing left to lose."* Well, the adage certainly applied to him.

He was up early the next morning. He set the thermostat as low as possible and pulled the blinds on all the drafty windows. The small copper lamp in the corner of the living room remained on from last night. He turned it off and replaced the bulb with a fluorescent one and turned it back on. He made the beds, including Miranda's. She had torn off the sheets and left the quilt dangling over the iron frame. He picked up the pile of sheets from the clothes washer and put the sheets back on and stuffed the old feather pillows back into the cases. He thought it might be comforting to smell her scent in the bed after his return and cringed to think what Miranda would make of that. He picked up magazines she had left on the floor, an empty pack of cigarettes on the bedside table. He took her ashtray downstairs and put it in the dishwasher. It was odd how life worked out. He had always had an aversion to smoking. In his mind it was not feminine, and yet every one of his women had smoked. Miranda needled him about his weight, and he nagged her about the smoking. She had tried to quit many times.

He put away a couple of books he'd been reading the night before and took out the garbage and set the plastic sacks in the back of his car. He picked up his traveling bag and the laptop, glancing around at the familiar details of his life: worn rugs, the lumpy sofa, a rickety rocking chair. The blackened stone of the fireplace and the splintered flooring seemed to rebuke him, reminding him of all the domestic chores he'd neglected, even after Karen's death, when there had been time to do whatever he wanted. He had to admit he'd been lazy when it came to the basic mechanics of maintaining a household.

He locked the house and walked slowly down the basement steps and climbed into his Jeep. On his way down the mountain, he felt a sense of relief at leaving the past behind. Far above him, on its icy pinnacle, the house seemed to bid a mournful good by. Its doors were locked, the shutters closed, as if it harbored a secret.

As Jack threw the twin bags of garbage into the landfill, he felt as if he were shedding some indefinable burden. He glanced around at the monotonous landscape in the gray, early morning light, and felt a sense of exhilaration. He was leaving Leadville behind. He stopped at the ATM and walked along the narrow, broken sidewalks to the Windjammer. There he sat down at a table in the corner and tried to compose himself. He'd been alone so long that he wasn't sure he could summon the emotional energy to reconnect with society. It had been hard enough accommodating Miranda, but to venture out into the world again on the dubious undertaking she had conceived seemed for the moment as crazy as it did the morning after she arrived.

Thinking of New Haven brought back the sense of humiliation he had felt as a newcomer to New York City thirty years ago. What a hayseed he'd been, he thought, thinking of his silly dreams of success. He had landed the beautiful Felicia, and he had sincerely thought he'd made it – that the world would open before him, opportunities piling up like stacks of currency, but it hadn't worked out that way. His success had been short lived and empty. In fact, it had been so ephemeral that now looking back on it, he wasn't even sure he had actually written a book others read, before it was forgotten by everyone else but him.

Miranda liked it, though, he reminded himself, smiling over his coffee.

Across the room a family of four sat eating in silence. Except for the kitchen sounds, there was nothing to indicate that anyone in the room had feelings, he thought suddenly. It was as if the whole scene was as lifeless and flat as the house he had just abandoned. Jack stood up and threw a ten dollar bill on the table and walked outside. The cold smacked his face, another rebuff. In the distance the trees were heavy with snow and gray in the blend of sky and rock. No wonder they named the town Leadville. It was time to move on, time to get out of the place before it swallowed him up in its dismal landscape. Before he had closed too many more doors and grown as limited as the place itself. It was a small-person town, he thought, hitching up his jeans and pulling at the collar of his parka.

His lizard boots rocked slightly as he walked back to his car. He sat in the freezing Jeep, glancing at the old buildings of the downtown and the gray-pink sky arching over them. Ribbons of charcoal clouds crowded the horizon beyond the town. The silence of it all engulfed him with a sense of futility and shame. He started up the car and turned the heat to high. As the heat dried out the bottoms of his Levis and penetrated his damp boots, he felt his mood change. The sun rose higher, and the sky turned yellow and scarlet. The ribbons of charcoal suffused into a thinner, all pervasive blend of violet and orange and red, and then it all turned into a sky so blue and perfect it made him want to cry. Jack reached up to pull his dark glasses down from the visor then thought better of it. He squinted into the sun and drove on.

The trees were beginning to thin. Yellow leaves coated the snow-packed streets. School buses lumbered along the winding roads, stopping to pick up serious faced young people, reminding Jack of human need and responsibility. He was glad his life hadn't come down to that. Children had been the one condition upon which Miranda would have agreed to marry him had he not run off with Felicia. Now both of them were childless, and what did it matter in the scheme of things? They were free while the others in their high school graduating class still tried to please a generation of entitled adults. Jack was grimly aware that he would not have been a patient father. His own father had been exacting and judgmental, his mother disengaged, he had slowly come to realize as he grew older. He'd always claimed she was the perfect mother, but since Karen's death, he was beginning to acknowledge her indifference. Karen had been more giving to the town children than his own mother had been to him. Karen took an interest in kids, volunteered in their schools, went on field trips when room mothers were not available. At her restaurant, she often treated the less affluent children to a sundae or a sandwich. At first her affection for the children annoyed Jack, but he'd learned to accept it. He supposed his annoyance had been the result of his own possessiveness and the fact that young people simply bored him. Still, he admired Karen's maternal instincts.

The airport was almost empty. He sat down in the corner and read the opening chapter of Dostoyevsky's *The Idiot*. He had wanted to re-read all of Dostoyevsky for years but hadn't felt ready to deal with the author's existential questions. As a young man he had read all of Dost over and over again. He and Miranda had had many discussions of the books. They had read them together, oftentimes reading passages aloud to each other. All that intellectual stimulation now seemed a distant memory.

Karen and he had shared many interests, but not a passion for literature. He wondered if Miranda still read as voraciously as she had then. Her ideas had inspired him to read more carefully, to think more deeply. To realize now that he didn't know if she still read with such passion made him feel abandoned, although why he felt that way he could never begin to explain. He supposed it had to do with his current sense of loss, so profound it had indeed unsettled him. He didn't know who he was, what he wanted. With a start, he realized he was as clueless as he'd been as a young man. Perhaps some men never grew up, never gained the insight needed to grapple with the world. Miranda had accused him of such over the years; maybe she was right. When you thought about it, the two did have a history, still echoing through their separate experiences. It wasn't likely that would change even with Don Parrish in her life.

When it came time to board the flight, he heaved his laptop and travel bag up into the luggage compartment and promised himself that he would not write nor even think about writing. This once he would observe the world around him, as Miranda would under the same circumstances. He would note the way people interacted, the demeanor of the stewardesses, the simple, open way children stared at him as they passed his seat and wandered to the back of the plane. He would avoid the unhealthy meal and refrain from an alcoholic drink or two. Letting the past go meant making some changes, he told himself.

Instead he ate the tasteless omelet crammed with bright orange cheese and drank two Bloody Marys'. Rather than talk to the pleasant middle aged woman seated next to him, he stared out the window and thought about Dostoyevsky and whether there could ever be a man of Myshkin's goodness. He had never known anyone who struck him as innocent. Rather, he saw people as conniving and ruthless, like the people surrounding Myshkin, whose tragic end exemplified man's fate, as far as Jack was concerned.

He awoke with a start when the plane landed and groggily stared at the gray New Haven skies. What was he doing here?

Chapter Eight

He rented a car and drove through the downtown. The place hadn't changed much in the thirty years since he'd last been there. It still possessed a seedy ambience, as if corrupted by the financiers whose citizenship once granted it a tenuous respect. Yale University, with its magnificent and crumbling façade rose from the rubble of the ruined city. Empty buildings, abandoned lots, and graceless architecture mingled in a bleak montage. The streets were rutted, lined by mismatched buildings, abutting broken curbs and cracked sidewalks. There was a sense of neglect, even abandonment in the deteriorating asphalt, the grimy masonry and rotting cornices, the stench of garbage and diesel. It was a depressing place, Jack thought, and wondered how a person could enjoy such a dreary environment. According to his information, the professor's wife still lived in the city.

He hadn't meant to call her right away. In fact, he told himself he needed to do additional research so that when he requested permission to write her husband's biography, she'd be impressed by his knowledge of the man. He reminded himself that she was a widow, perhaps still bereft, unlikely to be amenable to talking at length about her spouse, however much she might want him remembered by the scientific community. Now, after being reminded of the city's deteriorating state, Jack was not only curious about the man whose achievements were legendary, he was also intrigued by the idea of a widow who chose to remain in New Haven. It would seem that what had kept her there for years had been her husband's position at the University. Jack reasoned that like a lot of professors, Theodore Hudson chose to live close to his lab rather than commute from any one of a number of scenic bedroom communities nearby. It was obvious to Jack that New Haven was not a safe place for a woman in her circumstances. So why had she remained in the city after her husband's death?

He drove past her house, noting the graceful Queen Anne architecture and the wide, expansive porch. It was a gray-clapboard, three-story home with garnet-colored shutters and trim. Above the leaded glass door was an oval stained-glass window in the same color scheme. Beautiful in an old-world way, with its turrets and ornate moldings, it immediately struck one as the kind of house that demanded a lot of maintenance. A wooden ramp for the handicapped extended from one end of the verandah out to the driveway. Was the woman an invalid or did someone else with a disability occupy the residence? After driving by the house and around the neighborhood of similar homes, Jack realized the old homes he remembered as falling to wrack and ruin in the seventies and eighties, were being reclaimed. Workers installed new siding; painters assembled scaffolding, glazers replaced old windows. There was the sense that some of the city's past vitality was being restored. Jack parked his car across the street and studied the professor's home for clues to his character. The paint on the upstairs level was peeling. The grass needed mowing. A gate leading to the back yard had a broken hinge and swung back and forth in the wind.

As he stared from his car window, the front door suddenly opened. A woman stood on the verandah, looking vaguely up and down the street. She was beautiful in a classic sense: tall, with refined features, a slim figure, expressive eyes, but what stood out in Jack's mind was a traditional elegance apparent in the way she moved and in the chignon loosely coiled at the nape of her neck. He hadn't seen such a hairstyle since he was a young boy in West Texas, where the old women still plaited their hair. Her demeanor and the way she glanced cautiously around her, gave him the impression of a reserved and very controlled woman. She noticed Jack then quickly looked away. To conceal his discomfort at being discovered staring at her home, he grabbed the map of New Haven and pointedly studied it.

When he looked back at the house, she was pushing a young man in a wheelchair out onto the porch. As Jack watched, she pulled a red knit cap over his head, gently pleating the rim, and then went back into the house. She brought out a heavy blanket and placed it over his legs. The young man made a comment that caused her to smile. The boy was startlingly handsome with no resemblance to his mother that Jack could discern. His hair was black and thick, his torso wide and well formed. Yet the blanket could not conceal the fact that his legs were short and frail, probably atrophied. He had a naturally colorful complexion and wide, alert eyes that seemed to follow every nuance of his mother's expression.

She wheeled the boy down the ramp and out onto the sidewalk without looking at Jack. From his open car window, he heard the sound of her voice blending with the young man's as they worked their way down the street amidst the falling leaves. Jack had forgotten how beautiful a season fall was in the east. The scene was lovely indeed with the woman gracefully walking behind the wheelchair, animatedly talking and glancing around her at the flaming sugar maples. He watched till her figure blended into the shadows far down the street. For a moment he imagined what else their eyes took in – those two so devoted to each other that even a stranger could feel something special in the air around them. He didn't want to relinquish the scene.

He drove into town and found the cheapest motel available. The parking lot was full of cars and spotted by wads of chewing gum and oil stains. A dingy vestibule smelled of dusty furniture and bathroom disinfectant. His room had a moldy odor; the windows were streaked, and there were black stains on the carpet, but he told himself it was good enough and better than a lot of places he'd stayed in. He thought of Karen's bungalow and experienced an unexpected surge of nostalgia.

After he had showered and surfed the Internet for information about Theodore Hudson, he decided to call the woman. By then it was late afternoon, and the shadows through the open curtain were thick and oppressive. He was hungry, but he didn't want to dine after dark. He suspected that in New Haven, one was subject to any sort of crime or indignity. The motel did not have a restaurant so he would have to go out, but first he would call the woman.

She answered the phone quietly, perhaps groggily, as if she'd been sleeping or was distracted. He felt the weight of some vague distress on her part and had the urge to relieve her of any unpleasantness.

"Mrs. Hudson," he said, more than a little unnerved by a voice that did not match the personality he'd observed earlier. He was expecting more vitality, maybe an effusive rush to talk or even a New England reserve, a native imperiousness – anything but the seemingly fragile, somewhat tentative response of the woman. "I'm the man who parked outside your house this afternoon."

"I beg your pardon," she said.

"I was looking at a map of New Haven," he went on, "because I wanted to be sure I knew where you lived. You see, I want to write a book about your husband. The world should know more about Professor Theodore Hudson."

There was a long silence over which he heard the drone of the air-conditioning beneath the plastic curtain and the sound of a car door closing in the wretched parking lot. He felt a tightening in his chest and neck. He steadied his free hand against the side of the bed and waited.

"You realize there have been others," she said wearily.

"I'm sure there have," he said. "But I can assure you, I will give the project my heart and soul, nothing less. A great man must be remembered. The truth of his life must be told."

"I see," she said. He heard the creak of what sounded like bedsprings.

He felt his heart beating hard, almost painfully. It occurred to him he was getting too old for any kind of stress, if this simple petition put him at such an obvious disadvantage. He tried to relax. "I have time right now to devote myself exclusively to recording your husband's legacy, if you'll just give me permission." When she said nothing, he added, "I'm a freelance writer, and if I get busy later, I won't have the amount of time I would consider necessary to do justice to Theodore Hudson's life."

There was a long pause. He told himself not to talk further but to wait. He had said too much already, revealed his insecure and anxious nature. His instincts told him this was not the kind of woman you pushed or manipulated with half-baked flattery.

"I presume you have credentials," she said at last, in a more relaxed tone. Now he was certain she had been sleeping. Her voice was strong and measured, true to his image of her.

"Yes," he said, feeling his confidence wane in the presence of her strength. *One lousy out-of-print novel!* She'd dismiss him immediately. He thought of Miranda and her sense of purpose, the enthusiasm she'd aroused in him, and suddenly his sense of failure lifted, and it all seemed do-able again. He closed his eyes against his pathetic image in the dresser mirror across from him. His sagging shoulders and limp mouth taunted him. It made him so angry he ventured, "May I make an appointment, and we'll discuss my qualifications more completely?" He was perspiring, he noticed, feeling like a child back in school, in the process of being interrogated by the teacher who knew he hadn't read the assignment.

"Wait a moment," she said. He heard what sounded like bedsprings again and the rustle of clothing. "I'm going into the kitchen. Hold on."

When she picked up the phone, he could hear classical music in the background. Outside his hotel a thunderous rain storm was in progress and the room was cold and dank. "What did you say your name was?" she asked.

"Jack Pierce."

"You're from Yale?"

"No, I...I..."

"Good, because I've turned down several writers from here. I'm not sure I want to have Ted's story done right now, but if I decide to go ahead, I don't want the writer to be from Yale." She sighed as if she regretted talking to him in the first place, as if explaining herself was more than she had the energy for at the moment. Hearing her weariness endeared her to him.

"I know how you feel," he blurted. "It's so soon and all. Sometimes it's hard to discuss the life of the person you're still grieving. I'm sorry to intrude, really I am." To his astonishment he was trembling with emotion.

"You're very considerate," she said. "But you don't really understand."

Her words, gentle as they were, nevertheless rebuked him. He felt as if she had slapped him in the face. He didn't know what to say. His stomach rumbled, reminding him that he hadn't eaten since that terrible omelet on the plane.

"I really want to understand," he burst out.

"I know," she said. "I'm sure you're a very good person."

"But I'm not," he wanted to say. "I'm a fool and a loser and as ruthless in my own way as a man can get, but there are things I care about." Yet he said nothing. Words eluded him. What could a person honestly say in these circumstances? That he needed a job desperately? That a close friend depended on him to do the story? That a lunatic suggested the project? To his surprise she seemed to take his silence for agreement.

"You may come tomorrow, if you'd like," she said soothingly, transparently trying to relieve pain for which she mistakenly assumed responsibility. When he didn't respond right away, she added, "I'll make you lunch. We don't go out much here."

All he could manage was a timid thank-you. He waited, holding onto the phone cradle with a desperate strength. Until that moment he hadn't realized how important the project had become in his own mind.

"I'll see you around one," she said and hung up.

Jack put the phone down and sat in a stunned silence, listening to the thrumming of the rain on the windows for several moments before he regained his composure. The walls seemed to comfort him, the drab room transforming itself before his eyes. Outside the blackness of the rain-soaked night could not diminish a sense of elation.

As he drove through the downtown streets of New Haven, he thought how the smoky light from the old street lamps conferred a quiet dignity on the town's cracked concrete. The subtlety of shadows and falling rain obscured the peeling paint and angry faces of passersby. The city didn't seem so bad without the scrutiny of sunlight. He was reminded of past times sitting in bars in New York City and New Haven in the early seventies, listening to Kris Kristofferson. It all seemed so long ago, he thought sadly, those times when one felt wrapped in the gauzy cloth of hope, as he had been then. Where had it all gone, he wondered. He thought of Bob Dylan's elegiac laments. Of Martin Luther King, John Kennedy, Robert. Somehow their idealism had died with the times. The world had changed on a dime, sometime in the eighties, he guessed. One day everything had seemed different, but he wasn't sure at the time just how or what had changed. He just knew it had. He could tell it in the faces of people, in the literature and media. A lot had been written on the subject, but in Jack's mind no one had pinpointed the nature of the change.

He thought of Theodore Hudson and presumed he had embodied some of the idealism of that period. To write his story would be an honor and a service to himself and all members of what had then seemed to its critics a confused and immoral generation. He liked the idea of affirming something. He would be recapturing the past in the only way possible for him. The more he thought about the project the more excited he became. He couldn't wait to discuss the subject with Miranda.

He ate a pizza at a hole-in-the-wall place close to the university and looked around at the young people drinking pitchers of beer. The place was mellow, consisting of quiet conversation and no music. He sat in the back corner of the shallow parlor and watched a pretty young girl in a skimpy top down glass after glass of dark ale. Her hair was cut close to her face, emphasizing large eyes and black brows. Her lipstick was bright red and smeared her glass and the napkin with which she kept wiping her face. Just as Jack finished his food, the girl stumbled to her feet and followed her date out of the room. Jack watcher her stagger on down the street, grabbing her boyfriend's hand as she disappeared into the night. The scene reminded him of Felicia and her tendency to drink too much. He wondered if now in her later years she was still as bored and tedious as she'd seemed then or if she'd reinvented herself as a working woman, an idea she often tossed out, but which he'd felt was an unlikely role for a hedonist. She lacked the discipline. More likely she'd married any number of callow men by now. Jack had kept in touch with his other wives, but until now he'd thought very little of Felicia. The marriage had been a mistake. They had had so little in common that leaving her had been as easy as walking out on a boring movie.

He drove back to the hotel. There were few people out, and the roads were quiet. By the time he drove into the parking lot, he was exhausted. He drew to a stop right outside his room and let himself in. The air-conditioner had been going strong, and the room felt like a morgue. He turned the thing off and went into the bathroom. He removed his clothes and turned on the shower. Then standing for a long time under the hot blast, he let himself think of women, of life, whatever. His mind seemed to drift from subject to subject in a bizarre association of images. He thought of Miranda. He'd call her tonight, even if it was late. He imagined her asleep on her four-poster bed with the old headboard she'd painted mauve, her hair spread out against the dark pillowcase, like an aura, and her white hands resting on her stomach. In the light from the window she'd look about thirteen, her countenance calm, her body curved into itself. She'd be dreaming, and the flickering expressions of her closed eyes would expose an esoteric imagination she hid from others. Well, she couldn't conceal that from him, now could she?

He dialed her number. It was late but Miranda never seemed angry when he called, and she often stayed up late, reading or watching a movie. Even when he awoke her late into the night, she'd always seemed eager to talk. Of course, it had been awhile since he'd dared to do that, but he was sure his call would be welcome.

The phone rang and rang. No answering machine responded. He hung up feeling strangely unsettled. He turned on the television and watched a movie till he felt himself grow groggy. He must have drifted off because he was faintly aware of a loud commercial. He opened his eyes and looked at the clock. It was three in the morning. The room was humid and warm.

He pulled the covers down and lay on his back, hearing the sound of traffic through the walls, recalling his first year in New York City and how hard it had been to sleep there with all the noise. Eventually he'd grown accustomed to it. All New Yorkers got used to the constant racket, he knew, surprised that he hadn't missed the excitement of the place these years he'd been buried in Leadville. He hadn't been bored one day in the city. That period in his life had been full of new experiences, and he'd known even then he was growing in ways that surely his writing would someday reflect. At the time, he'd wondered how Miranda would react to the man he was rapidly becoming. He'd once had the temerity to believe he was invincible and had returned each year to his Texas high school reunion with a renewed sense of a man going places. He was the successful *author*. Now so many years later that the details were fuzzy and incomplete, he wondered when it was that he stopped attending those gatherings. He had ceased to feel important, but he realized now that he should have kept in touch with his old friends. Miranda had. He should have been concerned about them, not only about his own success. Every year on the date of the reunion he had felt a pang of nostalgia for the tiny town that had nurtured him. But he'd felt shamed, too, and wondered why. Wasn't a man allowed to be less than a success? He supposed not, recalling his parents' stern expectations, how disappointed they'd been when he dropped out of the mediocre Texas college his parents had saved for. His mother had wanted him to be a lawyer.

The image of the professor's wife rose in his imagination then the face of Miranda as she'd headed on down the icy mountain road. With a start, he realized Miranda was still on her way back to Texas, moving steadfastly though all those drab Texas towns with their parched mesquite and tottering barns. At the moment he missed her so much he could hardly believe it. No doubt she had a cell phone. He cursed himself that he hadn't even asked for the number. Lying there in the darkness in the meager hotel room, he felt as alone as he ever had in his life. What was he doing? Where was he going with his life? For a moment he wished Miranda hadn't appeared, reminding him that being alone and single wasn't all it was cracked up to be.

Chapter Nine

He hadn't slept well. The noise of the parking lot awoke him more than once. Memories of Felicia twisted him into agonies of regret. He hardly ever thought of her, but when he did there was the guilt that he'd never tried to make their last months together tolerable. Instead he had taunted her, denigrating her intelligence, her seeming lack of discipline, even her beauty. He was certain that when they finally separated for good, she believed he hated her. Well, he did then, but he didn't now. It's just that whenever he recalled her, he grew angry at himself, at the shallow man he'd been then to have taken up with a woman like Felicia. Everyone else seemed to have her number. They'd all tried to discourage the romance — even his mother, who could barely stand to be in the same room with her. Still, he had not seen their basic incompatibility until it was too late. By then, they'd come to depend on each other for all the wrong reasons.

She liked to party and drink; he enjoyed the freedom he had to write as a result of her money. They had struck a wary peace since his being an author granted her the intellectual status she craved, and her social position allowed him access to the literary connections he needed to survive. Looking back it was surprising their marriage lasted as long as it did. During that time he never wrote anything worth reading. He'd gone through four agents who'd all given up on him. When at last he left Felicia, she weeping so hard he almost couldn't do it, he had to go because if he didn't, he knew he'd never write again, so self-battered had he become in those eight terrible years.

Afterward, he'd never called her, never written. When her image floated up from the abyss of his unconscious, he'd curse her in his mind's eye: her selfishness, her vanity, her depravity. After they parted, he'd told himself she was a slut whose beauty had suggested the virtue he couldn't claim in himself. He'd thought classic beauty, such as Felicia's, was analogous to Truth or goodness, as the poet Keats suggested. *Beauty is truth, truth beauty; that's all ye know on earth and all ye need to know.* Well, the poets were wrong, he decided. Of his wives and lovers, Karen had been the most beautiful inside. What of Cleopatra or Delilah or Helen of Troy? A man had to learn to see through appearances, and for some inexplicable reason that was difficult for him.

Miranda told him he should be over his anger at Felicia by now. She was what she was, said Miranda, who never judged anyone. He supposed it was her line of work that made her so reluctant to see the dark side of people, although she wasn't above giving him a hard time. Why was that, he wondered. He decided it must go back to the time when they loved each other without reservation. She was still angry with him for leaving her and moving on to the others. During the years of their youthful courtship, the idea that there would be a time they wouldn't be together was unthinkable. They had predicated their futures on each other. Such was their shared absolute, what romantics lived by. Curiously enough, after their various disappointments, they still sought solace in each other. He told himself that it would always be that way, but with Don Parrish in the picture, he wasn't so sure.

Don Parrish. He might have guessed the attraction had he been anything but self-absorbed and cocky in those days. When he thought about it, the man had been lurking around just waiting for Miranda to move on. If he hadn't left for Nam, he'd have made his move, Jack was sure now. He had to admit he was surprised he hadn't, but then maybe he had, and Miranda, so loyal and honest, had simply never told Jack about it. It had been plain then that Don liked Miranda a lot. In those days she'd been the queen, the personification of what it meant to be young and imaginative and open to the times. All kinds of people had been in awe of her and her idiosyncratic ways, her tendency to see the world in a grain of sand, as Blake would say. Her depth had always astounded him, but looking back, he supposed her insights had grown heavy on him. He'd actually started to yearn for someone less complex, with whom it wasn't necessary to share so much. With whom he could retreat into his own imagination without the responsibilities of extension or whatever it was that made demands on one's time and self.

The day was wearing on, Jack noted, finally leaving the dreary room and stepping out into the parking lot. A gray mantle lowered the sky. Beyond the motel, cars drove along the entangling arterials of New Haven. He walked across the street and sat down in the coffee shop on the corner. He took out the notes he had on Theodore Hudson. What had surprised him in his research was how little mention there was of the professor's family. Despite the mounds of information on his discoveries, his multitude of articles, books and lectures, the press coverage of his various causes, what was decidedly lacking was a profile of the man himself, the spirit behind the body of work, or the family connection to the messianic zeal with which it appeared the man had pursued the mysteries of immunology. He had been a passionate advocate for ethics in medicine and life, as if the two were inextricably bound. He had been short listed time and again before he won the coveted Prize.

Research supported the fact that he was indeed one of the foremost scientists of the times. Beyond his scientific accomplishments were the many philanthropic and social causes he launched and supported. An advocate for the family, he'd lectured extensively on its importance to the survival of the human race. That a Nobel Prize recipient would argue that healthy bodies were nourished in healthy families gave further impetus to the Focus on the Family and other such groups. His work on behalf of AIDS patients was legendary, resulting in his receiving numerous grants that benefited Yale's labs and libraries and sent him on lectures around the world. His assistance to Doctors without Borders, his commitment to solving the mysteries of Malaria, Ebola, and Tuberculosis, and his willingness to lecture tirelessly in the far reaches of the Third World imparted to him a legendary status. Nor did he run from controversy; he was often at the center of debate as he argued scientific axioms not always popular with the establishment. At Yale he had fought the powers that be on numerous causes. Yet he had persisted in the face of unbelievable opposition to forge new constructs that continued to cause seismic shifts in his field of study. Now that he was gone, one wondered what the impact would be on the funding for immunology at Yale. Jack would have to dig deeper for that information; nothing he had uprooted to date touched on that important question. No fellow researchers here had commented publicly on the impact of Theodore Hudson's untimely death. Only the president of the university, in his boilerplate tribute for the media, seemed to recognize the dearth his death represented. Jack found that fact strange. In his judgment there weren't that many men in the sciences who were known to the general public, and none of the stature of Theodore Hudson, so why was the academic community so mute on the subject of his demise?

Jack had done enough research to know that this omission was the beginning of an important part of Theodore Hudson's story. He thought of his widow's reluctance to have a Yale person write the book. He recalled the body of past media coverage before the man's death, its tendency to portray him as an icon, the leader of his generation's scientific contributions, a world figure of political and social consequence. This was a man who was invited to the White House, the subject of documentaries, a pundit in his own right. And yet, he'd been dead a year, and not one Yale scientist was quoted as to the significance of Theodore Hudson's accomplishments. It was as if he'd already been forgotten, but Jack couldn't imagine that was so. Something dark and unwarranted, no doubt, dwelt beneath the silence here. He was determined to find out what it was. He speculated that it was probably due to jealousy in a competitive, possibly megalomaniacal academic environment that his legacy had been, for all practical purposes, denied him.

With a start, he realized it was time to meet Mrs. Hudson. He went into the coffee shop's bathroom and studied his appearance in the mirror. His beard was trimmed, his clothes well coordinated and appropriate for the occasion. His eyes weren't swollen as they often were when he lacked sleep or had been reading too much. He looked as presentable as he was capable, so he left the coffee shop and went to his car, satisfied. He thought of Miranda and wondered where she was in her long journey back to West Texas. It struck him as odd that she hadn't called, but he reminded himself that she'd always been an undependable communicator, calling him when she chose and then disappearing back into her own life for months or even years. Well, they had a bargain this time; he expected to hear from her soon.

By the time he arrived the sun had come out, and the houses along Whitney had assumed the grandeur of their past. Recently a collection of rooming houses, many of them formerly lovely old homes, had been reclaimed and restored as private residences. The Hudson house was exquisite, he decided, curious to see its interior. He walked up the concrete ramp and rang the doorbell. A magnificent leaded glass door with an iron security panel allowed him to see into the house's entryway. An Oriental carpet stretched across dark wood flooring and under a French armoire. Two straight-back, Windsor chairs sat opposite it. On one was piled a stack of books. To his astonishment there was a copy of his own book, *Tainted Souls*, still in its original, tattered cover. Even the title struck him as dated now.

He hadn't opened the book in twenty years and had long ago decided it wasn't any good. Well, the woman had done her homework.

She was at the door immediately, radiant in the light from the porch. Her hands turned the key to the dead bolt; she waited for him to enter and removed the key and placed it on the top of the armoire. When she turned toward him again, a gracious smile made him feel immediately at ease. "Would you like some iced tea?" she asked, looking up at him as she led him into the kitchen. She was of medium height, he decided, slender and somewhat delicate in bone structure. Her eyes were dark and riveting, with the faintest suggestion of Arabic or mid-eastern descent. It was an intelligent face with high, slender cheekbones, a long, graceful neck, and full, unpainted lips. He found himself staring at her classic features as an artist would a Vermeer or a Rembrandt. "You're beautiful!" he said, without thinking then was horrified that such an obvious *faux pas* should escape his lips under the circumstances.

"Well, thank you," she said, laughing. "It's not every day that a stranger tells me I'm beautiful."

"I'm sorry," he said. "That was truly stupid."

"Trying to take it back?" She laughed again.

"Oh, no, I mean..."

"Why don't we just start over?" she said, pouring him a glass of tea from a pitcher on the counter. It was a large kitchen with tall cupboards and wainscoted walls. A tribal rug of scarlet and coral hues stretched beneath a round, claw footed table. Leaded glass windows looked out on a yard of deciduous trees and blue grass. He could see a patio table and chairs beneath a fruit tree and beds of pansies and impatiens. He had a sense of order and restraint but also of warmth in the tidy, colorful environment. Gold, red and amber leaves fell gently from the old trees out back and spread across the lawn and up against the fence. To Jack, this was the loveliest scene he had ever observed in New Haven.

"You have a gorgeous yard," he said, continuing to survey the autumn beauty. He'd always loved the turning Aspen of Colorado's falls and hadn't expected to be moved by the beauty of this place. His pleasure took him by surprise, as it appeared to have her as well.

"I've never been to Colorado," she said, "Although I've always wanted to see the Rockies. Ted was there often and always promised to take us sometime, but it just never worked out." There was the faintest suggestion of disappointment in Mrs. Hudson's voice. Jack held his tongue and waited for her to continue. "I guess that won't be happening now," she finished. She held up his glass for him. "Well, why don't we go outside then. It's quite nice out."

She picked up a plate of cookies from the counter and led him through the back door onto a slate covered patio. They sat down at the wrought iron table. She passed the plate to him, and he took one of the cookies – a molasses one with sugar on top, his favorite. It had been months since he'd eaten a homemade cookie, and it pleased him, reminding him of childhood and the old pleasures of the past. He couldn't remember one of his wives or women friends making cookies for him, although before Karen's death, he had made cookies for her.

"I have a confession to make," she said, as she took a bite from her cookie. Over them the trees whispered, and the sun filtered through the golden branches. Still warm out, the air was mildly humid and smelled of ivy and boxwood, a scent that conjured up visits to the country when he and Felicia left the city for weekends all those years ago.

"Yes," he said eagerly, almost lost in the flashing reverie of the Berkshires in the fall.

"I knew almost instantly who you were."

"You did?" he said, astonished. He remembered how his voice had trembled from self-consciousness and the sense that he was insinuating himself too early into her grief-laden world. It had been hard to broach the subject and extremely difficult to continue when her voice had seemed unenthusiastic. But he had pushed himself anyway, feeling an obligation to Miranda more than anything.

"I read your book when it first came out. I thought it was marvelous. I always wondered why you didn't write another one."

"I saw it on the chair in the entryway, but I thought you were just doing your homework. It would never have occurred to me that you knew of my book."

"I was an English major," she said. "I still read most of the touted current fiction. Before Ted and I were married, I taught at Wellesley. I actually had aspirations to write myself, but then David came along." She looked down at the sparkling diamond on her finger. Her dark eyes seemed to turn gray as the sun disappeared behind the clouds. There was a long pause. "And everything changed."

"David?" he said.

"Our son. He has Muscular Dystrophy. Would you like to meet him?" Her smile was so gracious, her face so alight with expectation, that Jack was touched by something he couldn't name. He felt a general warmth suffusing him with a sense of promise. Nevertheless he reminded himself to be cautious. Most men were charmed by beautiful women. Jack liked to think he no longer was.

She stood up. "I'll get him." Before Jack could say anything in reply, she had opened the back door and was calling into the house. "David, darling... David?"

Jack sat back in this chair and thought about the two of them on their walk yesterday. He recalled the harmony of their movements through the enveloping trees on Whitney Avenue. In his mind's eye, he saw the boy, his face upturned, questions flowing from his lips and her measured responses. Jack had been struck by their unity of spirit, of something more than the harmony of mere compatibility and habit.

She wheeled him out onto the slate patio and poured him a glass of tea. Jack watched as the boy thanked her and raised the glass to his mouth. He had on a clean white shirt and blue jeans that revealed the fragility of his legs. Jack was again struck by how handsome the boy's face was. His eyes and complexion were clear. His skin had a rosy glow, his black wavy hair was shiny and thick. He reached out his hand to Jack and looked him full in the eyes as if he were used to meeting people. When he spoke, it was with a strong, deep voice.

"Mother really liked your book," he said. "I haven't read it yet, but I will. Soon."

"You don't need—"

"But I want to," he said, turning his wheelchair to face away from the sun. He adjusted the blanket in his lap and scanned the shadowy areas at the back of the property. A squirrel made its way across the trail of leaves to the fence. David's eyes followed the creature with interest.

"Please call me Ann," the woman said as she seated herself next to her son. She sipped some more from her tea and gave Jack an earnest look. "I'll call you Jack, if you don't mind."

"Certainly," he said, noticing the chignon at the nape of her neck, the white blouse beneath a fitted herringbone blazer, the long skirt hanging to her laced button boots. The clothes, the hairstyle, the wispy curls around her face gave the impression of a woman from another era. And yet she exhibited beyond her natural reserve a refreshing openness and forthrightness he found attractive and welcoming. He wondered that she maintained such warmth in her personality after her year-long ordeal.

"I've prayed a long time for just the right person to come along. There have been several who approached us, but none of them seemed right." She looked over at David, who nodded. "And then just when I despaired of giving my approval to anyone now, you came along. I just knew right after you called that you'd do right by him." She looked away into the trees at the back of the property. "He was a very complex man, my husband, and I don't believe anyone who hasn't studied people could begin to understand him. God knows it was hard for us to grasp why he did some of the things he did." Her eyes opened wide then lowered to the ground as if seeing in her mind's eye some unfortunate scene, "but David and I realized we just had to have faith sometimes because Ted marched to his own drummer, and that was that. No force on earth was going to dissuade him from what he thought had to be done. He drove himself hard, harder than anyone I have ever known. For that he gave up a lot, too. There were so many times he wasn't here when we needed him, but we learned to share him with the world. His yearnings were so noble we didn't want to interfere." She watched her son for reactions, but he sat still, a serious look on his face.

"I was proud of my father," David said after a long silence. "I learned very young that he would provide, but that there would always be pressing demands he had to acknowledge. After a while, I accepted that."

"David's a very mature young man, for his age," Ann said.

"He sure is," Jack said, recalling his own immaturity at David's age, when nothing mattered but football and Miranda's kisses. Necking beneath the pecan trees of his parents' property and reading Tolstoy, Dostoyevsky, Milton. He'd certainly read a lot at David's age. "Do you read?" he asked the boy.

"All the time," David said. "A lot of non-fiction, science, philosophy, political science. I plan to major in physics at Princeton."

"Quantum?"

"Yes, how did you know?"

"Just a guess," Jack said. "From what I understand Princeton is on the cutting edge of Quantum Physics."

"It is," David agreed. "Dad wanted me to go there. He knew several faculty members."

"Not much fiction then?"

"Oh, yes. I like fiction, too. It's just I'd rather read about the world."

"I see," Jack said, recalling those were the exact words Karen used to explain her preference. She rarely read fiction. Try as he might, he could never persuade her to love novels or poetry, his two loves. Always for her, life was about the physical world. She read travelogues, biography, self-help books. She found fiction too abstract, too unreal, if one could imagine anyone arguing that, he thought, he who considered fiction more real than anything out there.

"Well," Ann said, standing. It was getting cool in the backyard with the shadows spreading across the yard. Outside he could hear the late afternoon traffic moving along Whitney. There were sirens in the distance. "Let's go inside and talk. It's too cold for David out here." She moved the blanket to cover his shoulders and wheeled him to the door. As she stepped over the threshold, she motioned for Jack to follow them from the kitchen into the room beyond.

He heard her taking David to the bathroom, the quiet murmurings of the two as the door closed followed moments later by the flush of the toilet and the water running in the sink. Jack found himself in a paneled room with a long Chesterfield sofa, brass lamps and several paintings. An old mantle clock chimed the hour. The brick fireplace smelled of charcoal or creosote. There were stacks of magazines sitting on the coffee table: *The New Yorker, Atlantic, National Review, The Spectator, National Geographic.* Many had yellow bookmarks in them. Despite the basic formality of the room, it had a cozy ambience with its many colors and the warm feel of the tribal rugs.

Jack sat back in the sofa and waited. It was a while before Ann Hudson returned. By then he was feeling he should go, that she must have to prepare dinner, that although she had been warm to him, now was the time she probably needed to herself.

"Don't worry," she said. "We can still talk. David needs to get his studying done." As if reading his mind, she said, "We generally eat late."

"So tell me," she said, "Why on earth did you choose to write about my husband when fiction is your love?" She sighed. "Your specialty."

He didn't know what to say to this beautiful woman whose grasp of character was as acute as his, most likely. He didn't want to lie, and he didn't want to schmooze so for several moments he said nothing.

Finally, he offered, "I wanted to write something truthful, something that would capture the greatness of your husband's generation."

"*Our* generation," she said knowingly.

"Yes," he agreed.

Chapter Ten

He heard the rumbling of the elevator and the wheelchair make its way down the upstairs hallway. A door opened and closed; there were the sounds of lights going on and a radio playing softly. Already it was getting dark outside. As he sat back in the sofa, the house settled into a peaceful silence. Ann Hudson moved about, switching on the lamps in the den. She withdrew, moving on down the hall to the entry, turning on the lights there. He listened to the muffled sound of her feet on the rugs and wood flooring and thought about the project ahead of him. He knew he wanted to do it, but he wasn't certain of his skills anymore. It had been so long since he'd written anything of merit, that it now seemed absurd he could pull off the authorized biography of the world's most eminent scientist. The thought struck him that the author should be someone from Yale, a distinguished scientist, not a washed up writer of fiction, who hadn't even graduated college.

Miranda had always said that what most defeated Jack was his lack of confidence, so he tried to imagine himself discussing the book with an admiring audience. He visualized Ann Hudson at his side, supportive of his efforts, Miranda duly impressed, his own parents glad to see their seemingly lost son once again successful. Over the years he had sensed their disappointment in him, and it had hurt. He had a sister who'd never amounted to much either, but he was the man in the family, his mother had always said. Jack suspected his father had disappointed her as well. Married right out of high school, what did his mother expect? They'd been dirt poor throughout his childhood; that's why looking back made Jack feel so terrible. Their meager savings had gone to assure him a college education, and he had dropped out, filled with the dreams of writing. Such hubris, he thought now. Was it also hubris to believe he could do justice to Theodore Hudson, to Ann Hudson? To Yale University with its concentration of the best and the brightest in every field? He felt suddenly overcome with the enormity of the task before him. It made him physically sick to ponder it.

"Here," Ann Hudson said as she placed before him a glass of white wine and an assortment of cheeses and crackers. "I'll be right back." He heard her walk into the kitchen. She was on the phone for a few minutes then returned with her own glass of wine. "Now where were we?" She sat down wearily on the opposite side of the room. Her hair under the faint lamplight was auburn, its wispy tendrils falling forward as she sipped her wine. "How can I help you to get started?"

He gazed over her head at the walls surrounding them, looking for pictures of her husband, but he saw none. Registering his sweeping gaze as one of curiosity, she said, "There are family pictures all over the house. Let me show them to you. I believe a person's character is somewhat evident in his face, do you?"

"I think it is," Jack said, getting up and following her. "Such a cliché' but often true," he added.

He followed her down the hall to Theodore Hudson's study, an oak paneled room with high ceilings like the rest of the house. A brass floor lamp with a red silk shade sat next to a wingback chair by the fireplace. Over the fireplace hung a magnificent painting of Ann Hudson as a young woman dressed in a gown she might have worn to her coming out party. The dress gave the illusion of swirling around her as if endowed with a life of its own. A vast walnut desk occupied one side of the room above which a gallery of family pictures framed in walnut spread in several rows up to the beam-crossed ceiling. Floor to ceiling bookcases lined two walls. Another tribal rug with hues of red, navy and maroon covered most of the flooring. A smell of linseed oil permeated the room. It felt masculine, bold, ordered. Jack wondered what it would be like to work in a room like this. He felt mildly envious of the quiet stability that appeared to have governed Theodore Hudson's life. Jack supposed that was another thing to keep in mind about the man: he led an ordered, disciplined life, one that was hard for Jack to imagine since he couldn't seem to keep his own small amount of possessions organized, let alone his comparatively uncomplicated schedule.

Every conceivable landmark of the Hudsons' lives seemed to be featured on the professor's study wall. The young couple beaming over an elaborate wedding cake, swimming on the beaches of Barbados, holding their infant son, standing next to Gerald Ford at a reception.

Theodore with Tony Blair, with Robert Gallo, Nelson Mandala, Bill
O'Reilly, Jimmy Carter, Sister Theresa, Depak Chopra, Dan Rather,
scores of important men and women. A picture of the Nobel Prize
banquet with Theodore at the head table, Ann and David flanking
him. Hudson's face was consistently kind and reserved, his bold, alert
eyes steady and seemingly sincere. The man was almost dashingly
handsome, Jack noted.

"Good looking man," Jack murmured.

"That he was," Ann Hudson agreed. "When I first met him, I
thought he was the handsomest man I had ever seen." She smiled;
clearly the memory was a good one. Jack surmised they had had a
happy marriage and that looking back was not painful for her.

"You two must have cut a wide swath," he said.

Ann Hudson paused. She looked at him curiously. "I suppose we
did. I never thought about it then. There was always too much going
on to stop and think about trivial things like that. Our social life just
didn't seem all that important then, frankly."

"And what did matter?"

"David, always. Assisting the poor. Keeping on an even keel. You
see, Ted was easily exhausted. He had to get his sleep. He'd push
himself until he dropped, literally. Then he'd have to regroup and let
things slide for a while. Sometimes it was hard knowing where he
was in that cycle, but then I'd get the drift and adjust to his rhythms.
Still, to be honest, it was baffling at times. I never knew if I was doing
the right thing."

"You mean he was an up and down kind of person?"

"I guess so. It wasn't that he was difficult, he just pushed himself
and then when he pulled back, he was, what you would say, very
restrained, very reserved, quiet. I have to admit that sometimes I
couldn't reach him then and would feel despairing."

She held up her glass and peered over its rim at Jack. The
chardonnay in the muted light looked orange. "I don't know why
I'm telling you this," she said suddenly. "I'm certainly being a jabber
mouth – something I hate, actually. I must be starved for someone to
listen to me. I'm sorry."

As he watched, tears started down her cheeks. Jack rushed
to reassure her. "No, please, don't stop. I'm sure every wife of a
famous, multi-talented, energetic man feels similarly. It must have
been awfully hard keeping up with him, keeping on top of his moods
or whatever."

"You're very understanding," she said, a hint of sadness evident in the quiet, suppressed tone of her voice. "He wasn't an easy man, that's for sure."

"Most great men aren't," Jack said.

"Why is that? Why should an extraordinary human be exempted from normal expectations?"

"All men should be held to the same standard, all right. It's just that both you and your son seem to agree that your sacrifices were merited, that you aren't sorry you allowed him a wide berth. He had his work to do, which you valued. You admit it seemed more important." Jack hoped he was paraphrasing her correctly; this was what he thought he'd heard.

"Life is full of contradictions, isn't it?" Ann Hudson asked, taking another sip of her wine and finishing the glass. She held it up to the light, circling it in her hand. From upstairs the sound of classical music drifted downward, enveloping them. She got up and walked over to the stereo and put in a C.D. It was Mendelsohn, and for a moment he thought of his own dark corner for writing, of the sacrifices he had made in the name of art, the women he'd lost over its constant demands. Make that over *his* need to write, as if any need justified the retreat from family ties. Maybe Theodore Hudson did not shirk those responsibilities, but Jack knew he had many times over the years. Only Karen had seemed to accept that.

"I'd be the last person to begrudge Ted's life work or to complain about him. I loved the man. He was larger than life, so incredibly *huge* in every way. It was an honor to be married to him. Truly."

"You mentioned contradictions. What do you mean?"

"I was so proud of him and yet so jealous of his time." She covered her face with her hands. The sounds of Mendelsohn drifted between them. When she removed her hands, her eyes were full of tears. "Oh, I'm so ashamed. So ashamed that I couldn't see beyond myself when the whole world was waiting on what he might discover. And now he's dead, and I can't call him back to do the world's work."

"I'm sure you were there for him, even if it doesn't seem so right now. Grief plays cruel tricks on us. You'll see things in more perspective as time goes by." Jack thought of Karen and his own regrets. He wasn't sure he was being honest with Ann Hudson, but he felt he was in the presence of a sincere, empathic, good person, and it wouldn't be right to acknowledge neglect or pettiness on her part. She wasn't that kind of a woman.

"You're very kind," she said, "but I know where I've erred. I've thought about it a lot since that terrible night when the police came and informed me my husband was dead."

Jack felt something ebb from her, a dissipation of energy that left her limp and tired. She suddenly looked older and pale as she got up and took his glass with hers into the kitchen. He heard her walking around the kitchen, the fridge opening and closing, the final crescendos of Mendelsohn, even David's bedroom noises as he worked his way through his homework upstairs. It was as if all sound were more acute to him right now, as if somehow he was experiencing communication in its most intense state, even though nothing now was loud or jarring to his consciousness. It was as if something were allowing him access to another level of perception, something which he'd never experienced before. With a jolt, he realized this explanation in his conscious thinking sounded like the weird experiences Miranda described. With that understanding, he thought of Miranda and wished she were there to provide insight into the complicated emotions of Ann Hudson. Miranda was gifted that way, whereas he felt limited when it came to grasping the nuances of women's behavior.

She appeared before him, glasses of wine in hand. She handed him one and sat back down. "Well, this is quite the initiation into the project, isn't it?" Her face was flushed, and she seemed a little disoriented as she reached for cheese and crackers.

"Actually, I think this is all relevant to the task before us," Jack said. "I need to understand what kind of man Theodore Hudson was, and you're helping me. I've had so many questions—"

He stopped suddenly. Ann Hudson had covered her face and was sobbing as if her heart would break. Her whole body shook convulsively, her narrow shoulders trembling violently. There was no choice. Jack had to go to her.

He took her in his arms and pulled her up from the chair. "I'm so sorry you feel bad," he said. "I'm so sorry."

"Now you're going to write that he neglected us," she said, her angry voice sounding over the Mendlesohn, over all the subtle, innocuous noises in the tranquil house. He could hear desperation and frustration, an outpouring of grief so irrational and terrible that it frightened Jack, but he held on to her, quelling the violent trembling of her shoulders by the sheer strength of his body. He was almost angry with her for feeling the way she did.

"I'm messing it all up," she said with finality. "I want you to memorialize the good work he did, his valiant efforts to right the wrongs of the world. I don't want you to expose his limitations! Please understand that I of all people know what a generous, people-loving, magnanimous person he was!"

"Do you think I don't know that? Do you think I don't realize how much you admired him? That you have his best interests at heart? Of course I do," Jack said. "You're being honest, that's all. And you're still grieving. All of this will seem different when you start to heal. And personally, I feel the book will help you do just that."

For a moment, he thought he saw something profound in the way she sat back in her chair and clasped her hands on her lap. Her eyes swept the room as if she were seeing it and something else — something terribly important — in a new, fresh light. She wasn't simply buying Jack's reassurance about her part in the marriage to Theodore Hudson, she was seeing herself apart from him and perhaps the world. She was *seeing* something for the first time. Jack wondered what it was that could instantaneously convert her hyper vigilant emotions into a steadied calm.

"I do think that's enough for one day, don't you?" she said at last. Behind her the grandfather clock chimed, and Mendelsohn softly ended. Jack rose from his chair, reluctant to leave the warmth of the old house, the music, the sense of physical comfort. *Home,* he thought. *Home.*

Chapter Eleven

Back at the motel, Jack felt restless and confused. He'd spent an enjoyable afternoon with Ann Hudson, but something was lacking, and he couldn't put his finger on what it was. He wanted to talk to Miranda and was angry at himself that he hadn't nailed down their means and frequency of communication. It seemed the two took each other for granted, falling into habits they'd once lived by – without time constraints or rules – in those years when breaking the mold *was* the rule, when so much was relative and up for negotiation and time wasn't a priority. Age changed things. Now his sense of mortality weighed on him and he did most everything in a timely fashion. He wanted Miranda to do the same. He had to admit they were no longer cut out of the same mold; the years had changed them. He was at time's mercy, even if she were not.

He hated motels. He had avoided them all his life. One never knew what lurked in the mattresses, under the aged carpeting, along the surfaces of bathroom fixtures. He supposed he could get used to a five-star hotel, if given the opportunity, but nothing short of that struck him as desirable. Even when he had been on his one book tour, when they'd arranged decent lodgings, he'd hated the impersonal, over-decorated ambience of the places. He loathed the nights out in restaurants and the inevitable return to the room with its gaudy bedspread and poor lighting. Since then he'd had to rent inexpensive rooms from time to time, and the situation always left him moderately depressed. This particular one verged on seedy and made him feel diminished by its shabbiness and want of aesthetics.

He turned on Fox News Channel and watched O'Reilly, wondering if he considered Hudson an ally. Who really was Theodore Hudson anyway? In Jack's experience scientists tended to be progressive yet Hudson's emphasis on the importance of the family fed into the conservative agenda. Much of Jack's research cited support by

leaders of the right for Hudson's stances on everything from abortion
to homosexuality. Yet Hudson had rejected their position on the so-
called "Day-after Pill" and voted Democrat in the last election. His
vocal intervention into the Darfur situation and his condemnation of
Saddam Hussein suggested a bipartisan outlook. His dossier was full
of philosophical and ideological contradictions such as those. Hudson
had been reluctant to condemn Kevorkian, whose sole mission was
the practice of euthanasia. Jack decided his research to date was too
superficial. What better source for the truth of Theodore Hudson
than the vast, well endowed library of Yale?

He was soon absorbed in the copious file on the man. He sat
down at a long oak library table and pored through several articles,
taking careful notes on index cards which he dated and documented
precisely. A kindly librarian at the Leadville Library had compiled an
extensive file for him and counseled him on how to do the research
himself once he arrived at Yale. Previously Jack had done most of
his research on the internet; this was his first piece of biographical
writing.

Most of what he was reading he already knew from his previous
sources, but he continued, finding the repetition helped to reinforce
his sense of the man. His curiosity now drove him as much as
Miranda's encouragement. The human personality with all its quirks
and subconscious motivations was what interested Jack. He realized
that delving into the life of Theodore Hudson would be as fascinating
as it got.

He read by the green light at the table for several hours before he
realized he was hungry. He closed up the file and left it at the reference
desk to resume reading tomorrow before he visited Ann Hudson. He
looked forward to visiting with the woman again, surprised he hadn't
been intimidated by her wealth and social position. Instead he felt a
kinship with her, something he never would have anticipated back in
Leadville. He was reminded of Miranda and her hysterical insistence
that he undertake the mission. He couldn't help but wonder what set
her on Hudson's track. Annoyed she hadn't called, he put her out of
his mind.

He stopped for dinner at Claire's by the University. He sat in
a chair in the back and watched the people as they came in. The
crowd had dwindled to a few stragglers, mostly young people. He
spread out some of his papers and went to the line to order. When
he returned, a young woman was perusing one of the articles on

Hudson. He felt offended that someone would be so bold as to read his stuff. When she saw him staring at her from across the table, she said, "Oh, sorry." She must have registered Jack's annoyance, because she rushed to add, "I knew the man. He was my advisor. He had quite an influence on me." Noticing he was still frowning, she went on, "He was a great teacher, like I mean truly GREAT. I could have listened to him all day, you know. I don't think I've ever seen such charisma. Why, he could talk for hours. Without notes, you know, like he just knew everything." She set her backpack on an adjoining table and sat down. "So why are you reading about him?"

"Just curious," Jack said. Was this how Yale girls talked? If so, they'd changed a lot since he'd spent time in New Haven. She looked like any young woman out there nowadays – plain, colorless, straight hair, on the plump side. She noticed his sizing her up and grimaced.

"Yeah," she said. "Like don't tell the truth."

"What makes you think that isn't the truth?" Jack asked, annoyed at her unearned superciliousness. It was the modern woman's sense of entitlement that drove them to be audacious.

"You're going to write about him," she said, piercing him with a knowing look. "So why don't you just admit it and be done with it?" She smiled wryly, turning away from him and sitting down. "Honesty is the best policy, you know." She had a look of disdain on her open face. He didn't know what irritated him more, her intrusion into his private life or her judgmental stance. He decided it was both. The girl was annoying, hardly worth the time to set straight. It didn't matter. She was already lost in her own thoughts as she scanned the menu posted above the counters.

"You're a hard little one, aren't you?" he couldn't resist saying.

She glanced at his plate of a baked potato, string beans and fish. "That looks good. Think I'll get some of the same." She flounced off to the ordering counter and pointed back at Jack's plate. "I want what that man has," she said in an authoritative voice.

Jack bent over his plate, looking down rather than observe her self-important expression as she waited before the cash register. He'd always liked Claire's but he couldn't recall ever talking to anyone while eating there. A young person at that. It seemed at the moment remarkable. Then he recalled that he was in the position of searching for information about Professor Hudson, so why was he closing out this possible source?

When she returned, he stood up and pulled out her chair for her. "When you're done eating, I'd like to talk to you about him," he said, trying to sound kindly and professional, although he was still put off by her abrasive manner.

"Fine," she said, "but you'll have to talk to me now cuz my boyfriend's picking me up back at the dorm, and I have to hurry." With that, she got up and moved to his table, throwing her backpack on the chair beside him. She sat across from him and talked with her mouth full, "So what d'ya wanna know?"

He hated Brooklyn accents. He almost frowned, but he restrained himself and smiled pleasantly. "Everything."

She sniffed. "Why doesn't that surprise me?"

"Name's Joline," she said, reaching out her hand. She wore purple polish on nails chewed to the quick. Her fingertips were yellow, probably from smoking. Looking at her closer, he could see she had a rather nice smile but the bleached blonde hair, her shorn cut and the tight sweater and jeans gave her a cast-offish appearance. "I was his best student," she said. When Jack didn't respond, she said. "Bet you don't believe that, do ya?"

"What difference does it matter what I think?"

"Full scholarship," she said, her mouth tightening over the fish. "Not many of those here, ya know." When Jack still said nothing," she said. "You're not impressed?"

"Well, as a matter of fact, I am," Jack admitted. "Since I didn't even finish college, much less get into Yale."

"Oh, yeah? I thought you were probably one of *them*."

"Them?"

"The professors here." She cocked her head and looked at him out of the corner of one eye. She reminded him of a caricature of a woman, trying to act mysterious when there was no mystery there. "Course Ted didn't associate with them much. He was a 'loner.' Know what I mean?"

"I know what a 'loner' is, but how would you know that sort of thing?"

"We were friends."

She couldn't have surprised Jack more if she'd told him they were lovers. He couldn't imagine what a man like Theodore Hudson would talk about with a girl like Joline.

"He even took me out sometimes." She seemed to gauge his response. When Jack said nothing, she continued, hurrying her speech as if afraid he might lose interest. "It's not as if I'm a complete *drag*," she said, searching his face for a reaction. "He thought I was funny." When Jack still did not comment, she said. "You don't believe me."

Jack measured his words. "It's not that I don't believe you, but it wouldn't be advisable for Theodore Hudson to date a student. It doesn't sound like something a man in his position would do."

"That's because you didn't know him," she said. "Ted liked a good time more than anybody, and he didn't care about silly things like social position or *appropriateness*. He was his own man."

"From what I have read, I'll grant you that," Jack said, trying to keep her talking. He didn't believe a word she'd said so far.

"You know, there's a lot of people don't know about New Haven," she said, looking Jack straight in the eye. If he hadn't sensed a basic authenticity in the girl, he'd have thought she was coming on to him. Her look was sharp and searching for something in him. He refused to look down, and eventually she turned her gaze on the wall menu. "Wanna buy me dessert?" she asked. "I'm really hungry. Ted always bought me a piece of cake."

"You come here often?"

"A lot since Ted passed. Not much before then, but he always liked this place. Said it was the next best thing to home cooking." She looked sad, and there was an obvious tremor in her voice, but Jack wasn't buying performances anymore. He'd learned to wait women out, to see what they truly were before he believed them.

"You came here with the professor then?" Jack asked. He doubted if Hudson would have been seen with Joline in this most public place. A lot of professors hung out here for coffee or meals.

"Sometimes," she said. She watched him closely. "You still don't believe me."

Jack said nothing.

"Okay, I'll prove it. Ask me who his favorite author was. When Jack didn't respond, she said, "Go on, ask me!"

Jack thought about it. He could ask Hudson's wife who it was and verify Joline's truthfulness. He decided to play her game. "So who was it?"

"Who but Dostoyevsky?" she asked, her mouth stretched straight and trembling, causing her to look older and pathetic. She was not a pretty girl.

"I didn't know he was a reader," Jack said, thinking what a coincidence it was that he'd just been rereading Dost, his own favorite.

"Was Hudson Russian?"

"He was, but I bet you didn't get that from your research." She looked at him sideways, her head turned to the window where a young man stood staring at her from outside. He was tall and thin with dark glass frames and a thin jacket.

"No, I didn't, as a matter of fact."

"I'm Slavic, too. I suppose that's why he told me. I don't think people know that because, you see, Ted was adopted when he was ten, right here in New Haven."

Despite his initial dismissal of the young woman, he now felt she did know the professor well. Either that or she was delusional. There had been several in-depth stories on Theodore Hudson, and not one of them had mentioned he was adopted, nor that he was Russian by birth.

"I gotta go," she said, shifting her head toward the window. "Sam gets mad when he's kept waiting. He was supposed to meet me at the dorm, but oh, well."

With that, she got up, pulling her backpack from the chair. "You'll take care of this for me, won't you?" she said, pointing at the empty tray.

"You bet," he said, at a loss for words. He stood up to take back her tray. "Oh, by the way," he told her, "I'd like to offer a rain check on the dessert." He forced a smile even though Sam was glaring at both of them.

She looked surprised. "Well..." She looked back at Sam through the glass and smiled sheepishly. "Sure. See you tomorrow. Same time, same place." She laughed and dashed out of the restaurant, leaving him impatient with his own plodding mind-set. He should have worked harder at establishing rapport with the young woman. As it was, he might never see her again. He gathered up his things and rushed outside, looking for her in the thickening crowds of people roaming the streets. He walked up and down the block, trying to get a glimpse of her and her boyfriend, but he didn't see them, just scatterings of other couples enjoying the mild New Haven night.

Back at the motel, he looked in the telephone book for Hudson entries. There were many, so he sat down and dialed them one by one. He began each greeting with, "Are you by any chance the parents of Theodore Hudson?"

Every person who answered said no.

Disappointed, Jack tried to divert himself from the subject of Theodore Hudson. In the first ten years of his writing, he'd acknowledged he was obsessive about his work. Once he began a piece, he would think about it constantly. That had been the only way he could write – by immersing himself in the tapestry he himself wove. He couldn't say it had been like that for at least a decade. The years had taken away his concentration and his will. These days he wrote mechanically, one could almost say, without heart. He was acknowledging for the first time the changes time had wrought on his talent. The realization made him feel splintered, half alive. He thought of Joline and her silly enthusiasm over nothing. He supposed that was what age meant – the fraying of that, like so much else. How to keep it going, he mused. He had a notion it wasn't only Ann Hudson who stood to gain solace from his book.

When the morning sun awoke him, he let himself visualize the day's events before getting up. During the night, his mind had worked its way through various reveries. Oddly, he'd felt Karen's presence, and he had yielded to it, grateful that his longing could still summon her. He felt that when he slept well, it was because on some deep level the two of them shared something beyond words. There were so many things the human mind did not understand. Life didn't make a lot of sense. He wondered if someone of Theodore Hudson's intellect experienced doubt or frustration. Perhaps he accepted only that which could be proven empirically, as most scientists were taught. Or did one's faculties create reality, as the existentialist argued? What was truth? What was Hudson's truth? Was there such a thing as truth or was there only perception? Jack knew he wasn't alone in wondering about the big questions all men asked. He almost laughed to recall how strong had been his sense of moral certainty at Joline's age. His generation had felt it had all the answers. The Age of Aquarius, remember that? It was almost hilarious to realize their smugness had created a legacy of divorce, dysfunctional families, STD's, war, materialism, pollution, insomnia — you name it. Looking back, he was repulsed by the certitude he'd harbored in the face of complicated issues. His generation had perpetuated all the societal ills they'd protested. How hypocritical was that?

Chapter Twelve

Jack knew the devil was in the details, but so far the details he had were sketchy and contradictory. He wondered if he'd be able to validate enough information to make the book an assessment of both the man's professional contributions and the extent to which his own family background and marriage had contributed to his life's work. There was no doubt that Theodore Hudson had benefited Yale's reputation as a leader for societal advancement, but more importantly, he had been one of the few examples worldwide of solitary humanitarian achievement. He was truly a legend in his time.

It seemed to Jack that Professor Hudson and Yale had been inextricably linked in all the causes for which Hudson stood. With him gone, there had been no other leaders of his stature to succeed him. His former causes failed to ensure today's headlines; the swirling controversies he aroused had disappeared from public discourse. Yale's preeminence in the realm of world affairs had sharply declined while stalwart academicians from Harvard, Princeton and the University of Virginia had seized the limelight, pursuing other goals. Jack felt a sense of urgency to present Hudson's story before his legacy was lost in the shifting sands of academic politics. The *word* was vital in this case, Jack mused, wondering what Miranda would say about that. For himself, he couldn't remember when a cause had so absorbed him.

Ann Hudson had invited him to lunch. He'd reviewed the Yale files all morning, again taking meticulous notes. He had arranged for appointments with fellow faculty members, lab supervisors, Yale administrators, even the department secretary. He felt that after tomorrow he would have enough information to proceed with purpose. Hopefully, Joline would make her appearance tonight. He'd developed a long list of questions for her. He had still not found documentation that the professor had been adopted, nor that he was of Russian descent. He didn't know whether to believe Joline or not. On the one hand she seemed forthright, but there was something suspect in the way she reacted to the young man outside and in the surreptitious way she encouraged a sort of intimacy between her and Jack, but then Jack wasn't used to being around young women either and may have misunderstood her intentions.

By the time he arrived at the Hudson house, his mind was full of data, and he felt confused. He had a list of questions to ask Ann Hudson, but he hadn't reviewed it sufficiently and was fearful of offending her. Moreover, he was reluctant to conduct himself as an interrogator, sensing in the woman a New England reserve that wouldn't submit to aggressive tactics. The very questions Jack had about her husband might be viewed by Mrs. Hudson as a violation of their privacy. Thus, the question in Jack's mind was how to uncover the intimate details of the man's life without offending her. He hoped it was possible.

She opened the door in the same gracious and radiant manner she had the first day. He felt immediately relieved. They had indeed established a kind of intimacy where self-consciousness did not appear to be a factor with either of them. She again offered him iced tea and led him outside to the patio table on the verandah. More leaves had fallen since yesterday, and the yard was covered in them. The trees were starting to look spare against the brilliant blue sky. The air was mildly humid with a faint breeze. From somewhere a dog barked, and he could hear children playing in a yard nearby.

It all seemed so conventional, sitting in this beautiful yard in a well tended home with the sounds of dogs and children, that Jack felt for the first time in his life he had missed out on a certain traditional rooting that ordinary families took for granted. He had never owned a house, never been around children, hadn't owned a dog nor wanted to. Home had served to be where husband and wife alighted to pick up after the demands of the day or to eat, sleep, drink or read. For his wives, it had not been a refuge, a sanctuary, as he supposed this one was. The realization made him sad. It was obvious Ann Hudson cared about her home. The music playing, the art, the comfortable furniture, the pictures of family and friends, even the smells of linseed oil and something cooking, spoke to a person who loved her home. It revealed someone for whom aesthetics and comfort mattered. Jack, who had never been materialistic, who often claimed with pride, that he "owned his possessions, they didn't own him," could not begrudge the woman her possessions. They had been chosen as gestures of caring and justified their expense. He was surprised he had this reaction since normally he was critical of large homes and deftly placed objects that served only as ornamentation. Such had seemed wasteful to him, excessive. He considered himself a minimalist. Aesthetics hadn't mattered.

"Is David at school?" he asked as she sat down opposite him at the patio table. A leaf had landed in her hair, and she reached up to remove it. "He is," she said. "I took him this morning since I had to stop by the grocery store. A bus generally picks him up."

"He likes school, doesn't he?" Jack asked, realizing he was following his line of questions without intending to.

"Yes, he does," she said. "He's always enjoyed learning. Chip off the old block, I guess. Both Ted and I were ambitious students. I still consider myself a student of the world. I bet you are, too." Her clear eyes and open manner endeared her to him. It seemed she could talk about anything, and he found her refreshing. He had expected from her prim appearance and ram-rod straight posture an inhibited, possibly opinionated woman, but that didn't appear to be the case.

"I wouldn't want to stop learning," he said. "So where does David go to school?"

"He attends the lab school here. It's excellent, as you can imagine. I give his teachers enormous credit for what they do with the kids."

"A sort of 'whole kid' approach, would you say?"

"Why, yes. How did you know?"

"Just a good guess," he said. "Not all that prevalent in the east, I would think."

"I think it is unusual around here, but Ted insisted on that approach. We haven't been disappointed."

"Was your husband involved in the school?"

"He was instrumental in planning the science curriculum. He made sure there were field trips, a strong forensics club, mentoring programs, drug and alcohol education, lots of things. He was a visionary in education as well so it's not surprising he made himself heard in David's school. As you know, he's been commended for his own teaching since he began his career. Former students still comment on his teaching."

"And what do they say?" Jack asked, feeling at home, something he had not anticipated. Her welcoming personality encouraged talk. He assumed Theodore Hudson had been the same kind of person.

"That he cared about his students, that he enjoyed the classroom." She paused, looking out at the red and gold landscape, at the withering Irises along the back, waiting for their winter sleep. "He could spot the disadvantaged kid a mile off. Those tended to be the ones he targeted for mentoring, or whatever you would call personal attention. Although he had come from an affluent background, he respected the ones who got here on sheer talent, and those were the ones he wanted to get to know."

Jack thought of Joline.

"Did he bring those kids home?"

She looked at him curiously. "Why no, he didn't." It's interesting you should ask that. I never thought about it before, but he did take them under his wing, and he often reported to me what he felt he'd accomplished with them." She seemed to be lost in thought for a few moments while Jack tried to think of other questions he'd formulated. "He was particularly interested in three that semester he died. There were two men, one from West Virginia who'd been orphaned at four and raised by a widowed grandmother. He had a terrible twang, and Ted tried to help him speak more grammatically and without an accent." She laughed. "I'd never heard language used that poorly by a smart person before. It made you cringe. The other boy was from Washington, D.C. and he mumbled terribly. I couldn't understand anything he said, but Ted turned him around as well. It was exciting to witness the transformation, although he didn't bring them here, to answer your question."

"Any girls he singled out?" Jack asked.

"There was one," she said. "Her name was Joline. She was a strange girl, Ted said. I never met her, but he said she was brilliant. She was from New York City and had never lived in a real home, just foster care, where she'd somehow managed to learn on her own. She read constantly. Dostoyevsly was her favorite author. Imagine that? Ted believed anyone could benefit from a solid home and enough family income, even a good example by the parents; but the deprived and disenfranchised were also capable of amazing achievement if they had appropriate encouragement. He was there for that kind of kid in particular. I admired him for that."

"As well you should," Jack concurred, curious about Joline, but he reminded himself he would hopefully find out more about her situation tonight. "What about your husband's attitude toward his peers?" Jack ventured. "Did he feel comfortable in the Yale milieu?"

"I'd say he did," she said. "It's a very competitive environment, as you can imagine, but he served as department chair in the eighties.

We were invited to other professors' homes. He was consulted for advice on various issues. Yes, I'd say he was very comfortable at Yale; he never talked of leaving or going elsewhere despite the fact that he was always being approached by other universities. Yale was his home, and then, of course, there was David. He didn't want to upset his education or tear me away from my friends. He was very considerate that way."

"I would think there would have been some friction among his peers."

"You mean because so many of his causes were controversial?"

"Yes, I would think others might resent his clout when he opposed a colleague's views. I've read where that happened fairly often."

"You're right," she said, but the unusual thing about Ted was that he didn't take criticism or even rancor personally. He was a rare man that way. I used to tease him that he didn't have an ego, like the rest of us."

"And what did he say to that?"

"That his manifested in different ways."

"What did he mean, do you think?"

She glanced at him with her lovely bohemian eyes, her face devoid of expression. "Why, I don't know," she answered, looking off into the distance behind him. "I never thought about it before. I guess I didn't attach enough meaning to certain things then. Now it seems awfully important, doesn't it?" There was an unmistakable element of fear in her eyes as she seemed to ponder the past. "At any rate," she said sadly, "I never saw him act in an egotistical manner. *Never.*" She sat totally still for a moment, rigidly upright in her demeanor. "He was the most self-less person I have ever known."

The telephone rang inside the house. She got up. "Will you excuse me? I'll be right back."

He looked around at the leaves slowly falling, a vast carpet of red and yellow, pushing up against the fence where the wind had flung them. It was fall, he thought, smiling. That had been the time of year he always disliked since it was the harbinger of winter, the season he hated. Far up in the mountains of Leadville that meant insulated window coverings closed a great deal of the time, shutting out the spectacular canyon views, fires constantly burning to keep the house warm, decks and driveways that always needed shoveling. The list went on and on. Winters were exhausting and depleted his enthusiasm, but when spring came – generally late in Colorado – he was always happy. He loved the mountains then, the aspen leafing out among the pine, the rocky landscape taking on a pink hue at twilight and in the morning when he stood out on the deck with his coffee. There was no air more rarified than that in Leadville – dry, crisp and pure. With a start, he was realized he missed his bungalow, his bed and books, the old pine flooring that suited him just fine. It was an aged house housing an aged man, and all that was as it should be, he knew. He felt he was changing somehow when just days ago he'd been embittered and angry by all the things in life he couldn't control.

Death did a number on you, he knew that. He wondered that Ann Hudson could smile and be gracious under the circumstances. He knew he hadn't been able to muster a grin since Karen passed. Any little detail would remind him of their time together, and he'd withdraw from people, even the situation he was in at the moment. He decided it was good he got out of Leadville because he was feeling stronger now that he could put his grief on hold, if only for a while. The woman, though, was remarkably self-possessed, he decided. She had kept the home going and was there for her son. Whatever personal grief she felt, she did not let it subdue the moment. Somehow she had learned to make the present work, and he admired her for that. He knew that if he didn't have this project to work on, he'd have been wallowing further and further into the morass of self-doubt. Thank God for Miranda, he thought. Speaking of the woman, where was she? His annoyance was turning to anger. Why hadn't she called? He thought of Don Parrish, and a cold, hard resentment took possession of him. *The son of a bitch!*

"You look quite relaxed there," Ann Hudson said, returning to the table. She had a platter with sandwiches, a salad and a soup tureen. He stood up, taking her arm to steady her.

"Let me," he said, taking the tray.

"Just hold it for a minute, will you?" She spread a checkered table cloth over the wrought iron. "There. Now you can put it down." She set out cotton napkins and went back into the house. She returned carrying the pitcher of tea. Today she had on a long, fitted jacket and tapered pants with boots. It was an equestrian look and it suited her. Although she'd worn a dress last time, on both occasions she gave the impression of subtle formality. He couldn't imagine her riding with one of his female friends in West Texas, with dusty chaps and a jaunty, sun-curled hat. Ann Hudson looked so fresh and impeccably neat one wondered if she even sweated. And still, Jack felt comfortable with this woman of cultivation and means. Well, that was a new one, for sure. He thought of Miranda and wondered what she would think of Ann Hudson. He mused, it ought to be interesting.

"You mentioned your husband's commitment to the less advantaged students," he began, as they both started to eat the lunch. The sandwiches were creamed cheese and fresh cucumber on rye. The soup was a crab bisque, and the salad of fresh greens and vegetables had a light vinaigrette dressing, French, he guessed. The woman was a good cook, he could tell. She had an artistic flair in presenting the food – with kale garnishes and strawberry and orange slices served on what appeared to be antique dishes. He had never tasted bisque that flavorful.

"Yes," she said. "Over the years, he has helped so many... Every year he seemed to spend more and more time working with them."

Jack thought of Joline. He wondered if Ann Hudson knew her husband had taken her out alone.

"So you were fine with that?"

"I was," she said. "Teaching is really about young people, isn't it? You know, I wanted to teach. I think I might have, if David had been okay, but he became my special pupil. Teaching is a calling, I think. So many of the professors here are more concerned with their fame as authorities or authors, but Ted remained primarily committed to his teaching and, of course, his relationship with his students. His truly was a higher calling."

Jack thought of the praise Joline had heaped upon the man. She'd clearly been impressed with his teaching.

He thought for a minute. There were so many things he needed to know, but one question seemed more important than most. "What can you tell me about his parents? I can't for the life of me find anything about them."

"I know," she said. "I find that interesting, too. In fact, Ted rarely mentioned them. They lived here, you know. Before we did, actually. To be honest, I never met them."

"That's odd," he couldn't help but say. "Why was that?"

"They went to Yugoslavia right before we were married."

"You mean they weren't at your wedding?"

"As a matter of fact, they weren't. It was the oddest thing, but I didn't question it at the time."

Jack was beginning to wonder a little about Ann Hudson. A lot of things seemed to happen around her without her asking questions.

"Where was the wedding, if you don't mind my asking?"

"Greenwich, where I grew up. Ted arranged our honeymoon in Barbados. He said at the time that his mother wasn't in good health, but as the years wore on, he never visited them, nor did they come here. It was odd, I'll grant you that, but he told me they'd never been a close family and that he had more or less let them go during his Princeton days. He'd seemed so alone when I met him that I didn't doubt what he said. Besides, I loved him for his melancholic ways. I guess I felt he needed me. Later when he found his voice, so to speak, his causes and his teaching compensated for his sense of aloneness. He was the kind of person who would turn his own personal suffering into something that would benefit others."

"Any siblings?"

"He was an only child."

Jack noticed she had not mentioned adoption. He'd wait on that one for now. "What did his father do for a living?"

"He never told me," she said. "But they were quite comfortable, obviously. He showed me the house he grew up in. It was in Deep River. Very nice. He said he'd enjoyed living there because it was quiet and conducive to enjoying the outdoors. At first we thought about living in the area, but Ted wanted to be close to the lab so he could work at night, if he needed to."

"So Ted was raised with a certain privilege," Jack ventured. He didn't know how to establish that, but it seemed important.

"Oh, yes," she agreed. "Saint Phillips Academy, Princeton, University of Chicago. His family traveled all over the world. He'd been everywhere and had an appreciation for all cultures. She poured Jack more tea. "I think the traveling cultivated a compassion for the poor. He told me once that Africa had changed him forever. Later, when he saw what was happening with AIDS there, it was all he could do not to tear up when he talked about Africa. He loved the country."

"Did you two travel a lot?"

"No, we didn't. Ted did, though."

"You didn't want to go with him?"

"Before we were married, I did a lot of writing. I liked being at home, alone. I was enrolled in the doctoral program here, made friends, got wrapped up in that life, I guess. I'd traveled a lot all my life, so it just didn't seem that important to me."

"So your husband traveled alone, for the most part.?"

"Yes." She seemed suddenly embarrassed and self-conscious. Her face flushed, and her hands wrapped around her cup trembled as she brought it to her mouth.

"Of course, now I wish I'd gone with him more." She looked up at Jack over the brim then looked down. "We never know how long we have with those we love. I wish now I'd done a lot of things differently."

"I know what you mean," he said.

"You do?" she asked vaguely. She seemed lost in thought.

"The woman I lived with died a year ago."

She looked at him, clearly astonished. "I'm so sorry. I had no idea—"

"It's okay," he said, tired at the mention of it. "I'm getting used to it."

"Getting used to what?" she said, a hint of cynicism in her voice. Or was it sarcasm? He wasn't sure.

"The self-blame. Isn't that what you're talking about?"

"Indeed," she said.

"Well, that's what I mean, but we could all do things differently if we *knew* what lay ahead, but the simple fact is we don't know. So we should be forgiven for acts of omission."

"Perhaps you're right. At any rate, your words are comforting..." Her eyes glassed over as they had on so many occasions in the last two days. She seemed to be following something in her mind's eye. "To get back to your question of why I didn't accompany him on all those trips abroad—."

"I didn't mean to put you on the defensive," Jack rushed to add. "You don't have to tell me everything."

"But I want to. It's important to me that you understand." She scanned the yard as if searching for something. "You forget I've read your book. I consider you a seeker, like myself." She looked him full in the face as if sizing him up. "Don't you see? I need a seeker."

He was touched by her confidence, that she saw in him what he thought he saw in her: an unusual depth of character. "Go on," he said, too moved to say anything else.

"I was going to say that after David came, well, traveling just seemed impossible. Ted understood."

"Would you say you two had a close marriage?"

When she hesitated, he said, "You don't have to answer that either. There are ways of handling that part of his life without revealing confidential stuff."

"I've thought a lot about that since his death. We had so much in common. I was desperately in love with him when we married. And you know from your reading what a fascinating man he was. He always had something going on. He was absolutely vibrant. I was in awe of him, I must confess." Jack could tell she felt enormous respect for the man, but it wasn't clear whether she truly loved him. She hadn't answered Jack's question.

"You must understand," she said, "That David's condition made a big difference in our lives. Before he came along, I was available in ways I couldn't be after that. I guess it's fair to say we drifted apart afterwards, but that happens when children come along, and I don't think we drifted far. I'd say for the most part we were there for each other." She seemed to be thinking about it more. "All in all, I'd say we had an excellent marriage," she finished. "I have no regrets, and I'm sure he had none."

Jack believed her. The woman struck him as someone incapable of lying. To him everything she said and did had the ring of authenticity. Where Ann Hudson would come up short, he decided, was in her inability to see things from different angles. She appeared to focus on one aspect and ignore the others, such as the question of her husband's family. Jack felt most people in her circumstances would have asked the hard questions, but she hadn't, instead trusting in his judgment and perspective. Thus, she had never gleaned the truth of it, and the truth of it mattered, Jack thought, almost angry at her. What else, Jack wondered, had Ann Hudson missed in the years of her marriage to Theodore Hudson?

By the time he left the Hudson home, Jack felt tired and confused. The memory of Ann Hudson sitting in the splendor of her yard with the faintly regretful expression on her face made him feel sad and dissatisfied with his own performance. He was afraid his direct line of questioning might have frayed the bond they'd formed and forced upon her a wary resignation. He didn't want that. To him it was important that this experience be rewarding for her, that he not contribute to regret or sorrow, as had happened to him with thoughtless friends and acquaintances after Karen's death. He sensed in Ann Hudson a superior intellect's acute recognition of irony. He was sure she realized all the implicit paradoxes of her husband's untimely death. She would have analyzed them a thousand times over, so when she claimed their marriage was a good one, she had arrived at the conclusion after careful reflection. So he believed her. Jack also felt that she had been part of the inspiration for Theodore

Hudson's various causes, including his devotion to the less fortunate. There was an idealism apparent in Ann Hudson's appreciation of her own husband. For her, greatness was measured by selflessness, and Hudson would have been similar, if they were as well matched as she claimed. Jack believed they were.

He drove slowly into downtown New Haven, thinking back over the interview. He felt flattered by her assessment of his character, the fact that she'd retained him because of what she'd gained from reading his book. He decided that the afternoon had probably gone okay or he would have sensed her disappointment. Her face hid nothing, he realized, having stared at it enough over the last two days.

Jack parked close to Claire's and walked around the building and in the front door. The place was almost deserted. He did not see Joline and experienced a tug of disappointment. He sat down at one of the tables by the window and looked outside at the thickening darkness. He was a little early and would wait an hour to be sure he didn't miss her. He took out his notes of the interview with Ann Hudson and added in comments and underlined points. In the margins, he added observations of her reactions. Something was knitting at him, but he wasn't sure what it was. He realized they had actually covered a lot of material.

He felt he was beginning to understand the man. From what his wife said he was very caring. His sense of social justice took him in so many directions, but what Jack wanted to know was how deep those feelings really were. Obviously he cared about the poor and the disadvantaged, but did that capacity for compassion and concern extend to his own wife for the burdens she experienced caring for their son? It struck Jack as odd that she didn't travel with him, and he wondered whose decision that had been. The fact that he had disowned his family struck Jack as very telling. Jack knew a lot of men who professed sensitivity and empathy, but when it came down to being there for someone, were mysteriously absent. Such people, Jack had decided, were, in fact, emotionally shallow. They avoided emotional involvement. Jack felt he knew because before Karen he had been one of those men. Yet Jack hadn't been damaged by a lack of love from his family; his failure to connect on a deep level had resulted from his poor choices in women, women he simply couldn't stay with for various reasons, much less trust his emotions to. Whatever had happened to Theodore Hudson to make him abandon his parents had to have been serious; it was a part of the man that had to be understood before the man's story could be told. Surely Ann Hudson had some theories on all that, but on that score she had remained silent.

Jack had just decided to leave when Joline came in, smoking a cigarette and looking more bedraggled than ever. This time her hair was black and hung in greasy strands beneath a knit cap. There were shadows under her eyes, and her nose was red. When Jack looked closer, he noticed her eyes were glassy and that she wasn't walking steadily.

She staggered toward his table and sat down opposite him. He noticed her lips were dark and her skin so pale she looked unhealthy.

"You all right?" he asked.

"Fine, fine, fine..." She looked around the room and dragged on her cigarette. Her purple nails were chipped and torn, as if she'd been doing the gardening or something physically demanding. Her intelligent eyes that before had sought out every detail on his person and otherwise, now appeared sluggish and disinterested.

"How about a piece of cake?" he asked. "Some coffee?" He stood up. "I'll get it for you."

"No, I have a surprise for you. The cake can wait."

"Now whatever could that be?" he asked, turning around to see if her boyfriend were lurking in the shadows in the back by the bathroom or out the window where he'd waited before.

"I guess we'll see if you have the mettle of Dr. Theodore Hudson," she said, stomping off ahead of him, her cigarette lighting up the semi-darkened restaurant. She led him outside where the air had cooled and the sounds of traffic intruded on his thoughts. He felt temporarily disoriented by the speed at which she walked ahead of him, her legs awkwardly shuffling, her gait unsteady. He was fearful she'd stumble and fall into the busy traffic so he rushed up beside her and walked along the curb.

She'd tottered several feet before she turned to him, seemingly disoriented, and inquired if he had a car.

"It's around the corner," he said, pointing down the street in the direction from which they had just come.

"I have something to show you, if you'll accompany me. You wanted to understand Professor Hudson; well, then, I'll take you somewhere that will give you some insight. But you must realize that nothing is as it seems. Always keep that in mind, and you'll eventually understand."

He had no idea what she was talking about, but he was along for the ride till Miranda deigned to show her face in New Haven. Once again he was angry she had not bothered to appear or get in touch with him. Somehow he knew that if she were here with Joline, the situation would be easier on him. As for the way it was going down, he felt old and stodgy around a brilliant young student, even if she was accommodating.

"You're sure you're okay?" he asked as she stumbled into his car and dropped heavily onto the seat. Her cigarette was dislodged and fell in the gutter. She sighed heavily and stared out the windshield. It had started raining and the streetlights and windshield glittered with moisture. She shielded her eyes from the bright lights and thumped her temple, as if trying to clear her head.

"Here's the deal," she said. "We're going south. Just follow my directions." She held her head with one hand and continued to shield her eyes with the other. "Take this road as far as it will go till we're out of town, then turn right."

He did as he was told, and soon the traffic thinned out and the wide road gave way to a narrow curving one where there were few cars. The rain was falling thicker, and the street was black with no headlights and no houses. Jack hoped she wouldn't get him lost and he couldn't find his way back to the city.

"Turn in there," she said, pointing to an old weather beaten house with dark windows and the faintest suggestion of light from deep within. Gnarled, untamed trees surrounded the structure. There were several cars parked under the trees behind a battered fence. No light was on at the door, and the darkness of the night with no moon and the black rain gave Jack the creeps. This was not a destination he would have set out for on his own, but he sensed Joline knew as much about her beloved professor as anyone, so he would be patient for now.

Chapter Thirteen

Jack followed Joline up the crumbling concrete steps to the front door. Leaves had gathered on the unprotected porch and in the cracked urns perched haphazardly at the top of the stairs. Water spilled from the eaves and gathered in pools around shrubs and trees. It was so dark outside that without the car lights he could hardly see. From far away there was the screech of a fire engine and the rumble of New Haven traffic, but here it was strangely silent except for the wet leaves quivering in the wind and Joline's heavy breathing as she reached for the iron railing to steady herself. He wished he'd brought a flashlight. The door was black and gouged with deep gashes that were sharp to the touch. Looking closely, Jack could see that the small window in the door's center was cracked. Through it he could see a pale, luminescent light from deep within. A dark stairway stretched out from one end of a small entryway. He stepped aside for Joline to open the door, but she hesitated for a moment then turned toward him.

"So you're ready for this?"

"Well, I don't know," he said. "Do you want to fill me in?"

"It's best if you just experience it," she said, sighing deeply. The rustling of wet leaves seemed to swallow her words. "Well, let me think." She stepped back from the door and looked at Jack. He followed her eyes deep into the blackness beyond the trees. He felt his heart pounding, and put his hand protectively on his chest.

"Scared?" she asked, watching him closely. He was reminded of her hungry eyes that first night at Claire's. He doubted she missed many details. Right now her vision fastened on the naked door, the dangling shutters, the dead leaves spilling from the broken urns. She stamped her feet on the ancient welcome mat and turned the door knob. She held it there without pushing the door open, waiting for Jack's response.

"If you're game, then so am I," he said, moving closer to the door.

"Remember, things aren't always what they seem." The door creaked open into a dark hallway. They could dimly make out the side stairway, ascending to another floor and a plastic garbage can at its base. Jack could see paper debris along the hallway floor, pieces of food, wrappers, tin cans. The place smelled of spoiled food and neglect. Jack resisted the impulse to cover his nose and followed Joline down the hall past a bathroom with its door open. Inside he could see the white toilet seat covered with filth. The room reeked of vomit and piss. He hurried down the hall to an open space that must have once been the kitchen but was now so dilapidated the cupboards were hardly recognizable as such. Their doors were falling off the hinges; spider webs hung from them and in the corners where the weak light from the window glazed the room in a charcoal sheen.

"Nice place," he said.

"Isn't it?" She walked past an old table to the fireplace which looked like a gaping orifice. Someone had stuffed cans and wadded newspaper into the hole. Beside the fireplace was an old armchair with stuffing spilling from several openings. On the mantle sat a kerosene lamp and a packet of matches. Jack took the matches and started to light the lamp.

"No," Joline said. "Not now."

Jack set the lamp back on the mantle and listened. From upstairs he could hear the faint sound of rock music and someone walking around.

"Is there someone up there?" he whispered to Joline.

"Probably just Yvonne," she said. "She spends a lot of time here."

"She doesn't live here?"

"No one does." Joline took off into the darkness beyond the fireplace. He followed her into what must have once been a dining room. Torn curtains hung on one window and the other had none, only a broken shade that stretched forlornly across cracked glass. Rain had trickled in through the breaks and stained the sashes. A large wood table stood against another wall with four chairs at various angles. There were cigarette butts everywhere and more garbage and debris. Despite his reluctance to venture anywhere in the house, Jack felt immediately curious about its function and who the upstairs occupant might be.

"Interested in seeing more?" she asked, watching him closely. He felt the object of a prurient curiosity. She had certainly settled down from her spacey, possibly intoxicated behavior at the beginning of the evening. Her words now seemed measured, possibly calculated.

"I presume there isn't any danger," he answered, "So why not?"

"All right," she said. "But remember what I told you." She led him through the front room which was as dreary and bare as the others. A broken lamp sat on an orange crate, its cord wrapped around the base. There was a dark, sticky substance on one side of the box and pieces of torn paper everywhere. Jack smelled something in the walls, but he wasn't sure what it was. It lingered with the unmistakable odors of mildew, vomit and waste. He resisted the urge to cover his nose. For some mysterious reason, it crossed Jack's mind in a Miranda-sort of insight, that this structure held a truth he sought. The thought scared him, but he refused to let fear stop his quest. *This matters*, he thought, suppressing a vague fear.

Joline led him back, past the bathroom stench, through the hallway to the entry. She glanced outside at the brooding trees and turned to the stairway. "Watch your step," she said, briefly turning around. In the spare light, he noticed a hard, determined look on the young woman's face as she mounted the steps, her noisy shoes clunking on the broken stairs.

Jack held tightly onto the splintered railing. It was loose, and he didn't want to fall. His balance hadn't been what it used to be, and he secretly feared falling whenever it was dark. The downstairs emptiness gathered Joline's footsteps and echoed them upward, creating the impression of crowds walking in the silent house. Before they reached the landing, a door creaked open, revealing a faint, blue fluorescent light. A tall black woman stood with her arms folded, cigarette smoke swirling from her fingers.

"Joline, is that you?"

"Yes, Yvonne. I brought him."

"Bring him in, please."

With that, the woman stepped aside while Joline led Jack into a shabby room with a television going in the corner. It was a single room with thick, frayed drapes covering a large window. On an old deal dresser incense burned on a teak tray, its curly spire ascending to the broken light fixture on the ceiling. The scent of sandalwood wafted over a dusty, mildewy undersmell. A bed with a red satin coverlet dominated the space. Jack had the impression of a bordello or a crack house, so devoid of luxury or comfort was the place. Even the satin coverlet was frayed and stained, the mattress so lumpy Jack would not have been surprised if its stuffing were cornhusks. He'd seen beds like that among the shanties of the West Texas migrant workers. Their homes had smelled similarly. It was the stench of poverty, his senses told him, although it was nothing compared to the filth downstairs.

"May I get you a drink?" the woman asked. Although she had dirty dreadlocks, her beauty was undeniable. There were dark circles under her eyes, but the shape of them was what drew his attention. Black as any he had ever seen, they slanted upward, imparting an exotic quality to her face as a whole, which was perfectly symmetrical with a sharply defined nose and thick, sensuous lips. Her teeth were perfectly straight and white. Taller than he, she cut an imposing figure, standing in that austere room with the faint light of the television screen illuminating the interior. For some reason, Jack was drawn to the woman. She eyed him coldly, her eyes scanning him from head to toe.

"So you're the one who's going to write about him," she said in an accusatory tone.

Jack said nothing.

"I googled him," Joline said. "He wrote a bestseller back in the seventies."

When the woman didn't respond, Joline said, "It was acclaimed, actually. At the time, he was fairly well known."

"Have you read it?" the woman asked.

"I just found out about it. I will, though."

"Who's he answer to?"

Joline turned to Jack. "Well?"

"Don't most writers answer to themselves?" he asked. He was starting to get annoyed. If it hadn't been for the woman's stunning beauty, he'd have walked out, but there was something mysterious and unbelievably seductive in the way she moved and spoke. Her extraordinary looks merely enhanced her unusual presence. He stalled, unsure what else to say, while she tapped her feet, as if listening to a song no one else heard.

"Yvonne, he's a nice guy. Believe me. I brought him here to talk to you. He just wants to know more about Ted. You know so much more than I do."

Joline turned to Jack. "She's known him for years and years. They grew up together, didn't you, Yvonne?"

The woman inhaled her cigarette. Its red glow moved fast in the dim room, and Jack watched it, mesmerized by the circular, orange pattern. She walked across the room and turned on a lamp. A ragged chair sat by the window. She lowered her body into it and continued smoking. Her intense stare still roamed his body. He felt naked, exposed. His face felt warm, and he turned away from her. He walked over to the bed and sat down. Joline joined him.

"He died here," the black woman said in a monotone.

When Jack said nothing, she pointed. "Over there. By the bed. Beneath the fucking night light." Her voice quavered, her mouth twitching in an unnatural manner. Tears gathered in her lovely eyes till she wiped them away with one hand. "He wouldn't want me to cry," she said through clenched teeth. "He always wanted me to be upbeat. I wasn't supposed to be sad or angry or ugly."

But she did sound angry, Jack thought. Very angry indeed.

"You were a source of joy to him, Yvonne. You know that." Joline reached in her purse and brought out a newspaper article. "I got this from the *Hartford Courant*." She handed the piece to the woman, who read it and looked up.

"This article is about the book. It says here that Ann Hudson is cooperating with you."

Jack said nothing. Around him the room seemed to shrink, holding them all hostage to something indefinable but terrible. Once more, he thought of Miranda and wished she were here to help him make sense of the moment. It was as if there was something else going on besides the scene before him, some truth that hid in the walls or among the spider webs on the ceiling. Jack shivered from the cold of the place, from something imperceptible that caused him a sudden sense of anxiety. Joline looked at him; their eyes met. "Don't worry," she said, touching his leg beside hers. "There's nothing to fear."

He tried to heed her words, but something inside him caused him to stand. "I really must be going," he said, looking behind him at the open door and the dark hallway at the top of the landing. He listened for sounds outside, but all he could hear was the rain dripping from the eaves and the sound of the woman inhaling her cigarette.

"I have work to do. I must be going."

"Wait," the woman said. "If you want information, you'd better get it now." She made an elaborate show of smoothing her dreadlocked hair and turned back to him. "You'd better get me while you can. Who knows how long any of us has left? Especially those of us who like to take risks. Right, Joline?" The woman rolled her eyes and frowned at the drab interior. "Not much of a pleasure palace, is it?"

"What do you mean?" Jack asked in spite of himself. He was exhausted. All he felt like was going to bed, but the woman lured him on into the perilous waters of her personality. He could feel the danger she posed, the danger she'd lived by, no doubt, but he felt helpless to resist what he considered to be some truth only she possessed, and for that he was desperate.

"What do I mean?" she repeated. She looked at the plastic clock on the wall above the bed. "This, Jack Pierce, was the other home of the renowned Theodore Hudson. His sanctuary from the pressures of the vulture-driven world he scorned. His castle," she finished, a low, rumbling laugh escaping her parted lips. "It was here he did most of his writing. He prepared his speeches on the bed you're sitting on." She stood and walked over to a small bookcase by the television and brought out a folder. "And it was to this house, not the mansion on Whitney, that he brought his special students." She sat back down in the chair and resumed her smoking. "You see, it was I who loved him. It was me he needed."

She tossed the folder in his lap. It fell open to a sheaf of papers with an old photograph on top of a thick stack of others. Jack stared down at a portrait of a young, slender Yvonne in her high school graduation garb. Her smile was innocent, her eyes bright and clear. Around her neck was a small cross. The photographer had caught a girlish mischievousness. Jack felt sick at heart to see the altered awareness so evident in the mature Yvonne. One could grasp without trying the darkness her experience embodied. It was evident in the room itself, in the dearth of books, the smell, the dark circles under her eyes. The squalor of the bed, its satiny desolation, and the lumpy sloping of its used spaces merely reminded Jack of the timeless homilies preached him all those lonely Sunday mornings in bleak West Texas churches. With shaking hands, he shuffled through the other pictures, his heart sick with knowing what he didn't choose to. There they were, as young lovers at what appeared to be a picnic in the woods, on a deserted beach at twilight with the red sun behind them in the reflection on the water. Dancing at an all-black gathering at someone's home. Before the Eifel Tower, wearing matching cowboy hats. Standing on the steps of the Taj Mahal, hoards of begging children crowding them upward. In every picture the two smiled, comfortable, happy in the presence of the other. The last one was of them attending a play, Yvonne looking as she did now, a black, sexy dress emphasizing her slender body and prodigious height with her huge bangled earrings dropping almost to her shoulders.

Stunned, Jack sat still while around him the room seemed to echo another silent truth, one he knew he could not face at the moment. He felt physically ill. The image of Ann Hudson rose in his imagination, the sight of David Hudson in his wheelchair, planning for Princeton. He thought of her words that day, her gentle manner, and the injustice of her lot smote him as cruelly as anything he had ever experienced. For a moment he considered running down the stairs and out the door, driving off to the airport at La Guardia and never returning to New Haven and the bereft widow whose grief had touched him irrevocably. But, he reflected as instantaneously as intuition or telepathy, truth was not something you could contain in a sealed jar and be done with it. Like Pandora's Box, the truth would out, and the big question always was how you were going to deal with it. He didn't know, but like the shadow that has no sentience but still follows relentlessly, he would follow that something out there. Here. And that something would help him to understand

Chapter Fourteen

They drove home through the falling rain. It came down heavily and without respite. Along the winding road the trees bent into themselves, thick and dark in the scant light. Occasionally he would glimpse Joline's profile in the reflection from a passing car or the moonlight wavering through the trees. She stared fixedly ahead as if lost in thought. He wanted to say something to reassure her or at least thank her for trying to help. He hoped to see her again and talk about Theodore Hudson in more depth. Mostly he wanted to apologize for his own want of courage back there. He could not forgive himself, and he doubted that once Miranda heard about the evening, she would either.

However, try as he would, he could not share with the girl his dark fears, nor could he begin to explain the strange effect the woman Yvonne had on him. Right now in the utter blackness of the countryside, he could not forget her face, the way she stood at the top of the landing, as if challenging him, them both. Nor could Jack ignore the seductive, hand-drawn circles of cigarette light he felt she used to lure them into her sphere. It was clear to Jack that the woman wielded an unnatural influence over Joline, and he wondered if this was what Theodore Hudson intended when he invited his protégés to the isolated place. That he should expose young people to the obviously experienced and possibly profane Yvonne made Jack feel sick at heart. And yet the woman's appeal was such that even now on the lonely, moonlit road he was thinking, not of Karen, but of the tall black beauty whose body language and few words left him feeling confused and powerless. Because of loathsome truths she seemed to embody, he felt fear and a need to protect Ann Hudson, Joline, Miranda, even himself from a danger he could not explain.

"Why did you feel it necessary to take me there?" he asked Joline as they were nearing the lights of New Haven. Beyond them the rain-slicked roads were almost empty and the quarter moon so far above them, it seemed remote and unimportant. He was trying to sort out the experience as they wended their way among the trees and deserted roads, yet he was still at a loss as to what the experience meant. Still baffling him was the role of the cipher, Yvonne.

"You wanted to understand the man," she said, her voice somewhat husky, a monotone, for once, as she spoke, staring straight ahead at the shabby, neon-lit mélange of New Haven by night. "Sometimes you have to *see* things for yourself. Most things are not what they seem, you know."

"I'm quite aware of that," he said, affronted that she would see him as falling short in the ability to discern people and situations for what they were. In fact, Jack had long ago decided that with the exception of certain beautiful women in his past, he was a pretty good judge of character. He liked to think he understood people fairly well. How else could he have written the novel he did? And, in fact, hadn't that understanding of human nature been the basis of his acclaim? Of course, Joline had not read his book, he reminded himself.

"What do you think drives a great man, if it isn't an inordinate curiosity?" she asked. "And perhaps that curiosity drives him to suffer as well." Although Jack cringed to admit it, she had lived a life of unbearable hardship; she did know more than he about human suffering and deprivation and possibly degradation – the whole nine yards, he thought in a flash of compassion for the girl. He saw her pale, intelligent profile, the hard set of her lips, the ridiculous, wayward chaos of her hairstyle, and the thought occurred to him that her wounds were incapable of healing, unless someone helped her to achieve a clarity of vision. For Jack there was a narrow line one walked in the presence of threatening elements one didn't always understand but which gave off their own sense of confusion and cold. He realized he was afraid for her and for all those like her. He hadn't experienced such threats to his understanding when he attended his small Texas college in the days before the world changed on a dime, as he liked to describe the sixties and seventies. It was one thing to brush casually with inexplicable forces out there, but quite another to enmesh oneself in them, as he was afraid she might have.

"I don't know," he said. "Didn't curiosity kill the cat?" He tried to inject some humor into the painfully serious evening, but his heart wasn't in it. The stakes were too high.

To his surprise, her mouth opened wide, and she turned and stared him full in the face. He had the impression she was astounded by the remark, that for her it held a basic truth she hadn't considered. "Oh, God," she said, and turned away from him to the sodden nocturnal landscape.

It took a few moments driving through the neon-lit streets to realize that his comment had registered in her mind as applicable to Hudson. That a cryptic observation could elicit such a reaction made Jack realize how impressionable the girl was, and with a start, he understood how even the wisest young person could so easily be derailed by the curiosity which drove anyone of intelligence. That she had already experienced so much in her life did not necessarily make her wise and could have even perpetuated a misguided quest for the thrills of life embedded in the arcane or profane, as the case might be. He stopped the car. "Please don't misunderstand me," he said as he reached over and pulled her toward him. He held her shoulders, delicately, as if she were made of eggshells so as not to present the impression of someone sensual and needy. "Joline," he said. "Did it ever occur to you that Hudson, for whatever motive, did not have your best interests at heart?"

"It most certainly did," she admitted. "But I trusted him. I believed in him." She seemed to rest in his arms quite comfortably. "You have to realize that we didn't have a physical relationship or anything like that. He was like a father to me."

Yeah, right! Jack wanted to say. *Great father he was!*" But he said nothing as he held her for a few moments and hoped that nothing had happened out there in that God-forsaken place that would irrevocably affect her capacity to trust or love or live a life without regret or remorse. He held her for a few moments more as they listened to the rain fall on the car and the swish of cars rolling by in the gaudy light. It surprised Jack that the two could feel at ease after what had transpired earlier, but it was clear that between them a hurdle had been overcome.

"I'm taking you home," he said, removing his arms. She turned again to the window and watched a dog sniffing a pile of plastic bags outside a gas station. Thin and lame, the wretched creature began to paw at the bags, spilling their contents across the sidewalk.

"I know how that dog feels," she said.

Jack watched the dog. It had found a chicken carcass and was devouring bones and flesh, its slimy beard catching the bright lights of the strip mall behind it.

"You've been that hungry?" Jack asked.

"Figuratively speaking, yes." For a few moments she said nothing, but then her words started anew, a flood of speech as if long withheld and bursting out of her. "You can't imagine all those terrible places," she said. "The inhumanity, the dog-eat-dog nature of foster homes and their like. People use you and abuse you and they don't care. There's no one to turn to, no systems in place. No sense to it." She looked down at her hands clenched in her lap. "The irrationality of it, the ugliness, the depravity—"

He presumed she was talking about her life in a series of homes, the challenge to her sense of security and self-value that the experience presented. Jack reached over and patted her hand. "But you're so smart," Jack said. "If anyone can overcome a lousy upbringing, you can."

"Can one really overcome a deprivation of love?" she asked, her voice faltering.

"Oh, Joline," he said, overcome with pity. "I think so. It must take an awful lot of focus and effort, but I'm sure it can be done."

"How do you know?" she asked.

He thought for a moment, the thumping of the rain sparking a rhythm to his thinking, a sense of reassurance in its steadiness, its predictability. "You said *deprivation of love,*" he reminded her. "Well, maybe you just have to fill up that hole, that space with something else, something fulfilling." He had to admit he wasn't sure what he was saying, but he knew it was true, as swiftly and surely as he'd known there was something threatening about the woman Yvonne. Yet he couldn't explain beyond that one fragment of insight. He couldn't go on.

She looked at him sadly. "I'll think about what you said."

Since he could say nothing more, he started up the car and drove past Claire's. Of course, it was empty this late at night. A thin light shone from a back room, and he was reminded of the house in the country, its dreadful shabbiness and neglect, the rotten stench of desecration. He thought of Joline's behavior tonight and of her reaction to his inarticulate advice, and he suddenly had confidence in the girl's ability to make her life work for her. Just like that — out of the blue — with swift and solid certainty, he knew. He felt relieved, and his hands on the wheel relaxed as he turned to meet her eyes.

"I'll see you tomorrow?" he asked.

She opened the car door and stepped out into the rain. Behind her the ancient gargoyles and spires of Yale University awaited her.

She turned to face them and then turned back and bent her head and smiled down at him.

"Same time, same place," she said, before running across the way and up the steps to her dorm.

By the time Jack sat down with Ann Hudson he had convinced himself that she knew of her husband's double life and would probably discuss it with him before he went any further in his research. She would most likely suggest that he keep that part of Hudson's life secret and focus instead on his many achievements. After all, that approach would satisfy the need to immortalize Hudson's work and to honor Yale as well as protecting her and her son. Yet Jack found the idea hard to accept in the light of how he viewed the woman. She had seemed honest and straight forward. Was it possible that she was unaware of Hudson's propensities for risk taking? Jack had to admit it was a stretch to believe a woman of Ann Hudson's intelligence and sensitivity could be unaware of her husband's conduct. He had been at Yale for too many years for his behavior to remain a secret. By now any unsavory truths would have been exposed. The woman did not strike Jack as someone capable of denial. He saw her as one who would face the truth head on, no matter how unpleasant. It was this characteristic that had driven her love of literature and her capacity to deal with her son's physical condition.

Today she was dressed in a long skirt and a fitted jacket that emphasized her small waist. Her hair was pulled back with tendrils at her temples and her chignon in its usual immaculate form. Her face was flushed from walking with David. She ushered him in the front door and to the back of the house, where she sat him down on the leather sofa. "I'll be a minute," she said.

He heard her go up the stairs and open the door to David's bedroom. She closed it behind her and was there for a few moments before the door opened again, and she descended the stairs. She had Mozart playing on the stereo, and there were cooking smells coming from the kitchen. As usual, the house had about it an air of order and comfort. He glanced around at the books lying about, the stack of compact discs, the magazines she had open on the coffee table, and he wondered anew what it was that Ann Hudson expected of him. He doubted she would want him to lie. He decided at the moment she was descending the stairs that he was right about her — that she was incapable of deception. That could mean only one thing: Theodore Hudson had deceived her all those years of their marriage. He then felt a loathing for the man that was so intense it frightened him. It occurred to him that he didn't want to write the man's biography unless it was steadfastly honest, but how could he expose the truth of the man when it would be so devastating for Ann Hudson and her son?

Jack thought about Miranda and wondered again why she hadn't gotten in touch with him. He needed to discuss the dilemma before he went much further. He needed to understand what she already knew with her keenness of insight and compassionate view of human frailty. Why were the two of them aligned in the purpose of writing about Hudson, if he weren't the honorable man they believed him to be?

"So how are you?" Ann Hudson asked as she handed him a glass of iced tea. She had a lightness in her step and a joy he hadn't seen in her before. If he'd had to describe her to date, it would have been a woman who'd suffered and done so with dignity and grace. He'd have said she was a classy woman, an interesting woman, a very astute woman, but he would not have said she was ebullient, happy in the traditional sense, or even vivacious. Instead, she appeared defined by her sorrow – accepting of it, grateful for what she had, and focused on making David's life as well as her husband's as meaningful and as comfortable as possible under the circumstances. As such, she was the good mother, the good wife, the stoic in the face of adversity, but not the joyful woman for whom destiny had been kind. If he'd had to select a word that most described her, it would have been "serious."

"I'm fine," Jack said. "Working away."

"They're being helpful?" she asked.

"*They?*" Jack asked, wondering if she knew whom he'd been getting information from. He thought of Yvonne and Joline, the dark house in the country, and he felt a chill go up his spine. For a moment, he even wondered if Ann Hudson were having him followed, but before she answered, he knew again that she wouldn't do that. *Where was Miranda?*, he thought, in a torrent of frustration. He needed to talk to her. *Now.*

She must have glimpsed his discomfort. "Why, the Yale librarians, of course. I should warn you that Delaney, the head archivist, didn't much like Ted."

"Now why was that, do you think?"

"Professional jealousy more than anything, probably. The man has a superiority complex, it seems to me. He and Ted were on several committees together – you know, research ones, that sort of thing. Ted said the man had always been rude to him." She frowned and sat down across from Jack, crossing her legs beneath the folds of the long skirt. "Delaney is gay and quite temperamental, but I don't know how that would equate to rudeness. I've always found him to be kind, actually."

Jack thought of Yvonne and the seedy environment of the house in the country. After having thought a great deal about the scene last night, he wasn't sure what to think. One couldn't help but regard the place as a den of iniquity, but then again that alone couldn't possibly explain the room upstairs, the woman who spent so much time there, Joline's seemingly ineffectual efforts to help him understand something that Jack knew was eluding him so far. *"Things aren't always what they seem,"* she'd reminded him more than once. Certainly what they seemed was pretty terrible, even if Ted Hudson were absent from the premises. The fact that Hudson had any involvement with the woman or that students frequented the place was anathema to the reputation of Theodore Hudson, one of the greatest men of his time. Provoked by the thought that he was indeed assembling an elaborate puzzle, Jack tried to clear the cobwebby confusion from his mind and focus on the woman here who held truths equally important. *One thing at a time,* he told himself. *Don't get tangled up in other webs of deception until you know for sure what is going on right here. Listen carefully. Stay in the now, don't jump ahead.*

"You're pretty candid about this Delaney's attitude toward your husband," Jack began. "Any others you feel might have tried to denigrate your husband's reputation? Do you know of any colleagues who for whatever reason, didn't want your husband to receive recognition?"

He could tell by the slight blush and sudden glance outside that he had struck a nerve. Her eyes seemed to focus on something beyond them, some image in her mind. She set down her glass and got up. He watched as she walked into the study, deep in thought. He sat back and listened to Mozart, the falling crescendos he loved, the way the music filtered up the stairs and hovered outside David's door. He supposed the boy was studying and admired him for his diligence. He wondered how close the boy and his father had been.

He'd almost forgotten what he'd asked, so absorbed had he become in the music and watching the leaves falling from the trees outside. The sun had come out and the outside scene was once again flawless in its natural simplicity. It made him want to walk somewhere, to get outside and enjoy the last of the autumn beauty.

She swept back into the room with a pile of papers. "These are the various committees he served on at Yale," she said. "All the members are listed. I have them listed by their phone numbers so he could call people when he needed to. He often had to miss meetings due to his travels. I think some of the members resented him for that." She handed Jack the pile of papers. "Beyond that, I don't know. He was a loner, that's for sure, but I don't think people resented him, if that's what you mean. He was such a hard worker, and his clarity of vision and prestige in the field were assets to any committee, I would think."

"You mentioned that you and your husband entertained colleagues and they you. Were you privy to gossip then or were the occasions primarily professional and formal in terms of behavior?"

She thought again. "I guess you would say that Ted did not indulge in gossip. He and I never talked about his colleagues' private lives. It simply wasn't a topic of interest to us, not even when he was having departmental difficulties with someone. But he was interested in their professional accomplishments. He read all their publications and gave his feedback. In that way, he really encouraged his associates. I'm sure they appreciated that because few were as attentive to his work, even when it made national headlines. I did notice that."

"Did that bother you?" Jack asked. "Did you feel he was slighted?"

Again, she thought for a while. "I think I did at times," she admitted. "I guess that's why I didn't encourage Yale people to do his biography."

"And there were requests from his colleagues here?"

"Students, yes. Professional acquaintances, colleagues, no." She said nothing more, perusing his reaction. "What do you think?" she asked at last.

"I'd venture to say there was indeed professional jealousy. One could hardly imagine a man of our times having more prestige as a thinker, writer, activist. Why, he was larger than life, that's for sure. It would take an unusual man indeed not to arouse some defensiveness or jealousy among his associates, but that doesn't diminish his stature nor does it explain why no one from Yale requested your authorization to write about him. I must admit it doesn't make sense to me."

The phone interrupted them. Ann Hudson left and went into the kitchen to answer it. He vaguely heard her talking then she was standing over him with the receiver in her hands. "It's for you," she said. "A woman."

Jack took the phone with a sense of relief. It had to be Miranda.

"Yes?" he said, waiting for the familiar voice, intent upon giving her a piece of his mind for not calling sooner.

"Jack, I'm here in New Haven."

"Boy, am I glad to hear from you," he said.

"I hope you weren't worried, but it does take a while to drive here."

"You drove?"

"Well, you needed a car, and so did I. Heaven knows how long this will take and I couldn't expect you to hold onto a rental for long."

Despite Jack's annoyance of a moment ago, he was glad to hear Miranda's familiar voice and grateful to her that she did bring her car since Jack had been fretting over the expense of his rental car. He could hear Ann Hudson in the kitchen moving about so he didn't want to say much, but he didn't want to let Miranda go before they had agreed to a meeting. "When can we get together? I need to bring you up to speed as soon as possible."

"Where are you staying?"

He told her.

"I'll see you there in a couple of hours, if that's okay with you."

"Sounds good," he said and hung up. For a moment, he sat still, listening to the music and feeling more settled than he had since he arrived in New Haven. What had once been a city that repelled him, it was now the home of Ann Hudson, whom he respected and liked. However, it was also the site of things he didn't understand, and in that sense he felt strangely disconnected from the mainstream here. It was in this town of prodigious intellectual pursuits that most people would feel daunted, he knew, but until last night the thought that he would feel intimidated by the culture had not presented itself, no matter what his concerns had been until now. He was glad Miranda was back to ground him, to help him make sense of the ambiguities he'd witnessed. He wondered about her trip out here alone, her parting from Don Parrish, the information on Hudson she'd managed to glean since he saw her.

"Are you ready to have something to eat?" Ann Hudson asked him from the kitchen. He rose and went to her.

"You bet," he said.

She led him into the dining room where the faint glow of an elaborate crystal chandelier suffused the dark room with light. She had three places set at a massive walnut table with thick legs. Along the walls were various sized oil paintings in a variety of styles and frames. With the crimson walls and paintings, the room presented a sense of old world ambience. A large soup tureen sat in the middle of the table and three salads with fish on top. A basket of bread gave off a smell of yeast. Jack was suddenly very hungry.

"David?" she called to her son, and immediately the door upstairs opened. Jack could hear the sound of the elevator descending, the door opening again and the creaking of the wheelchair along the wood floors.

Chapter Fifteen

"So how's the paper coming?" Ann Hudson asked her son as she spooned soup into his bowl. It was a fish chowder, Jack noticed, instantly hungry. She had set flowers on the table and changed the CD to one Jack didn't recognize. Although the room was somewhat dark, it had a feeling of warmth with the soft light from the chandelier and the fire burning on the opposite wall.

"It's going really slowly," David said. "Today I definitely have writer's block."

"I know how that feels," Jack said.

"What do you do when it happens?" David asked, taking the napkin from the table and putting it on his lap.

"I generally use it as an excuse to do something else," Jack said, laughing.

"We could go for another walk, Mother," David suggested. "Then I would have spent the whole day doing nothing."

"I'm sorry, honey. Maybe you should lie down for a while and plan on working later in the evening, like you sometimes do."

"I'll do that." He looked over at Jack. "So how's it going with the book?"

"It's coming along," Jack said. "There certainly is a plethora of information on your father out there. I should be able to write a lot about the man."

"He was remarkable. Everyone said so, anyway."

"So what did your dad and you do together?"

"Dad wasn't into sports, but neither was I. So sometimes we went to movies or to the park along with Mother. He took me to the museums around here; we went to all the art exhibits. Dad knew a lot about art. He was pretty busy, though, so it wasn't like we spent a lot of time together."

"Did he attend your school activities?"

"I'm a debater. I've been in forensics for years and Model UN, Science Club. The usual for those of us who aspire to an Ivy League education. Yes, he attended my debates and presentations when he was in town."

"David starred in the school play this year as well. It was a first for someone in a wheelchair. I was so proud of him. He actually demonstrated a flair for comedy."

"Thanks, but it wasn't a hard part."

"Yes, it was. You were the star." She seemed intent on giving him credit when he preferred to minimize his involvement. Jack wondered if he was always self-effacing, a quality in people Jack didn't particularly admire. He'd seen too many politicians and schmoozers adopt that sort of diplomacy to court approval. "Everyone praised his performance," she finished.

"I was fine," David said. "Let's just say that being an actor would be hellish for me. I didn't enjoy the experience, but I wanted to prove to myself I could do it. And that I did. So now I can move on and try other things and not be fearful."

"Did your father teach you that?"

"Teach me what?"

"To conquer fear, to challenge yourself to try new things?"

David thought for a moment. "I guess he did. He was always challenging himself to try new approaches, to see things from different perspectives. He said there were many routes to truth and many truths to rout. He was a seeker, and I think I became a seeker, too, due to his example." David's mouth trembled slightly. He glanced sideways at his mother. "Mom's always been a seeker as well." David seemed to reflect more on the subject. "Perhaps that was Dad's greatest legacy. He did inspire me to really *see*. Since I intend to be a scientist, too, that turned out to be a gift he gave to me. I'm sure that someday, like at this very moment, thanks to your question, I'll realize that legacy again and be thankful once more. Like my dad and mother, I hope to benefit from knowledge beyond the money it earns me or the prestige or power my position affords. No, I just want to learn, to develop my imagination, and to see where the knowledge I acquire takes me. That's what matters."

"And that is what your father instilled," Ann Hudson said. "He would be so happy if he could hear you now." She smiled across the table at Jack. "You see, Ted's parents didn't seem at all interested in the workings of the world. Ted was so disappointed in them that he couldn't share what he learned or talk about issues or simply pursue his imagination in creative activities. They wanted him to be an athlete and major in business. His intellect was lost on them, it seems. It was the big disappointment of Ted's early life."

"And still he pursued learning to the extent he was admitted to exclusive schools. It's amazing what a strong will can accomplish, isn't it?" Jack eyed David, noticed his serious face unclouded by petty emotions such as envy or the need to impress.

"I didn't realize Dad's parents didn't value learning," David said. "But then I never met them either. They didn't visit, and he never talked about them to me."

"We are close to my parents, though." Ann Hudson offered.

"Yes," David said, seemingly lost in thought.

The grandfather clock on the landing sounded. Ann Hudson moved to collect the plates. "Let's have a quick dessert and then you can get on with your paper, David," she said soothingly. "I'm sure it will go fine now that you've had a break from it."

"I think it will go better now," David agreed, as if a block to his imagination had indeed been removed for the time being.

By the time Jack left the house on Whitney Avenue and drove back to the motel, it was getting dark. He hoped Miranda would arrive soon because he had forgotten to tell her about his appointment with Joline. There was a lot he wanted to discuss with her before then.

As Jack drove up into the motel parking lot, he was surprised at the warm sense of satisfaction he felt seeing Miranda's SUV parked outside his unit. He could barely see her torso though the windows, her thick mane of wayward hair standing out in the moonlight like dried grass. He quickly parked and walked over to the driver's window. She got out of the car and threw her arms around him. "Oh, Jack, you can't imagine how happy I am to see you! I've been so bored driving those interstates. Honestly, I don't think road trips are my thing."

Jack held her close for a few moments, his head buried in her hair, the natural smell of lime reminding him of the past, the way she'd always been. Whatever place in her heart Don Parrish filled, she was the same woman he'd known most of his life. Holding her was as natural as eating or sleeping, as comfortable and pleasingly so as listening to good music or eating a particularly tasty meal. He wondered if all aging people felt similarly, as if the simple unadulterated nearness of people one loved were enough to mitigate the various disappointments of life. With Miranda right this moment, he felt wrapped in a cozy blanket of familiarity similar to the warm predictability of Karen's presence before her terrible decline.

"We are quite the pair, aren't we?" she startled him by remarking. "We can't be together for long, and we can't be apart indefinitely. Oh, well.... Such is life, I guess."

He left it at that. But he knew she was right.

"Come in," he said. "I have a lot to tell you."

"Nice place," she said, surveying the drab room with its countless carpet stains, the dusky walls and shabby bed covers. "I can't blame you, though. I wouldn't want to spend a lot for a room in this city either."

"You don't like New Haven?"

"It's not exactly your quaint New England town, is it? You forget I hate cities – all the noise, the people, the cars..."

"I used to hate this place," Jack said. "They're fixing it up; it isn't so bad. Mrs. Hudson lives on a lovely street, you'll see."

"So what's she like?" Miranda asked, turning toward him and throwing herself down on the bed. She tucked her boots beneath her legs and looked up at him mischievously.

"Well, she's quite beautiful."

"Of course," Miranda said. "You must really like her, then."

"How so?" Jack asked, somewhat annoyed.

"You've always put too much stock in a woman's looks." The faint curl of her lip, the way her eyes looked downward, the detached tone of her voice revealed to Jack that she was offended.

"I'm sorry," Jack said, "but beauty is beauty. You can't expect me not to notice."

"Men, artists, I hate them all!" Miranda said. She glanced around the room at the forlorn paintings of faded flowers. "You should look into the human heart more and less into the shallow configurations of external beauty."

"If I took your advice," Jack said without thinking, "I'd be listening for vibrations and looking for ghostly presences. I'd be a nut case like you!"

It took only a second before he knew he'd gone too far. Her face crumpled with disappointment and fatigue. Her lovely eyes grew dim in the meager light. "Thanks a lot," she said after a long moment of silence. To Jack who had been waiting to see her again, this was the defining moment, what had always happened when they got back together after a separation. They cared about each other, but neither could resist an impulsive need to possess or dominate the other, even if true commitment between them was impossible. Ah, the complications of Miranda love, he thought sadly. Of all love…

"I'm not a nut case," she said evenly. "And you should know that by now."

"No, of course, you aren't," he said soothingly. "I didn't mean that. I don't know why I said it even."

"You said it because I implied you're shallow."

"Well, right," Jack said. He could feel himself getting annoyed again. Her impertinence, her tendency to judge him, the sense of inferiority her judgments implied smote him as they always did. Such observations not only diminished him, they made communication impossible. They broke the wary intimacy the two insisted on establishing but then let fray just as easily. There was no figuring the why of their actions, but to Jack at the moment, they both seemed egomaniacal, part of an obvious power game they insisted on reenacting. To him they should be beyond this petty, elliptical banter. They'd known each other too long and been through so much that at least now with all the water under the bridge and all the bridges they'd each burned, it was time to be honest and direct, if they were ever going to establish a meaningful, lasting relationship.

"I think we need to be more honest with each other," Jack said.

"*Oh, please,*" she said. "You don't know how to be honest."

If he'd gone too far moments ago, she certainly had just now. "What are you saying?" he asked, totally surprised at the hostility, the hollow flatness of her voice, the voice he generally thought of as warm and musical in its own way. The voice that moved entire groups of people to action and truth. He felt suddenly ashamed. Why was it he couldn't get through to her, he her most ardent fan?

"I've always thought I was very honest," he said quietly. His words sounded tentative on the muffled air, blending with the traffic moving past, the faint sound of the heating system. From long ago, the image of a skinny girl in frayed jeans with fresh, unadorned cheeks and eyes and lips, plaid shirts hanging down to her knees and rancher boots recalled to Jack in his agony and frustration the innocence of the girl then. He was reminded of her pure motives and natural compassion for animals, people, all the lost and disenfranchised people out there. She'd always had the need to help, and from that single orientation itself had emerged a complex woman of the world, one who wasn't afraid to mingle with the hurting masses and minister to the deformed of body and mind. Who was he to call her personality into question; who was he to question her validity? He, Jack Pierce, who'd languished in Leadville after failing in Texas and New York. He who'd abandoned his wives at the first sign of conflict. He who'd invited failure with his refusal to work out the conflicts in his muddied personal life. In a flash of insight, he realized that Karen had indeed been unique for accepting him as he was; most women would have expected more. Most women would have demanded more.

"I'm so sorry," he said, groaning with the effort it took to apologize. "You don't need that. You deserve people who appreciate your goodness, not a loser like me who lashes out at the truth, who doesn't want the burden of extending himself. Who simply wants everything nice and easy," he finished, feeling so depressed that for a moment all he was there in New Haven for vanished in a cloud of doubt and self-recrimination.

"Oh, Jack," she said, "I didn't mean that you take the easy way out. I didn't mean you are shallow or a loser." She jumped up from the bed and threw her arms around him and buried her face in his chest. "I just meant that you run from the truth sometimes, that you dream to make the world the way you want it, that you avoid life by doing so. You *escape* life rather than *live* it. You try to make the world the way you want it rather than accepting it for what it is!" She threw herself back on the bed and turned away from him. Her shoulders heaved, and he wanted to comfort her, but he couldn't.

He sat down on the other bed and watched her sobbing shoulders and felt the pain of chastisement again for the thousandth time. This time it was his own silent judgment that wreaked its cruel justice. For once he saw his own terrible limitation himself, through his own eyes as if he looked down a deep, dark well of his own murky intentions and failed dreams. They bobbed along an uneven surface like plankton scavenging depleted resources. *I'm such a failure, he thought. What have I accomplished with my life?* The woman on the bed, the dreary motel room, even the radiant face of Ann Hudson coalesced into a dark smear of personal truth. He vowed he would change his life, right now, in New Haven. He would redeem himself from the legacy of his past. He would listen and learn and help the world in his own small way, as Miranda had done. He told himself that only this focused effort could deliver him from his own self-loathing. Not success or love or even pride in his writing could redeem him now. He had to fight to relinquish his fear of failure, his sense of inferiority, his dearth of understanding. For once he would have to submit to a truth beyond himself, beyond his own petty yearnings. And if that meant a diminishment of his Self, well, so be it.

He walked over to Miranda and took her frail frame into his arms, feeling the bony limbs, smelling the lime, the sweet skin he'd known so long ago. "Ann Hudson is a beautiful woman," he said, "but I hope you appreciate that what I see in her exceeds her physical beauty."

Miranda had stopped sobbing. She looked up at him. "I know that," she said. "I guess I was just a little jealous."

"You are, too, you know?"

"What, beautiful?" she asked, a scornful look replacing her sorrow.

"Yes," he simply said.

"Hmmfff..." she said, but the antagonism had passed. He waited a few moments before he drew away from her, then told her briefly about Joline. She followed him out the door and they left for Claire's in her truck.

Chapter Sixteen

"So tell me more about your Joline," Miranda said. "She sounds interesting." On both sides of the car the neon lights of the city gilded the windows with a gaudy sheen. Jack drove slowly, deliberately, attuned to Miranda's presence and his own fears of disappointing her. He drove past Ann Hudson's house without informing Miranda and noticed the Tiffany lamp in the entryway window, the quiet sense of peace and order the house presented to the world. He recalled the orderliness and subtle masculinity of Theodore Hudson's study, the grace and elegance of the spiral staircase and chandeliers. Theirs was a home where every opportunity to provide comfort and beauty had been seized and finalized. The image of his home in Leadville rose in his imagination, and he suddenly wished he were there, before the open fire, looking out the window at the snow-covered canyon. The sentiment filled him with joy. He liked the idea that home finally meant so much to him. It occurred to him he'd buy new furniture for the place, finish the deck railing. All the domestic tasks he'd avoided in the past seemed suddenly worth doing, important to the new Self he was cultivating. He looked over at Miranda, noticed her delicate profile against the color outside, and wondered at the epiphany that had driven her to plumb the mind of a genius she'd never met. For once, the sheer mystery of her insight rose in Jack's mind as a call to action, a belated encouragement to the fulfillment of his own repressed longings.

Jack thought about the girl Joline – her drab, unusual appearance seemingly at odds with the sharp, inquisitive mind that had removed her from the streets of New York City to the privileges of Yale University. "She strikes me as someone totally without fear," he said in answer to Miranda's question. "She's been through a lot, and I suppose that someone who's had her experiences knows what real fear is and no longer is hostage to it." Jack thought about the filthy house in the country, the depraved Yvonne, the intimacy Joline claimed with Professor Hudson, and he knew the girl's knowledge of humankind was profound, cultivated by a deprivation most people would never understand. Like a feral dog, she had grown up in abject misery and loneliness, refusing to be defeated, pursuing her own dreams that to anyone else must have appeared ridiculous. Yet she had persisted in her search for knowledge and education. That didn't mean she had banished the demons of her past, but in her way she had at least held them at bay. A close associate of Hudson, she still had her wits about her, still courted a subtle conventionality that would serve her well in the long run – after the bohemian life of a student had served its usefulness and the need to meet the outside world on its own terms demanded its due.

"She's a remarkable young woman." As he pronounced those words, it immediately occurred to him that they were the very ones Ann Hudson' had quoted her husband as using to describe Joline, and the awareness moved him to a sense of kinship with the man he'd never known but whose life had had its own share of sorrow and deprivation. Jack thought of his own mother – a silent presence in the home whom he'd always described as generous, a perfect mother. With a start, he suddenly realized that he hardly knew her. She'd been an elusive personality, always at her domestic tasks, preoccupied with the narrow routines that defined her life, while he, the quiet, introverted Jack had pursued a life of the imagination to fill up the moments of solitude and loneliness one experienced in the vast stretches of the west Texas farming community he and Miranda had grown up in. It hadn't been till Miranda walked into his life that his experiences at school or home seemed endowed with anything resembling joy. There had been little joy in his parents' house. The scream of poverty seemed to stifle everything else, to justify his father's tyranny over him, his mother's matter-of-fact stoicism and lack of emotion, his own lack of interest in school. He couldn't wait to get away from the smothering structure he called home then and from whence his father fled at every opportunity, leaving his mother alone with her regret and her tired faith that anyone could see was nothing more than an excuse for the deprivation she wore in the pursed set of her thin lips. His negative thoughts surprised Jack. He felt guilty. *Where had they come from?* He'd never felt this way before. He supposed it was the strain of trying to understand Theodore Hudson, the man. Jack told himself that he was wrong in his perception of his mother; she'd been there for him – always. But the moment had yielded its sorry truth, and Jack understood it. The realization left him empty and sad.

"You okay?" Miranda asked, eying him with her all-knowing sentience. He looked into her eyes which seemed to see him in all his inferiority and nakedness. He felt like a small boy again, refusing to eat corn and boiled potatoes and submitting to his father's blows. How small he'd felt. There were so many kinds of deprivation, he thought, sighing.

"Something wrong?" Miranda persisted. Her eyes were moist, and he knew she sensed the humiliation of his remembered past. Once more she'd read his mind. Only this time her uncanny ability quelled the anger that generally rose to the surface in such moments of remembered impotence.

"Mother," he said. "I was thinking of her."

Miranda reached over and patted his hand on the steering wheel. She said nothing, but he felt her empathy. "You were always so protective of her."

"Yeah," he said, not sure what Miranda meant. Protective of her or protective of himself? He'd always wanted to believe she'd been good because that meant he had the capacity to be so as well. It didn't matter, he told himself. The past was gone forever. He'd moved on long ago. There was the now and the future and then death which came to everyone. It served no good to dwell on grievances or regret. After all, his mother had had her own crosses to bear, he thought, recalling the consequences of his father's infidelity which he and his sister had learned about only after he'd passed away from an early heart attack. *Nothing was what it seemed,* he told himself, thinking of Joline's repeated refrain at the dreary house in the country.

"It's touching a nerve, isn't it – this whole thing?" Miranda looked outside at the sign in front of Claire's. Jack had stopped the car and placed his hands in his lap, reminding himself of hours spent in quiet desperation in a skewered wood desk on hot Texas afternoons, trying to avoid the teacher's scrutiny.

"I guess it is," he admitted, "although I'm not really sure what is getting to me. Maybe you're right, I'm still trying to dream my life rather than face it for what it is."

"Why do you say that?"

"What did you think of my mother?"

Miranda looked down. She seemed to regard her slender white fingers with incredulity. "She was all right."

"No, what did you really think?"

"What difference does it make?" Miranda said, taking his hand. "She was your mother, you loved her. That's all that matters."

"Did she love me?"

"Of course, she did. She must have. All mothers love their children." She gazed inside the bright windows of the restaurant at a girl reading a book. "Let's go meet Joline."

Gone for the moment was his interest in Joline, but he stepped out of the car and walked around to Miranda's side and helped her out of the car. He felt vaguely disoriented, but Miranda's hold on him as they walked into Claire's steadied him, and when he caught sight of Joline at the familiar spot in the middle of the place, he found himself glad to be seeing her again and to have Miranda at his side to lend insight into the girl and her version of Professor Hudson.

"Hi," Joline simply said when Jack introduced Miranda. Joline put down her book and smiled vaguely. She had on a nubby brown sweater that was too tight for her plump figure and unbecoming to her hair and complexion. Her hair had been pulled straight back from her face, emphasizing her full features and pallid skin. Jack doubted she ever took time with her appearance, as if her looks really didn't matter to her. He decided, that like Miranda, Joline operated on a different wavelength from most women he knew.

"Hi," Miranda answered, sitting down opposite the girl. "I've really been looking forward to meeting you. Jack said you were quite remarkable."

When Joline looked surprised, Miranda rushed to say, "He used those exact words, and I can assure you, he doesn't say that of many women. In fact, he rather tends to underestimate women in general."

Jack felt a rush of annoyance but told himself Miranda was just trying to make Joline feel comfortable.

Already Joline's indifference seemed to be melting away with the genuine interest Miranda showed in her. Jack had to admit Miranda's social skills were enviable. Her openness and clear interest in others seemed to endear her to most people she met. After they got to know her better, people bonded deeply with her firm sense of direction and her quiet acceptance of everybody, without judgment. Everybody but him, Jack thought bitterly. She was his harshest critic.

"Jack said you knew Professor Hudson well."

"Theodore Hudson was my dearest friend," Joline said, twisting her index finger over a ring on her opposite hand. It had a pink stone set in a silver setting. The girl looked down at her hand. "He gave this to me on my birthday last year," she said, tears welling in her eyes. "He said I deserved to have something special since I was special." She regarded Miranda with an ironic expression. "I suppose most people would take that statement with a grain of salt, but I knew he meant it. He never lied. With words anyway." She looked down at the pale stone in the dusky light from the window. Tears gathered in her eyes and gently fell on the hand in her lap. "I really miss him. I wonder that I can go on from day to day, knowing he won't ever come back. My one and only true friend."

Miranda looked at Joline with big, suffering eyes. In the scanty light, they were opaque, huge in the diminutive bone structure of her face. Her mouth trembled involuntarily, and for a moment words refused to issue from her lips but sat instead frozen and lifeless on the still air. All Jack could hear was her ragged breath, trying to force out sounds of support. *"Alone."* Miranda finally said, nodding as if to an unseen force behind the girl. *"You aren't alone,"* she said. She took Joline's hand in hers and held it there on the table scarred with countless names of callow predecessors: Tyler, and Jon and Samantha...Bill, Edward, Tory... *"We are none of us ever alone..."*

"Oh, but I am," Joline said, refusing to be placated. She wiped her eyes and shrugged her shoulders. "The truth hurts, but I can take it." She squared her shoulders and gave Jack an imperious look. "One learns to persevere."

"Yes, indeed," Miranda said. She didn't move her hand away, but there was something in her breathing, in the silent, still way she held her shoulders that was reassuring and final. The three sat at the table as a bell rang in the kitchen and a group of noisy students pushed in through the outside door and crowded the line to order. They were insistent and full of themselves, but the three at the table were immersed in their own quiet drama. Jack was surprised that he felt connected to the two women and not ashamed of his undivided attention nor embarrassed by the tears that even now sat in his eyes like permanent glass fixtures.

"Why are you here?" the girl asked Miranda.

"It was my idea to write about Hudson. My idea to memorialize his achievements. His story needed to be told. Someone had to do it." The words rushed from Miranda's lips as if she were in need of discarding them as quickly as possible.

"I...I....thought it was *your* idea to write his biography," Joline said, eying Jack with clear suspicion. "You said—"

"It was Miranda's idea," Jack affirmed. "She convinced me how important it was." Jack glanced around at the tables filling up around them. He registered the complacence in the young people's faces, their feigned indifference to fear and surprise. He saw their petty sufferings in a glance and felt a deep gratitude for the women on both sides of him, for their quiet acceptance of themselves and their willingness to reach out to him and include him in their collusion with fate or destiny or whatever one called it that occurred with or without man's assistance. It was a game, he thought, but a most serious one, and he needed to be reminded from time to time that the stakes were indeed very high.

Joline seemed to follow Jack's surveillance of the room. He watched her gaze shift around from person to person — to the polite server at the counter, the cashier with her stern impertinence, the busboy clearing half-emptied dishes. Her hand still clasped the ring reverently, but her eyes seemed to see it all and take in the ironies of the microcosm with a stoic withholding of judgment. He felt certain she understood so much more than he and that her insight was something she took for granted, a part of her that she had trusted all her life to lead her where she needed to go. To Jack at the moment, that constituted a kind of faith he'd never contemplated before. A sort of extraordinary gift beyond human comprehension. It was a rare moment for Jack: to see the world in a grain of sand, and his whole body responded with a surge of expectation. Everything beyond the little table seemed to melt away and the three of them were transported to another place — beyond aggravation and senseless blame. Beyond regret...

"It doesn't really matter whose idea it was to write about his life," Joline was saying. "It only matters that the truth of the man be captured. Because, believe me, Theodore Hudson was an extraordinary human being."

Jack thought of Yvonne and the secret den of their sensuality, and he almost recoiled at the girl's words. Surely she wasn't so innocent that she didn't realize the dark side of Theodore Hudson. It was possible he'd corrupted her, that his feelings were self-indulgent and terrible, but Jack kept his fears to himself, convinced he held in his consciousness only part of what the man was, as Joline herself had warned him.

"So what made him so extraordinary?" Miranda asked, reminding Jack that she, too, must have her own unique insight into the man and, perhaps, her own apprehensions.

"He accepted the fact that his exceptional talents were God given and that his responsibility was to manifest them in all ways. It's for that reason and that alone that he drove himself beyond human endurance."

"You mean that he was tireless in his efforts to improve the lot of those suffering terrible diseases?" Miranda asked.

"Oh, that and so much more," Joline said, looking off into the distance as if she could visualize the man out there. "He once told me that he could *feel* human suffering as we would a cut or a stubbed toe."

"But how could he do that?" Miranda asked.

As if she didn't know, Jack thought, — she who was cut out of the same mold.

"You're like that, Miranda," Jack said testily. "If there's one sad soul in a room, you find him." Jack thought of all the times in those restless sixties and seventies when he couldn't find Miranda at a gathering, only to locate her finally, listening to the sad story of some hopeless itinerant whose emotional crashes had become habitual. It didn't matter, she had a nose for the sick, the sad, the misunderstood. With a start, he wondered if that's what attracted her to him in the first place. Had she seen him as the sad, lost Jack Pierce, the boy whose parents were too absorbed in their own petty destinies to recognize they had a lonely, unfulfilled son? It was a bleak thought and he dismissed it immediately.

"You know, he's missing a kidney, don't you?" Joline peered at Jack.

"No, I didn't realize that," Jack said, thinking of David and Ann. Did they know? He doubted it. Ann Hudson would have mentioned it.

"What happened?" Miranda asked.

"He gave it to a student we knew. A kid from West Virginia, who had Acute Kidney Failure." She patted Miranda's hand. "That's why he limped all last semester. He had it done in Washington so no one would know. He was supposed to be at the World Affairs Conference, but he wasn't. He was at George Washington Hospital. I visited him there."

"The man wasn't a spring chicken," Jack noted. "There had to be risks for him."

"And his family," Miranda finished. "Did they know?"

Joline shook her head. "He said his wife would never condone such a thing on his part, so he didn't tell her. He worried, though, when sepsis set in, but the doctors got it under control right away."

Jack wondered how Ann Hudson would react to that information. Surely she would have minded the risk it posed to their family. He understood her feelings on that. It was one thing to help discover new treatments for disease and to minister to suffering humanity in various ways, but to put one's own life on the line when he had a family to support seemed to Jack nothing short of irresponsible. What drove the man to such an extreme measure?

As if reading his thoughts, Joline responded: "Love."

When Jack and Miranda looked at her aghast, wordless in their incomprehension, Joline continued. "For suffering humanity," she said, as if that clarified anything either Jack or Miranda could accept as a rational explanation.

"I told you, his favorite author was Dostoyevsky," Joline said, averting her eyes. "Perhaps you should read him."

"I've read every book he wrote," Jack said, sputtering with indignation.

"So have I," said Miranda, cocking her head in wonder. "To think there are people out there that selfless..."

"Oh, please," Jack said in spite of himself. "The man must have been a nut!"

"Why would you say that?" Joline demanded. "It's a noble act to give of yourself like that. And that's just one instance of Ted's altruism. He gave of himself in every way."

"According to his son, Hudson wasn't so generous with his time," Jack said, annoyed that the women before him would condone such misguided altruism. You took care of your own first, he told himself, before you extended yourself beyond your own family. Jack thought of Ann Hudson and her purity of demeanor and he was sickened at the betrayal Hudson's actions revealed.

"He was always giving things away," Joline continued. "Money, books, tickets to events. There was this guy in my anatomy class who was gay. He got really sick and wasted looking. Ted looked everywhere for help, but the hospital here required insurance and the boy didn't want his parents to know he was sick. Finally Ted drove him to the Mayo Clinic and paid for all his bills for a year."

"What happened to the boy?" Miranda asked.

"He died before he graduated. Ted visited his parents and told them the boy was gay. He prepared them as much as he could, but they couldn't accept it. They didn't attend the funeral, but Ted did. He had the gravestone made and wrote the obituary."

"Did others know about this?" Jack asked. "His colleagues? His students?"

"He kept it secret," Joline said. "There was no use in advertising his efforts. He just wanted to do what was right. For those who suffered." Joline looked from Jack to Miranda and back again. She held Jack's earnest stare. "You see, he was indeed a saint, but he'd be the last to admit it."

"I see," Jack said, but he didn't really understand. Such selflessness was beyond human comprehension, if only because it took so much effort to get one's own affairs in order, to live up to the responsibilities of a father and husband or son. He thought for a minute, shielding his eyes against the mirthless crew hovering along the walls, whose discussions were punctuated by denunciations of the Iraq War. What did he, Jack Pierce, know about anything?

"He had a prodigious capacity for idealistic love," Joline said. "Don't you see?"

Chapter Seventeen

"Boy, that was interesting, wasn't it?" Miranda remarked as they climbed into her car outside Claire's. It was raining again, and the smell of diesel hung in the air. Jack felt tired. It had been a long day with too much going on. The truth of Theodore Hudson, which he had thought would be straightforward and flattering, had become murky. Attempting to understand the interplay of personalities involved was far more emotionally draining than he would have expected. He yearned for the simplicity of his life only weeks ago — before Miranda appeared, drawing him back into the world, as she had done before when it seemed to her he had retreated. She had always demonstrated an uncanny knack for sensing his withdrawal, whether it was on an emotional level as he delved deeper and deeper into his own writing, or actual physical reclusion, as he'd resorted to in Leadville after Karen's death.

He supposed when he thought about it that his writing really was an escape from the tumultuousness of life, as Miranda had always claimed. It was difficult for him to express his emotions. His Texan upbringing had taught him to ignore them, and only when they overcame him completely did they make themselves apparent and then in a fiery tempest that unsettled everyone around him. Otherwise he presented to the world a calm forbearance so that when one of his emotional outbursts occurred, people were frightened and amazed, having never guessed he was capable of such anger or hostility or whatever one wanted to call it. He considered himself a rational, controlled man, but his wives thought otherwise. Miranda alone sensed the despair that lurked beneath a mask of equanimity. She mockingly called him "well bred" when in fact, she saw him as a frightened child at times. She'd told him so, and he had not forgiven her that insult to his manhood. Reeling from the confusion of the last few days and recognizing his need for Miranda to ground him on this project, he had to acknowledge her insight. He needed life to be straight forward and without doubt. Although he did not believe in a god, he did believe in justice and rationality. If people tried hard enough, they should be able to make their lives meaningful and joyous. He believed in hard work, and if you didn't get it right the first time, you just kept trying until you did. It had never occurred to him that people couldn't get it all right, if they tried hard enough. Well, he wasn't about to give up, no matter how much of a failure he seemed at the moment.

Miranda said he was his own worst critic, and he supposed that was right, too. At the moment he felt he wasn't doing things correctly, that somehow he had lost his way in the process of truth gathering. He wasn't sure whether this was a failure of effort or imagination or whether he lacked the mental acumen required to understand the complex personalities he was confronted with. And, after all, what was truth but someone's perception? The trick here was to meld the various perceptions of the man into an integral perspective that was believable and still reflected all the facts available. Unfortunately, he Jack Pierce, knew too much about the man already. It was impossible for Jack to resolve the conflicting perceptions of the man, his vast contradictions. Oh, sure, one could nonchalantly allude to the complexity of a human being as if that were an asset, but to delve into the whirling dervishes of Theodore Hudson could be emotionally shattering. Jack hadn't expected to have to make sense of the man's personality. He'd thought his charge was simple: to record the monumental achievements of a great man. And he'd naively believed that a man of Hudson's remarkable accomplishments was an open record, as clear and definitive as a newspaper article. Instead he was dealing with a poem, a conglomeration of dissonant imagery and metaphor. He didn't know what to believe. Perhaps he should have stayed in Leadville longer before embarking on this project. He should have finished his grieving before plunging into ambiguity of this nature. It reminded him of his first college philosophy course, when he had to learn to think a new way and thus to open himself up to skepticism and nihilism. For surely on some level, that was what was happening to him again. He was doubting Hudson, and he was doubting himself. His head throbbed so badly he thought he would have a stroke. He looked over at Miranda's profile as she watched the cars speeding by. He noted the smoothness of her moonlit face, the eerie gleam of her pale eyes, the pursed, reflective lips that seemed to be chewing on unsavory truths as well; and he knew on some level he needed her to help him remain whole or to become whole. Sadly, he wasn't sure which. The whole experience was unnerving.

"You're awfully quiet," she said gently. He thought she sounded subdued as well.

"I don't know what to think," he admitted. "I probably shouldn't have brought you together with Joline till I had explained more about her and what she's shown me. To be frank, I was pretty bummed out by what she said tonight."

"Why?" Miranda shook her head in bewilderment. "I guess I expected surprises of that nature. The man is clearly selfless." She stared ahead at the traffic signal then turned to him, her complexion sallow in the amber light. "I'm ready for many other surprises related to the man. I really am." Jack could swear Miranda was turning weird on him again. He decided to keep quiet for a while.

"Well, come on," she said after several moments of silence. "*Talk to me*!" She had always hated it when he retreated into his own mind. She liked to share thoughts, not hold them hostage to herself, as she charged he too often did. "What did you think? What did you notice?"

Jack thought for a moment. The slick roads and the bright headlights were adding to his sense of bewilderment. He wanted to be alone, holed up in his cheap motel room with his thoughts and a bottle of Jim Beam. He wanted to tune it all out, all the hurly burley, and be done with it for tonight. He didn't want her questions, he didn't ask for her take on things, he just wanted to leave the impressions of today in a quiet place in the back of his head and watch some brainless cable news channel till he drifted off to sleep. Tomorrow in the clear light of day after due thought on his part, there would be time to ruminate on the character of the man, without interference and without fatigue.

"Don't do this, Jack," she pleaded. "Talk to me."

"Can't you just leave me alone?" he snapped. "Is it possible that just this once you could refrain from imposing your own extraordinary insight on me? I don't really care what you think." When her eyes teared up, and she turned away from him, he threw in, "Flap-mouth!"

He was immediately sorry, but he told himself she'd crowded him again. She had all the answers, she knew everything. "*Well, take that, Miranda*," he thought, "*You don't know everything, even if you think you do!*"

She must have been exhausted, too for her shoulders heaved with her sobs, so violently the front seat quivered with her exertions. "Why are you so cruel?" she finally flung back at him. "What did I do to deserve this?"

"You're a woman," he almost said, "and a damned poor excuse for that!" But he remained silent. Searing muscle spasms shot through his legs. His head felt like it was in a vice.

He saw her wordless plea for an apology move listlessly over the marble face. Her mascara had run down her eyes and formed black lines on her cheeks. Her nose was red, her skin paler than usual, her girlish features rebuking him with the sense that he had abused a child here. She reminded him of an animal kicked by its own master. He saw fear in her eyes and distress so acute it made him choke with regret and longing for the part of him that used to be naturally kind, that soothed Karen's final days and hours and buried her with a pure sorrow. Who was this other that lashed out at the one true friend his life still held? He swallowed his sense of self-loathing and peered ahead at the bright headlights. He said nothing while Miranda sobbed over the traffic sounds, over the hammering of his own heart, over all his petty grievances that he would never understand any more than he would the enigmatic Professor Hudson.

They drove on in silence. He stopped the car in the motel parking lot and walked around to her side and opened the door. The latch felt cold and heavy in his hand as he stole a glance at Miranda. Her smeared face jutted out from her graceful neck in the peculiar angle he knew so well, as if painfully enduring the slings and arrows of her outrageous fortune. He'd seen that expression before, knew it as well as his own fierce temper. It suggested victim and abuse and made him feel all the more angry, as if to quell his own hurt, he had to dig deeper, spite her more profoundly. He refused to speak.

He recalled the first time he'd felt this way with Miranda. She'd been elected homecoming queen at their high school. He'd seethed with rage at her telling of it. They'd fought so hard it seemed they'd never be able to resurrect anything close to the intimacy they'd shared to date. Always, later, she'd say he ruined the dance for her, that their one last chance to be happy together at that miserable school had been dashed by his own meanness. He hadn't seen it that way. He'd merely reacted to her arrogance and the prim way she'd announced the news, her self-importance diminishing him with every eager word. Months after that, he'd married his prom date just to spite her.

Nevertheless, he considered himself kind. He was a good listener. To his mind he'd never been cruel, but he knew his wives thought differently. He'd seen that look before, the caged-animal fear, the disappointment, the frustration compounded by his protracted silence. In Miranda's case, the shoulders would be squared, the jaw jutting in feigned defiance. She refused to be a victim, and he admired her for that. Felicia and the others withdrew into their shells, turtles bearing the historical burden of man's incivility to women. They were martyrs, as if the world expected their stoic endurance as second class citizens. He supposed he did have a mean streak, after all, or was it merely a short fuse, an inability to tolerate frustration himself? Miranda claimed his problems stemmed from self-hatred, but he had long ago dismissed that observation. Although he often considered himself a failure in the eyes of the world, he still saw himself as a generous and tolerant guy. He prided himself that his ex-wives, except for Felicia, were still on civil terms with him. Miranda, in her sarcasm, called those relationships "wary armistices," noting that the women's obsequiousness did not suggest affection, just a weary compliance for the sake of harmony.

He took Miranda's hand to help her down from the seat, but she tore it away from him and jumped down herself. She refused to look at him but followed him onto the sidewalk of the motel, her eyes on the sign.

"Good night," she said without looking at him.

"You aren't coming in?" he asked.

"No."

"We should talk. There's a lot to discuss."

"Tomorrow," she said.

"So what are you going to do?" He'd cleaned the room, expecting her to take one of the beds. That way they'd save money. He wasn't sure he could afford to stay more than a week if he had to foot the bill alone.

"I'll get my own room. That way I don't have to put up with your cruelty." She caught his eye and glanced quickly away. "I just don't understand why you have to do this." Her lip quivered in the defiant pose of her face, and he knew he should go to her and hold her, reassure her that he wasn't unkind. He could do that, and she would forgive him, as she had so often before, but he didn't want to. For the moment he had to reclaim some part of himself that might disappear under the capable tutelage of Miranda. With a start, he realized the extent to which his own fragile ego smote his chances for happiness.

Still, he could not go to her, and so he turned away, bereft. "Well, good night then," he said in a monotone, the familiar detachment settling into his manner.

"Good night," she replied, heading toward the neon-lit motel office with its huge "Vacancy" sign. Two Indian men stood outside the office, smoking cigarettes and looking upward into the blackness of the cloud cover. There was no moon tonight, no splattering of stars, just a sulpheric glow of dirty streetlights and the sheen of rain-soaked roads and sidewalks.

Jack thought of Ann Hudson and her comfortable home on Whitney Avenue, the sense of peace he felt there, as if somehow she'd accomplished the impossible. How did one in her circumstances accept the cruel twists of fate? How did she find the will to move on, to overcome the sense of multiple betrayals — she who'd merely tried to do right by her husband and her son? And then the question begged: Did she even know about her husband's dubious character? Did she wait up at night for him, silently resigned to martyrdom? He hoped not; he had a seething contempt for women who endured unfairness, going back to his mother's stoicism in the light of his father's philandering.

He supposed he'd sensed an indomitable strain in Miranda and knowing she would never accept his cheating had clung to her for protection from himself as much as for her sense of absolutes. There was no compromising where Miranda was concerned; right was right and wrong was wrong. It was the Texan Way, borne of the dry, desiccated West Texas Mesquite, the expansive blue skies, the terrible humidity that only hearty, willful people could long endure. The ragged land bred a certitude he doubted you'd find anywhere else. A sense of who you are and what you've known that no one could take from you, a knowledge that you could persevere, just push on through disappointment, illness, crushing emotional experiences because the land and nature's unpredictability had taught you that. You knew that, even if you didn't farm the land, like his dad did, or watch the effects of drought and fire and flood on your spouse, as his mother had. You simply knew its truths just by living amidst those who fought the land and subdued it for petty gain all their wretched lives.

He'd like to talk to his dad now, explain that he'd just had to get away from the land's angry demands, that his own dreams had overshadowed the dust of the farm and finally turned to dust themselves, but he knew that even if his father were alive, they'd never have this conversation. His father didn't know how to talk. Words eluded him. He'd never read books or dreamed of anything beyond simple endurance and physical pleasure. A plain, simple man who'd died of a heart attack in his early fifties, he'd been relentless in his insistence that Jack measure up to his own scrupulous standards of what it was to be a man. Jack's bookish nature, his sweet and affable ways, while charming to his mother, infuriated the distant man who sired him. *Flesh of his flesh...* Jack had rejected his father's "*great expectations*," as his mother had labeled them, his mother who did read books and could have gone to college had she not settled for the predictable life and married at sixteen the boy she'd grown up with. It was all water under the bridge now, he thought, wondering if either of his parents had brooded over the past as he did. He wondered if just once, they had doubted themselves. It had never seemed so when they were alive as day by day they met their own fates, his dad with a Texan swagger and his mother with pursed lips and a feigned optimism. It was the *Way*, he reflected, as bred in the bones as hunger or fear.

It hadn't taken him that far, though. But that must be because he did something wrong, didn't quite calculate the equation right, so to speak. He needed to figure that out, get it straight once and for all. He had to think about it, focus on it. Now while there was time.

He turned the key into the motel room and stepped inside. He had left a lamp on, and for once the dingy place didn't affront him with its shabbiness, its lack of amenities, the cold, dank feel of it. He threw himself down on the bed and stared at the ceiling. Again, he thought of Ann Hudson and her peculiar predilection for not knowing a lot about her own husband. At first, this seemed understandable in the light that she had the constant demands of a severely handicapped child to care for, but that explanation no longer seemed sufficient when Jack thought of the neglect Yvonne's presence in Hudson's life would mean for Ann and for David. It still struck Jack as unusual that she knew virtually nothing of his parents and had not pursued that information from countless possible sources: Theodore Hudson himself, the Internet, genealogical societies, whatever. That Ann Hudson, an intelligent woman, should know so little about her husband now struck Jack as extremely important and possibly suspect. It suggested either utter denial on her part or compliance in what to Jack seemed almost diabolical. He shuddered at the thought that she might be aware of the derelict house in the country, the lascivious Yvonne or the wayward Joline. That Theodore Hudson was a profligate Jack now had no doubt, but for Jack to accept that Ann Hudson collaborated in his unraveling or even accepted it as part of her lot was anathema. He visualized her face, smooth and open as a girl's, her graceful demeanor, the beautiful eyes, so quick to discern other things, such as character or need, and he couldn't believe that the woman who summoned his admiration had any responsibility for the terrible fall of Theodore Hudson...

Chapter Eighteen

Jack poured himself a drink and sat down on the bed. The taste of whiskey in the quiet calmed him. Outside a wind blew debris across the rutted parking lot. He watched a large woman and her husband enter the lot from the sidewalk, noted the cars jumbled along the road, exhaust streaming, horns blasting, the sounds of screeching tires, an emergency vehicle screaming into the roar. He thought about his home in the mountains and wished he were there with the pine whispering around him and the clear, blue, silent sky stretching over the white landscape. With a start, he realized he had changed back into a country boy. This surprised him since for years he'd longed for the insane busyness of New York City. Never bored there, always driving himself to write more, observe more, meet more people, he'd been sucked into the maelstrom as certainly as those on Wall Street whom he'd scorned for their driven ways. He'd left the place only because he'd had to. A failed author after years of not being able to publish his novels or short stories, he'd retreated from a New York City sense of failure to the relative obscurity of a no-name town in the mountains, so far away from his various homes that he had only to be there to avoid the expectations of himself and others. He'd enjoyed his anonymity; Leadville had many like himself — men who'd fled their dreams, their ex-wives, lovers, children, dreary occupations, the law. It was a place where people didn't ask questions, and Jack liked it that way.

It had been a while before Karen asked questions, too, although he sensed she was curious about his past. Straight up front he told her he'd been married four times and didn't want to go there again. He wasn't the marrying kind, he'd declared, not explaining why. Her large, round eyes seemed to see into the shamed child within, and she simply gave him full rein, never making demands, knowing you couldn't with a man like him, he supposed now, feeling sorry for that. Had he betrayed her in that respect, he wondered. He guessed he had.

He switched on the television and watched the news, his mind refusing to deal with Miranda and the hurt he had so intentionally inflicted. She was a big girl; she could take it. His memory searched the past in the dusty West Texas town where life in comparison to now seemed so simple, so predictable. All you had to do then was live by an obvious code. The values were instilled in you from birth, and you lived up to the expectations that went along with them, and you grew into a man who provided for his family and contributed to the community. It was what you were born and bred to do. And then the world turned on a dime, the old values were questioned and replaced till you didn't know what you thought anymore. You didn't know who you were, so you stumbled on, trying to create the new you, who just never quite found a home again but no longer fit into the snug world of certainty either. A line had been crossed and you couldn't go back, so you muddled through an increasingly murky existence, stumbling and falling all the way till you woke up one day and didn't know who you were and what you wanted, life had become so chaotic and purposeless.

The whiskey had done its job, and he felt good. A sense of well being pushed itself up through the brooding memories, reminding him that however lost he seemed, there was something inside him that still clung to hope and meaning. Somewhere there remained that idealistic Jack Pierce who'd intended to change his world with the stroke of a pen and make everything right, as if writing were magical rather than an act of faith, as he saw it now in his subdued homage to other truths he'd come to own in his long search. It was obvious to him in the moments when the whiskey loosened the subterranean speculation that what he lacked was faith in himself, and he didn't know how to get it back. He smiled to recall the cocky Jack Pierce of his youth — so raw and sure of himself. He wrote a good book then without much effort. He hadn't stopped to question himself, just writing it as surely and swiftly as one would drive his car to work. Easy. The book had poured out of his inner being. He'd had something to say, and his mind urged him on to the telling of it: through the lonely nights into the gray mornings, the endless weekends, the long winters and humid, diesel laden summers till it finished itself with a finality that was pleasing and as certain as his life had been till then.

He thought of Miranda and the disappointment on her face this evening. She'd believed in him enough to seek him out and urge upon him the biography of Theodore Hudson, a man she didn't know but also believed in. He had to admit Miranda had faith in the world — that it yielded its own brand of justice. And it was fair, she would argue. Karma. Theodore Hudson was a great man and as such deserved to have his due. Like Jack, Miranda believed those who served the world honorably would be rewarded. Hudson's story had to be told because Truth mattered to her. Well, they both felt that way, but perhaps they differed on what the truth of Hudson actually was.

Miranda had never been one to judge while Jack had always been quick to form opinions, take offense, see the dark motives behind a gesture. Why was that, he wondered. What made him so slow to trust, always in a state of perpetual wariness, anticipating the next shoe to drop? The next broken relationship? The next artless slap in the face? He didn't know the answer, but he did know he wanted to live differently. He wanted to feel free from fear, as he had when he was young and cocksure. He wanted to feel that what he did was fine, that *HE* was fine. That all his shortcomings and mistakes had amounted to the same errors of judgment others made and nothing more than that. He had only to find that old Self and let him go, like a good race horse feels its way naturally on the track, simply aware of its destiny on some gut level that words can't mince or analysis can't staunch. Where was that still, small voice that cheered one on to new heights and new achievements? With a start, he realized that this voice, or whatever you wanted to call it, had been the making of the man, Theodore Hudson. The man's massive achievements had to have had their roots in a relentless quest for truth. Jack also realized that Hudson, for whatever reason, had eventually chosen to ignore that still, small voice, and this had been his undoing. Greatness was a function of the *voice,* Jack was sure, in his mild intoxication.

The booze had done its job, and now Jack felt pleasantly high. He thought about Miranda somewhere in the dark, rambling confines of the seedy motel, and it made him a little nervous that she was alone and unprotected, but he dismissed his concern and poured another drink. In the background the television murmured on and the shadows filled the room with a gloomy blanket while he thought some more about the past and his disappointments. Ah, the sweet nuances of his self-inflicted suffering, he thought, for suddenly he saw his whole life as one of disintegration. It seemed to him at the moment that once he had been free and good and then he'd lost his way somehow. It was as if his mother had let go of his hand in a vast and impersonal shopping center, and he'd proceeded to buy the wrong things and wandered down aisles of junk food and mechanical toys and tried things that weren't worth the price, then returned them and selected again, only to make the wrong choices again. Again and again... It was the recognition of all the wrong choices, without even identifying them one by one, that smote him in the worst way. He wanted to call himself back from every last one of them, but there was no going back, only his present erring Self that cried out to be righted somehow. Was this Man's lot, he wondered: always wanting to be set right and not knowing how to do it? He presumed it was, and the awareness made him feel sadder than he could ever imagine.

He thought of Karen and the tears slid from his eyes and watered his face. They were so heavy they fell onto his shirt and dripped into the glass of whiskey, and he drank them, hoping for a sweet baptism, as if that were possible. He knew how Theodore Hudson felt when he entered that dreary house in the country and squandered the last of his will on the nefarious Yvonne. It wasn't love that propelled him into her sphere but a basic wantonness that was man's lot. The great and glorious Theodore Hudson, whose mind could outthink the greatest ones of his century, could not subdue the dark, driven daimon of his own nature till it unraveled all the good he'd accomplished and left in shreds the lives of those who mattered most. Jack looked deep into the glass of his own tears and need and saw the squandered lives of all men, and he felt such a heaviness in his chest he thought it would burst with a feeling he didn't think he'd experienced before — an emotional outpouring so unlike him that he felt as if he were watching a movie of someone else's life. There was a man who'd made terrible mistakes, and he was truly sorry for them and all the pain his poor choices had cost those others, but he didn't know what to do. The vast triviality he'd created when his being was capable of such magnificent potential both astounded and perplexed him. A light appeared from the parking lot. Brief and bright, it illuminated the shabby room then went out. Jack put down his glass and drew his arms around his knees and pulled up his legs on the lumpy chair and cried as if his heart would break with sheer compassion for the man, Theodore Hudson. He would not have thought it possible to feel so sorry for another person as he did now, and so he wept and wept as he'd never done before, in his whole damned, miserable life.

He must have fallen asleep in the chair because when he awoke, he was still wrapped in his own arms in the moldering upholstery, his head bent between his legs. Outside a bird sang its sweet song to an indifferent world, but Jack heard it as distinctly and true as he felt the urge to urinate or to move his aching limbs. He got up and went into the bathroom. From the mirror he saw his stubbled beard, the pale blue eyes awash in sagging skin and gray hair — colorless, bland, external features concealing the deeper essence, its unfathomability. Yet this morning Jack felt a sense of optimism, as if for once he'd plumbed it somehow, if only peripherally. He felt now he'd had a glimpse into the human heart, and it filled him with a sense of purpose and hope he would not have thought possible. It was as if he'd had a reprieve from sorrow, as if he'd experienced a temporary absolution of sorts. He felt like a recovered alcoholic who has submitted to the huge underpinnings of the universe in a last ditch effort to get out from under the dictates of his cold, hard, needy self. It was a good feeling, an overwhelmingly satisfying sense of for once being at one with the world rather than at odds with it. If Jack had been a religious person, he would have gotten down on his knees as his brethren did in the old West Texan church of his youth. Instead he composed a silent prayer to whatever it was out there that knew his feelings. For once he felt there was some true and abiding connective force that did wait for man to decide his fate. What that force was Jack didn't know, but he felt it as surely as he breathed the air or moved or talked. It was *THERE*.

He shaved and showered. As he dressed he listened intently to the bird outside, trying to take in completely the nuances of pitch and rhythm, as if to discern some universal language that must be there for the grasping, if only man were receptive to it. Jack parted the curtains and looked for the bird, but he couldn't see it. Somewhere it sang to all living creatures, as if to sing were its only function. It was a natural thing for it to do, something it didn't contemplate or question, it didn't analyze or craft, it simply sang as if not to were to be dead. It sang to live, and it lived to sing. For man it should be the same, if he were true to himself and his purpose. It seemed to Jack in his moment of understanding that speech or *logos* or whatever man wanted to call it, was a sacred thing, divinely inspired and as such part of that essence that pervaded everything. Jack had only to submit to it, as he had to his own sense of feeling last night, to be its instrument, and so he would, he decided.

He opened his laptop and let the writing carry him on into his own insight. He typed for a long time, it seemed, not even knowing what he was writing. It was enough that the words unleashed themselves from cement and appeared on the screen. They welled and coursed as a mighty river, and he felt his body move with them — over the falls and down the chasms till they tumbled onto the rocky shore, in an orgasm of sentences and paragraphs, true to something resplendent in him. He found himself smiling in gratitude as he hummed the words onward into the mysteries of his own mind. He'd written for a long time, it seemed, or at least the sense of his fingers was so, that when he heard the gentle knock at his door, he felt he was ready to stop for a while and gather steam before he proceeded. He exited the program and walked to the door.

Miranda had a paper cup of coffee extended to him. Standing there in the morning light with her frazzled hair and exotic features, she seemed the embodiment of his nocturnal epiphany. At least she would understand, he thought, still reluctant to share the evening's experience with anyone, but if he did it would be with her, he knew.

"Sleep well?" she asked, a hint of irony in the mere sweep of her eyes. She peered into the room's dim light. "Been writing, I see."

He felt diminished again, resentful of her easy perception into his world, her seeming insight into his habits and personality, but he reminded himself that he had nothing to hide so why should it matter if anyone saw through him? What difference did it make in the scheme of things? What was there to hide, after all? What was the use? It struck him that all his life he had submerged parts of himself, as if underneath the clothing there lurked a monster people would reject if they saw it for what it was. The secretiveness he had indulged in all these years now struck him as absurd, and he briefly wondered why he had found it necessary. Smiling into Miranda's open face, he was reminded of his mother and the thought occurred to him that he'd been afraid of her. This was a truth he had never acknowledged till now, and it made him feel sad. He had always admired his mother, but now with an insight borne of the evening's funk, he realized he'd never really known the woman, perhaps had known her about as much as he knew any of the women he'd been intimate with, with the possible exception of Karen, who had in her way, dismantled the barriers to intimacy — she possessed of the truth of suffering and the cruel indignities of dying. And here was Miranda, he thought, the strange object of his past longings, a soulmate of sorts, he realized, respecting the irony of that as he did of her preference for the insipid Don Parrish.

In the instant what he noticed most about the woman was not her radiantly open face, the eyes perusing him without judgment, the diminutive, suppliant demeanor meant to please and not threaten. What he couldn't ignore was the strength she nonetheless exuded. She was a person comfortable in her own skin and all the vicissitudes of life could not unravel that basic sense of self. Still uncertain of where his new found insight would lead him, he envied her her hard won independence.

"Go ahead," she said. "Take it." She thrust the coffee into his hands and turned to the parking lot. "Did you hear that bird? Lovely, wasn't it?" It struck him as odd that she would know he, too, had heard the bird's longing refrain. *How did she know these things*, he wondered. What had seemed so threatening in her suddenly lessened as he gratefully accepted a shared affinity for nature, perhaps for all living beings, although he wasn't yet sure about that. He just knew he was glad to see her.

"Come in," he said, taking the coffee. "I missed you last night."

She looked at him curiously. Her eyes in the bright sunlight were lavendar, her pale skin as white as the painted brick of the building. She looked at him sideways, cocking her head, smiling. It was the old Miranda of decades ago, the mischievous smile on her face and the sardonic sense of humor he'd loved then. Without thinking he bent over and kissed her on the lips, a friendly, open, non-sexual kiss that lingered for the moment in the sun with the bird's sweet pleading till she gently pushed him away. "Did you have a change of heart?" she asked with the same faint sense of sarcasm he'd resisted and resented all these years.

"I did," he said, truly repentent. "I'm so sorry about last night. I want to say I didn't know what came over me, but I have an inkling," he admitted.

"Something about fear?" she said knowingly.

"Maybe," he said, again impressed with her insight. "I wish I could say offhand what I was afraid of, though."

"It's always the truth," she said.

"I think I know the truth. It's just I don't want it to be that way."

"Maybe you don't know it all; maybe you know only the half of it, if that. Maybe the rest of it is just sitting there waiting for you to discover it." She stepped past him into the dim room and glanced around her. She plopped down into the same lumpy chair he'd sat on last night and sighed heavily.

"That was one strange conversation with your friend Joline," she said.

Jack sat down on the bed and sipped from his coffee before he replied. It had bothered him that Miranda had accepted all that Joline said. He hadn't believed much of her account. Or at least he had felt she didn't have all the information and that her untamed upbringing, the constant exposure to the dregs of the world, had negated her ability to discern the enormity of the situation with Theodore Hudson. In Jack's mind, her acceptance of the man's depravity was to be expected, but he had been bothered by Miranda's blithe acceptance of Joline's perspective. He had always counted on Miranda's moral authenticity to equip her to separate perception from reality, and this time he felt she had let him down. This time her laser eyes and wisdom about people had failed him and her. He realized that he'd resented her for that. He'd trusted her to see more, know more.

"Joline is a product of her past," Miranda said, "but she sees in the man that which you yourself should."

"How so?" Jack asked, irritated.

"The moral dilemmas here are pretty defined, aren't they?"

"What do you mean?"

"There were things he probably couldn't tell his wife."

"Such as his terrible needs, you mean?" Jack said, testily.

"You sound as if you have a stake in the man's character," Miranda pointed out, "When really you are writing about his achievements, which are not debatable."

Jack thought about that. What she said was true, but could you separate the man's work from the man himself? Could a morally bankrupt man produce noble achievements? When did the moral imperatives begin and end? One could say, perhaps without dispute, that Theodore Hudson was driven to produce, and what he chose to accomplish were noble acts and noble achievements. Jack guessed you had to give the man that: his motives for the betterment of mankind were laudable. That fact no one could deny, could they? The waters had muddied again, and Jack felt confused. Again, he was surprised at Miranda's defense of the man. He told himself she didn't know Hudson like Jack did and so she spoke out of faith. From out of nowhere he heard in his mind's eye Joline's voice cautioning him: *Things aren't always what they seem.* So what? Jack told himself. So the world wasn't simple and predictable and tidy, subject to time-honored rules, so what did that say? That everything was relative, and that's why he and others should overlook moral depravity? He doubted any reasonable or moral person would look at the world that way, so why should he?

He decided to tell her what he knew.

"Theodore Hudson was not the kind of man you think he was. He was a profligate, a lousy father, a lousy husband, a raconteur, if you will. Why, he led young men and women into corruption," Jack said, so fiercely angry he hardly knew what to do with himself. He who had no children, who didn't even particularly like children, was offended by Theodore Hudson's exposing them to decadence and God knew what. Jack thought of the sleazy bedroom upstairs in the country house, of the sleek and sensuous Yvonne, her knowing eyes that had seen everything, and he felt like vomiting all that awareness away. He didn't want to know it, didn't want Miranda to have to deal with it.

"Jack, you seem upset." Miranda eyed him with concern.

"You're damned right, I am," Jack said. "It makes no difference to me if a man decides to abuse drugs or succumb to a sexual addiction or become an alcoholic, but to encourage the same in vulnerable young people, well that is a sin if there ever was one. I cannot forgive a man who would do that."

Miranda continued to eye Jack. Under the staid resolution of her glance, he sensed bewilderment.

"I'm right about this," he said. "I must be right."

"I'm sure you are," Miranda said, reaching over to pat him on the leg. "It's just that I've never known you to get so wrought up over anything to do with kids."

"I know. Quite unlike me, isn't it?" He wondered what this meant himself.

"Going back to your mother," Miranda said.

"Why? Because everything goes back to the mother?" Jack said contemptuously. "Mothers are always the brunt of all criticism, aren't they? Easy to pin a whole slew of sins on them!"

"That isn't what I meant, Jack." Miranda's eyes swept around the neglected room, falling on the dingy prints of flower bouquets over the beds. She stopped and peered at the faded greenery, the pale yellow flowers, the blotched matting and sighed as if the scene of lifeless flowers filled her with a sorrow she couldn't express. Outside the traffic hummed its dull roar and the sound of the air conditioning sputtered to an abrupt stop. "I simply meant there's more to this subject than you realize. It's not like you to get so wrought up over a man's actions."

"Hell, I guess."

"So something else must be bothering you, something you can't quite put your fingers on."

"Oh, give me a break! Miranda, the psychiatrist!" He could hear the contempt in his voice and remembered the scene of yesterday and the pain he'd caused her. He didn't want to hurt her again, but her condescension antagonized him and he didn't know why. He had the urge to lash out, but this time he resisted it. To his surprise she smiled, a slow, calculated gesture of affirmation. They were in this together, her smile said. Nothing he said or did would affect that. They were a team.

The conspiratorial, bemused expression gave way to her standing. Then she walked over to his chair and reached down and hugged him. "Oh, Jack, you're just too good, you know it? The world isn't simple, for sure, but you make too much of the moral ambiguities. That's what I mean about your mother, don't you see? Maybe she was so judgmental that you can't allow yourself any leeway in the moral questions we all face. Maybe her nature made life hard for you to navigate, harder than you deserved."

"That's ridiculous," Jack said without thinking. "That's what mothers are for — to teach kids right from wrong."

"I agree," Miranda said. "But sometimes they go too far, wouldn't you say?"

Jack thought of Karen and her tolerance of all people, her natural acceptance of people as they were. It would never have occurred to her to be judgmental. So it was with Miranda as well.

"That's why you are so hard on yourself," Miranda said quietly.

He thought about that and decided she was right. "But that doesn't excuse the man," Jack said. "What he did was wrong. Absolutely and irretrievably so. There are moral absolutes, aren't there?"

"Maybe he had a judgmental mother. Or father. Maybe he felt there was no one there for him. Maybe he was always alone. You know, the judged always feel alone. And those who judge set themselves apart." Her beautiful eyes smote him with the clarity of her moral vision. At the moment, as in so many past ones, he loved her to the core of her being. He loved the way she thought, the way ideas moved in her like a turbulent stream that resolved itself as it swept downward.

Once more he thought about what she said, what he knew of Theodore Hudson, and he believed her. He recalled the conversations with David and Ann Hudson, and it all seemed clear for the moment. Perhaps Hudson's parents hadn't known how to handle a genius. They hadn't bargained for that. Jack thought of his own mother and realized her silent presence had been emphatically detached for all her seeming righteousness. The dutiful wife and mother, she'd been there but not there, always preoccupied with the rituals of domestic protocol. The woman had done what was expected of her, all right, but she'd performed her role with a pronounced lack of flexibility and warmth. It wasn't that she was cold, but that she was remote, distant, as cool and dependably so as a machine. She was rational and responsible but without heart in the sense that Jack desired that in someone close to him, as he was fortunate enough to experience in the generosity of spirit of both Miranda and Karen. Few men were so lucky, he thought, grateful that such a boon should happen to him in his later years, unsure he would have appreciated it so much when he was young and clueless.

And so it made sense to Jack that Theodore Hudson had happened into a family that couldn't cope with his extraordinary acumen and curiosity, his evolved sense of responsibility to his fellow man. Chastened by his moral certitude, his monumental goals, they fled and left it to him to carry out his lofty plans. Frightened and full of his own unresolved conflicts, the man had still pursued his dreams to the neglect of his physical self, which demanded its own fulfillment nevertheless. Theodore had married the beautiful, intelligent Ann but then found himself unable to deal with his own son's limitations and those his condition placed on the family and marriage. Like his own step parents, Theodore Hudson suffered from an inability to cope with circumstances beyond his control. Like Jack, his mother, so many out there, Theodore Hudson, too, had difficulty being flexible in his approach to the human needs of those close to him. It was something he had never experienced; he had no role models. Dutiful and correct, like Jack's own mother, Hudson performed the roles assigned him but without the imagination that fired his accomplishments outside the family. He was first and foremost a scientist. His loyalty was to the earth, to the body of intellectual thought, to furthering man in his quest for an ideal world. And as such, the man had exceeded his own expectations, most likely, but if he was the man Jack thought he was beginning to know, he also had a yearning for personal love and enlightenment. He needed the kind of love he himself couldn't offer so he lived a lie to gain a substitute for his longings.

Jack thought of Sonia, Dostoyevsky's downtrodden heroine of *Crime and Punishment*, Jack's favorite, and he realized that Yvonne was Hudson's own symbol of suffering. Recognizing that, Jack could see where his connection with her was not simply decadent but borne of a mystifying altruism. He doubted he would ever understand the workings of Hudson's mind on that issue, but he felt the relationship indeed was not what it seemed, even if it had contributed to the man's disintegration. It pleased Jack that his understanding of the man allowed for his own reservation of judgment, for the time being anyway. Otherwise he wasn't sure he could carry on with the project, so vile did the man's actions strike him without some sort of psychological explanation. He had to hand it to the women in his life that he would go so far as to consider any psychological justification of a man's immoral behavior. Jack also thought it interesting that it didn't seem that Hudson depended upon Yvonne for adulation or acceptance, the typical expectations of emotionally weak men. No, Jack was growing certain that on the contrary, Yvonne was the beneficiary of his largesse and that his needs were not merely of the ego, as would seem the obvious explanation. The understanding freed Jack at last from judgment and enticed him onward in his quest for Theodore Hudson, the man.

Chapter Nineteen

"Tell me everything you know," Miranda said, sipping her coffee. The day had brightened and the light entering the room glittered with dust particles, coating Miranda's features in a gauzy haze. They could hear the rattle of the maid's carts along the rutted sidewalk and the opening and closing of doors nearby. Jack swallowed the last of his coffee and began to describe his various meetings with Ann Hudson, her son, the experiences with Joline. He finished by describing Yvonne and the wretched hovel in the country.

"I know," Miranda said in a voice so quiet Jack could hardly hear her.

"You know *what?*" he asked.

"The squalor he died in, the bleakness of the terrible place."

"Why didn't you tell me about that? Then you know about the woman?"

"The beautiful black lover?" she asked. "Of course, I knew..."

"*But how?* How could you know that? Have you been here before? Did you know Theodore Hudson prior to your weird dream experience? You said—"

"I know," Miranda said tiredly. "I told you the truth. I never met the man, never knew him."

"Then how could you possibly know about Yvonne? The squalor? *How he died*?"

"I just saw it all. He reached out to me from someplace we'll probably never understand, and I responded."

"But how did you *know* it?" he persisted. He felt the object of an elaborate hoax. It was like the old times when she tricked him into complacence or threw up barriers to his understanding. He was not in the mood for her esoteric conclusions. He wanted facts.

"He asked me to *remember* him, and I just saw it all..."

"Well, that makes a lot of sense!"

"Some things don't make sense," Miranda said. "Not in the way *you* expect, anyway."

"Oh, please," Jack said. "Just get on with it. What else do you know?"

Miranda seemed to make a pretense of thinking, cocking her head and shifting her eyes as if seeing beyond the room into the pit of Hudson's consciousness. As he watched, her eyes ceased their random search and stopped, boring into some scene in her mind's eye. They opened wide and expressionless and fastened on whatever it was, gazing unflinchingly at something beyond the pale. Whatever it was she saw was so utterly *there* that Jack could almost feel its presence himself by the intricate reactions of her throat and chest as they heaved to an arcane rhythm. Jack continued to watch her closely, fascinated by the changing tapestry of her face as it took up the movements of her body. The sound of her breathing filled the air and gave sustenance to the room as Jack hung on, feeling part of the ride on a pale horse of her creation. Then it was as if he were back in the dank, smelly room in the country outside New Haven, inhabiting the spider-webbed walls, the thick, gross drapes laden with the noxious odors of cigarette smoke, meth, marijuana, heroin, crack. He felt he would gag, but he clung to the experience nevertheless. He was learning to admit the unpleasant truths into his conscious awareness, he realized with gratitude. He felt freer than he had in a long time, more open to the mysterious fabric of the cosmos and the silent messages of his own heart. All he could do was wait, he knew in a flash, and he did just that, his eyes fastened on the shifting lexicon of Miranda's expressive body. He didn't know what to think, but something beyond ordinary experience was happening, and it was real, and he had to admit, *true*.

Her body stilled, the glazed eyes regained their focus, Miranda smiled, as if to another aspect of herself. She rolled her eyes and stood up. "Well, how crazy did that seem to you?" she demanded, wrapping her arms around her shoulders and shivering.

"Pretty strange, all right," Jack agreed, confused and reassured at the same time. He didn't understand how Miranda knew what she apprehended and how, but he no longer doubted her. He recalled the images of her life on stage in the little church in West Texas — the charged atmosphere, the lamentations of the old and infirm, the ecstatic, passionate gratitude of the visitors to the humble shrine in the middle of the prairie with its whited sepulchre from pioneer times, straddling the hills over which the pilgrims traveled on their journey to the albino healer, already a legend in her time. She was the stuff of prairie lore, Texas myth, and tabloid journalism. If there were those who debunked her gifts, there were plenty who swore by her, most particularly her parishioners, who never doubted that she was divinely inspired. Few of them questioned her; none opposed her. For some reason she escaped the pettiness so often directed at spiritual leaders, even though she summoned her congregation to controversial causes and steadfastly urged them on to newer and more risky endeavors. Their pied piper, she could have led them through the gates of Hell, Jack had often thought, amused but skeptical. He wondered if she ever questioned herself. He knew that on occasion he had expected the congregation to rebel, but they hadn't, and that, too, mystified Jack. He guessed it was her powerful presence in that ramshackle place that produced such an astounding effect, but in his heart he knew her appeal came from within. Whatever that essence was it defined her charisma. He believed it was nothing less than an unflinching, relentless quest for truth. She felt she knew that which most people sought their entire lives, so she would not be quelled till all of her followers subscribed to her vision as passionately and as selflessly as did she. He thought of Don Parrish and knew why the man loved her. He loved her for the same reason they all did. She was both harridan and redeemer, activist and peacemaker. To Jack she had always been an enigma, but to Parrish and others, she was the embodiment of Christian values. They loved her for the example she unwittingly set. For Jack, she was too complex, and he faulted her for that. He didn't want to spend his life with someone who baffled him. He preferred women he had a chance of understanding. Concrete women. Simple women. Women whose demands were not excessive.

"Anything you saw I should know?" Jack asked, a little reluctant to inquire of her results.

"He didn't mean to die," she said. "It was an accident."

"Drugs?" Jack asked.

"Partly," she said. "There was more to it than that, though." She looked around the room, sweeping in the impoverished aesthetics. "He was broken in many ways, and he knew it."

Before he could ask her more, she stood up and walked to the window. She stood in the morning light with the sun on her face. "I want to hear the bird before I go," she said. "And then you'd best be getting on to Ann Hudson's house, don't you think?" She smiled impishly at Jack. "I bet you really like her."

When Jack said nothing, she laughed and walked outside.

"I hear our bird," she said from the curb. "Time to get to work."

They had more coffee at Claire's and talked about strategy. Miranda thought Jack should visit Ann Hudson alone, but he wanted Miranda to be there. "You need to understand the situation at home," he said. "You should meet David. So much of Theodore Hudson must be related to the tragedy of the kid, don't you think?" Jack watched Miranda for her reaction, for the moment uncertain of his recent theory.

"Probably," Miranda agreed, "But I prefer to visit his office first, meet some of his colleagues. I feel the need to focus on his professional life to begin with." She held up the folder of Jack's research. "Besides, I want to study the file first — get to know him my way." She had out her reading glasses and had begun perusing the thick sheaf of papers. "You should just go on and meet Ann, as per your routine. Then we'll get together later and debrief. You take the car, I'll find my own way to the Immunology lab."

"All right," Jack said, looking out the window at the pedestrians moving along the downtown sidewalk. Today Claire's was full. Several tables had been put together to accommodate a professor and group of students who talked earnestly about various social causes. Among them was the young man who had accompanied Joline the first night Jack met her. Thin and tall, he had a weeping mustache over thin, stern lips. Jack wondered what the girl saw in him. He reminded Jack of a voyeur — one who lurked in the shadows to watch rather than participate. Even now amidst a group of ardent young people, he stood apart, detached and critical, a haughty expression on his angular face.

When Jack looked up again, the man was studying him with a shrewd, knowing look. It made Jack feel uncomfortable, but he didn't think to mention it to Miranda, who was deep in concentration, the spread of papers angling across her side of the table, her forehead furrowed. "You didn't mention his favorite author was Dostoyevsky," she threw out just as he was getting up to leave.

"Yeah, quite a coincidence, isn't it?"

"You mean because he's yours, too?" she asked. "I was thinking it interesting because if that's the case, Hudson was different than what I was thinking."

"You mean the depth? You didn't think he had it?"

"No, I meant he understood people, literature, but that I didn't see him as torn—"

"Torn?" Jack asked.

"Between the two sides of his personality, don't you see? Dostoyevsky might have been bipolar or schizophrenic, even. Remember how obsessed he was with the idea of people having two sides to them: the dark and the light? Remember Myshkin and Rogozhin? Innocence and evil. I'd say Dost was obsessed with the idea of crossing the line between good and evil. I can't think of another writer who explores the dark side of man better than he." Miranda stopped, looked away at the man friend of Jolines, as if she sensed his unwavering stare, then back at Jack. "Don't you agree?"

"I do," he said, watching the young man follow Miranda's every gesture. He seemed to hang on her words. "That's what we always liked about his books. He had terrible Epilepsy, you recall."

"After facing an execution squad," Miranda said. "Yes, I remember. The Emperor was trying to teach him a lesson, all dissidents a lesson."

"Dost was a student then. There was no freedom, no dissent. Just the Emperor's edicts." Jack had first grown to love Dostoyevsky's work when he was a poor student at the no-name university he eventually quit. That had been during the time of the student riots on campus, the universal movement to increase the rights of the disenfranchised. He thought of the Black Panthers, the Weathermen, the Feminists, war protesters, Students for a Democratic Society, the Hare Krishna's, Hemlock Society, Affirmative Action, Kent State, S.I. Hayakawa. The assassinations of John Kennedy, Robert Kennedy, Martin Luther King... All the upheaval of the times washed over Jack in a torrent of conflicted memories. In his mind America was then in the throes of a national nervous breakdown replete with drug abuse, broken families, divorce, runaways, psychotic, lost people everywhere, a so-called "sexual revolution," and he knew even then as a young man that it would take years to heal the soul of America after all that turmoil and the rubble of Viet Nam. He pushed the memories from his head and focused again on Miranda and the task at hand.

"Think Hudson protests against oppression on college campuses, his being a professor?"

"Maybe. He was a conservative, though. He believed in authority, a strong army, restricted government. He wasn't exactly championing change."

"Hmmm..." Miranda stared at her hands, at the silver ring encircling her finger. She pulled and twisted it, watching the finger turn red and raw. "You think he related to all the untreated disease that Dostoyevsky writes about? You know, the Katherine Ivanovna tuberculosis, the hordes of ill people who couldn't seek healing because they were poor?"

Jack thought of the young man Hudson had taken to the Mayo Clinic and wondered if Miranda wasn't on to something. Perhaps Hudson had been ill as a child, Russian orphans often were. The idea of a frail young Hudson seemed plausible, another complicating factor for the parents, who perhaps were old world stock suddenly saddled with new world dilemmas. Dysfunctional families were the subjects of Slavic writers, for sure, but the overwhelming realities of raising a genius in a radically changing culture would have made it hard on the Hudsons, Jack was willing to bet. "There's no research available on the early part of Hudson's life. Maybe we should hire a detective."

"We can do that," Miranda said.

Driving to Ann Hudson's Jack was suddenly seized with self-consciousness. He'd learned so much since he'd last seen her, that he was afraid she'd detect a difference in him. He knew her to be a student of human nature, and it frightened him to think she'd guess he was withholding information. Still, he couldn't tell her what he knew. He just couldn't add to her suffering. It didn't seem fair to Jack that a woman of her quality should have to endure any sorrow, much less the realization that the man she'd loved had betrayed her for decades. It seemed preposterous that Theodore Hudson had gotten away with his petty self-indulgence or that he'd been a beneficiary of even a small part of the love she had to give. Jack felt himself grow angry to realize the sacrifice she'd made of her life when any number of men would have cherished a woman of Ann Hudson's exceptional character. Jack would be willing to bet that single colleagues of Theodore Hudson watched the beautiful Ann Hudson and secretly planned a way to woo her. That was the way of men, Jack mused, certain he would have been one of them himself, had he been in her sphere.

He drove up the familiar street and parked outside her house. He was reminded of his first day in New Haven and his surreptitious stakeout of her home, his view of her walking David down the tree-lined street in the early afternoon, the seeming sense of closeness the two shared as they ambled along the way, oblivious of his scrutiny. It struck him as a major coincidence that she had read his book and even more coincidental that she had decided on him as the authorized biographer of her husband when there must have been so many others who sought the honor.

Jack sighed to think how things had gone since then. He wondered if she had resisted the other offers because she suspected Hudson's colleagues knew of his unsavory involvements, but he dismissed that idea almost instantly. Ann Hudson did not know, he was certain. She was not the kind of woman who could live a lie. She would never submit to a sham marriage. All the more reason Jack could not reveal what he knew. To do so would be a violation of her heart and his own. He didn't know how he was going to keep it from her, but he would.

She met him at the door, her eyes bright and warm as they always were. She had her hair down for the first time since they'd met, and he found her lovely with the curls falling around her shoulders. She had on gold earrings, and they flashed in the light from the sun at her back, trailing through the long hall from the living room window. Today she wore a dark green skirt and black sweater. A single strand of pearls dipped below the scoop neck. To Jack she was as beautiful as he'd seen her to date, flushed and perky as she looked up at him with quiet expectation.

"Well, the man about town," she remarked, leading him into the family room and fetching a glass of tea. Jack sat opposite the Monet prints and thought about Miranda and what she was doing, whether word would get back to Ann Hudson about her interviews of Hudson's colleagues. Jack worried that Miranda might reveal something he didn't want Ann Hudson to hear about. He wished he'd cautioned her more, but then Miranda did her own thing, whatever Jack advised. She didn't like to be managed, and so he had no choice but to let her do things her way.

He sat back in the sofa, smelled its leathery scent, and searched through his notes. There were questions he wanted to ask Ann Hudson, but he wasn't sure he should. He decided to do what he'd done to date: give her a wide berth and listen carefully. She would let him know what he needed, he told himself. It had happened before. Then he would ask follow-up questions and see how that went. It had worked so far; it would work again.

She swept into the room with the tray of tea and cookies and sat down beside him on the sofa. He could smell her perfume, the faint scent of shampoo. She set the tray between them on the sofa and looked around her at the sun slanting across the framed prints. He could hear the birds singing outside and the muted rumble of traffic down Whitney. Sitting in her presence, surrounded by her possessions, he felt oddly out of kilter, a sort of displacement for the moment, as if he were an interloper, but he dismissed the idea. She had invited him; he belonged here for the moment even if her world was a foreign one to the likes of Jack Pierce, who'd never owned art, attended the symphony, or graduated from exclusive schools that catered to the rich and privileged. He'd never known luxury or sought it, even when married to Felicia. Material things hadn't much mattered to him. Having never experienced abundance, he didn't know how to spend money beyond the pleasures it would purchase. Aesthetics had never been a concern when arranging his living space although he was visual, all right. Sitting in the living room of Ann Hudson reminded him of the distance they bridged when they conversed: the gap in their upbringings, their pasts. It made him sad to think that materiality could so distance people. He sensed a kinship between them, but that one difference spoke volumes. She would always have the sense of how one manipulated her environment with luxury items while he would not have noticed the kitsch of people's lives, so incidental did such choices seem to him. As Miranda had noted in the past, "You live so austerely. You can afford better." He was fearful of comfort, the easy life too much materiality represented. He knew he never wanted to be so comfortable in his surroundings that he'd be fearful of losing them or moving on. Materiality imprisoned one as surely as children or financial or emotional obligations. He looked over at Ann Hudson as she poured the tea. He didn't want to think about it.

"You asked about Ted's parents," she began. "It is odd I don't know much about them," she admitted. She held up a photograph and handed it to Jack. "I found this in his study, at the back of a folder that wasn't labeled. It must be of his parents."

"No identification, nothing?" Jack asked, surprised.

"Nothing."

He studied the picture. It was black and white and of a fine material. A woman and man stood, holding the hand of a boy of about ten. The child's face was overly serious, fearful, Jack thought, feeling a sudden pity for the boy. The parents were somewhat short of stature with wide angular facial features and dark, curly hair. There was a definitive Slavic look about them, apparent in their rigid bearing, their sharp, perspicacious stares, the old world apparel.

Jack was reminded of a Latvian family he knew in Sweetwater, their austere home, the rigid rules, the beatings for small infractions. He wondered if Ted Hudson's parents had been as unforgiving as they. The Latvian family had moved just before Jack left home. One of the boys had run away in the process. It was rumored he joined a group of hippies heading for San Francisco. No one blamed the boy. It had been a hard, miserable life for the children of that family. Oddly, Jack's father had praised the Latvian father's discipline, which everyone else saw as harsh, but then Jack's father had been harsh as well. His uncle had often remarked that he didn't know how Jack endured his father's beatings. As for Jack, he couldn't even remember them. It was as if they'd never happened to him, so closed had he become to memories of that sort. Miranda claimed his poor memory was just one more example of his repression. Perhaps it was, but why would he want to remember his own father brutalizing him? Miranda had urged him to remember everything, acknowledge everything, but he'd resisted her then and he did so still. Yet seeing the unflinching set of the little boy's face and the clouded, sorrowful expression in his eyes, Jack knew that the boy had suffered, and with the realization of his abuse, Jack acknowledged his own. He refused to dwell on it, but the understanding fortified him and validated his life somehow. He could give himself credit for a measured growth, even a forgiveness of sorts for those who had so cruelly wronged him. The recognition lightened the load of his own responsibility and lent him strength to assume other obligations, he knew, in a sudden moment of self-discovery. Ah, the legacy of the past, how it weighed one down, reduced one's options till he recognized it and learned from it. So much to learn. A lifetime was not enough, he thought, imagining Theodore Hudson at the moment of death, still muddling through the dark landscape of his own creation. Fearful and contrite and subject to impulses beyond his comprehension.

"What is it, Jack?"

He roused himself from his reverie and looked at the woman. She had her hand on his wrist that held the notebook of questions he wanted to ask. It was purposely closed, and she looked down at it now, as if the thought occurred to her that he was indeed hiding from her some despicable information.

"I was just thinking," he rushed to say, a flare of embarrassment warming his face.

"About what?" She seemed so concerned, he had to answer so he pushed himself to say anything that would placate her curiosity.

"About my own parents," he blurted. "How judgmental they were, how unforgiving."

"You see that in Ted's parents, do you?" She took the picture from him and gazed at it a long while. "He never said an unkind word about them."

"Did he tell you anything about his past?" Jack asked in spite of his resolution to let her decide on the line of questioning.

"He didn't like to discuss his childhood," she said, fingering a strand of her hair. "He was strangely mute on that subject. He'd talk about anything else, he was a great conversationalist, but he made the point clear from the beginning that the subject was off limits, so I didn't pursue it. I did wonder sometimes, when I recognized inexplicable behaviors on his part, just what had provoked his tirades, his petty displays of anger, but I just assumed it was really his own business, and that was fine. I didn't tell him everything about my life either. We were both keepers of secrets."

Jack vaguely wondered what secrets a woman like Ann Hudson would have, but he didn't pursue it. As she would probably say, it wasn't his business. And it wasn't, but Hudson's secrets were his business. He intended to know the man whether she revealed all she knew or not.

"Anything else you have that might shed light on your husband's childhood?" he asked.

She thought for a minute then got up and went into Hudson's study. When she came back, she held in her outstretched hands a wooden figure, the kind of toy that is several wooden pieces within one, each smaller than its outside container. Each piece was the same rounded body of a peasant child with full pink cheeks, tattered clothes and angelic eyes. She opened the figures one by one till at the last, she stopped. "It's so small," she said doubtfully. "There wouldn't be anything in here, would there?" She opened the last tiny figure. Inside was a tightly wadded piece of paper. She slowly unfolded it, straightening it on her lap. Jack could see the faint fountain ink on the parchment — small, precise, foreign-looking penmanship.

Ann Hudson let out her breath in a long sigh of relief. She handed the parchment to Jack, who held it up to the light. The thin sheet of paper appeared very old and was folded in many places. The faint brown ink had no slant and the words were very close together. Jack put on his reading glasses. The page smelled faintly mildewed as he held it up to the light. He read aloud:

Dear Son,

By now your parents are in the Balkans. We will soon arrive in Albania, where we belong. I couldn't settle down amidst familiar surroundings without explaining a few things you must have wondered about. Your father and I loved you even though we were not blessed with an understanding of your unusual personality. Since you were so unhappy with us, now that you are old enough to make your own way, we are sure that our departure will not affect you adversely. Although America was kind to us, it is our wish to return to our own culture. We thought raising a Russian orphan would fulfill us, but you were always more American than we. Perhaps we were too hard on you, insisting on values we grew up with when you wanted to be allowed more choices. We are sorry for that now. We respect what you have accomplished in your short life. We admire your intelligence and ambition. We hope you won't judge us too harshly for our shortcomings and for leaving. We wish you well and will always remain your parents should you ever need anything. The house is yours. Perhaps you will bring your wife there someday and have your own children running on the property. We sincerely hope so.

Please tend to your health, always. Stay in touch with Dr. Kerkoff. He has always had your best interests at heart. And forgive us our desire to be home once again.

Katarina and Jules

Jack reread the letter and set it down on the coffee table. "Where did you find this?"

"It was in the very back of the last drawer in his file cabinet. I must have missed it the other times I looked there."

Jack thought about the note. The one piece that stood out to him was the mention of the boy's health and a Dr. Kerkoff, presumably a local doctor Jack intended to look up. The letter seemed to support Miranda's theory that Hudson had personality issues, perhaps a disorder of some sort.

"Did your husband have any health conditions?" Jack asked.

For a moment Ann Hudson hesitated. A flush rose from the curve of her sweater upward, bathing her face in a crimson glow. "I'm not sure what the diagnosis was but he saw a psychiatrist regularly, one here at Yale. I could look up his name for you," she said, getting up.

She went into her husband's study and came back with a business card.

Yeffim Sloboda, Psychiatrist, Yale Medical School, Jack read aloud. "Did you know him?"

"I never met him," she said. "Again, there were parts of Ted's life he wanted to remain private. I didn't want to intrude."

"I understand," Jack said, although he wasn't sure he wouldn't check up on his wife to understand what kind of psychiatric problems she had. He'd want to know.

"You think I should have checked up on him, don't you?" Her eyes held him, and Jack could feel her probing stare, searching for any clue that would reveal his criticism of her.

"He could have been a pedophile, a sex addict, bipolar, schizophrenic, a lot of dangerous conditions," Jack blurted. "Yes, I think I would have pursued the subject."

"You weren't married to Ted," she said quietly. A weariness had stolen into her voice. Jack didn't know what to say. It occurred to him at the moment that maybe Ann Hudson hadn't leveled with him after all. She hadn't told him about the psychiatrist before, nor had she offered anything he hadn't already uncovered in his research. Perhaps she wanted a mere whitewash of the man's life. Maybe she didn't want him to probe too deeply. Quite possibly he got the authority to write from her because he was so ill prepared to do the job. Suddenly Jack felt sick at heart. He hadn't realized till that very moment how important it was to him to render this man's life honestly and completely.

"What if you were to find out some really terrible things about your husband?" Jack asked. "What would you do?"

"I...I..don't know. I don't expect there is anything terrible about Ted out there." Her voice quavered, and she held her hands up to her face. "You'd have to know Ted," she said after remaining silent for several long seconds during which Jack's heart thudded uncomfortably. Something inside of his chest hurt, and it frightened him.

"Don't you see," she burst out, "He was the most generous, kind, and honest man I have ever known! His talent didn't hold a candle to his generosity of spirit, his compassion, his basic goodness. Ted would give his last dime to anyone who needed it. I couldn't have asked for a more wonderful husband. If he had his faults, they were small in comparison to his virtues. If he had a *condition*, then he had one, but that didn't take from what he was. He was still Theodore Hudson, the man I loved, the Nobel Prize winning scientist, a genius, a leader. Don't you see, I was proud to be his wife, proud to share his life with him, in awe of his talents. Don't ask me such a question, as if Ted Hudson were an ordinary man. *He was not an ordinary man. He was extraordinary! I loved him... I loved him... I loved him..."*

With that, Ann Hudson broke down and sobbed into her hands. The walls held the echoes and Jack felt the pain as if it were his very own. He had the urge to put his arms around her, but he held himself in check. It was not for him to presume a friendship at this juncture. Nor did he feel she would want it. He searched for the right words to console her, but he didn't know what to say.

Her sobbing continued till he thought he would break down himself, so bad did he feel and so impotent. Outside the sun faded from the trees, and the traffic sounds rose louder on the late afternoon air. Jack thought of Miranda and the lab atmosphere, the prim, earnest faces of the men who worked there, and it was as if he were seeing all mankind in the context of their own feeble cries for help. Did no one ever consider the possibility that even the gifted sometimes need help, he wondered. It wasn't only Ann Hudson who took her husband's needs for granted, it was every person who did so, and it was every person who was denied help or understanding as a result. No, it was not her fault that she didn't know Theodore Hudson as well as she might have, it was the fault of every human being who blithely sought out his own happiness without taking time to understand the others out there who needed help. He knew he'd never been attuned to others to that extent. He thought of his wives, his lovers, Miranda, his mother, and it hit him with the force of a thunderbolt that he had never really thought deeply about anyone's feelings but his own. Oh, he'd made a pretense of doing so, but he hadn't really cared. But, he reminded himself, he did care now. He cared that Ann Hudson was crying out of grief and disappointment and confusion and perhaps out of feelings of deep inferiority. It hurt him to hear her as nothing in his life had hurt before. Against his own inclinations, he reached over and gathered her in his arms.

"There, there..." he said, smoothing her lovely hair back from her face. "Don't feel so bad. I'm not critical of you, you must know that. You did what you thought was right at the time, and that's all anyone can ask of you."

She didn't look up at him. Her shoulders continued to heave against Jack's chest, and he patted her and spoke kindly. Then finally she stopped crying and gently pulled away. She wiped her face with a napkin from the tray and stood upright. She gathered the tray and cups and went into the kitchen.

Chapter Twenty

Jack left the Hudson residence feeling that whatever occurred in the future with the book, that Ann Hudson deeply loved and admired her husband, as Jack had believed before. If anything, she worshipped the man. Surely she did not know of Yvonne or his other indiscretions out there in the old house. It was a part of his life she had not been privy to. She had respected his right to privacy, and Hudson, as far as Jack was concerned, had abused that freedom and David's and her trust. Jack was convinced she knew more about his health than she had told him, but he felt she would reveal what she knew on that subject as time went on. The letter from Hudson's mother convinced Jack that he and Miranda were indeed formulating some theories about the man that might bear out after further research. He smiled to think that so much of their insight had a basis in their study of literature, but Miranda's intuitive abilities enabled her to see further than the clues a sophisticated understanding of people could provide. He had to admit that Miranda's glimpse into the human heart was paranormal, but he was beginning to accept her observations without question.

He drove to Claire's feeling a sense of accomplishment. Although his time with Ann Hudson had been cut short because of her emotional fragility, he knew he would be able to take off where they ended the session and catch up tomorrow, if necessary. He wondered how Miranda's experience at the lab had been. He doubted she had found out much that was new there. Jack had found most of the professors and their students to be uncooperative. Only the secretary of the department had been willing to talk to Jack in more than a few sentences, and she had not imparted any personal observations or new facts. What had been insightful about the experience was the sense of the working atmosphere of the place. It was apparent to Jack that most of the scientists and students worked relatively independently and did not socialize or extend themselves in any way. It was an every-man-for-himself environment, as far as Jack could tell.

He parked the car outside the restaurant and went inside. The place was deserted except for three people sitting at different tables. One was the young man who'd been with Joline and who kept staring at Miranda earlier in the day. He looked up when Jack entered and met his eyes. Jack nodded to him then found a place by the windows. He set down his folder and walked up to the counter. The man rose and walked over to him.

"I'm Sam Levy," he said stretching out his hand to Jack.

"Jack Pierce." He clasped the frail warm hand.

"I understand you're writing about Professor Hudson."

"I am." Jack turned to the person behind the counter. "Small black coffee," he said.

"He was my adviser."

"You're a molecular biology major?"

"I was," he said. "I'm a Ph.D. candidate. Immunology. I help supervise the lab."

Jack was surprised at the man's comments. He didn't seem like a scientist, but he did seem a little older than most of the students Jack had seen around campus. As Jack looked at him now, he decided the young man had a time-worn appearance, as if he were older than he probably was. To Jack he appeared pale and possibly not well. His skin which stretched tightly across his face was sallow, and his thinning hair was dull and badly cut. He pulled out a pack of cigarettes and lit one, inhaling deeply as if desperate for a smoke. His fingernails were ragged and dirty. He wore a long, old-fashioned overcoat which gave him a look of shabby formality or vintage ethnicity, such as pre-revolutionary Russian. Jack smiled at the man's sense of style, so unusual for the trendy times, either at Yale or any college campus.

"Let me buy you coffee," Jack said. He glanced at the array of coffee cakes spread out along the counter. "How about some cake?"

The man nodded. "Thanks."

"Why don't you join me," he said to the young man. Jack walked over to the table where he had set down his things and watched Sam Levy gather up his backpack and a spiral notebook and pen. He placed the pen and paper in his pack and picked up his coffee and cake and walked over to Jack's table and sat down. The cigarette still hung from his mouth and trailed its smoke throughout the restaurant. Jack noticed the man limped as he walked with the pack over one shoulder. He seemed to breathe heavily with a rasping irregularity. When he sat down, his eyes surveyed the restaurant then came to rest on his paper cup. He did not look at Jack but sat still and waited.

Jack found it a little disconcerting that the young man who had approached him did not speak or make eye contact. His eyes continued to roam the restaurant for several seconds till Jack decided to cut to the chase. "So what can you tell me about the man?" he asked, looking Sam Levy right in the eye. He wasn't sure he could believe anyone who didn't look at the person he was engaged in conversation with. He thought of Joline and wondered what she saw in the man — she with her gregarious personality and keen understanding of people.

"He was an evil person," Sam Levy said without looking at Jack. His cigarette had burned to a stub, and he took it between his thumb and finger and flung it on the floor then stepped on it. He looked around him and lowered his voice. "He got what was coming to him in the end, though, didn't he?" The faintest light moved in his eyes as he made contact with Jack by a barely perceptible smile then turned away so that Jack was looking at his long, angular nose and the strange mustache that suggested poverty and ill health.

"I don't know what you're talking about," Jack said, attempting to lead him on.

"I think you do," Sam said. "Joline told me she'd been honest with you."

"Sam, I know what you mean, if you're referring to what goes on at that house out there, but I keep trying to understand the other factors that might have made him vulnerable to such behavior. It's hard for me to believe that Theodore Hudson was a dissolute by nature. His wife, others, thought the world of him. He certainly showed the purist kind of altruism."

"All an act," Sam muttered. "Hypocrite. Chameleon, that's what he really was." Levy drew out the pack of cigarettes and lit another. "He always played to an audience, and people fell for the act. Great actor, I'll give him that."

"Chameleon?" Jack prompted. "Explain what you mean."

"If you had traditional values, you know, like you valued the sanctity of life, or your folks had taught you to avoid substance abuse or fornication till you married or," he seemed to be searching the room for examples, "revulsion for promiscuous sex," he'd pretend to have those values by referring to his mother's virtuousness or his wife's or anything that would leave the impression that he was as moral as you. But really it was all a sham, what he really wanted was to get you in a compromising situation, and eventually he would succeed. Ask Joline what he did with her her very first week at Yale."

Jack thought of Joline and her seeming defense of Hudson. He was reminded of the kinship she and Yvonne shared, of Joline's fervent claim that Hudson had been her best friend. Jack recalled that Joline had said Hudson was like a father to her. Evidently the professor was someone Joline trusted completely. So what was the truth here? Jack felt he was again back at square zero, waiting for so many other pieces of the puzzle before he knew anything, really.

"So what did Hudson do that first week at Yale?" Jack asked.

"You'll have to ask her," Levy said. "I could have killed the man myself for that." His cigarette was down to the signature stub and he spat it onto the floor then mashed it with his shoe. He wore old black combat boots with leather laces, Jack noticed. "You know how vulnerable Joline is," Levy said in a gentle voice. "You know what she's been through, everyone does. Hell, the girl's a walking miracle, if you ask me. And then she takes up with this creep, and he does a number on her, like he does all the women, and then there's nothing right anyone can do after that. She's ruined, and that's the end of trying to save her."

"You were trying to save her?" Jack asked, trying to keep Levy talking.

"She's a good person deep down," Sam Levy said. "But she has a lot of baggage, and she needs positive influences to give her courage, to support her good side. Know what I mean?"

"Of course," Jack said. "We all need support, good influences. We all need a chance to rise above our birthright, to show what we can do with our lives."

"That's what Joline achieved by getting to come to Yale in the first place," Jack said. "She wanted so desperately to prove herself. She knew she was a quick study, but she had no models or bases of comparison by which to measure her intellect. At times she thought she'd gotten in to Yale because she was poor and disadvantaged, but that was a very small part of it. They don't accept you here unless you're truly bright, and she had brains, I tell you. She is brilliant."

"That's something for you to say, a Ph.D. candidate in Immunology under the Nobel Prize Recipient, Hudson."

Sam Levy said nothing. For one brief second his eyes found Jack's then he slowly resumed his optical journey around the restaurant.

"What went on in that place was bad enough," Levy continued, "but there were other things the man did that were even worse."

"Such as?" Jack eyed Sam Levy, noted the curl of his stern lip, the narrowly spaced eyes, the taut skin paler and more sallow in the brightening afternoon light.

"He was an extremely cruel person. It was as if he derived sadistic pleasure from destroying people."

"Are you sure, Sam? This just is not ringing true. I just came from his wife's house. She claimed he was the most decent, honest, generous man she'd ever known. Her son says the same thing. Why, these are bright people, too, you know. You can fool a lot of people, all right, but we both know how hard it is to hide the truth from those you live with."

Jack looked at the man again. He listened to his ragged breath and watched the wayward eyes resume their journey. He noted that they had made eye contact no more than twice all the time they were conversing.

"Are you sure you don't have an axe to grind, because it doesn't make sense that a man of Hudson's achievement, considering the nature of those accomplishments, could subvert everything he had lived for to date. I'm sorry, but I just can't believe he did all the evil things you suggest."

"He corrupted me, too," Sam Levy said, "and I resented the dependency I experienced as a result, but even then I tried to please him, as Joline did, till finally with me, I stopped the whole damn, vicious cycle of craving all the wrong things. I got myself back together, and I played the game because my folks aren't rich, and I needed the financial help my teaching assistant position and manager of the lab provided me, but I broke the deeper ties. I did, and it was the hardest thing I ever did, I can tell you, but I stopped going there. I got off the meth and the heroin and I started eating right. They say you can't get off meth, but I did, and I did it alone because there's no way I could afford to go to rehab."

"What you have to do you have to do," Jack said.

"I'd been clean for a year when Joline came. I warned her about Hudson, but she didn't listen. He had her fooled from the first day they met. A lot of talk about doing good for humanity, and authors they both liked, which suggested he had a conscience and concern for the underdog, confessions about his orphan background and his seeking out a priest to help him find God. All horseshit designed for a young, impressionable woman who wanted to believe in goodness and people after her terrible upbringing. But that's the way he operates: he says what he knows you want to hear, and you buy it because why would a person lie about his life, his past? You don't think people do that so you believe…"

"He was an orphan, " Jack said. "He did like the author, Dostoyevsky, as he told Joline. His work shows he did care about the downtrodden, the poor, the sick, the disenfranchised. It doesn't appear to me it was all a lie."

"You believe what you want to believe," Sam Levy said, "but my definition of evil is one who lies just because he can. To confuse. Such people have no scruples. Theodore Hudson would do anything for his own self-gratification. There are no limits to the man's ego. No limits to his need."

"What are his needs, then?"

"Besides the harlot, Yvonne, to be on top, to seek thrills to divert himself from his fears and anxiety, to corrupt others so he wouldn't feel alone in his degradation."

"You're pretty convincing," Jack admitted, "but you talk like a psychologist rather than a scientist. How did you acquire such a knowledge of human behavior, anyway?"

The young man's face reddened. Blotches rose around his pale neck. He lowered his voice so that his rasping breath sounded with the quiet murmuring, "I haven't told Joline, but when I was a child, some things happened to me that messed me up for quite sometime." He looked off into the restaurant with a vague acknowledgment of some image he seemed to hold in his memory. Jack watched his face cloud with anger and shame. "A priest," he said, to Jack's earnest expression. "A family friend, my dad's oldest childhood companion." He cleared his throat; Jack felt Levy was holding back tears, and he didn't want to make the confession any more difficult than it was so he sat quietly, taking in the trembling voice, the red-shadowed neck and face and the moist eyes of the man who had struck Jack as a bystander to life, one of those who'd withdrawn from the fray and choose instead to watch the struggling masses from a safe distance. Well, no wonder. Jack would, too, if he'd experienced such a violation.

"You said Hudson was sadistic. That suggests you feel he gets off on bringing people down." Jack had to admit that if he were to define "evil," it would be the perpetuator of personal destruction. He'd always despised the gossips of the world, the slanderers, even politicians with their cruel, contentious ad hominem attacks on people. It had always seemed to Jack that one's name mattered in the scheme of things. That you worked hard to establish your good name, your word meant something, and to have anyone take that from you with gossip, innuendo, false accusations, well that was the ultimate sin, as far as he was concerned. A man could be wrong about another, that happened all the time, but he shouldn't put his condemnation to words — that was wrong, just plain wrong.

"My experience with him was anyone who stood in his way was subject to attack, but what surprised me was how often the victims were women. Boy, the man must have had a piece of work for a mother, all right."

Fleetingly, Jack thought of his own mother and her quiet detachment, her pretense of involvement when one could argue she hadn't really been there as a source of emotional support. Looking back, her emotional absence in that tired house was all too apparent now. He thought of his father, always angry about something, the affair with a neighbor's wife that went on for years, his cruel tirades directed at his only son and Jack's own passive rebellion. He almost flunked out of high school, dropped out of college. One could wreak psychic disturbance or terrible loneliness in a child by that alone. He wondered about the woman who'd written her son the good-bye letter and he thought he saw behind the small, precise penmanship a woman who was eager to divest herself of the responsibility for raising a genius, a child's whose needs were extravagant compared to the simple ones of his peers. The thought made Jack very sad for the man. At least, his own mother had remained a physical presence in the home. He knew he'd needed that — till Miranda came along, anyway.

"If you show him up, if you challenge him, if you're one of his competitors, he'll squash you." Levy went on. "He has his ways of destroying anyone who's a threat, whether it's a colleague or merely someone in his circle of friends who has a dissenting opinion. He'll humiliate you in public, he'll attack your character in private, whatever, but he'll do what it takes to come out on top. Like I say, he's dangerous because he doesn't exercise limits of any kind. And he's so brilliant, he manages to cover his tracks. I know some graduate students who transferred to other universities because they were afraid he'd come after them."

Jack thought of Joline, and he feared for her. "Did he ever attack Joline?"

"Not to my knowledge. She was so in thrall, he didn't have to."

"Any names you can give me?"

"Yeah, there was this guy who was gay, and Hudson told his folks because the kid wasn't in Hudson's camp as to the way the lab should be run. The kid planned to blow the whistle to higher-ups because there was mismanagement of federal funds, but he came down sick. Suddenly he was gone, and no one knew where he went. The rumor was Hudson put him up at the Mayo Clinic for a while, but he died very soon of AIDS — and not from being gay but from drugs, from sharing needles at the shit-hole house when Hudson was *there*." Levy looked Jack full in the eyes and let his glance linger there, watching for his reaction. At that moment Jack felt certain Sam Levy was telling the truth. "His name was Simon Shirovna."

"What about someone whom Hudson gave one of his own kidneys? Is that true? Joline mentioned that."

Levy's eyes wandered off around room as if rehearsing to himself how he'd answer that question. He took a long time to respond while Jack thought about Miranda and wondered what was taking her so long. He'd expected her back at Claire's by now, but then again, she'd ensnare anyone into talking due to the sheer magnetism she exuded and her own brand of attractiveness. He imagined she'd have a few interesting stories by the time she met up with Jack.

"He did do that, and to be honest, it seemed totally selfless on his part," Sam Levy said at last. "I didn't want to attribute any nobility to the act myself, knowing his ruthlessness, but I had to give him that, it was out of some pureness or goodness or whatever. I still can't believe it, and to be honest, there were other good things he did. It's just that I *know* what the man is."

"Do you want to give me that man's name? I could follow up on that aspect."

"Josef Chizzick. He left school but works at the hospital here. He should be in the directory." Levy glanced at his watch, a beautiful old one with a gold face, and looked up at Jack. Again, he looked into his eyes and smiled. Jack felt the experience had bonded the men in some indefinable way and it felt good. He sensed Sam Levy felt relieved to have shared his own, tragic story to a non-judging listener.

"Just one more thing," Jack said.

Sam Levy looked down at Jack still sitting. He was hauling his backpack onto his shoulder. Jack could hear the telltale rasp of his breathing and hoped his health was all right. At the moment he seemed more energetic than he had and certainly more at ease. "What's that?" Levy asked, again looking Jack in the eyes. His own suddenly appeared dim, as if the light had gone out of them, Jack thought, noting the dark shadows surrounding them. He hadn't noticed that before and wondered if the tension of the personal disclosure on his part was taking its toll on him. Jack felt bad if that were the case since he'd taken a liking to the enigmatic young man.

"How much do you think Theodore Hudson relied on Yvonne?" Jack was thinking that if you could identify a characteristic in a woman that would be a singular indication of the man's need for her, it would be the inspiration she provided him to develop himself in the ways he thought important to his happiness. For Hudson, that would be his imagination, his altruism, his scientific investigation, his social causes, his writing. A larger than life human being, it would seem he would need most the woman who supported and inspired his efforts to express himself. Yvonne had said he wrote there in that squalor of the upstairs bedroom, and that bothered Jack, knowing the tasteful, quiet domesticity of Ann Hudson's home. To her for whom aesthetics and comfort obviously mattered, it would be devastating to find out her husband had preferred the filthy environment of the home in the country to do his best work.

"They'd been together a long time," Levy said. "Since childhood, evidently. He actually told me that one night at the house after a couple of joints." Levy looked out the window, and Jack turned to follow his gaze. Miranda was passing by, her hair standing out around her like a huge aura of white and silver. "She's beautiful," Sam Levy said. "You're very lucky."

"I'm afraid she's not mine." Jack smiled. "Too bad, huh?"

"Yeah." The man's eyes followed Miranda as she walked in the door and over to them. Her face was flushed from the outside air, and Jack had to admit she was at the moment knock-down, drag-out gorgeous. He was seized with a longing to have her back on the terms of the past, before he had so stupidly been attracted to Felicia and what seemed then the good life, so seductive to a provincial Texan boy full of himself and his dreams. She hadn't really been a support to him, and he hadn't looked to her for that anyway. He'd simply used her, he had to admit now and it made him feel bad. He knew he'd have to seek her out and somehow resolve their breakup. He owed it to her, he decided.

Miranda walked up to them with an expectant look. "You must be Joline's boyfriend," she said, reaching out her hand to him.

"How did you know?" Levy asked, a deep flush covering his face. He stood awkwardly before her, taking in her electric presence. It wasn't the first time Jack had seen men go ga-ga over Miranda, not even the first time a young man had done so, but it reminded Jack of what he'd lost all those years ago, and he felt a sense of loss that was so keen and so deep, he thought he might cry. He heard himself sniff and pulled himself together as best he could.

"Oh, I just know things," she said vaguely. "You look like the quiet, steady type, the kind of guy she'd be attracted to. She smiled sweetly. "The kind of man she'd need."

"Quite the judge of character, aren't you?" Sam Levy said, smiling. Jack noticed his eyes had ceased their perennial journey around the room and now fastened on Miranda with an eager attentiveness.

"You might say that," Miranda said, never one to minimize her talents. "And Joline," she added, "is brilliant and imaginative and fearful of being constrained. She'll drive you crazy, but she'll love you till the day you die." Miranda looked at Jack, gave him the thumbs up. "So what do you have to say about your efforts today?"

"I'd better be going," Sam Levy said, nodding at Miranda. He turned to Jack, an inquisitive look on his face. "What was it you wanted to ask me before Miranda arrived? Oh, yes," he said. "Yvonne." He hesitated a moment, clearly evaluating whether he should discuss the subject in Miranda's presence. He glanced at Miranda, holding her eyes for but a moment.

"I think she was the means to his self-destruction," he said, turning to Jack. "He didn't love her, but he did need her. They'd been together a lot, he'd come to depend on her to relieve his anxiety, to tolerate him when he got nasty. He had a terrible, dark side, you know. We all knew it." He looked around the restaurant and lowered his voice. "More than once it occurred to me he might be insane."

"You can't be serious," Jack said, shocked by the intensity of feeling in Sam Levy's voice as much as by the disclosure itself. If Ann Hudson hadn't seen aberration, how could you believe that? Jack reminded himself that the facts were the facts in this case, but he still couldn't reconcile that with her account, David's. It didn't make sense that Theodore Hudson displayed a side to others he didn't reveal to his family. Families were always the harbor of those deceptions, weren't they? How could one keep such a secret, Jack wondered. He doubted it was possible.

"He had a mental illness," Sam Levy said. "I'm just not sure what it was. In the grips of whatever that condition was, he'd do anything." There was fear in Levy's expression that moment, Jack felt, and it sent a shiver up Jack's spine to sense it. Jack glanced at Miranda. She was studying Sam Levy with a fierce scrutiny, her lavender eyes boring into his, moving around his angular features, over the disdainful curve of his lips, the hard, steely eyes, his trembling hands with their empty gesticulations. Sam Levy was clearly nervous, and yes, truly frightened, Jack surmised. No one would feign that.

"Wait a minute, Sam," Miranda said. She had stopped staring at him. She seemed to be listening to another voice or something in her own imaginative mind. Thoughts flashed in a succession of images, a flickering of her eyes that Jack had seen before, but it never failed to unnerve him, as if there were another world out there to which only she had access. It was eerie and rather repelled Jack, but there was no repugnance in the face of Levy, who regarded her with a quiet fascination, his face softening as he watched the changing landscape of her face. His antagonism of a moment ago vanished, replaced by a tender solicitude Jack would not have thought possible in the angry young man.

"Yes?" Sam Levy said gently, looking directly at Miranda, seemingly finding solace and understanding in her clear, open expression. She had a shy smile on her face as if she clearly understood the power she had over this young man and didn't want to compromise his will with the strength of her own personality.

"How would you describe the way Theodore Hudson acted when he seemed ... *insane*?" She held his eyes and seemed to study him for his reaction as well as for the information he would impart. Again, there was that riveting intensity that made Jack uncomfortable, but it didn't appear to faze Levy, who still hung on her every word. People poured into the restaurant, it was getting noisy, but the two of them seemed lost in their own private conversation. Jack was sure that Miranda for the moment had forgotten Jack. This was between her and the young man and about truth. Jack sullenly looked down at his feet, utterly put off by Miranda's dismissal of him.

"Generally Professor Hudson was accommodating, accepting of people. He had impeccable manners and a sort of courtly bearing. Since his memory was so sharp, he never forgot people's names, he could converse with anyone on just about everything." Levy scanned the restaurant, noting the crowds. "Perhaps we should sit down," he said, seating himself and putting his backpack on the floor beside him.

"Of course," Miranda said, sitting across from him. Reluctantly, Jack pulled out a chair and sat down. He pulled out his notepad.

Levy resumed talking with his voice lowered. "But sometimes, whether it was at the house out there, under the influence or not, or at the lab, he'd erupt into these violent arguments. When he did, he was mean, so unforgiving it made you cringe."

"You mean he would attack colleagues, students?" Miranda asked.

"Mostly students," Levy said. "Mostly women and often the women he liked the best, which struck many of us as really odd. We learned to spot his changing moods and avoid him when he was edgy because we never knew where his irritability would go."

"*Irritability...*" Miranda said, nodding. "Did his irritability seem to have a seasonable component?"

"I don't know, but he'd be hyper for a while and then he'd blow at seemingly insignificant comments, events. It was like an explosion. Terrible. Mean. Unprovoked. You just couldn't guess what was in his head, but he'd tear into you and totally demolish your self-esteem, as if he really enjoyed tearing into you. He played mind games as well, sort of tricking you into a vulnerable place, getting to find out what your Achilles Heel was, you know, that sort of thing."

"Sadistic?" Miranda asked.

Levy nodded. "Very. When he did it to me, I totally broke down. Here I thought he cared about me, really liked and respected me, and then it was like I was a vile fly on the wall. He brought up things I didn't even know he knew about me. My past, my psychological problems, all sorts of *secret things*." I stopped trusting him after that. I never felt at ease with him again."

"Do you think he sensed your relationship had changed?" Miranda asked,

"Are you kidding?" Levy rolled his eyes. "It was like he had no recollection of how cruel he'd been, how totally over the top he really was. The man never apologized. Go figure."

"It sounds like a personality disorder," Miranda offered. "Maybe he's bipolar or has Borderline Personality Disorder. Both have a narcissistic component."

"Oh, he was narcissistic, all right," Levy said. "At first you wouldn't guess it because he was calm, methodical, and he didn't talk about himself at all. He tended to draw you out, to really listen, like you were a very interesting person, like he cared about people. But actions speak louder than words and soon you realized that everything was really about him, about maintaining an image, about seeking approval to allay his fears of inadequacy." Sam Levy shook his head in disgust. "Whatever way you looked at it Theodore Hudson was about himself, and he'd do whatever he had to do to maintain his psychic equilibrium, and if that meant cutting you down to size and destroying you, he'd do it in a heartbeat. I know... *I know*," he said, a look of perplexity on his face. "I've never known anyone like that."

"I have," Miranda said. "And I agree with you, Sam, that kind of mercurial personality is very disarming in its charm, but it tends to be predatory because, as you suggest, the maintenance of their facade and what they truly want to be is a constant balancing act. They need adulation to counter the inferiority, so they work at building up an audience, so to speak." She touched Sam Levy's hand in support. "I think you're pretty wise about people," she said, "but it's hard for me to dismiss nobility of spirit in a man of Theodore Hudson's accomplishments. There's got to be more to the story, some explanation. I don't think our work is anywhere near done," she said, looking at Jack for the first time in the long conversation. "I bet the truth is much more complicated."

"You sound just like Joline," Levy said wearily. "She kept insisting I didn't really know the man, that he had generous impulses. Blah-blah-blah," he said disgustedly. "From my vantage, she just didn't get it."

"Sometimes women see more in an insecure man's reactions than mere cowardice or cruelty or even, mental illness." Miranda stood her moral ground, but Levy didn't seem offended by her reluctance to accept everything he'd said, nor did he seem bent on thrusting his biased perspective on her. He nodded as Miranda spoke and earnestly listened with an accepting expression on his face.

"I know what you're saying," he said. "People are complex, and we all have our dark sides, for sure, but it's the capacity on Hudson's part to arouse sympathy in women that contributes to the power he eventually achieves over them. Joline just couldn't see how he used that to ensnare women," Levy said, sounding angry again. "You're lucky he's dead, Miranda. He'd have gone after you for sure!"

"Why?" Miranda asked, surprised.

"He liked to get inside intelligent women's minds and manipulate them to doubt themselves. That was his game, that made him feel powerful. Maybe some weird kind of revenge."

"I don't think he'd have conquered Miranda," Jack interjected. "She's tough in her own way."

"So is Joline," Levy reminded them. His intelligent eyes bored into Miranda's. "He'd have loved your beautiful mind. Its inquisitiveness, the imagination of it, its knowing what so many don't know..."

"I know nothing," Miranda said, but Levy didn't seem to hear her.

"There might have been some misogyny there, or maybe he just came into contact with women who happened to be the best and the brightest out there. That's Yale, after all. He looked away at the people lined up at the counter, "But we know he was hard on men, too. It's not like it's all tidy and conclusive. He was indeed very complicated, but that doesn't excuse his viciousness, the lying..."

"It doesn't," Miranda agreed. Jack could see the confusion in her face and knew the session with Sam Levy had discouraged her.

Levy took out the pack of cigarettes and with trembling hands took out one and lit it. The sound of his ragged breath filled the space around them.

"You should give that up," Miranda said.

"Smoking? I'm always trying to quit. I will one of these days."

"Me, too," Miranda said. "I'll quit if you will." Her voice, her face were earnest in the fading light. "Say you'll quit," she said in the charming way Miranda had of presuming an intimacy among people who liked her."

"Why not?" Levy said. "I've quit a lot of worse addictions." He threw his cigarette on the ground and stubbed it. "There!"

"I will never smoke again!" Miranda said, laughing. "This will have been a fateful day, thanks to you, Sam. Hear that Jack?" She took his arm. "It's never too late to change."

"Just be careful," Levy warned. "Hudson's dead and all, but I tell you the man is dangerous." He thought for a minute. "In fact, I don't like the fact that Joline has anything to do with Yvonne. That woman is as bad as Hudson, as far as I'm concerned."

"Have you talked with Joline lately?" Miranda asked.

"She's upset with me," Levy said. "She won't talk to me till I let up on Hudson." He sighed. "She still thinks he was the greatest man of our times. She really cared for him." Sam Levy looked at Miranda and said in a sad voice, "She just doesn't get it."

"What?" Miranda glanced at Jack and then back to Levy.

"That there are evil forces out there. And she should be more careful." He slung his backpack over his shoulder and stood up. Without another word he walked with straight shoulders and eyes focused ahead, out the door of the restaurant. He didn't turn back to say goodbye.

Miranda watched him, her head cocked, her knowing eyes ruminating over something in memory or the esoteric nether world she inhabited on occasion. Then silently, wordlessly, she got up and began walking out of the restaurant.

Jack waited momentarily to regain his own psychic balance, then followed her out into the early evening dusk of New Haven.

Chapter Twenty One

"The mystery goes on," Jack commented as he helped Miranda into the car. "Just when you think you have a handle on the story, it takes another detour. Doesn't it throw you, all these contradictions?"

"Not really," Miranda said. "I was expecting this sort of thing."

"What do you mean?" Jack remembered only her certainty of the man's greatness when she presented her proposition in Leadville. He was certain she had not prepared him for the ambiguity of the situation.

"What about all that talk that I would be *serving mankind* by telling the story of this great and noble man, whose story just had to be told because "the truth mattered." Isn't that how you put it, Miranda? I don't hear any caveats in that, do you?"

"If I'd told you anymore than I did, you wouldn't have taken it on, now would you?"

Jack thought about that night in Leadville, the raging blizzard and Miranda's car edging its way up the precipice. She'd endangered her life by arriving that particular night in the middle of a storm, and as she'd told it, had pushed herself in driving all the way from Texas in a relatively short time. She had felt the errand compelling enough to urge the project on Jack with every feminine wile of which she was capable. Now that he thought of it that was the only time Miranda had asked a favor of him. She'd always been too proud to ask for help, especially of him. The realization made Jack feel oddly affirmed. He had done that for her, and it felt good now, even if he was frustrated.

Jack felt that he was the kind of man who didn't get confused, who saw the world for what it was: basically logical, governed by immutable laws that even if he didn't understand them, gave the diurnal functions credibility. He'd taken physics and chemistry, mathematics, psychology, philosophy, history, and literature in his college experience; and although he quit before graduating, he felt knowledgeable about the abstract and physical workings of the world. He read a lot, his interests were varied, and he associated with intelligent people. It was unusual for him to feel confused, and he didn't much like that. He told himself he could work his way through the situation and the resulting understanding would be worth it, but he did resent the uncertainty and the enormous effort necessary to resolve the contradictions the project would eventually require. He wanted to get back to his own writing, to forge ahead with the ideas that were crowding his mind lately.

"Would I have taken it on?" Jack mused. "For you, I would have."

Miranda smiled sweetly. "Thanks," she said. "I have lots to tell you."

"Dinner?"

"Sure," she said.

They drove to a restaurant Jack had spotted on one of his drives before she came. Inside the place was half full. They were seated by the window. Miranda looked out at the traffic surging by in the darkness. "Pretty busy place, New Haven," she said. "It will sure be nice to get back to Texas. I don't think cities agree with me."

"I'm beginning to feel that way, too," Jack admitted, thinking of Leadville, the little house hugging the hillside, the sounds of the aspen whispering overhead, snow coming down so silently it surprised you when you saw the thick blanket piling up over the rocky outcroppings. Jack missed the quiet, all right, but mostly he missed the crisp, clean mountain air. To him New Haven smelled of diesel and neglect, overflowing dumpsters and dog urine, debris. He'd been a vocal critic of the heaping mine tailings in Leadville, of the ramshackle commercial buildings in need of paint and repair, the dated infrastructure, but he decided he appreciated its lack of adornment, its mismatch of modern and antique structures, the seeming lack of standards the town government imposed. Now it struck him as authentic, true to its rustic nature and the wild mountains it claimed as home.

"Yeah, let's hustle through this and get back to our homes!" Miranda said.

Jack detected a brutal homesickness in the woman, and that was okay, he told himself, but if she pined for Parrish, that would piss Jack off big time.

"Maybe you just want to get back to your lover with the forked tongue," Jack suggested.

"If you're going to talk like that, I'm leaving," Miranda said, rising from her chair, her pale face flaming. "I don't know where you get off thinking you can talk to me that way. Either you get a handle on it, or I'm out of here!" It was the first time she had ever leveled an ultimatum at him, and the firmness of her voice made Jack flinch. With a start, he realized he no longer had the upper hand with Miranda. In the past, she'd been cowed by his demands, the fact that he didn't allow her to challenge him or talk back, but here she was naming her own terms, and he knew if he didn't oblige, she'd be out of his life as fast as he'd deserted her all those years ago. It was tit for tat, and she knew it, and he realized it now. For a moment the realization saddened him, but then he decided that he no longer wanted to control her, that her resistance wouldn't arouse his anger anymore. He'd changed although he wasn't sure how it had happened.

"I'm sorry, Miranda," he said, and he meant it.

They sat in silence till the waitress came and took their orders. Then both sat back and waited for the bottle of wine. He'd selected Chianti for her because it was her favorite, and he could tell she was pleased by the gesture. Miranda seemed to be mulling over something. Her eyes had a far off look and her expression was grim.

"So what did you find out today, if you don't mind my asking?" Jack finally said. "You know, I tried to interview several of the lab assistants, profs, students, but most of them avoided me. If they did talk, they did so unwillingly and didn't reveal much. That's when I got the impression the lab was not a comfortable, open place but one where people performed their experiments, did their reports, said nothing to each other, and hustled out of there at the earliest opportunity."

"I had the same impression," she said. "It's a cold place, all right."

"I thought Hudson was supposed to be such a caring professor," Jack said, recalling Joline's words the night they met. "So why doesn't his lab reflect that?"

"I got the impression someone had told everyone not to talk," Miranda startled him by saying. Jack hadn't considered that. He'd just felt it was a competitive place and people didn't want to take the time away from their work.

"What gave you that impression?"

"Two women, actually. Both worked for Hudson, one was a doctoral candidate. They answered all my questions in monosyllabic responses. You know, I really prepared for the interviews. I had a lot of questions, but their reaction pretty much shut me down." She sighed, "The men were more cooperative. I talked to one who was pretty negative about Hudson. He works over at the hospital halftime."

Jack wondered if he were the same person Sam Levy had mentioned. He'd said the man had dropped out of the program. It occurred to Jack that perhaps Levy didn't know all the facts concerning Hudson's critics after all. It seemed possible that Levy was wrong in his assumptions. Jack hoped that was true because he still dreaded meeting with Ann Hudson unless his concerns were laid to rest by the facts.

He checked his notes. Josef Chizzick was the name Levy had given him. His notes showed Levy had indeed claimed he'd dropped out of school and was working at the hospital full time. "Was his name Chizzick?" Jack asked.

"I think so. Polish. That sounds like it. My notes are in the car if you want me to check."

"We'll check them later. What else did he say?"

"He said he hated the man."

"Did he say why?"

"He said Theodore Hudson was a fraud. He claimed some of his discoveries were in fact achieved by his assistants, but that they never got the credit because he blackmailed them!" Miranda studied his face. "You don't believe that, do you? It seemed so far-fetched to me, and Chizzick clearly had some problems of his own."

"Like what? Jack thought of the gay young man Hudson had taken to the Mayo Clinic.

"He had scabs and pustules all over his face, and he was absolutely manic. I had to keep walking around, following him because he couldn't sit down or remain still. It was the weirdest experience. I've never been around someone that hyper, and it made me so nervous it was hard concentrating on what he said. He talked faster than anyone I've ever met." Miranda mimicked the jerking gestures of the man and rolled her eyes like someone crazy. It was a funny imitation, Jack had to admit. He laughed along with her, recalling old times when they'd spent the night talking and laughing, never tiring of what the other had to say. It seemed odd that after all these years, they could still be so comfortable together.

"Do you think the guy's on drugs?" Jack asked.

"I do," Miranda said. "Meth perhaps."

"Geesh, maybe that's why he's back in the lab."

"To keep his access going? Maybe," Miranda said. "But why would he trash Hudson if he needed him for the drugs?"

"Perhaps the place has closed down by now."

"We need to get in touch with Joline," Miranda said. She took out her cell phone and looked at the directory. "No call from her," she said. When Jack looked surprised, she said, "I called her earlier and asked her to call me back. I meant to meet with her after I met up with you at Claire's. Then I got sidetracked by Sam and forgot. I hope she's okay."

"She's a big girl," Jack reassured her. "She can take care of herself."

"Probably better than you or I," Miranda said. "Still, I didn't think she seemed quite right the other night, like she was confused or maybe keeping something to herself." Miranda thought for a minute. "Yeah, something's wrong," she said, rising from her chair. She punched in a number on her cell phone and went outside. The waitress returned with the Chianti, and Jack thought about pouring himself some but he decided to wait for Miranda. He liked the way she savored Chianti, like a child drinking her chocolate milk. Even in her maturity she made a dramatic show of appreciating the simple pleasure of drinking wine.

He looked around. The place had a cheerful, bohemian ambiance with burlap tablecloths and bright linen napkins in various colors. The walls were decorated with colorful Italian pottery, and every wall was painted in a different dark earth tone. Jack found himself wondering if Ann Hudson ever dined here. He felt she would like it and decided to take her to lunch there. Thinking about her made him uncomfortable. He was still worried that he'd unconsciously reveal an unpleasant truth or that he'd feel compelled to tell her all he knew. Jack had never been one to keep secrets, and he didn't want to start now. She'd trusted him to be fair to Hudson's legacy, and that's what Jack wanted more than anything, but he was beginning to realize that she probably didn't know her husband as deeply as she intimated. He presumably had a dangerous secret life he'd adeptly concealed from her. Incredibly blind to his weaknesses and so supportive of him, she probably wouldn't accept the truth of the matter when it was presented to her, by him or anyone else. Jack had the nagging sense that no matter what he did in the days to come, he could not win.

Unknowingly, he had assumed an impossible position and now faced a complicated moral dilemma he would have to resolve sooner or later.

He poured himself some of the wine and looked around for Miranda. Through the windows he could see her standing alone, bathed in the neon pink glow of the restaurant sign. She appeared animated and strong, and other patrons were watching her with interest, Jack noted. Suddenly she was done with her conversation and closed up the phone. He watched her look into the restaurant. She seemed to think a minute then punched in another number and waited. He wondered who she was calling now and repressed his irritation at being kept waiting. He drank the glass of wine and kept watching her. After a while, she closed the phone. Then suddenly she was walking through the door and approaching him, her eyes glittering with excitement.

"You won't believe it," she said. "Joline's in Las Vegas!"

"What's she doing there?" Jack stood up and helped Miranda into her chair. She smelled like the outdoors.

"She wouldn't tell me." She looked at Jack in the knowing way that was totally Miranda — impish, secretive, certain. "Something's up!"

"So who else did you call?"

Miranda regarded him with surprise. "Spying on me, huh?"

"You were right out the window; it's not like I had a choice."

"You could have looked over your notes."

"I'd rather watch you."

"Well, thank you," she said. "That's a very nice thing to say."

"Although I was getting annoyed," Jack confessed. "The wine was waiting."

Miranda glanced at the bottle sticking out of the linen cover. "It *is* Chianti, isn't it?"

"Just for you."

"And you started without me?" Miranda's dramatic expression of annoyance pleased Jack, reminding him of their easy intimacy these days. She was like the girl next door now that they'd both had their years alone and with others. Miranda had never been wild, even in the days when women insisted on sexual equality. She'd always been discrete and restrained, considering the times then and now. Jack doubted she'd had other lovers besides himself and Don Parrish. He admired her for that as much as for her adventurous spirit that endowed their times together with a sense of immediacy he enjoyed.

He was living in the moment, he realized — mindful and attentive — while enjoying a cherished closeness with this rare creature.

"You abandoned me," he said. "I didn't feel like waiting."

"Oh, poor boy," she said. "Poor, poor callow boy!" For some reason her chiding reminded Jack of Felicia. She'd used that word for Jack a lot. He'd bristled then, and he felt his irritation rise now. He told himself Miranda didn't have it in her to mock, but that was simply rubbish, she'd used sarcasm as a weapon with him many times.

"Don't call me *callow*," he said, hearing the irritation in his voice.

He watched surprise register on her face followed by pain. Her mouth wilted, and the bright gleam of her smiling eyes faded instantly. "You aren't going to be mean now, are you?" she said, studying his face.

"I'm not mean," he said, further annoyed. Why couldn't she let things drop? Why did she always push and push?

"Sometimes you are," Miranda insisted. "When you feel slighted. It's really rather childish."

"You were rude," Jack reminded her. "You left the table and didn't even tell me where you were going or how long you would be."

"I did what had to be done, Jack. I can't answer to you every minute." She looked down at her hands lying in her lap. "Would you pour me a glass of wine, please?"

"You can pour it yourself," he said, turning away. He made a pretense of watching a pretty young woman feed her toddler at the table next to Miranda.

"Well, so I will," Miranda said. She parted the linen and took the bottle of wine out of the jug. She poured the large glass to its rim, slowly as if teasing Jack. She had a serious, knowing look on her face, but her hands trembled. The glass was so large that she had almost finished the bottle by filling it up so full. Just a small amount remained, which she carefully returned to its place in the jug. "There," she said. "I think I have enough to endure whatever outrageous insults you choose to level at me tonight!"

"Well, if you want to leave, we can leave," he said evenly.

"Oh, I think I'll drink my wine," she said demurely. "Nothing like a big glass of Chianti to dispel the fears."

"As if you have any fears," Jack said in spite of his intention to remain silent.

"Oh, but I do," she said.

He thought about that. Miranda had never been short of nerve. To Jack it seemed anything was possible for her. She seemed to breeze through life, accomplishing so much in a seemingly effortless manner while he plodded along, taking his time, always second guessing himself till he'd reached a hard won perfection or at least as close as he felt capable. Miranda, on the contrary, did everything slap-dashedly, and yet he had to admit what he saw her do was superior — from her sermons, to her writing, to the advice she gave others. She'd earned straight A's in college without studying. She took her masters one year when she felt bored and flew through the experience, finishing in record time and publishing her poetry on the side. Her first book came out at the same time a publisher picked up her thesis on the healing arts of the desert southwest. She was a remarkable woman, he had to admit, and sometimes she just made him feel inadequate. It was as simple as that, he realized, feeling down. He never meant to hurt her, but he repeatedly did, and so he faulted himself for his insecurities, and that made him overreact to her self-confidence.

"You don't expect me to believe that you have any fears?" He noted the crinkles around her eyes and presumed she had another sarcastic blow to his self-esteem in mind.

"If you weren't always so preoccupied with your own concerns, you'd know I do. We've discussed this subject many times, in case you've forgotten. It always follows one of your mean outbursts, but you never listen. You don't want to think anyone else has problems or worries or anxieties. You don't want to hear because you don't really care. Your own life swallows you up. You don't look outside your routines, your circle of friends, yourself..." Her voice had reverted from its habitual vivacity to a monotone — slow, laborious, dull, so unlike her that he felt chastened by the truthfulness it revealed in its slow murmuring, like a confession made under duress.

"So what are these so-called *fears* of yours, anyway?" he asked, certain she'd make some flip response that revealed nothing. In so many ways, Miranda was a cipher. Jack felt she didn't allow much scrutiny into her innermost self. She had a way of avoiding revelation, but then Jack didn't expect that in a woman, either. Perhaps he'd never asked the right questions, he realized. They said women liked to talk about themselves, and maybe Miranda wanted to, but there had never been the audience such openness would demand. Jack promised himself he would ask more questions of her from now on. He acknowledged his own self-centeredness in that regard.

"In answer to your question, I'm afraid of death."

"Aren't we all?" he said, feeling she was being evasive again. She wasn't telling him anything unique, anything *intimate*. She was watching him closely. She had leaned forward on her elbow, cradling her face which had become more earnest by the moment. Her intensity permeated the air around them. He almost felt he could hear it crackle with electricity.

The waitress served their food and Miranda moved to accommodate the plate, but she resumed her pose of concentration immediately. She continued to scrutinize him with a morose look on her face.

"Death should be a bridge," she said. "Of all people, I should have the faith to accept it, but I'm so afraid..."

Jack put his hand on hers. Her food steamed between them. "Miranda, of all people I know, your transition to the other side will be as easy and serene as your other accomplishments."

He suddenly had the sense that she had retreated into a world of her own. Gone was the seething passion of moments ago. Her eyes were filmed and without focus. It was the weird Miranda again, but he refused to be put off by it. She seemed to be viewing a scene in her mind's eye.

"What is it?" Jack said.

"He was *so* afraid!"

"Who?" Jack hadn't touched his food, nor had she, but he told himself this one time he would be there for her. He wasn't going to defer to food, the perusal of the room, even to the memory of today's interviews. If she needed his attention, she had it.

"Theodore Hudson was terrified of death."

"How do you know? He was a man of faith, of so many altruistic projects, so many good deeds. He must have felt he did his part to make the world a better place. By most accounts, he exemplified the Christian spirit."

"I saw into the pit of his fear, and it was terrible," Miranda revealed. "Like those dreadful drawings in the Hare Krishna's *Bhagavad Gita*, so punitive and fiery, like Dante's inferno. She shuddered. "It was indescribable but horrible beyond words. I haven't been able to shake the images, but thank goodness, they only come at night. If I thought about them during the day, I wouldn't be able to carry on with this project."

"You probably took it all in at the time, but I bet those dark images will fade as the memory grows old. It's because you recently experienced the Hudson vision that they trouble you, but they'll go away."

"You think so?" she asked.

He still held his hand over hers. "Yes," he said with all the conviction he could muster.

"I hope you're right," she said at last. "You know, I really felt for the man. He was in such agony."

"I can imagine," Jack said. He took his hand from hers.

They ate in silence for a while. Jack thought about what she said, and she seemed to be mulling over something.

"I didn't really think he could be a bad man. He was just so afraid which would make sense with anyone under the circumstances."

Did you understand the circumstances?" Jack thought about the place in which Hudson had died, the squalor, the compromising situation. He wondered if Ann Hudson knew the house, had visited there, or if she'd merely identified his body at the morgue and accepted whatever explanation was fed her. There had been no coverage of the professor's death that identified the location. It had merely been reported that he'd been at a gathering of friends in the country, when he'd experienced a heart attack and died of natural causes. There had been no inquest, no autopsy. Yvonne's name had not been mentioned. Jack wondered about that. Had Yale silenced the media? He decided to check with the sheriff's office.

"Jack, do you believe in evil?" Miranda asked suddenly. She had drunk most of the wine, he noticed. Her face was flushed and her eyes sparkled in the candle light.

"I do."

"I never have, really. I see people as just falling short of what they might become, simply flawed or whatever. But intentionally *evil*, I just never believed that. It's hard for me to believe there's a destructive force out there, intentionally leading men astray. No, I don't see things that way. Yet I could always imagine those people who were simply not there in terms of compassion or gentleness; to me, they needed more time to evolve, that's all. I still have a hard time envisioning a dark spirit, for instance." She stopped eating and placed her fork on the plate. "But I'll tell you something: *Whatever it was Theodore Hudson experienced that night seemed evil to me.*" She shuddered. "I was *there*." She had such a look of torment on her face that Jack had the urge to take her hand again, but he didn't. He continued eating. The candle at their table flickered and went out.

Miranda reached in her purse and pulled out a lighter and lit the candle. "We must keep the light going," she said tonelessly.

"Don't be afraid, Miranda. There's nothing to fear."

"Oh, but there is," she said. "You'll see."

Jack didn't know what to say. He knew from experience there were times you simply didn't reason with Miranda. The shadows closed around them as the night deepened. Outside the blur of traffic lurched and slowed and waned. Pale, amber lights showcased the magnificent spires and turrets of Yale University. Jack thought of Joline and the evening he'd taken her home and she'd rushed up the Gothic, concrete stairway to her dorm room. She'd seemed to him then strange and wise but sensible, too, and unusually honest. To have showed him the derelict house and introduced him to Yvonne now struck Jack as astonishing, given the fact that he was writing about the man she had adored. She must have known on some level that Jack's visit there would arouse serious doubts, might even cause him to abandon the project. What was she thinking?

"Look, Miranda, I wonder if Joline simply ran away."

"Why would she do that?" Miranda asked, glancing around the room for the waitress, who was taking an order at a nearby table. She raised her hand with the wine glass in it.

"More wine?" Jack asked. "Don't you think you've had enough?"

She made a face at him. "One more glass," she said, "won't hurt a thing."

When the waitress arrived, Jack ordered another bottle, and they sat drinking the wine, Miranda growing giggly as Jack continued to inquire about Joline.

"She'd be crazy to leave Sam," Miranda said. "He clearly loves her."

"Maybe it got too hot here," Jack said. "Maybe she had something to hide."

"She probably went off with some guy for the weekend. She's that kind of girl, isn't she?"

Jack didn't know. What did he understand of young women these days? For that matter, what did he understand about any woman? He thought of his ex-wives, even Karen or Miranda. Did any man really understand those baffling creatures? Whereas with Miranda her otherworldliness had always frustrated him, it was Karen's seeming inordinate compassion that had been hard to understand.

With respect to any of his ex-wives, who could guess what they were about? Go figure.

"Someone might have pressured her not to talk." Jack thought of Yvonne. He wouldn't put it past her to harass Joline, if she wanted to, especially if she still allowed young people to use the place to hang out and indulge their vices, as Jack assumed they still did. He doubted the situation had changed from a week ago. Someone like Yvonne would perpetuate the self-destructive habits of a lifetime, he was sure. There would be no respite, even after the untimely death of her lover, but that didn't mean she would want the situation to be known by anyone outside the fraternity of users and abusers she'd encouraged over the years.

"Maybe it's time I meet Yvonne," Miranda said, reading his mind.

Chapter Twenty Two

"Why don't you come in for a drink?" Jack asked as he pulled the car to a stop in the motel parking lot and climbed out and walked around to Miranda's side. The air was thick with the promise of rain and the diesel fuel from a day's deliveries. Jack's eyes swept the littered lot and rested on the neon vacancy sign, its garish cotton candy pink an obtuse reminder of all his failures. He told himself he needed companionship when all he really wanted was the sweet sense of security that had always eluded him since high school when Miranda had been his cheerleader and the future stretched forward like a plush carpet amidst the War and civil strife and cities burning — Kent State, Haight-Ashbury, Washington, D.C. What a mess people made of their lives, he reflected. At least he wasn't the only one. Even America, with all its vast resources and brilliant people couldn't do it right. He thought of Hudson, whose talents were prodigious. If he couldn't get a handle on the irrepressible needs of the conflicted spirit, who could?

"I thought you said I'd already drunk too much," Miranda said, still miffed. She took his hand and stepped down. Her pretty lips were pressed into a firm line, and she refused to look at him. Her face was flushed from the wine and the cool outside air. He didn't care about the stunt with the wine; he even understood her pique. He'd baited her with his comments about Don Parrish so he deserved her petty attempt at revenge, he knew. He was no longer angry, now mollified by her presence and the wine, which had been very good. He didn't want to let the evening end, and he suspected she didn't either.

"All right," she said, tossing her head in the imperious way he generally disliked. It suggested she'd won that round, and he was always sensitive to the notion that he was the one that held onto the past while she was emotionally self-sufficient. The last thing he ever wanted was to appear needy. He guessed she knew that and generally was careful not to flaunt her own independence, but now that he knew about Parrish, he simply could not let it go. The idea that she had any kind of intimacy with the man aroused something in him he didn't know existed – a muted yet powerful rage that Jack could hear in his temples at the mere thought or mention of the man. He supposed at the root of it was an unseemly jealousy she would find hilarious, if she knew. Jack had always been careful to conceal petty emotions. He was certain Miranda had never seen this side of him, and he wanted it to remain that way. In Jack's book, you didn't give a woman the upper hand. He prided himself in his noncommittal ways. It seemed to him that his withholding had always been the secret of his success: women ate out of his hand in those first whirlwind weeks of love and intimacy. However, he had to admit that his power over them didn't last. Before he knew it, they'd moved on – those poor wounded birds, and all his pleading fell on deaf ears. He knew he had to change, but he didn't know how. He thought of Gary Cooper, the Texan ideal, and he wanted to be like him. At the same time he recognized he was more a J.Alfred Prufrock, so fortified against rejection that he'd lost the capacity to feel the simple joy of spontaneity, the very quality in Miranda he most liked.

> *In the room the women come and go*
> *Talking of Michaelangelo...*

How he'd always loved that poem despite the fact that it concerned a pathetic old man whose life had consisted of incomplete and broken relationships. Prufrock had been afraid, Jack knew, but of what? Maybe of women and so much more – the fear of not being in control, of not appearing strong, of being misunderstood. Those were all fears of the miserable man, Jack realized and thought of Hudson. Perhaps Hudson did fear women. It would explain a lot. Long ago, Felicia had accused Jack of being a woman hater, and he'd dismissed that charge then. Well, maybe he was. You couldn't count on women. They came and they went, always looking for a better deal, a more successful partner, more freedom, more pleasure. He was sure he would never know what it was they wanted, but he told himself the subject was beyond him, as it was beyond Prufrock. He guessed that despite their claims to the contrary, neither he nor Prufrock wanted to be understood. Not really. And this Miranda knew in her intuitive heart that grasped those subtleties of human nature.

> *I grow old…I grow old… I shall wear*
> *the bottom of my trousers rolled…*

Similar to Prufrock, he would age and fossilize like all the other old men of a certain vintage, and he would look back on the desecrated landscape of his life and regret that he took himself so seriously when if he'd merely let down enough to just once allow one woman to reign triumphant — without resentment, without a false sense of entitlement, without feeling a bitter disappointment borne of the injustice of it all, then he might, he just might have gotten over all that silliness of ego and ignorance and shame and simply grown up. It must be what Miranda meant when she cocked her head in an ironic gesture and called him "clueless." She meant, of course, that he still didn't get it, and now that he thought he knew what she meant when she acted that way, it made him sad.

As Yeats would say, this was *not a country for old men*, this day and age of women usurping the powers of men, their own entitlement taking precedence over tradition and history and common sense. He had a glimpse of what Arab men held onto and why they hated the West. Just where were ordinary older men supposed to go in this new age of super women and overly ambitious young men? He felt squeezed out of his heritage and wondered if other men felt similarly, or was his anger merely the result of his own failure of will? Of talent? Of heart…God forbid. He didn't know the answer anymore than he knew how to change. He just knew that it was no longer a man's world and in his mind that meant there had to be a lot of angry men out there besides himself. The trick was to grow beyond anger and fear. The trick was to acquiesce somehow to the way things were or one would literally disintegrate from the unfairness of it all.

Those dying generations at their song…

Ah, Yeats… This was the domain of Miranda, he thought contemptuously. It was the realm of the poet to ponder life's paradoxes and cruel truths. It was not for him to contemplate the ways of the world but to render them in stories that were precise and true, unclouded by ambiguity and abstractions. He noticed Miranda had turned around and was waiting for him. She stood at his motel room door, eyeing him with a knowing expression.

> *And I have known the eyes already, known them all—*
> *The eyes that fix you in a formulated phrase,*
> *And when I am formulated, sprawling on a pin,*
> *When I am pinned and wriggling on the wall,*
> *Then how should I begin*
> *To spit out all the butt-ends of my days and ways?*
> *And how should I presume?*

Was he going mad, Jack wondered briefly. To be obsessed with poetry, of all things, was new to him. He hardly ever read poetry and had to be recalling it from college days decades ago. The fixation struck him as womanish and frightened him. It occurred to him that Miranda had somehow lay open the path he now traversed, as if her introspection had miraculously produced this alien fodder, poetry, and conveyed it somehow through the paranormal workings of her mind. Telepathy, of course, he thought then dismissed the idea. He definitely wasn't himself tonight, he realized, concerned.

Nevertheless, he followed her to the door and willingly unlocked it. The stench of overused air freshener blasted him. He turned on a light and held out a chair at the small table for Miranda, who gratefully slumped into it, stretching her long legs out into the middle of the room. She looked very pale, he noticed, her mouth drooping, eyes red with strain. As he put his keys and wallet down on the dresser, she fished in her purse and brought out a container for her contacts. In the dim light she deftly plucked out the contacts and placed them in the solution, screwed the container closed and placed it back in her purse. When she looked up at him with faint pink irises, he realized he'd never seen her without her contacts, not ever, even when they were kids. It was a shock to see her thus revealed, and for a careless moment, he couldn't look away. In certain lights and under various circumstances, Miranda had exuded a sort of ethereal quality, he'd always supposed had more to do with her persona – the esoteric yearnings of her substantial mind – rather than her unusual appearance, but now looking at the pale eyes and skin, the thin, almost wrath-like figure, her fantastically sculpted classic features framed by the tangled, wayward sheath of hair, he was struck by the absolute anomaly of the woman. Oddly enough, even in her revealed freakishness, she was beautiful.

"Tired?" he asked, sinking down on the end of the bed. He walked over to the fridge in the corner and brought out another bottle of Chianti. He saw her eyes open wide, and a gentle smile formed on her lips.

"Ah, so sweet..." she said. "I don't need anymore to drink. You go ahead." She stretched out her legs till they rested on the end of the bed next to him. Instinctively he reached down his free hand and clasped her little boot. He was reminded of when she was a girl and always so clumsy in the snow or ice. She'd grasp him so hard it would hurt, and he'd hold her tightly as he watched her little boots plod skittishly over the slick sidewalks.

"Just a little more," he advised, opening the bottle. "You wouldn't want me to drink alone, now would you?" He poured a little of the Chianti into a plastic cup, wishing he'd taken the time to buy a couple of decent glasses.

She took the glass he offered and looked around the room. He'd closed the drapes before he left, and the room hung heavy with shadows. She set the glass down on the table and wrapped her arms around her shoulders, sighing heavily. "It was quite a day, wasn't it?"

"Pretty confusing, all right."

"I thought Sam Levy was interesting, to say the least." Her eyes sought his, studying him. Jack felt himself squirm under her scrutiny. He waited.

"That man is a walking contradiction."

"How so?" Jack asked, puzzled. To him Levy was a type, the young, insecure, inexperienced boy on scholarship to a prestigious university, cowed by the authority and privilege surrounding him. Sam Levy reminded Jack of himself when he first arrived in the Big Apple or later when accompanied by Felicia to extravagant parties, he'd felt like an interloper, still the child of dirt poor sharecroppers in a hick town. There was no escaping your past, he thought wearily, and the past repeatedly slapped you in the face when you least expected it. He thought of Ann Hudson, groomed for her position as the wife of a world famous man, and he wondered, as he had before, that he didn't feel diminished around her. Perhaps Hudson had, he thought, Hudson who had his own genius to deal with, not an easy task.

"He's suffered so much," she said, reaching for the wine, "And yet he doesn't seem to realize the extent of Hudson's torment. I would expect more compassion from a man like Sam Levy."

"He has it for Joline," Jack pointed out. "He certainly looks out for her, don't you think?"

"Yes, he does," Miranda agreed, "But it's not the same as the depth one generally acquires from terrible suffering."

"Unless that suffering results in a perversion of love," Jack said, trying to smile, but his lips felt frozen and would not move.

"What do you mean?" Miranda's eyes, absorbing the color of the Chianti, were rose-colored, wreathed in the yellow light from the dingy glow of the lamp.

"Come on, Miranda, you know what I mean," he said, exasperated.

"You mean that abuse or whatever can cause one to be devoid of feeling or tending to hate rather than care?"

"Something like that," Jack said, not willing to discuss the subject further. What did he know? How was one to explain a dearth of caring in another human being? It was all conjecture, and it frustrated him.

"Man is born to love, not hate," she said — dismissively, it seemed to Jack in his wine-dulled state.

"If he's shown how," Jack corrected her. "If someone loves him. You don't know Levy's situation. Maybe he had uncaring parents, like… like…" She watched him intently, her face registering a pity he hadn't noticed before in all the years they'd known each other. "Like Hudson's parents," he finished.

"Oh," she said. "Maybe." She took the wine glass and held it before her face, gazing into the crimson dullness of the plastic. "Or Hudson's time in the orphanage could have deprived him of his potential."

"Like the rhesus monkeys in the studies on maternal neglect?" he asked, wondering if the famous experiment had been conducted at Yale.

"Yes," she said, still studying his face as if she expected something more from him. With Miranda, more was always expected, he thought bitterly. She could be so unforgiving at times.

To Jack, Sam Levy was just a kid. He had his whole life to get it right – to learn compassion or generosity or self-discipline, while she'd always been wise beyond her years due to her vocation and the unique plight of being born physically different. He told himself she didn't understand that most people probably had to make a concentrated effort to grow beyond being self-serving and, all right, *clueless!* You didn't get the impression Gary Cooper was compassionate when he shot down thugs on the main street of town and watched them die. It seemed to Jack that Levy was entitled to his hard feelings regarding his mentor. Hudson had not only failed him professionally, but he'd played mind games with him, resorting to a subtle, diabolical control over the young man. That struck Jack as soul murder, terrible beyond words. And words were the instruments of destruction, Jack thought. Well, words meant something to Jack; they were indeed sacred. One had the responsibility to at least try to get them right and true. For that beyond all else, Jack faulted the eminent Theodore Hudson, and he wondered if words had been part of the game he employed at home in the warm comfort of the house on Whitney.

"Levy isn't dishonest, though," Jack observed. He was watching her face closely as her features seemed to disappear into her own psychological terrain, one he couldn't visualize or understand, so he merely waited, seemingly recovered from the impatience of a lifetime.

He didn't know if she'd heard him. He could hear the repetitive rumble of the traffic outside and the monotonous hum of the old fridge. His mind drifted to the earnest face of Levy sitting in the restaurant, his tendency to avoid eye contact and the bluntness of his claims. Jack had trusted the man, and he still did. There was the ring of truth to his account; it jibed with what Joline had said and what Jack observed. Yet, he mused, it was unusual for Miranda to hint at another's shortcomings, as she seemed to be doing with Levy.

"Impartial truths are sometimes the greatest lies of all," Miranda said, her eyes focusing on him at last.

"Only if the rest of the story was intentionally withheld," Jack countered, thinking of Levy's acknowledgement of the donated kidney. "I don't think Levy withheld the truth, do you?"

"Maybe," she said, her face inscrutable.

"But why would he do that?" Jack pressed.

"To protect Joline."

"From what?" Jack thought of Joline's quiet strength, her sturdy physical presence, her brilliance, and he couldn't buy that concept. Levy spoke the truth, as far as Jack was concerned, and that was that.

"Why is she in Las Vegas?" Miranda had poured herself more wine and now looked at the glass with the faded stare he associated with her insights.

"Maybe she got out of Dodge before Yvonne got her," Jack joked. It wasn't a funny comment and was met with silence. Miranda continued to stare at the wine glass, moving it lightly in her fingers.

"How about to get an abortion?" Miranda said tonelessly.

"Give me a break!" Jack sputtered, angry at Miranda for suggesting the idea. In his mind's eye he saw the girl, her round, open face, her truthful observations, her blind loyalty to the man who'd recognized her brilliance. Street smart, she wouldn't fool easily, he thought, trying to consider Miranda's suggestion rather than dismiss it without consideration. But it was insane, wasn't it? Yet Miranda had talked to her...

"Did she tell you that?"

"No."

"Then where on earth did you get that idea?" he asked. He thought of the last time he'd seen Joline and the seemingly disoriented manner she'd projected. She'd seemed confused all right, somehow disconnected. Jack had thought she was on something.

"It would explain a lot," Miranda said, studying him. "It could be Hudson's."

"Or it could be Levy's," Jack almost shouted. He felt stupid.

"It's just speculation," Miranda said, but it makes sense to me. It's not the time of year to disappear from school, so late in the semester. Joline wouldn't do that unless she had a reason. Her education matters to her."

"You're right about that," Jack offered, "But you can get an abortion in New Haven."

"Maybe she was afraid Sam or Hudson would find out."

"Maybe neither knows she's pregnant."

Miranda nodded, her elliptical manner annoying him once again. He felt she knew more than she was letting on, and it irritated him.

"Are you holding out on me?" he asked.

She sighed heavily and looked away, beyond the shadows of the short hallway to the dark, indefinable cave of the bathroom. "Just let me work out a few nits," she said and rose from her chair.

"But the night is still young," Jack reminded her. "Don't go."

To his amazement, she wandered over to the bed next to him and lay down. She stared at the ceiling for moments before turning to him. Her eyes swept his face for clues, it seemed, to what he really was after all these years.

He found himself doing the same with her, searching her familiar face for the meanings she now embodied – after the disappointments that had knitted them and unraveled them, after the ecstasy and expectation that had once seemed their destiny, after the friendship that had lasted beyond the details of their separate lives. He felt he at last knew the woman, that he could see beyond the hypersensitivity, the seeming loopiness, the perspicacity that unnerved him, to the simmering heart of the lonely woman in the moldering motel in New Haven.

"Oh, Jack," she said, her voice quavering. She reached up her outstretched arms to the ceiling. "Where are we, really?"

He went over to her and took her in his arms in a silent recognition of their platonic relationship these days. He felt her slender, supple body respond to him in a way that was heartening after all these years apart, but he knew it was the wine and the fatigue and the uncertainty of it all that laid bare their separate vulnerabilities, and out of respect for her and the yearning for truth that hung on the dank air as palpable as their lost innocence they both yearned to regain, he did not press for what seemed an unwise intimacy.

Chapter Twenty Three

"Why don't you stay here tonight," Jack asked her. "We'll go get your stuff. That way we can cut down on expenses." When she looked puzzled, he added, "It's not like we have to be intimate. It's not like we don't know each other well enough to respect each other's privacy." When she still hesitated, her eyes looking off into space, deliberating his request," he said, "I suppose you're worried about what Parrish will say." When she still said nothing, he persisted, "Aren't you?" Why did it always come down to Parrish these days, Jack dimly wondered.

"Oddly enough, I think Don would understand," she said quietly. "You don't know him. You have no idea how generous he is, how much he trusts me. And anyway," she tossed her mane of hair and looked him in the eye, "He knows we got over each other years ago!"

To hear her say that cut Jack to the quick. He guessed he harbored a vague hope that she still wanted him, as he'd suspected for years. After all, it had been she who kept the friendship going by getting in touch with him. She still sent birthday and Christmas cards. Occasionally she called, slightly tipsy about a problem or just to chat. Whenever that happened, the years slipped away as they talked, and he sensed she enjoyed the conversation as much as he. They'd always been on the same wavelength. He had to admit she was still his best friend, and even during the years with Karen, he'd thought of Miranda, sometimes longingly. But he'd told himself they weren't suited, and in truth they weren't. She was too right brained for him, too unpredictable, too emotional, too sure of herself, too crazy. She could happily live on the edge, he realized, while he needed someone steady and certain, not someone who continuously asked the questions and never knew the answers or seemed unperturbed by the intellectual mess her own inquiring mind created.

No, living with Miranda might be exciting, all right, but it was fraught with a danger Jack felt he recognized in the disorder of her home, the lack of routine in her life, the poetry that simply wrote itself as if channeled by an unknown source, the manic vitality that made him feel old and sluggish by comparison. Somehow time had preserved her from the slowing down that crept over him like a rash, throwing him into states of confusion and entropy. When that happened, he'd have to stop and rethink what it was he was doing, then slowly regain his emotional balance and go on. For him anymore, confusion was a frequent visitor, but being with Miranda again reminded him that she rarely experienced uncertainty, merely plowing on like Don Quixote into the world of her own creations. It's not like he wouldn't like to be like that, but he couldn't and so he felt like her sidekick, and it wasn't how he wanted to feel with a woman he loved.

He thought of Karen and her sweet compliance, her willingness to suffer fools gladly, himself included, and her concrete approach to life. You might say she was a pragmatist, savvy in the ways of the heart and so tolerant it made you want to cry after the torment Jack had experienced from those who weren't — the women who always saw through you and demanded more and more till you couldn't begin to meet their expectations and didn't even try.

Jack sighed heavily over the sounds of traffic outside, over the humming of the fan, over the drumming of his own heart that he realized that very moment had slowed, awaiting Miranda's response, as if it really mattered more than he wished to acknowledge after all these years. He guessed it had always been like that: his waiting for her, he thought in a flash, chagrinned he hadn't understood that before.

"What is it, Jack?" Miranda's eyes were on him again, searching his face. She looked very tired and pale, vulnerable in her prone position and the thinness of her body in the shadowy bleakness of the room.

"Nothing," he said.

"Of course, I'll stay. We should save our money, and then you won't have to wait on me in the morning if I sleep in." It had always been a joke between them how she slept so soundly and late whereas he was up at the crack of dawn and hated to wait for her. She'd always claimed she needed the extra "dreaming time," and he presumed that was true for someone whose knowledge came from another dimension, probably visited in sleep.

Jack shrugged. "You don't have to. It's just I thought it made sense, you know."

"It does," she assured him. "May I have this bed?"

"Whichever one you want," he said, feeling his sense of gloom diminish. "I'll leave the notes I've taken from Ann Hudson right here, if you want to read them. And here are the ones I wrote up after the visit at the old house. Notes on the woman, Yvonne."

"I'll read those first thing tomorrow. Maybe we can go out there together."

"I think you should meet Ann Hudson as well."

"You're sure about that? You seem to be doing fine without me. She might not be so open if I trot along. After all, you're the writer she admired, you're a man and handsome at that. I might inadvertently create a wedge or somehow impede her openness. No, I think you should do that part alone, as you have so far."

"You're not curious about her?"

"Of course, I am, but I think I should stay away — for now, anyway. Besides, you have it under control; you don't need me."

"Okay," he said, relieved. She was right, and he appreciated her confidence in him. He thought of Ann Hudson and knew she wasn't the kind of person who easily confided in others. Once more Miranda had intuited the correct manner in dealing with the woman.

"I think we'd better get some sleep." Miranda stood and gathered her purse over her shoulder. She looked around the room and pulled back the sheets on the bed she'd selected. "Let's get my stuff," she said, heading for the door.

Jack followed her out the door into the parking lot. Clouds covered the sky. There were no stars tonight, just a wash of grey in the opaque blackness. He thought of Ann Hudson and her quiet demeanor compared to Miranda's boldness. It was Ann Hudson's reserve and shyness that endeared her to Jack, but it was precisely Miranda's spunk that appealed to him as well. He guessed the two women were so different from each other that they had little in common and probably wouldn't hit it off. It made him smile to think of Ann Hudson visiting Miranda in her home in Texas, seeing the endless bric-a-brac overlain with the dust of twenty years or more and the bizarre choices of art on the fading walls. Ann Hudson's disdain of disorder was evident in the gleaming order of her house and the absence of newspapers or possessions lying about.

"I'm on the other side," she said, leading him around the corner. "I just have one bag to move." And that was Miranda, too, Jack thought, imagining Ann Hudson would have brought several suitcases or a trunk. He had noticed her taste in clothing, a far cry from the jeans Miranda always wore.

"Still traveling light," he observed.

"Always," she said. "Clothes don't interest me anymore." Jack thought they probably never had, remembering her two or three outfits when they were together, although in those days she wore long skirts and nubby sweaters or tee shirts. He'd joked then that she had no sense of style, and she'd replied scornfully, "I dress to cover my body. Period." Occasionally she'd wear a sweater or top that emphasized her figure, but that was rare. "I'm just a country girl," she'd remind him. And except for when she conducted services in her black skirt and jacket with the white silk blouse, she wore jeans and a sweater, true to her West Texas roots, he presumed. At her request, he followed her into her motel room. On the bed table a huge bouquet of scarlet roses stood in silent majesty amidst the motel squalor. Miranda rapidly threw the bathroom articles into the bag and handed it to Jack. "I have to take these," she said, turning her back on him and gingerly drawing the bouquet into her arms. It was an awkward bundle, but she managed it expertly, smelling the roses as she left, and followed Jack out of the room.

"From Parrish?" Jack asked, and she nodded. He walked ahead of her to his room and opened the door for her. "It's been a long day, all right. Do you want to use the bathroom first?"

"You go ahead," she said, placing the flowers on the bed table between them. The fragrance filled the room at once, reminding Jack of his mother's rose garden and all the tending it took to maintain it. It had always been Jack's job to water it, and when he'd failed to do so, the roses had withered and died and his mother had worn the forlorn expression of the bereft. He'd felt terrible then and promised himself he'd never be so neglectful again, but surprisingly every year he managed to forget a time or two, and always there was the same expression on his mother's face — so sorrowful he'd felt guilty for weeks. He'd supposed then the sadness was due to the idea of something beautiful dying before its time, but he wasn't sure now why his mother had gotten so overwrought each time he didn't water the roses. Well, that was indeed water under the bridge now, he thought, admiring his pun.

He hurried through his bedtime routine, cleaning up the area and placing his stuff in a ziplot bag. He could hear Miranda talking on the phone and assumed she was talking to Parrish. Her voice hummed on the silent air, the bed creaked beneath her body, and outside a siren shrilled into the darkness. On Whitney Street, they were probably tucked into bed, resting from the day's labors. Perhaps Ann Hudson dreamed of her husband, not knowing his dark legacy, remembering him as a young man or as a first time father. Jack wasn't privy to the private grief she experienced at night, when the shadows stole across the room, ushering in a host of regrets. He assuredly did not know what doubts hovered beneath the surface of her confident claims. All Jack knew of Ann Hudson with certainty was that she was fervently supportive of the man she knew as her husband, the father of her only child. Had she wanted another child, Jack wondered, or was the burden of caring for David too great to consider it? Or was the marriage so compromised that she never considered the possibility?

There were so many unanswered questions, Jack thought, wondering how he was going to proceed. He could be honest or not, wretchedly informative or quietly withholding and thereby supportive of the man who'd probably manipulated the Yale faculty among others into backing him on a multitude of worthy causes over the years. It was his achievement that drove the massive support of the man, not his character, Jack was certain. People had willingly turned a blind eye to the man's faults in hopes he would continue the furthering of research, of great and noble social causes, of values so entrenched by the Right, that to expose him would imperil their own ministry. Hudson was an icon as no man out there today was, and the world needed heroes more than ever before. Jack told himself it would not be he that exposed the man for a fraud and hypocrite. To do so would violate something in himself that longed for truth and beauty. How had he gotten himself into this mess, he wondered, thinking of Miranda and her uncanny ability to move him to action, even when he wanted nothing more than to grieve or rest or simply wait till he'd gathered what little strength he had left to put one foot in front of the other till balance was once more regained.

Jack thought of Yvonne and the simmering tension of her sensual body, pacing to steady itself as it wandered around the decrepit house in the country. In his mind's eye he could imagine Hudson there, dying as Yvonne had said, in his love nest, beneath a nightlight. With a start, he realized the papers hadn't mentioned he died there. In fact, they said he'd died at Fleming Hall, alone in the middle of the night. His body hadn't been discovered till the next day when students and colleagues arrived to be stunned by the corpse lying in a pool of blood on the lab floor. It was then the police visited Ann Hudson, who Jack realized, had not reported him missing. It occurred to Jack that this very fact might be the sole indicator so far that Ann Hudson did indeed have some knowledge of her husband's illicit activities, or wouldn't she have been worried enough to contact the police? At the very least, the facts suggested that she was accustomed to his remaining out all night. Perhaps she was used to the excuse that he had work to do; maybe she even believed he spent his time alone in the lab at night. If so, she wasn't the intelligent woman he'd considered her to be. Jack found it hard to believe any woman would buy Hudson's story.

He finished cleaning up the bathroom. On the other side of the wall, the bed creaked, but there was no sound of Miranda talking. Jack walked back into the room to see Miranda with her reading glasses on, studying his notes on the visit to the country house. She was frowning, and her eyes were terribly bloodshot. "So Yvonne said he'd died there," she surprised him by saying. "I thought he died at the lab." Her voice had an edge to it, Jack noticed, and decided she was more tired than he thought. "I think I'm going to get sick!" She put her hand over her mouth and gagged. Jack thought she was going to vomit and took the ice container and held it under her chin.

"Don't worry," she said, weakly. "I'm not going to throw up." She made a pretense of reading his notes then looked up at him with anxious eyes. "I hope I didn't give you a bum steer. I believed in him. I believed in the vision."

"What vision?" Jack said sharply.

"Angels," she said. "They surrounded him. And there were all these people crying over him, praying for him. They said he was the greatest man of the century. They said he was a saint, that he helped the poor and ministered to the sick. They said I had to get someone to tell his story so that his good works could continue through others." Miranda doubled over as her stomach writhed in agony. She turned on her stomach and placed a pillow beneath her abdomen. He'd seen her do this when she was a young woman and her intense temperament had churned up worries she couldn't physically bear without a stomach ache. He'd bring her selzer or Pepsi to quell the heaving, but the process of quieting her organs often took most of the evening. He left the room and searched the motel grounds for a pop machine. He put in his money and brought out a diet Pepsi and took it back to the room. Miranda still lay face down on the bed with the pillow beneath her stomach. Her face was paler than before, and driblets of saliva ran out of the corners of her mouth.

Gently he pulled her up from her prone position and held the can so that the Pepsi dribbled slowly into her mouth. She let him help her and when finally she belched a few times, she took the can herself and finished it. "Oh, Jack, I'll never forgive myself if I was wrong about the man," she said, tears filling her bloodshot eyes and flowing down her cheeks, smearing her makeup. "I mean, he *came* to me!" Her face revealed so much bafflement and vulnerability that Jack felt a surge of protectiveness. It was a rare thing for Miranda to doubt herself, and that she clearly did right now held its own unique charm.

"Ah, Babe," he said, soothing her with his arms around her shoulders, still hearing her furious heartbeat and feeling her tears gush down her face next to his. He had never seen her so broken, and he rushed to dispel the disappointment and frustration and probably most of all, the sense of being wrong, something so hard for Miranda, who had such certitude, such faith in her powers that being wrong constituted nothing short of a crisis. "We'll make it right," he said, surprised by his own words. Some things simply could not be made right, Jack knew as certainly as Miranda knew her god and her powers. That people made incomprehensible decisions and terrible mistakes was not new to Jack, and he recognized that even as he spoke, he didn't mean what he said. In a flash he thought of Joline and her words: *Things are not always what they seem...* Perhaps the truth was hidden in the saga of the man. Maybe he and Miranda simply had to look deeper and keep their minds open. Maybe there was more to the story that would somehow exonerate Hudson and restore some dignity to their quest. He hoped so.

"I'll never forgive myself if I've led you into something sordid and... and..." Her eyes were slits of venom, he thought, darkened by anger and recrimination, "and ... and... *evil*!" She spat out the word as if disgorging a noxious food.

"There... there...," he said, pulling her back into his arms to avoid the sight of her distorted face. It was not the one he knew and loved but one possessed of a dark and cunning force that truly alarmed Jack. "You're getting overwrought. Let it go, all of it. You did what you thought was right, and it probably was. Keep the faith," he advised, as brightly as he could, hoping not only that his words soothed her broken confidence, but that he was right.

Later Jack lay awake, listening to Miranda's breathing in the darkness. It was slow and relaxed, he noticed, relieved. Although he could be annoyed by Miranda, he never wanted her to be upset. That she felt so deeply and passionately made her more vulnerable to disappointment. She'd always been a perfectionist, and most things came easy for her. He'd rarely seen her fail at anything, but even the slight mistakes of a lifetime troubled her, and she worked hard to avoid repeating them. Perhaps that was why she sought out Don Parrish. What rankled Jack about the man was his sense of entitlement. Parrish deserved to do what he wanted with his life but most people didn't have that choice. Parrish was intelligent and ambitious, and everything he did, he did well, from his tennis to golf, to speaking before an audience — something Jack could never do without agonizing over it — or simply shining at a social function. Always the golden boy in their youth, Parrish had unwittingly aroused the scorn of most of the guys Jack knew for his conventional upper class ways and his proclivity for always being right. It had never occurred to Jack that Miranda would choose him, and that truth stung Jack with its unfairness. It was as if she'd discarded the values she and Jack had harbored for a lifetime, as if she had in the process rejected all that Jack was. He told himself he was wrong about that, but the thought persisted, driving him into a frenzy of jealousy and self-hatred. All his hard won confidence seemed at stake when he thought of the two married and living in Dallas.

He got up and used the bathroom. He drank two glasses full of water and thought about Ann Hudson. What had attracted her to Theodore Hudson? Didn't a woman of her nature seek out a moral purity in her husband, or had she been different before the birth of an imperfect child somehow altered her? Jack couldn't imagine her living the unfettered life of a hippy or activist of her times then, but maybe he was wrong and she had indeed surrendered to the wantonness of the sixties. Jack knew many whose conventional lives and fortunes belied their dissipated pasts.

And then there was Joline, he thought, whose life had been marked by neglect and disorder, and yet she had risen above her birthright as surely as had Hudson. That had to be the bond between them, Jack surmised — the fact that both of them were orphans of neglect. Their extraordinary minds had set them apart so that in the end they listened to their own voices to propel them forward in the world. He wondered about Joline and if Miranda was right about her needing an abortion. And if so, whose child was it? It repelled him to think it might be Hudson's, but on some level he felt it was. He recalled how her face lit up at the mention of the man. She adored him, it was clear. Sam Levy loved her, but that didn't mean a thing if she were smitten by the professor. Jack understood how Levy could hate Hudson if he knew Hudson had seduced the girl. There was a sense of moral purity about Levy. He was a man of convictions, Jack was sure. The man might make mistakes but in the end he would do the right thing.

He smelled the roses and thought about the past, silly things like the corsage he'd bought her for their first prom, the dusty road they walked to school each day, his mother's tired reticence. He wanted to make things right— now, before it was too late. Mortality weighed on him like a lead mantle. He had countless regrets he couldn't seem to discard. They were part of him and as such he reckoned they would remain till he died and passed on. He tried to imagine what it would be like — dying — and decided it would be a blessed release. From himself, from all the mistakes and the grievances and the endless remorse. He might feel as light as a feather without all that baggage that flattened him more each day he lived and toiled with so little satisfaction. He felt like waking Miranda to ask her if she ever felt that way, but he didn't because she needed her sleep and because she looked like an angel with the moonlight trailing across her face and the lack of care on her softened features.

He smelled the flowers and finally dozed off into a dreamless sleep.

Chapter Twenty Four

He'd been dreaming of West Texas, he realized, slowly coming awake to the sound of the television. He could hear Miranda in the bathroom, moving around, the faucet going. He wanted to hold onto the imagery of the wide fields of cotton and the mesquite in their gnarled glory, dotting the vast openness. All his life he'd wanted to get out of Texas, and he mercifully had, but the dream reminded him of what he'd lost by doing so. He guessed he missed the big sky, its flushed brilliance in the morning and evening. The fragrance of Miranda's roses washed over him, their heavy scent sending him back all those years to one late afternoon before Miranda when he'd talked a girl into going to the cemetery after school so they could be alone. There they had sat on a stone bench and necked passionately till suddenly Jack felt uncomfortable, and so did she. Frightened, they looked around, vaguely aware of an unseen presence. Jack could still remember how his flesh crept and the sweat drenched him under his light shirt. The girl's breathing grew ragged and irregular as they both spotted the mangled wreaths of roses and carnations, countless bouquets of dying flowers, broken tree limbs and sodden grass all piled into a huge mound of decaying vegetation. He could smell the fermenting grass, so sweet and pungent, it sickened him, but underneath it all lingered the powerful odor of the roses, reminding him even then of his mother's garden and his responsibilities. The girl and he had never gone together anywhere after that and when they saw each other in the halls, they'd looked away, ashamed of their fears no less than their forged intimacy. He'd learned later that she'd told her friends he was afraid. He'd felt shamed, but then Miranda had come along and he forgot how a twit of a girl could steal his manhood with a few well chosen words.

"Sleep well?" Miranda asked. She stood above him dressed in the plum top she'd worn in Leadville. Her hair was wet and sleek, curling around her shoulders. She looked rested and had her contacts in. There was no trace of the telltale redness of the night before.

"I dreamed of Sweetwater," he admitted.

"Don't tell me you have made peace with Texas after all these years!"

Jack laughed. "Maybe I have at that," he granted.

"It's not a bad place, you know?"

"Not a bad place to have come from, but to spend your whole life there?"

"It wasn't so bad," Miranda said, reaching down to smell the roses. She went into the bathroom and brought out a glass of water and poured it into the vase. "Aren't they beautiful, Jack?"

"I guess," Jack said, "If you hadn't just been dreaming about them."

"What do you mean?"

He told her about the girl and the sickening smell of the roses heaped amidst the other dead things. "I remember thinking of Mother's roses, my tending the flowers. Do you remember that?"

"Yes," she said. "Your mother loved roses, didn't she?"

Jack couldn't remember if she did or if the yield of the sweet blossoms had proven something to herself and others. His mother did a lot of things for show, he realized, feeling sad.

"Jack...?"

She still stood over him, looking down at his face. She had gathered her purse and the notes he'd shown her. She set them on the bed and pulled on her coat and hat. "*Let it go*," she said, walking toward the door. "I'll meet you at Claire's. I'm walking."

"Let what go?" he wanted to ask, but he presumed she meant memories of his mother. She'd claimed he had issues with her he'd long since repressed. He didn't think so. Miranda didn't know everything, he told himself. Last night was proof of that.

After she left, he raised himself up in bed. The scent of the roses was overpowering. He turned off the television and sat there for a while, trying to decide what Miranda and he should accomplish today. He knew he had to see Ann Hudson, but for Miranda the house in the country and meeting Yvonne would be a priority. He wished Joline would call. He wanted to be certain the girl was all right, that Miranda's hare-brained theory was dead wrong. He liked the girl and was surprised how much he wanted her to succeed with her lofty goals after the deprivation of her childhood. He wondered how a girl like that did it. To shed the sense of abandonment and sheer want and apply herself to learning had required a strength of will Jack could hardly imagine. And that she should establish herself in the foremost university of her specialty was equally extraordinary. Hudson had been her mentor, he reminded himself. Somehow Jack didn't believe he would have violated her, despite Sam Levy's contention. Theodore Hudson had been an advocate for the family. He certainly would not have condoned an abortion. Jack doubted Hudson would have allowed his own fetus to be destroyed, nor could he envision the two of them together. He didn't believe Joline would betray Sam Levy. If she did, then Jack was indeed a poor judge of character. He dismissed the idea and got up to shave.

When he arrived at Claire's, he was surprised to see Sam Levy drinking coffee with Miranda. It was clear the two got along well. Jack envied their easy familiarity, but then he reminded himself that he, too, was lucky enough to enjoy that camaraderie with Miranda. Moreover, he and Ann Hudson were getting along better than he would have anticipated. He felt that he had gained her trust and that she considered him her equal. It pleased him that she'd admired his novel and that she'd chosen him to write her husband's story over all the qualified candidates at Yale.

When she saw Jack walk in, Miranda jumped up and ordered him coffee. As he sat down with Levy, she handed him the coffee. She'd poured in the cream and brought him a slice of cake.

"Thank you," he said, smiling at Levy. The young man drank his coffee and eyed Jack solemnly. "We just had a chat about your friend Hudson. Seems he was awarded the grant he'd sought just before he died. A million dollars to finance the AIDS recovery effort in Uganda." Levy's voice was laced with bitter sarcasm. Jack thought he detected malice.

"So what happens to the money now?" Jack asked.

"It still goes to the Institute," Levy informed him. "The others, Joline, too, will benefit. The money will be well used," he said, his brittleness lapsing into a monotone. "At least, it will help Joline. She needed an up-to-date computer to handle the stats."

"Where is Joline?" Jack asked.

Levy shrugged. "She disappears every once in a while."

"But her classes," Jack said. "Should she be missing them? The work she does for the Institute?"

"She's never gone long," Levy replied. "Maybe a day or two."

"You don't know where she is?" Jack studied the young man's face for clues. There was more color in his cheeks than in the past, and he looked healthier. Jack wondered if it was because he'd quit smoking.

"No, I don't know where she is," Sam Levy said, looking away out the window to where a bus was unloading its passengers. For a moment, he seemed distracted then he looked at Miranda and smiled. "So I hope you haven't lit up since we agreed to quit the nasty habit."

"I haven't," she assured him, smiling back.

"About Joline?" she said. Jack held his breath, hoping she didn't intend to share her thoughts on Joline's disappearance. "Does she do this often?"

Levy looked at his hands. They were long and thin, spread out against the table top. He seemed uncertain how to respond to the question.

"Sometimes she gets freaked and just needs a change of scenery. Then she's off. I don't always know where she is." He leaned toward Miranda and looked up into her eyes. "Yet she never goes when we have something planned. So my guess is she'll be back tonight because I told her I'd take her to the concert at Wellington."

"How nice," Miranda said. "What sort of music?"

"The Slavic composers, of course." When Miranda hesitated, he added, "You know, Mozart, Dvorjak, Mendelssohn...

Mozart was Viennese," Jack corrected, "and I believe Mendelssohn was German."

"Sorry." Levy looked embarrassed. "I guess the two played at the Grand Opera House in Prague. At least that's what Joline said. She wanted to go, so I scraped up the money to pay for it. Spent a whole month doing overtime at the lib so she'd better show up."

"I'm sure she will," Miranda said, surveying the restaurant. She stood and walked over to a small woman of Oriental descent and began talking. Jack couldn't hear what she was saying, but the woman looked familiar. He was sure he'd seen her around the department.

"That's the secretary for the Insitute," she informed them when she returned to the table. "I talked to her yesterday, but she didn't know then that the grant had been awarded. It's the talk of the University today," she said. "Everyone's excited about it. I guess Hudson was indeed the gift that keeps on giving."

"Give me a break," Levy said and rolled his eyes. He retrieved his backpack from the floor and stood up. His long, gaunt body towered over the two of them. He threw a dollar bill on the table and ambled out of the restaurant. Miranda and Jack watched him walk past the outside window and cross the street. He resembled a chimney sweep in a Dickens novel, Jack mused, noticing how Miranda's gaze lingered on the young man, following the lanky sway of his walk down the street till he disappeared into the crowds.

"I want to go to the house in the country," Miranda said without preliminaries. I want to meet Yvonne."

"Sure," Jack agreed, "but without Joline, it might be difficult." He thought of the beautiful black woman and the sense he'd had then that he was there by her largesse that had something to do with her affection for Joline.

"Isn't she there all the time," Miranda asked. "I got the impression that was where she lived."

Jack thought about that. In fact, she had indicated it was her home, but Jack hadn't believed anyone could live in that hovel. He recalled the filth of the downstairs bathroom, the dank smell of the moldering walls, the rotting kitchen cabinets, and it seemed to him the place, like the infamous House of Usher, was destined to fall down around itself, as bereft as the inhabitant herself, who presumably sought oblivion over salvation. "I don't know how to contact the woman," Jack said, but we can always pay her a surprise visit."

"Thanks, Jack," Miranda said, taking his hand as they got up to leave. "You're probably paying a visit to Ann Hudson?" She searched his face, her discerning eyes taking in the set of his shoulders, the subtle sense of elation the thought of the woman aroused in him. "I'll meet you here afterwards."

"What will you be doing?" he asked, curious.

"I don't know," she answered, "but I'll think of something." She gave him the mischievous look he remembered from childhood when she'd suddenly take off ahead of him on her bike and dash down the steepest hill, frightening him half to death, daring him to follow her. And he always did, just as he complied this time. She was the one with the ideas and so he followed the maze Miranda's mind materialized till it all began to make sense. He hoped it would this time.

"We won't be in any danger out there in that place?" she asked. "We'll be there after dark, probably. What if there are other people there?" She watched him closely. "I mean, people from the lab, those we've interviewed. What then?"

"We don't have to go in," he said. "Don't forget, I was there at night. There was no one else around, except for Yvonne. If we see others, we won't go in. Fair enough?" He gave her the hands high sign, and she returned it.

"Until later," she said, getting up to go. "Same time, same place." She left, and Jack went over his notes.

He wrote down several questions and rehearsed them in his mind. Ann Hudson would be expecting him any minute now, but he had the impulse to delay the meeting. He walked out into the sunshine and climbed into Miranda's car. Today he was oblivious to the bustling traffic and the ubiquitous diesel. He thought of the dismal motel room and the heavy scent of the roses overpowering everything, like the reek of bathroom disinfectant in a sports bar.

> *In the room the women come and go*
> *Talking of Michelangelo....*

There was time, he thought suddenly. He stopped at the florist and bought a dozen red roses for Ann Hudson. He dismissed the thought that she might consider the gesture somehow compromising or inappropriate. She needed some token of their unspoken pact to honor her husband, so he obliged without compunction. The scent of the roses filled the car, but it no longer bothered him. He'd made peace with the roses just as he would with the paradox of Theodore Hudson and his inscrutable wife.

She met him at the door as she always did, the same endearing smile on her face. He never knew how to describe her dress since her fashions varied. This time she wore a black silk jacket with a short skirt and emerald green silk blouse. Her hair was swept back behind her ears with tortoise shell combs revealing diamond studs in both earlobes. With her hair down, she looked younger and somehow less constrained, despite the formal attire. She had nice legs, he noticed for the first time as he handed her the flowers.

"My favorite," she said. "Thank you." She smelled the flowers, then holding them aloft, moved away from him, making a pretense of surveying the porch. "I should have swept it," she said, pointing at the debris, "but time got away from me."

He detected a slight nervousness in her this time, but he attributed it to the flowers and let it go. Perhaps it had been too bold of him, but he told himself she would appreciate the gesture, and she deserved an unexpected token of appreciation.

Again, he followed her into the family room. A fire burned in the fireplace, casting an orange glow around the room. He sat down in the sofa and glanced at the now familiar paintings and through the opening into Theodore Hudson's study. Empty, it gave the impression of premature abandonment. She had removed the pictures from the desk, he noticed, and the portrait of her above the study's fireplace. He looked around the family room to see if she had hung it elsewhere, but he didn't see it.

"So, anything new in your research?" she asked, the faint tremor of nervousness now more pronounced than at first. She had taken great care with her appearance, he noticed, wondering if that revealed a new found self-consciousness or merely the desire to re-capture the past. Her hands on her lap trembled, the brilliant flickering of her diamond reflecting off the tired walls. Jack felt the urge to flee for some inexplicable reason, but he held himself straight and regarded her with what he hoped was equanimity. She stooped and placed the flowers on the coffee table before them. "Thank you again," she said. "I think that must be the first time anyone ever gave me flowers."

The statement, wistfully rendered, shocked Jack. "You must be kidding," he said, without thinking.

"No."

Jack felt suddenly very sorry for the woman. He must have given flowers to dozens of women. It was expected of a man, wasn't it? He didn't know what to say so he remained silent. He noticed she appeared agitated, and he wanted to relieve the tension between them, but he couldn't think of anything to say. The silence stretched into an awkward interlude over which the throbbing crescendos rose and fell. She stood up to reduce the volume and turned to Jack expectantly, her face composed.

"I've had some disturbing phone calls," she began. Her voice had become softer, more quavering, and her eyes shifted uneasily around the room. Jack suddenly felt something had changed between them, but he was at a loss to explain what it was. For now, her eyes were steady, as if willed to remain impervious to his questioning gaze. He had the sense that she was withholding something, a sensation he had not experienced until now.

"You heard about the grant?" she asked, watching him closely for his reaction.

"I did. Congratulations. The legacy lives on."

"You believe that?" she asked.

"Of course, I do. Don't you?"

She paused, choosing her words carefully, he thought. He was reminded of women he'd known in his past. Secretive women who'd fled to other lovers and other lives, forgetting him entirely, as he soon forgot them. Oddly, he was beginning to feel suspicious of the woman for whom he'd felt affection only moments ago.

"It could die with him, you know?"

"Theodore Hudson is a legend in his time. I wouldn't worry," Jack said. "His reputation will outlive both of us."

"Yale does seem pleased," she acknowledged, her hands still trembling, the magnificent diamond's reflection flashing on the opposite wall. "I'm actually surprised."

"Why?" he asked, stunned by her doubt. She'd always been so positive about her husband's achievements, his courage and candor. Jack had never detected any skepticism about her husband, but he realized that moment that something had indeed changed in her. Now he was certain she harbored fears that threatened her seemingly fragile sense of the man she claimed to know so well.

"The calls," she said, taking out a handkerchief from her blazer pocket and holding it to her nose. Tears had formed in her eyes. "They say such dreadful things about Ted." She wiped her nose and glanced around the room as if searching for something. Jack followed her erratic gaze. It was the frightened look of someone who expected something terrible to happen.

"What do they say?" Jack asked.

"That Ted was evil, that he corrupted young people. That he .. he..." She stopped, suddenly unwilling to go on. A brilliant flush spread across her face. She looked at Jack with a stricken expression he'd seen before in the faces of those told their son or daughter had died in Iraq, their son was a pedophile, their spouse was in jail for murder — all the horrible fates that awaited man. She looked away from him so that he could no longer see the agony and fear in her. Her voice pounded out the words loud enough to be heard in the extremities of that quiet house. *They said he'd led a secret life with a Negro woman he'd known since childhood.* She paused and lowered her voice. *"That would be Yvonne,"* Ann Hudson said in a whisper. *"And she is a devil!"*

"Who said these things," Jack asked.

"I don't know." Ann Hudson stood and then seeming to think better of that, she tottered on her heels for a minute then sat slowly back down. "Some calls are from women, others from men."

"How many have there been?" Jack asked, wondering if Levy had called. He didn't think Levy was the kind of person who would deliberately hurt another human being. He knew what it was to be traumatized and some true part of him would not inflict such hurt on anyone. Jack was sure Joline hadn't been one of the callers either. The only person Jack suspected was the amoral Yvonne, who must have nurtured a vile hatred for her rival all these years. Ann Hudson was right, Jack reflected, to consider the black woman a devil. Jack had never felt so repelled by another human being, yet he reminded himself that Joline seemed to accept the woman as a confidante, no less. He recalled the two women in the vile room and Yvonne's insistence that Hudson did all his work there, that he died there in that squalor.

"There have been maybe ten calls," she said. "At all hours of the day and night since the grant was announced. Sometimes I don't answer the phone."

"The last call was from a woman. She claimed Ted died at her home. She said he'd over dosed on a cocktail of drugs. That he'd choked on his vomit." She turned from him and held her hands to her face. "Oh, Jack," she said, "I don't know if I'm strong enough to take this. I can't bear the idea of David hearing these lies." Her body was wracked with sobs. Jack reached out his arms to comfort her, but she drew away and stood up. "Excuse me," she said, running from the room. He heard her dash up the back stairway and run along the upstairs hallway. There was the sound of a bed creaking and the sobs intensified over the chimes of the grandfather clocks and the crescendos of symphonic music on the downstairs stereo. He wanted to go to her and comfort her, but he knew he couldn't. So he remained on the downstairs sofa while the shadows darkened the room and the outside landscape dimmed to blackness. From far away he heard ambulance sirens and the drone of rush hour traffic, and still he could not leave. He thought of Miranda waiting at Claire's, her anger and disappointment growing by the minute, and still he could not leave the woman to her misery.

At last, the doorbell rang, and when he answered it, a bus driver stood behind David's wheelchair. He handed over the contraption to Jack, who gently steered it into the house.

"Where's Mother?" the boy asked.

"She's lying down," Jack told him. "She's had a hard day."

You can go," the boy said to Jack. "I'll see to it she's okay." With that, David rolled the wheelchair to the elevator and went upstairs while Jack silently let himself out and made sure the door was locked.

"I thought you'd never come," Miranda said when he arrived at Claire's. Her mascara was smeared, and the lines beneath her eyes were accentuated by the light above the table. He could tell she was very tired, as he was, too, but he knew she intended to go to the house outside New Haven, where the man she'd bonded with had died a mysterious, untimely death. That infamous death had been concealed by an institution dedicated to the quest for truth. The ironies were too numerous to contemplate in his exhausted state, but he knew by the set of her brow that Miranda was bent on visiting the place and facing the vixen, Yvonne, whose image she'd seen on that fateful night of Theodore Hudson's demise.

So be it, Jack thought as he followed her out the door into the blackness of New Haven.

Chapter Twenty Five

"We can go now?" she asked, standing up and throwing her purse over her shoulders. She already had on her parka and the thick, red, knitted hat she wore in the cold. "What took you so long?"

He told her about Ann Hudson's calls, describing her behavior and the change he felt he'd noticed in her manner. "What do you think?" he couldn't help asking Miranda.

"She sounds upset, all right. The question is whether it's about her husband's relationship with Yvonne, which she might have known about for years, or the fact that the sordid information might get out and affect her husband's reputation and thereby the book she's so anxious to have written."

"*Anxious to have written*?" Jack asked. "I was under the impression she wasn't that interested in having his biography done."

"You probably thought it was because you happened to walk into her life, you a writer she'd admired, so she merely decided to let you do it because you are *you* — Jack Pierce."

He felt foolish and maimed by her acerbic observation, but he'd felt exactly as Miranda described. From the moment he'd first visited with Ann Hudson, he'd believed she chose him to do the project because she liked him. She related to him because she had enjoyed his book all those years ago. He now wondered who the con artist really was — he, Jack Pierce, deciding he was the best man to write a definitive piece on the foremost scientist of his time, so outside of his specialty and knowledge base — or she, the loving widow and supporter who mercifully didn't know her husband was a monster.

She noticed his face, the sudden onset of self-doubt, and she rushed to make it right. "Jack, I didn't mean she didn't like your book. I didn't mean she manipulated you, but we have to keep our minds open to the possible truths here, don't you see?" Something about the condescension in her tone, her more worldly view of life and human motivation, smote him with its validity and recalled for him his own miserable naiveté. He'd always been a dreamer, would always be. For one happy interlude, he'd felt he could do this project, and now he felt defeated again, lost in his own morass of failure and misjudgment. He knew if Miranda hadn't been there, peering at him so intently, always so careful of his feelings, that he'd have broken down and cried, so destroyed did he feel right now.

Instead he put on a face to meet her knowing pronouncements about him and Hudson and all worldly issues which dreamers like himself never understood sufficiently. Without missing a heartbeat, he put his own wretched ego on the back burner and steeled himself for the evening with Miranda. For the moment she was his only guide on the murky search for the truth of Theodore Hudson, and so he decided to embrace the effort with dignity.

"Let's go," he said, leading the way to the car.

It was a long time before either spoke. The quiet hum of the engine rose up between them, a treasured barrier to further intimacy. He reminded himself that she had said what she did, as a mother would do, to assist him in his pursuit. If he'd allowed his need for Ann Hudson's acceptance of him to get in the way of honesty in his work, then that would have been a terrible mistake. Yet recognizing the good behind Miranda's motives, he felt no better. Sometimes the truth was too hard to bear when ones very self was at stake. Couldn't she for once resist the impulse to put him in his place, when by so doing she'd reduced him as a man? It seemed to Jack in his hurt and frustration that a man's perspective is what Miranda lacked, and that Don Parrish or any other man would ultimately feel cowed by her uncanny knowledge of the inner workings of things. Sometimes a man needed to feel in charge, for God's sake. But with Miranda around the chances were that wouldn't happen. She was possessed of a rare certainty that wasn't likely to desert her.

They drove through the bustling chaos of New Haven out into the country where the traffic lessened and the serpentine roads demanded a reduction of speed and constant vigilance. Miranda turned on the radio to a country western station out of Meriden, and they both listened, calmed by the easy predictability of the genre. "So will it come out that Hudson died in that ignominious place, do you think?" Miranda's eyes darted everywhere, Jack noticed. She didn't want to miss any details of the dark countryside.

"I don't see how they can keep it a secret for long," Jack said. "It wasn't known drugs were involved either. Go figure."

"Who do you suppose was responsible for suppressing the information?" Miranda asked.

"I'd guess Yale pretty much runs the town."

"I don't know. Colleges don't usually control that sort of thing, do they?"

"Probably not," Jack agreed. "There's a lot of crime here, though. A lot of drugs, I'm told."

"So who would benefit from keeping it quiet?"

"A lot of people, I'd think," Jack said, recalling the huge amounts of money the Institute and various Hudson enterprises generated. Years ago a group of philanthropists had established the Hudson Foundation, which had swelled into the world's largest international relief fund. Jack wondered that Hudson had been able to devote time to his scientific inquiry and writing with all the demands of the various charitable organizations his foundation oversaw. Evidently he had proven himself as adept a CEO as a scientist, activist, altruist, and writer.

"Hmmm..." Miranda leaned back in the seat and seemed to be thinking. She was no longer staring out the windows at every detail. "You don't suppose he had anything to do with Russian intelligence, do you?"

Jack looked at her in surprise. "You've got to be kidding. What made you consider that?"

Miranda had the weird glazed-eye expression that used to frighten him. "Remember that professor of history in Colorado who'd disappeared when we were in Boulder in the late sixties?"

"The one they found had returned to Russia? I remember. Boy, that was a story of intrigue, wasn't it? All those shady characters that surrounded him." Jack remembered the authorities had finally linked the Colorado University professor to the KGB.

"Maybe Hudson was a communist sympathizer."

"If you're going to go there, maybe he worked for the CIA. Don't forget Hudson was an advocate for the family. He lived the good life. You should see his house, his possessions, his upper class wife. No, I think he enjoyed American prosperity, even if he had compassion for the poor and the suffering."

"It's just a crazy thought," Miranda said, seemingly dismissing it. "I just keep thinking of the parents going back home after all those years, just after the fall of the Iron Curtain. It just seems a clue to me — of something."

"You mean espionage of sorts?" Jack asked. "It sounds far-fetched to me. An immunologist as agent?" He could hear the sarcasm in his voice and rushed to tone it down. Already Miranda arched her back in defiance. He knew that look on her face and braced for it.

"Something like that. You know, you don't know everything."

"But why. That doesn't make sense."

Miranda's eyebrows knit together. She seemed to be concentrating on something from memory. "You said he loved a black woman. Maybe racism in America was an issue to him."

"Or inequality of every sort," Jack suggested. "The poor who couldn't afford decent health care, the AIDS patients who were denied hope till he and others came on the scene, the throngs of hungry people worldwide who never owned a car or house."

"Something like that."

"*Injustice*," Jack added. "Some people can get pretty worked up over that issue."

"He was an immunologist to start with. Do you suppose he had a health problem that drove him into that line of work?"

Jack considered the idea. He knew men who'd become doctors because their mother or father had a disease that couldn't be cured, but Hudson and his adoptive parents had been healthy, hadn't they? He'd been an orphan in Russia; maybe he saw Tuberculosis as a child and wanted to eradicate it. Perhaps he'd seen his own parents die. The possibilities were endless, he reminded Miranda, but maybe she was on to something. He secretly doubted it; she was merely using her intuition, but Jack was listening this time.

"There's the issue of economics, too," Miranda ventured. "I mean, Communism and Capitalism. He might have thought it unfair that so many in the world go without, while the rich have everything they want."

"Injustice," Jack repeated. There were so many kinds of it, Jack thought. He guessed that was why he didn't let it bother him anymore. It had once when the question was who went to Nam and who escaped that fate, when Negroes were denied their rights and women, too. There had been a time when his mind was geared toward fighting injustice, but somewhere along the way, he'd bought the American Dream of prosperity and so-called freedom. What freedom was there really when one's self-interest diminished the potential of others? Over those long years since the sixties, the issue of injustice had ceased to move him to action. The sixties aftermath had taught him how futile all activism really was. Man just kept making the same mistakes, and unfortunately that was never going to stop till the human species with all its conflicting motivations died out, and a superior one arose to claim the earth. Skepticism was the definition of growing old, he thought bitterly. He wanted to dream and to believe in something beyond his writing, but it was so hard. He looked over at Miranda sitting placidly watching the lights of houses on the deserted roads blur by her. She was more capable of accepting the contradictions than he. While he yearned to move on and make things happen, he felt paralyzed. Hudson might have thought he could make things different, but even he would have realized in the end, he really couldn't after all.

"Anyway, it's all food for thought," she said emphatically, brightening a little in her tone. She smiled at Jack from across the car and put her hand over his. "Yeah, life isn't easy for anyone, is it?" The gentleness in her inflection told him she'd rethought her words of earlier and that she was sorry in her own way, Miranda, who rarely admitted she'd erred.

They rode in silence through the winding roads till he found the house set back from the road, framed by dark scrub pine. There were no cars outside. Jack wondered if Yvonne was home, but he guessed she was because the light in her upstairs window was on and the frame open slightly to the cold air. From the car they both watched the window for a while till they saw a dark figure move across the exposed opening. "Let's go," Miranda said, hopping out of the car before Jack could say a word. Something about the dark beauty made him feel afraid to go in, but true to his word, he followed Miranda up the stairs to the weather-beaten door. They stood for a few moments, surveying the yard and listening then Miranda pressed the doorbell. They waited several moments and no one answered. The house was as still as death. Jack put his head to the door, listening. Nothing. He could hear no traffic sounds, not even the creaking of branches overhead or birds wailing. There was no wind, no rain, nothing.

"Kind of eerie, don't you think?" Miranda said, ringing the doorbell again. They could hear its muted sound from beyond the door, but no other noises broke the dead silence of the place. Before Jack could stop her, she softly pushed open the unlocked door. It gave off a popping sound that broke the silence. Both waited, frozen at the foot of the stairs. In the pale light from the door's small window Miranda looked like a lovely ghost. He stepped over and put his arms around her, waiting.

From upstairs came the sound of weeping — loud, insistent. It sounded as if someone were moving around, someone unsteady on her feet. Then the weeping changed to loud, deep groans as of someone in unbearable pain. Without thinking, Jack raced up the stairs ahead of Miranda. He followed the sounds to the door at the end of the hall where he'd met Yvonne the night he visited with Joline. He noted the peeling paint of the hallway, the smell of filth and neglect, the absence of adornment. A sliver of light shone from under the doorway. He walked up to the door and stood outside, straining to hear. Again, he heard the terrible groans, louder and more frightening than before. He touched the doorknob and waited a moment, but when the groan came again, echoing throughout the old house, he thrust the door ajar and went inside.

What he saw then he would never forget. Behind him Miranda stared with her mouth open in horror, tears filling her eyes and immediately splashing down her cheeks.

"My God!" she said. She clasped her hands together as if in prayer and moved her lips to some incantation that Jack recognized from long ago.

Blood tracked the carpet near the bed and spread in huge, gruesome patches to the hallway. Jack followed the grisly trail to the bathroom next door. There in the moonlight stood the dark figure of a woman, leaning over the sink, vomiting. Jack ran to her side.

"Yvonne?"

She turned to him with unseeing eyes. Her clothes were drenched in blood, her face discolored, her beautiful teeth stained with the substance. Blood filled the room. It covered the ancient tiles, the toilet seat, the sink over which she hovered, vomiting more into the receptacle as Jack watched helplessly. Her bloody hands held sheets of scarlet paper towels to her nose. While he watched, she moved over to the toilet, which was running and vomited again and again, her body wrenching violently. The groaning intensified, and before Jack could announce his presence, she fell to the floor, unconscious.

"Call 911," Jack said, dropping to his knees on the bloodied floor. It occurred to him she had AIDS, that she'd tried suicide, that she'd had a massive cerebral hemorrhage, but his thoughts were not of himself. His instincts took over, and he pulled the bloodied body to him and started to administer CPR.

"*Don't do that!*" Miranda screamed. "She has AIDS, don't you see? Stop it, Jack," she said when he didn't respond. He could taste the woman's blood in his mouth, smell her dirty hair, a scent of some terrible musk on her person that was overpowering. He could feel her breathing, irregular and terrible in its rasping efforts, but her eyes were closed and her body limp and unmoving. He continued his efforts, heedless of Miranda kicking his legs. "Stop it, Jack!" she screamed over and over again. It was all he could hear over his own desperate efforts, but he was helpless to resist the sense of what he had to do. He didn't think, he just kept breathing, as if to stop were to stop living. As he pumped his own air into her, their breathing became one process. It was then he experienced a sense of unity so profound it felt like he could cease living at that very moment and be lifted aloft by a presence that flooded his mind with brilliant imagery. He glimpsed a rain forest somewhere he'd never been but which was lush and beautiful beyond description. He suddenly felt a lightness, almost unbearable in its strange sensuous fulfillment. It was as if his body floated over the scene on the bathroom floor and watched closely what was going on, riveted by the details of the moment, studying it as one would a rare piece of art, dispassionate and analytical. He realized the sensation was as if he were writing about it rather than living the experience. Then after it seemed he had witnessed a lifetime in the moment, he felt a sense of inexplicable urgency. The lavish imagery of moments ago blurred and disappeared. The scene on the bathroom floor vanished before his eyes, and he felt a jarring sensation, like his body had fallen onto a hard surface. His ears rang and his skin felt sore. His tired bones throbbed with a searing pain. He was still breathing into the woman's mouth. Her body felt cold to the touch, and the blood still seeped from her nostrils and out the corners of her mouth. It emptied from the spread of her legs and pooled under him.

"*Do you realize what you're doing?*" Miranda kept screaming. Her shrieks filled the house, hurting his ears, but he held on, blowing and blowing till he could do it no more. Then in a fierce, shuddering spasm of every muscle in his depleted body, he fell down beside the woman and emptied his exhausted lungs in a long, drawn-out sigh that sounded over Miranda's screams and muted the violent beating of his own heart.

"Amen," he said, to no one in particular. At first there was no response. The house held a protracted silence while his heartbeat hammered on, swallowing the quiet.

He felt Miranda's arms around him, squeezing him so hard it hurt. "Oh, Jack," she shouted. "What were you thinking?" But even in his exhaustion, he noticed the tears springing from her tired eyes, the gentle smile slowly spreading across her face. "I guess you weren't thinking of yourself." She took out a washrag from the storage cabinet and stood before the sink, running the water. Then she took the washrag and knelt down beside him and placed his head in her arms and carefully washed him off. She did this several times while he lay still as death beside the woman, watching her. He didn't know if she was dead, but he could see no sign of her breathing. The blood that covered much of her face had started to cake and darken. There were several patches where the blood had worn off onto his own face, and the cleared spaces, he noticed were an unusual color, like raw umber rather than the rich bronze hue he remembered from that one night.

"I think she's dead," Miranda said, still ministering to him. He could see spiders crawling across the bathroom ceiling and dark mold spots in the corners. Webs stretched their silken threads from the light bulb and shower curtain and fell in gossamer strands down the hall. Lying there, he smelled the congealing blood, like meat cooking, and the faint odor of smoke in the walls. The smell of filth had always sickened him, but curiously it did not now. Instead he experienced a strange indifference as if he were accustomed to it, like a worker in a landfill or a coroner. This was the body triumphant, he thought, in dazed recognition. This was unglorified death.

The only emperor is the emperor of ice cream...

"Can you get up?" Miranda asked. She had thrown the washrag in the sink after cleaning his hands and face. Blood stained his clothes and shoes and he could feel its stickiness in his hair. He slowly raised himself up on his hands then sat up and finally stood. His legs quivered under him, but he kept putting one foot in front of the other till he was out of the bathroom and down the hall. His legs buckled on the first step downward, but he grabbed the chair rail for support. By the time he reached the downstairs, he had begun to breathe normally, his lungs filling up, his chest rising and falling. A curious sense of well being settled over him as he briefly sat at the broken kitchen table and waited for the police. From far off, he could hear the sirens coming closer.

After a few minutes, Miranda came downstairs. "I found this in the bedroom," she said, handing him a box. Jack took it from her and opened it. Inside was a typed manuscript. It had no title, and Jack couldn't tell who'd written it or what genre it was. Perhaps it was a memoir or maybe fiction in the first person point of view. He read a few paragraphs then gave up. "I'll take it with us," she said, walking toward the door. "It might help with our project."

"Anything else we should take?" Jack asked. "If we don't grab it now, the police will confiscate it, and we won't be able to use it."

"I'll check upstairs, if you'll run this out to the car." Miranda ran upstairs. As he walked out the door, he could hear her rummaging through the drawers in Yvonne's bedroom. He walked out to the car and put the box in the back of the SUV under a pile of Miranda's clothing. If the police searched the car, they would find it, but it was worth the risk. Jack could always claim Yvonne had given it to him. It occurred to him the car was parked a suspicious distance from the house, so he moved it closer. He had just gotten out of the car and returned to the house when the police arrived. He watched them drive onto the property from his perch at the top of the porch. An ambulance followed. Its attendants ran up the porch stairs with a stretcher.

"Where is the woman?" one of the men demanded.

"Upstairs," Jack answered, "but I think she's dead." He moved aside for them and followed the police into the house. The three ambulance attendants ran up the stairs and the police remained in the hall.

"She's in the bathroom at the end of the hall," Jack shouted as they opened the door to Yvonne's apartment. Miranda stood on the landing watching the men enter then slowly descended the stairs. She had a canvas bag over her shoulder which he presumed contained some of Yvonne's things.

The police waited in the downstairs hall. Jack followed them into the living room. The room was in the same state of squalor Jack had experienced the first time he visited the house. It reeked of various foul smells he couldn't identify. He sat down in the soiled sofa by the window and looked out at the dark shadows of the trees surrounding the house. The police lights were going, sending flashes of red and white around the yard.

"We need to make a report," one of the officers began. Miranda stole silently into the room and sat down beside Jack. She patted his hand and placed the canvas bag on her lap. She had blood all over the front of her plum sweater and down around the waist of her jeans. The soles of her boots were splattered. He reached up to pull back some of the white strands of her hair that the blood from his own body had stained. He wondered if you could get blood out of white hair.

The officers took their names and made a full report. Soon the ambulance attendants had removed the body and taken it downstairs and out the door. As Miranda and Jack watched from their seats on the couch, the ambulance slowly departed.

"We'll be in touch," the officers told them and took their cell numbers. Miranda and Jack left with the police still remaining. They drove in silence most of the way home. Miranda drove the SUV with a finesse he hadn't observed before. He still felt bummed out by the experience, the elation of the first moments of rescue having escaped and left in its stead an oppressive sluggishness. He tried to retrieve the overpowering sense of unity the moment of moving as one with that other corporeal form had achieved, but he couldn't. The ghastly scene in the bathroom kept coming to mind, and he'd banish it as best he could but he couldn't indefinitely. The sight of the blood and the horror of self-destruction washed over him in a terrible agony. He didn't want to talk about it with Miranda and looking at her out of the corner of her eyes, seeing her sweetness in the faint light, made him feel responsible for the sordid experience. He knew she wouldn't be able to let it go easily. She took all kinds of suffering to heart, but still tenaciously maintained a necessary innocence. That he'd been instrumental in a kind of moral corruption resulting from a dark knowledge that would never leave her, made him feel terrible.

"It's all right, Jack," she said, as if reading his mind. "I asked to go. I needed to know—"

"We could have waited." Just one more day and they'd have been spared the ugly scene.

"To look that kind of death in the eye is pretty terrible, isn't it?" She still looked like a ghost, he thought, so pale as if the life force had been drained out of her. Well, that kind of experience had a way of loosening one's underpinnings, that was for sure. For that reason, he thought of Don Parrish and granted the fact that he well might have changed after serving as a medic in Viet Nam. The ugly sights he must have seen while Jack managed to avoid the experience altogether with the help of Felicia's relatives made Jack consider the man beyond his memory of the boyish idealist, always angry at the world then for reasons, Jack was sure, had nothing to do with Viet Nam. His had been an angry generation, and he wondered now why that was. Compared to the times now, his coming of age years had been relatively idyllic, but some intangible energy coalesced into a movement that changed the country forever. Looking back on that, he wasn't sure what happened, and he wasn't sure he'd champion those same causes today. The world went on and on and on... oblivious to those who walked its soil for a short time. Jack didn't think man tended toward evil, but he certainly was fickle in his actions and shortsighted in his allegiance to truth. He thought of the war in Iraq, the seeming governmental failures that brought America into it, and he understood the country's bitter reaction. It still seemed there were superior ways to deal with aggression besides ground wars, but now he'd learned real fear when, in fact, he hadn't known it then. Driven by a false sense of empowerment and facile reasoning, he'd opposed Nam with something akin to messianic zeal. Now he wanted nothing to do with those decisions. He didn't know enough.

"I see a lot of death," Miranda went on. "I see the cold, inert bodies and I feel the absence of soul in them. They're just empty cavities at a certain point, and I know that." She looked him in the eye with a penetrating, unblinking stare, desperately trying to communicate. As in her sermons, she now had a riveting presence. She had regained her equilibrium, he reflected, and the animation that roused her to brilliant rhetoric in the small West Texas church had seized her again. "It's gotten to where death doesn't affect me, like it used to. I see the death in their faces, the absence of their spirits, but it usually seems fine. They've lived their lives, they've had their chance. It's the way life is. *Death happens...*

"But tonight I saw something I've never seen before. Something I can't even get a handle on. It tears at me and yet I still don't know what I saw." She was visibly trembling, but Jack kept staring at her, listening with his whole being to what she said so that maybe he could begin to understand it, too. He could still see her standing above him in the blood filled bathroom, screaming for him to leave the woman alone. He'd thought that odd, knowing her extraordinary compassion.

"A woman dying," Jack replied wearily. After the overpowering sense of unity he'd experienced then, he was now struggling to get out from under an oppressive sense of confusion about himself. It was as if the evening's nightmare had triggered a terrible doubt, not only in his sense of right and wrong, but in his own capacity to deal with life. He was afraid to acknowledge Miranda's trembling for fear the same response would consume him. He held tight to the canvas bag they had brought out of the house, almost soothed by her words and hoping she would make sense of the experience.

"It was much more than that," Miranda said. "Her vessel was not yet empty. I could feel her essence, and it was ... it was..." She turned to the side window so that he could not see her face over the mass of hair sticking out everywhere. "It was extraordinary, that's all," she said, at a loss for words.

He felt disappointed that she hadn't gone further with her explanation. He was relying on her to make some sense of the evening. He was confused and repelled by the memory more than he had been at the time. He wondered himself if he would ever get over it, but he didn't understand what he'd seen and why he'd felt so impelled to save the woman's life at the risk of his own health.

"*If you believe in evil,*" she said in a monotone, her face still turned from him, "*then you saw it tonight.*"

Chapter Twenty Six

Jack awoke early the next morning. The flowers were beginning to droop, and dried petals littered the bed table. Their heavy scent had lessened, overtaken by the musty smell of the carpet. Miranda still slept, her back to him, her body rising and falling in the stillness. On the table between them sat the canvas bag she had taken out of the house in the country. It was black with *Barbados* written in red letters. He hadn't thought of examining the contents of the bag last night. Then his concern had been with working out in his mind what had really happened out there and getting himself cleaned up. He had showered for a long time, cleaning his beard, washing out his mouth with soap and Listerine. Miranda had placed his bloodied clothes and shoes in a plastic bag and taken them out to the dumpster. She'd thrown out her own clothes, too, and washed her hair and body carefully. Afterwards, they had dropped into their respective beds, totally exhausted. They hadn't talked, both preoccupied and tense. When at last he'd heard her deep, rhythmic breathing, he'd been able to sleep as well, but he couldn't let go earlier. Now awake, he felt unclean again, as he had last night. Something in him felt violated, but he wasn't sure why. It had been his choice to help the woman. He might have been shocked by Yvonne and her gruesome plight, but the idea of her intimacy with Theodore Hudson was what truly offended him. He supposed that had more to do with Ann Hudson than anything else. A good woman, mother and wife, she shouldn't have had to deal with a Yvonne in her life.

He pulled out of the canvas bag a spiral notebook. Opening it, he could see it was a journal with pages of cursive writing in a bold, somewhat masculine penmanship. After reading the first paragraphs, he could tell it was Yvonne's. Also in the bag were three framed pictures of Hudson and Yvonne, one when they were very young and two on traveling excursions, one on the steps of the Taj Mahal, surrounded by begging children, another in Prague at the Grand Square. They were a handsome couple, Jack had to admit, exuding on camera an easy familiarity and lack of self-consciousness. Jack couldn't help but wonder if Theodore and Ann Hudson had enjoyed a similar relationship. He doubted it. Instead, he had the sense that theirs had been a marriage encumbered by responsibility and perfectionism. One could see it in the shop-worn smile of Ann Hudson, in her erect carriage and impeccable grooming, in the perfect manners of her son. Although Jack's heart went out to her for that conscientiousness, he felt sorry for her because in Jack's opinion it was such a woman who drove her man to another, less constrained companion.

At the bottom of the bag, wrapped in brown paper was a short typewritten manuscript. The printing appeared to be from an old typewriter with irregular keys that printed at odd angles. Jack flipped through the pages, trying to discern what the piece was. It was written in the first person and its pages were soiled and folded back, as if it had been read over and over. There were no markings that revealed who the author could be. Jack perused the first pages, noting they described an institutional setting — cooks, cleaning people, children. It was written in English with simple, direct language and recorded memories of the writer. Jack guessed it was Hudson's account of his experience in the Russian orphanage. He speculated it was written when Hudson was a boy, but the writer's precise age he couldn't determine. Almost lost in one corner of the bag were two small pieces of carved wood. Jack held them up to the light from the overhead lamp. They were figures of small children in peasant dress, one in trousers, the other in a plain frock. Jack turned them over. The carving of the girl had the name "Analise" inscribed on the bottom with the date 1943; the boy's had the name "Yeffem" and the date 1946. Both objects appeared expertly fashioned with careful attention to detail.

Miranda still slept so Jack decided to read part of the manuscript. Instead of glancing through it as he had earlier, looking for a paragraph that caught his eye, he began reading from the beginning. The paper had yellowed from time, and besides the soiling and folding of corners, it had some faint pencil markings in the margins. At the top of the first page, someone had penciled in printed caps: *EXTRAORDINARY MALADJUSTMENT.*

Jack read the opening paragraph following the penciled comment:

I, Yeffen Gorsky, of sound mind and character, do record this history of my life to remind me of who I am in the future, when finding my true identity, no doubt, will matter. Today I am an American by adoption. I did not seek this, but rather it was thrust upon me by caretakers who believed I had no other choice. Thus was I forced to leave the familiar surroundings of my childhood, my sister, Analise, and the village where I lived. Although Analise and I dwelled for years in the founding home in Bagen, we knew nothing better and were as content as possible under the circumstances. Our parents had died when we were small, of respiratory infections, we were told, and close relatives had brought us to the Home. There was no one to take us in since times were hard. The men in our village had resisted the Nazis to the last dying man and there was little food to spare. Analise and I understood the plight of the poor — we had lived it through our own parents — and did not resent being handed over to the Home. In fact, we thrived there until I was forced to go to America to begin my life with strangers.

Analise and I did not remember when we were first delivered to the Home. We were told I was two and she was four. Later we met some of our relatives who informed us our parents had died within a year of each other in their hut by the river. Father had worked in the mill, and mother had taken in sewing to make ends meet. Uncle Peter told us Mother died with her hands frozen stitching a frock. It had been a terrible winter, and there was no wood for burning. Both of our parents had been sick for a year, and their bodies simply could not withstand the injustice of that fierce cold. So many had died in the war that there were few men left to support their families, and the women had taken to working in the fields and factories and even some in the Home, where the cook herself was a widowed mother of three.

Jack noted the simple, smooth style of the writer. He knew that was unusual for someone raised in another language. It was obvious the young Hudson was a quick study, but what struck Jack most was the loneliness conveyed in the narrative. For the young Hudson, it had been a struggle to leave the past behind and part from his sister. He read on, feeling an overwhelming compassion for the boy.

In the next bed Miranda moved and stretched her arms. She turned to face Jack and seeing him reading the manuscript, asked, "What do you think? I just read a paragraph. Think it's Hudson's?"

"Sure sounds like it," Jack said, continuing. In the margin was the comment : *dirty little secret* in regular letters. He read on:

I was adopted when I was eight. It was odd how it happened. Magda came to see me in the morning after chores. She took me into the little office off the kitchen where she did the bills. There she seated me down in the worn damask chair I had never sat in before and fetched me a cup of black tea. It was the first and only time she had brought me into the office where she worked. Both Analise and I were afraid of her and her strict ways. We mollified her by carefully following the rules. Neither Analise nor I were ever punished although most of the children were, some of them very severely. Our parents had taught us obedience and respect for our elders, and that seemed to stand us in good stead at the Home. It would later assist me in my transition to America, where my adoptive parents were God fearing and demanding. In their case, I never grew used to the seeming tyranny of parents. It always struck me as wrong that adults should arbitrarily impose their own standards and expectations without considering the unique makeup of the child in question. All people are different, I have come to understand as a teenager, and I vow that I will respect my own child, should I ever have one, for his own particular personality, something I have not experienced in my American family. I rush to add that my adoptive parents have more than adequately provided for my material needs. It is only my soul they have wished to deny, but it is that part of me that feels so alone sometimes that I'm not sure I can go on, always looking back to the Home in Russia and remembering Analise and our short time together. I wonder if I shall ever see her again. My parents will not allow me to write her. Someday when I am grown and free of my parents, I shall visit the Home. They say you cannot visit the Soviet Union, but I shall find a way. Indeed I shall...

Jack read on about the experiences Hudson had in grade school and later. He was struck by what seemed to be an introverted personality who was curious and eclectic in his reading and academic pursuits. From an early age, he showed talent in the sciences, but clearly he was strong in all academic areas. There was no mention of childhood companions nor despite the brooding mood of the writing, was there any further criticism of the parents. There were lists of books he'd read on all subjects. The account affirmed Joline's claim that Dostoyevsky was Hudson's favorite writer of fiction:

Although as yet I possess no faith in an infinite being, it is still Dostoyevsky's compassion for the poor and his idea that man can will his own destiny by submitting to His will that intrigues me. I want to believe he is right and that someday I will find true faith which will martial my own unfocused will to a higher purpose. I want to accomplish much on behalf of the impoverished whose terrible needs are denied and neglected by so many Americans. America has too much; it fails its poor in its needless justification of greed. It is a self-serving culture indeed.

Jack could hear Miranda shut off the shower and knew he'd better get up. There was much to do today, he reflected. He'd be seeing Ann Hudson again and was concerned about how she was dealing with the calls and adverse publicity. He put on his jeans and walked outside to the newspaper machines and pulled out the day's paper.

There was no mention of Yvonne's death on the front page. Under Police Reports, her death was described in vague terms with no mention of her name, citing the necessity of locating next of kin before it was released. None of the sordid details were included nor an assessment of the cause of death. There was no mention of Hudson or the scheduling of an autopsy or inquest. Neither Miranda nor Jack was mentioned in the police report. Again, Jack wondered that the information was incomplete and whether someone or some institution was suppressing the information for its own purposes. It seemed unlikely and yet the deaths of both Hudson and Yvonne had been incompletely reported. Both had died in the same location, and yet in neither case, was the specific address cited. It was as if the house in the country did not exist.

Jack put down the paper and set his clothes out to shower and change. Miranda finished up and walked out of the bathroom, and he walked in. He turned on the shower and thought about what he had read. He recalled the little wooden figures and the photos of the couple. It all seemed to add up to a tragic story of a man whose genius had not been enough to protect him from the denizens of his past and his own failure to find peace in the present. It was an old story, Jack knew, the sort of thing you read about all the time, and yet it moved Jack in a way none of its predecessors had. Something about the serious, gifted voice of the young Ted Hudson in his adolescent memoir touched a nerve in Jack, and he knew he needed to take the young man's experiences to heart for some as yet unfathomable reason. He wondered what had prompted Miranda to take the particular mementos she had and what else she had found in the upstairs apartment that had been left behind.

He heard the telephone ringing over the shower and wondered who was calling. He toweled dry, dressed and walked back into the room just as Miranda hung up. "I'll tell him you called," she was saying. Beside her on the bed sat the open newspaper with Yvonne's death described in the police notes.

"Ann Hudson," Miranda said sheepishly. "I shouldn't have answered it."

"Why not? She might as well know about you," Jack said, wishing he had brought up Miranda's name before. It would have been so easy to have described Miranda's part in the project, but it had seemed silly at the time to mention that the idea to write Hudson's story had not been his own but the result of the paranormal experience of a friend. Jack could not imagine the seeming left-brained, orderly, refined Ann Hudson giving any credence to a Texas faith healer's visions of what happened that fateful night nor could he imagine what Theodore Hudson's dying state of mind was. It was too esoteric, too fantastic for anyone else to accept but Jack, who knew Miranda and who could no longer dismiss her powers.

"She sounded cold," Miranda informed him. "Maybe she was angry a woman answered your phone."

"Don't be ridiculous. She doesn't care one way or the other, believe me." Jack felt suddenly apprehensive at the thought of Ann Hudson. She had to be feeling alone and harassed after the barrage of telephone calls and the death of Yvonne. Jack felt certain she'd known of the woman all these years, but out of respect for her husband and son had not acknowledged it. To Jack that meant she'd in effect lied to Jack and her husband, and that bothered Jack, no matter what her motives might have been. He reminded himself that Miranda, too, had been less than truthful all the years she'd consorted with Don Parrish, who was married, even; and he felt disdain for both of the women. It was a matter of honor to Jack that one tell the truth at all times, and he prided himself that he'd done so with all his wives and women. Then he thought of Karen and his rush to assure her he loved her in those first few months of enjoying her hospitality. He'd known then he didn't love her, but he'd wanted to, even then. He'd told her he loved her because he'd sensed she needed to hear that and because he wanted to stay with her. He supposed all people lied to some extent and most could not or would not acknowledge it as if to admit such dishonesty were a violation of something grand in the human psyche. Well, man was not grand, he told himself. Man was ignoble, self-serving and weak; and lying in all its various forms was to be expected, so he had merely to adjust his expectations of himself and others. He had to learn to be more tolerant. He hoped becoming so wasn't merely a guise for relaxing his own moral standards.

"Well, she did sound miffed," Miranda insisted. "She asked who I was, obviously not expecting a woman to answer the phone. You didn't tell her about me, did you?"

"No, I didn't," Jack admitted. "What was I to say? Let me see, I could have said my weirdo friend had a vision of your husband dying. It was her idea I write about Theodore Hudson. What do you think? How does that sound for openers? Think she would have offered me the job then?"

Miranda said nothing. Her face turned a bright red, and she had the pained look he knew so well. He hated it when he hurt her like that, but even now it seemed to him as if she'd asked for it. There was in her question and in her face a rebuke, as if he'd avoided talking about her because he was ashamed of her.

"You just didn't want her to think you had another woman," Miranda said. "You wanted her to consider you available."

"That's ridiculous," Jack said. "That woman is so far out of my league I'd be crazy to encourage anything between us."

"Like Felicia?" Miranda said sarcastically. "I remember how you courted her behind my back. If she was too good for you, you sure didn't seem to think so at the time."

Jack guessed he had concealed a few things from Miranda then. By the time he broke off with her, he'd already asked Felicia to marry him. Miranda had accused him of duplicity, of wooing two women at once, but he'd staunchly denied it all. He realized now he'd felt a juvenile sense of entitlement then. He'd felt superior as a man whose needs were more important than those of his childhood sweetheart. It was his right to seek someone more educated, more connected, more beautiful. He hadn't counted on meeting someone as desirable as Felicia, so he couldn't be faulted. All this he had told himself at the time. He had been no more honest than Theodore Hudson, Ann Hudson, Miranda or anybody. What he had done was cowardly and dishonest, and he deserved Miranda's scorn, every last ounce of it.

"I'm sorry, Miranda. I should have told Ann Hudson about you. I just didn't know how to do so, that's all. Please forgive me."

Miranda appeared startled by his apology. It took a minute for his words to sink in. Then a slow smile started across her face. "I understand," she said. "Believe me, I understand. No problem." She shook her head knowingly. "I didn't expect you to tell her, not really..."

"I'll tell her today," Jack said, standing. He gathered his notes together. "Shall we have coffee?" When she nodded, he led her out the door into the parking lot.

When they arrived at Claire's, Sam Levy was waiting. He rose to his feet when they entered and went to the counter and ordered coffee and cake for both Miranda and Jack. He was dressed in the familiar great coat and combat boots.

"You heard about Yvonne," he said. Jack and Miranda nodded.

"You know she had AIDS?"

"We guessed," Miranda said, studying Levy. "We were there when she died, you know."

"You were? I didn't know you knew her." He studied Miranda as if he thought she was holding out on him.

"Jack took me there last night. I asked him to."

Levy looked from Jack to Miranda and back again. "You should have invited me along. I could have prepared you. I know Jack knew about the place, but I guess I didn't think Miranda would go out there—."

"That's nice of you to be concerned, Sam, but really I'm a big girl. And anyway, Joline prepared me to some extent. By the way, have you heard from her? Did you two go to the concert last night?"

"We did," Levy said. "She's back. We went over to the lab afterward so she could check on her experiments."

"How is she feeling?" Miranda asked.

"Fine, I guess." He seemed relieved. "She said she'd see you two this evening here, if you're available. She had some things she wanted to tell you, but she had a lot of work to do at the lab today."

"Was she upset about Yvonne?" Miranda asked. "I got the impression the two were close."

"Not close," Levy corrected her, "but they did have a bond of sorts."

"And what was the nature of that, do you think, Sam?" Miranda inquired.

Levy thought for a minute. "I think I told you they both adored Hudson. They believed in him." Sam Levy stared outside at the moving mass of cars then back at Jack and Miranda. "Like a lot of people, they believed the son-of-a-bitch walked on water."

"You said he did something terrible to Joline, but you didn't clarify what that was. Do you want to tell us about it?"

When he hesitated, clearly uncomfortable, Miranda reached over and touched his wrist. "He's dead, she's dead. Dead people can't tell tales or get even," Miranda reminded him. "Sometimes the truth matters and nothing else."

"You're still not smoking?" Levy asked Miranda.

"Clean since the day I made the promise."

"You don't look as pale," Sam Levy said, smiling at her. "Being clean becomes you."

"Thanks," she said, looking at Jack. His eyes were on Levy, a wary smile beginning. "Now, please tell me what Theodore Hudson did to Joline that was so devastating."

"He told her who her real mother was," Levy informed them. "Oh, he waited a significant amount of time, till she was his advisee, then he told her."

"And by then?" Jack asked, a dark suspicion forming in his mind, causing his stomach to cramp.

"By then she knew the woman and hated her."

"Anyone we know?" Miranda asked with a knowing smile.

She knows, Jack told himself, and sure enough, she did. Jack could tell by the set of her mouth, that firm, straight line it formed when realizing a truth she didn't want to acknowledge. He'd seen it thousands of times over the years they'd known each other.

"I really hate to say," Levy said. "She should be the one to tell you, and only if she wants you to know."

Miranda nodded her head sadly. "It's all right," she said. "I think I know who it is." Miranda spread her purse strap over her shoulders and rose to go. Jack stood up and reached to shake Levy's hand, but the other man didn't notice the gesture and remained seated.

"See you this evening," Jack said, turning to go. Outside the day was grey with dark clouds beginning to form.

"I'd tell you if I thought it was right," Levy said in apology to Miranda. She said nothing back but reached over and patted him on the shoulder. "There wasn't any reason other than just getting away that drove Joline to Las Vegas, was there?"

To Jack's surprise, Levy's head jerked upward at the question. He was paler than usual and saliva flew from his mouth. "What are you suggesting?" he sputtered then reached for a napkin and wiped at his mouth. He frowned at the two of them then rose and glared at Jack and Miranda. "Just what are you driving at?"

"Just a hunch," Miranda said quietly.

"You sure have a lot of those, don't you?" Levy said, frowning. This time he looked Miranda over, studying her face closely. "*Who* are you, anyway?"

"Just a woman who has a lot of intuition," Miranda said sweetly and started out of the restaurant.

"She'll tell you what she wants you to know," Levy repeated and sat back down. He watched them leave the restaurant. When Miranda turned to catch his eye as she left Claire's, he was talking quietly on his cell phone.

"So what do you think?" Miranda asked Jack as they climbed into the car.

"It appears something is going on with Joline," Jack agreed. "I don't know if your theory holds up, though."

"Could Yvonne possibly be Joline's mother?" Miranda said, a suggestion of doubt in her voice.

"Well, it would account for her getting accepted at Yale, all right. You'd think Hudson could have managed it, if he'd wanted."

"For a girl who might have prided herself on getting into Yale on her own, it would have been pretty disappointing to learn her parentage might have determined it after all," Miranda said. "Do you suppose Hudson kept track of her all those years?" Miranda eyed Jack solemnly from across the car. "That he knew her dire circumstances and did nothing, when she could have benefited from some guidance, a home, parents?"

"From what we're learning, anything seems possible," Jack said.

"Of course, she may not be Hudson's," Miranda asserted. "A woman like that, it could have been anyone's."

Jack thought about that. Of course she was right. In fact, it seemed unlikely Joline would have been Theodore Hudson's child. It was even possible he didn't know about the child till much after the fact. Something told Jack that had Hudson known earlier, he would have adopted Joline himself, but then he thought of the hatred Levy had for Hudson and that didn't seem right either.

"Levy did seem upset when you asked about Joline's health," Jack noted.

"I noticed that, too," Miranda said. She looked out the window at the shops of New Haven gliding by in the grey morning. She seemed to be working out something in her mind so Jack tried to make sense of the meeting at Claire's alone. Levy had indeed seemed preoccupied and suspicious of Jack and Miranda. Jack was convinced something had happened last night with Joline that had thrown the easy camaraderie of the three off balance. Jack guessed it had to do with how Joline had spent the weekend.

"You go see Ann Hudson," Miranda said suddenly. "Just let me off at the library. I'll see you at Claire's tonight."

When Jack showed up at the Hudson house, it looked empty. The gate to the backyard was ajar and leaves and debris swirled around the opening. Jack closed the gate and latched it and walked up the steps to the house and stood for several moments at the door before he pressed the bell. With the low cloud cover, the street noises were raucous and intruded on his thoughts. Since last night, he'd felt unbalanced. He wasn't sure why the sense of confusion had persisted, but it had and he was at a loss as to how to regain his equilibrium. He thought of the dying Yvonne and the waste her terrible death signified in his own mind. It seemed he had descended into a pit of dark knowledge, if you could call it that, and the awareness of it crept over him, unloosening more confusion and fear each time he revisited the scene in his mind. He had a bad taste in his mouth that no amount of food or drink would remove. It was a disillusionment he would carry with him for a long time, he felt, depressed.

Just as he was about to leave, the door was flung open. Ann Hudson stood on the threshold peering at him with steely eyes. As grey as the gunmetal sky, they showed no warmth this time, no acceptance, just a caustic indifference. He wondered at the change in her demeanor and considered that it might be due to the shock of finding out about Yvonne's death. Just how much trauma could a person bear without derangement, he wondered, recalling how she had insisted on the veracity of her husband. Jack was sure that Ann Hudson simply could not endure the truth of Yvonne's importance in her husband's life. That she might have known of the other woman made sense to Jack, but he was certain she never knew Yvonne mattered to the extent it appeared she had. Jack wondered what the police had told her and what he would need to impart. He could feel himself sweating in the bitter New England cold, but he suddenly knew he would tell the truth. It was no longer up for grabs. Instead time and the circumstances had mandated the truth. As Miranda would say, *the truth must be told.*

Jack wordlessly stepped over the threshold. For once he was startled at what he saw. In the hallway where he had first spotted his book, there were piles of paper heaped on the Windsor chairs and scores of full plastic bags scattered across the Persian carpet. Jack stepped around the bags and said nothing, following the retreating figure to the back of the house. Ann Hudson was dressed in black, resembling a woman in widow's weeds of a century before, her chignon more austerely arranged, without tendrils. Her jaw was clenched tight, and the high-collared lace blouse beneath her black suit suggested her Puritan heritage. For once Jack saw her as plain and without vivacity. The high coloring that to date had suffused her complexion had vanished, replaced by an unnatural, sickly pallor. All that gave life to her at the moment was an apparent anger she could not conceal but which seemed to own her utterly. Her voice was brittle and old, he thought.

"Just what do you intend to write?" she asked, her eyes boring into his with an intensity that made him look down. The house held an abominable silence. He guessed David was not at home. He sat down at the sofa as he had every time before and looked at her with astonishment. He could not believe the transformation of her features. She had lost weight, he was certain. The black skirt hung loosely from her hips, and she seemed to swim in the tailored jacket. Her hands were clenched at her sides, and she glared down at him as if she were scolding a recalcitrant child. "Just what are your motives, anyway?"

"What do you mean?" Jack asked, totally flustered. "I mean to tell the truth."

"And what is the truth?" she demanded.

Now that they were face to face, Jack felt the air seep out of him. He realized he'd been holding his breath on that long walk to the back of the house. He realized he'd been under a terrible sort of self-imposed pressure for a long time now – since he had begun to learn about Theodore Hudson. With a jolt, he realized how hard it was to suppress the truth. He had been prepared to gloss over it for her sake, to dedicate himself to idealizing the icon her husband was for the sake of perpetuating a myth. People needed heroes, and Theodore Hudson was one. It was an age that needed heroes, and Jack would gladly have spared Ann Hudson the truth of her husband's shady past, but he knew in that moment he could not have concealed the truth from her or anyone. He was incapable of that, he now realized. His only purpose was to tell the truth. Anything short of that he simply would not do. The awareness spread over him like a warm, protective blanket, buttressing him against the implacable set of her face. And despite the fact that on some level he felt a deep compassion and affection for the woman, this was not the time to compromise.

Chapter Twenty Seven

For once since Jack had met Ann Hudson, he felt in control. Later he would wonder why, but for the moment, he simply understood that this once he had unequivocally assigned his allegiance to Truth, and that by doing so, all other matters ceased to exert their trivial influence. He was his own man, and so he proceeded with the confidence it must have taken Theodore Hudson and all other pioneers of thought and deed to put aside their own narrow perspectives and surrender to that which transcended it all. In that moment he acquiesced to what had eluded him before and opened up his heart to the woman standing before him, doubt written on her lovely face as clearly and implacably as the sordid truths of Hudson's death rose in his own mind. He struggled only momentarily to find the words to answer her.

"Your husband," he began, "was indeed a remarkable man. A man for all seasons," he granted, smiling at her with the kinship borne of his search, "but he was a profligate as well. His death was sordid and terrible beyond imagining."

"Do you think I don't know that?" she screamed at him. Her clenched fists pounded at her thighs, only inches from his face. "Stand up, will you! I want you to look me in the face and tell me that is all you know about my husband!" Her face was red, a vein throbbed on her high forehead, and the eyes he had always thought soft and subdued blazed with fury and disappointment and scorn. When he hesitated, almost weak from the inability to adjust to the presence of this creature he no longer knew, she seethed, *"Now!"*

Jack slowly stood and faced her. He could feel the violent intensity of her presence, the pounding heartbeat and unfocused emotion, but he breathed of the air in that silent shrine of a house as if it were a balm for his own suffering and that of hers and others. He stood there eye to eye with Ann Hudson as Ahab must have before the mighty leviathan, and held his ground. "Of course that's not all I know about Theodore Hudson," he said.

"Then what else do you know?" she asked, her disgust as palpable as the blood coursing through the vein on her forehead.

And surprising even himself, Jack suddenly did know. As Jung and others had always said and he hadn't believed until now, he knew — without the specific facts to support his knowing, without the research finished, without Ann Hudson's own observations they had not yet thoroughly covered — that Professor Theodore Hudson was indeed a great man. In a flash of understanding, he saw a man moved to right injustice in the only way he knew how, a man devoted to truth as ardently as any seeker before him, a man who for the most part used his vast knowledge and creativity for the betterment of mankind. Hudson had blazed a trail that would be followed by others for a century or more. Jack saw it; he knew it.

"Your husband was the greatest man of his time," Jack said. "There won't be another like him for decades. I know that. His discoveries in auto-immune disease are just the tip of the iceberg, as you, no doubt, know. Because of him, AIDS will be wiped out by mid-century, as the scientists here at Yale finish the work he began. Perhaps you realize that he has left copious notes and files for others to use."

"Yes," she said. "He told me."

"And you know that he's helped a legion of young people finance their educations using funds he bestowed anonymously."

"He told me all that," she said.

"His foundation has combated poverty and disease all over the world, but most people don't know that he's seen to it personally that the most downtrodden have received the funds, not the fraudulent and the self-serving."

"That I know as well," she said, the venom disappearing from her voice. "That's why he traveled so much, so he could be sure the money really benefited the needy."

"Nor does the world even know how much his efforts assisted the starving in Eastern Europe, the legions of destitute Muslims from his native Slovakia. The poor in Africa, in Bangladesh, in India."

"How did you know that? Those efforts were secret."

"At great personal danger, he worked with the highest officials in our own government to end the dominion of the Soviet Union."

Ann Hudson stared at him with her mouth open. The color returned to her face, and she sat down in a chair opposite him. She grasped the arm of the chair and watched her ring glittering in the light from the window. Then with total abandonment she threw her head upon her arms and cried as if her heart would break. To Jack it sounded like the cries of a deep seated grief that had never before been expressed. The sound was almost inhuman in its departure from the standard sobbing sound of hurt or pain or frustration. There was a rattling in her throat, husky and empty at the same time. It reminded Jack of the wolves' cries deep in the canyons of Leadville. This time Jack did not try to comfort Ann Hudson. He sensed she required this untimely expression of grief more than she needed sympathy or compassion. For her the moment was fraught with fears she had harbored for a lifetime.

Without knowing how he grasped the unpublicized and undeniable facts of Theodore Hudson's altruism, Jack saw the man as endowed with a largesse of spirit carefully concealed for some deeply personal reason.

"Why?" Jack asked, confused, his emotions spent, his mind weary, "Why was your husband so bent on keeping his efforts secret?"

"You don't know the half of it," she exclaimed, lifting her head to reveal eyes that were red and swollen with thick streaks of black mascara marking her face, giving her the appearance of an old beadle. "He gave his blood. He experimented on himself. He... he..." she covered her face, her trembling lips refusing to voice the thought on her mind. She touched her lips as if to fortify their workings. "He injected himself with the HIV virus."

She bent down her head, covering her face once again. The grandfather clock chimed in the upstairs hallway. The light had grown dim in the house, and shadows were forming over the furniture. Jack looked out through the hallway at the leaded glass door, seeing the plastic garbage bags, like corpses, blocking the exit. He was reminded of David and his return home this time of day.

"We need to get you settled down," Jack said gently. "We can talk about all this later."

When she kept sobbing," Jack touched her arm. "Please," he said. "David will be home at any moment."

With that, she lifted her head and reached into the pocket of her jacket from which she drew a linen handkerchief. It was wadded and streaked with makeup. She brought it to her face and wiped beneath her eyes where the makeup had gathered thick and unsightly.

"Why don't you go upstairs," Jack said. "I'll wait here. If David comes, I'll tell him you went up to your room for a minute."

She smiled, a tremulous, jagged exposure of gleaming white enamel. "I'll just be a minute," she said, rising. She dashed up the stairs and down the hallway to the master bedroom. He could hear her in the bathroom, running water.

Jack waited, unsure exactly as to what had happened in this room. He was at a loss to explain it, but something strangely transcendental had clearly occurred. For what he'd told her he actually hadn't known for sure. It was as if that knowledge had crept into his subconscious somehow and then made itself known at the very moment it was needed to balance the wrong that might otherwise have been delivered in the name of truth. Jack might never know the origin of that urgent communication nor the process by which he understood it, but he knew whatever the source and however it was apprehended, this was the truth. A deep sense of fulfillment overcame him, and he sat back, numbed by the experience but curiously extended by it, as if he had pressed a torch into a hundred open palms.

He sat back in the sofa and closed his eyes. Upstairs feet crept around the room, but he wasn't listening. It felt good to ease back into the comfort of the sofa and let his cares slide away. He thought about the notes in his briefcase, about Miranda, surely researching this very moment in the vast archives of Yale University, and he knew she had much to tell him. He thought about Levy, a beneficiary of Hudson's altruism who didn't even know the extent to which he owed the professor for his future and his hard won independence. Perhaps this very moment he and Miranda were discussing this at Claire's and Levy for once had learned to see something he'd been blind to before. Jack's heart went out to the young man for his decency and honor and because he wanted to protect Joline, but his story of anger and vengeance was just one more testament to the fact that man made mistakes. Jack had been on the verge of a tragic mistake himself just moments ago, and the fact he'd come so close truly frightened him.

And then it settled on him like a lead mantle that *he just didn't know. Man didn't know.* If he could make the mistake he almost did earlier, then man was capable of worse ones, far worse ones, as a glance at history would attest. For the first time in years, Jack felt himself pray to whatever it was out there that saw beyond the veil. He wanted to be free of deception and illusion. He wanted to see the world in a grain of sand; he wanted to glimpse beyond man's suffering and error. He wanted to see into the human heart. All these things he wanted before he died, he realized in a flash of understanding that left him physically weak because for once in his life he felt a part of something huge and magnificent, as if to have been shown the secret of Hudson's life had revealed the very pulse and throb of human existence. He had a sense of the organic whole of things, of a vast, beneficent universe thrumming to an ancient chant, moving in its mysterious ways — timeless and infinite. It felt to him that moment as if he were back in his early days of college when he had felt that one central principle governed the universe, and that if he set his mind to it, he would discover it and lead his life by it. He'd long ago discarded that belief or hope or whatever it had been. Yet right now he felt the surge of that mindset again, and this time it empowered him.

He gazed outside at the old oak tree in the yard, its leaves brown and shriveled on the branches and littering the ground below. He watched a crow ruffle its sleek coat and peck at a worm in the yard. He saw the sun's muted glow in the west, spreading its light over a weary world, and he felt like the ancient mariner blessing the lowly water snakes. This was life as he knew it, and it was full of treachery and loss and uncertainty, but it was a good life nevertheless. Upstairs a beautiful widow paced the floor, still bereft. Across town, a church of black parishioners waited to bury a woman who'd died violently, her addictions and other transgressions quietly forgiven by a compassionate congregation. In moments a young man already dying of an incurable disease would arrive home, only to be reminded again of his father's untimely death and his mother's unceasing sorrow.

This was life, its essence broadened and shaped by human suffering. One couldn't avoid its ravages; one could only endure them with as much dignity and equanimity as possible. This Hudson knew, Jack felt, and this Dostoyevsky and Tolstoy and all those celebrated Russian writers accepted as facts of life. And this the young Joline and her friend, Sam Levy, had experienced as certainly as some more fortunate knew love and acceptance. Jack decided that even in his terrible and ignominious death, Theodore Hudson had known regret, for what was human suffering if it didn't center on man's awareness of his own limitations? Once again, Jack experienced the sense of the man, his heroic aspirations and his tragic inability to control his own impulses.

The doorbell rang, and Jack got up to answer it. Upstairs, he heard Ann Hudson open the door to the master bedroom and start down the hall to the stairs. Jack walked around the full sacks in the hallway and opened the door. The driver of the shuttle and he looked eye to eye at each other. Then David slowly wheeled himself into the entryway as Jack rushed to pull the sacks to the side of the hall for him to pass. Neither said anything, the steady sound of the wheels lifting on the air between them. Wordlessly Jack led David through the hall to the family room. There Ann Hudson had settled herself on the sofa, a magazine spread out on her lap. She read the page solemnly and looked up as David entered the room.

"I hope you had a good day," she said, closing the magazine. She got up and went to David, taking the handles and moving his chair to the sofa table.

"It's all right, Mother," David said. "I'm going upstairs right away to study a while before dinner. Nice to see you Mr. Pierce," he nodded at Jack. "I have a few more pages to write on my paper." With a deep sigh, he wheeled his chair down the hall to the elevator. In the silence they listened as the elevator doors parted and closed and David ascended to the upstairs and exited then rolled down the hall and disappeared into his own room where soon they could hear his stereo going.

"Excuse me," Ann Hudson said, getting up. "Something is wrong. I'd better check on him. Wait for me, and I'll be down shortly." She turned on the stereo in the family room and walked up the stairs.

Jack thumbed through a couple of magazines. He wondered if Miranda was waiting for him at Claires, but he knew she'd be okay without him. If she wanted to get in touch with him, she knew how. Without thinking he stood up and wandered into Theodore Hudson's study. He couldn't help but notice once again that the lovely portrait of Ann Hudson as a girl had been removed. Now in its place hung a framed picture of David along with a pair of Audubon prints. The study as a whole looked austere with its surfaces cleared of extra papers and files. It smelled of linseed oil and leather. It was meticulously neat with its absence of mementos and bric-a-brac and unmistakably deserted by the personality that even in its absence had formerly dominated the place.

"I'm getting it fixed up for David," Ann Hudson told him. She had walked in without his noticing her, and he almost jumped at the unexpected sound of her voice.

"Seems like a good idea," Jack said. "He won't have to go upstairs all the time now."

"Yes," she said wistfully.

"Whatever happened to the painting of you?" Jack asked.

She looked surprised at his question. At first she didn't answer. They listened to the quiet sounds of Mendelsohn before she said anything. "I put it in the closet," she said at last.

"Why not in the family room or the dining area?"

"It was painted a long time ago. A lot of water has passed under the bridge since then."

"Still, it's part of your history."

"Yes, but I'm in a different place now."

"I see," Jack said, although he wasn't sure what she meant by that. She still loved Theodore Hudson, that was apparent.

She sighed heavily. To Jack she sounded like her son moments ago when he wheeled his chair down the hall, absorbed with his school responsibilities and perhaps other concerns of which Jack was not aware.

"I have some things to say to you," she said. "Why don't we go into the living room." She withdrew from the family room with its familiarity, and he followed her down the entryway hallway to the front of the house into the dark living room. While he stood, she turned on two lamps and he sat down in a wingback chair by the fireplace and glanced around the room. He'd only glimpsed this room as he walked by it in the past, but it was lovely, too, he realized immediately. There was more artwork in this room, and the Oriental carpets were mostly red with dramatic colors of blue and green. He sat down on the Chesterfield sofa and waited. He wondered what she had to say.

She left for a moment and brought back a bottle of red wine and two glasses. She poured each of them one and left. She returned with a tray of cheese and crackers and sat them down on the coffee table and took a chair opposite him. Her hair was still austerely fashioned, pulled straight back from her face and knotted into a tight chignon at the nape of her neck, as if to deny her considerable beauty. Her black suit was plain, her shoes functional but unattractive. He had the impression today of a woman who had renounced her sexuality completely. She resembled an aging nun, not the beautiful and vibrant woman he'd come to know over iced tea.

"All the publicity is having its effect on David," she confided, clearly worried about her son. "He's so sensitive, it was bound to be hard on him. It's not such a large place that people don't know..." She looked up at Jack from her seat across the table ...just about everything." She sighed heavily again, this time taking a sip of her wine. "Oh, Jack, life is so hard."

"I couldn't agree with you more," Jack said, thinking about the events of the past few days. "David will be fine," he assured her. "He has a quiet strength, that kid."

She smiled at him gratefully. "You think so?"

"Clearly he does," Jack said. "I think you've done a great job with your son."

"We both doted on him," Ann Hudson said. "Ted was so proud of him." Her eyes searched his. She loosened the tight chignon, and the hair fell down around her shoulders. She suddenly looked much younger, more vulnerable. Yet the light in her eyes had vanished. The firm set of her mouth revealed how hard the last days had been for her. "I think Ted understood David, and David Ted. It was an odd alliance." She finished her glass of wine; her face was flushed. "You see, David knew about Ted."

When Jack said nothing, she went on. She held his gaze for several seconds over which the grandfather clock chimed its doleful refrain. "I mean about Yvonne, about the house outside New Haven, about the problems he had that he couldn't talk about."

The easy warmth of their relationship had returned, Jack noted with relief. The wine had started to banish his fears. "What problems?" Jack asked.

"You didn't know?" she asked, clearly surprised. "I thought you knew everything about Ted."

Jack thought about Dr. Kerkoff, whom he'd meant to track down but hadn't. Knowing Miranda, she'd most likely found out that information. "I knew about a Dr. Kerkoff," he admitted.

"Ted's been going to him for over fifty years. He was his pediatrician originally, but then he supervised all his care. When Ted first came to America, he was malnourished. His bones were weak, and he suffered from anemia. For years he had shots of various vitamins. Then he developed allergies, and Kerkoff helped him get a good allergist. Eventually, he developed Addison's Disease, which he struggled till his death to keep under control." She looked down and then above him at the oil painting in a gilded frame. "He wasn't physically strong," she said. Her voice quavered, and she set down her glass of wine on the coffee table and waited. "But he was all heart."

"Is that why you forgave him?"

Ann Hudson cocked her head, as if contemplating her reply. "You don't know the half of it," she said, repeating the phrase of a night ago. "Ted had some serious problems, and his Addison's Disease was the least of them."

"What do you mean?" Jack asked. "Addison's is pretty serious."

"Believe me, I know that. But what afflicted him the most was that which affected his brain, his will, his *intention*. You see," she said, "his plans meant everything to him. Oh, he had such hopes..." Her eyes were glassy as she looked past him into her own world. "Night and day that's what he thought about. His ideals totally absorbed him."

"Yes," Jack concurred. "I know."

"At the same time, he was his own worst enemy."

"How do you mean?"

"Have you ever heard of Borderline Personality Disorder?" Ann Hudson asked.

"Yes," I have. Jack thought of Felicia. He was sure she had something along those lines. He'd spent a year or more before he left her researching the various kinds of mental illness, but she had steadfastly refused to reveal to Jack what the psychiatrist she visited three times a week had diagnosed. She'd seen shrinks for years, Jack knew, but he had presumed at first that she merely followed the fashionable trend of women in her class. Yet her erratic reactions, the explosive anger that she displayed when drinking, her penchant for various addictions and her surrender to hedonism had long ago convinced him she had some kind of mental illness. After lengthy research he had decided it was most likely BPD. He had settled on that only after they'd been divorced for years, but he was certain that was her problem. It didn't surprise him that Hudson had that sort of illness. In fact, it struck Jack that BPD explained a lot about Hudson.

"I had a wife who suffered from that affliction," Jack admitted.

"You did?" she asked, her face softening. "Then you know you have to have compassion for such a person?"

"Why?" Jack asked, hearing the edge in his voice. He had never felt anything but contempt for Felicia.

"It's not like they have complete control over their emotions," Ann Hudson said. "Ted had been neglected and abused as a child. No one ever really loved him till I came along." She looked so sad as she said that that Jack felt like holding her. "And I did the best I could, that is, till David came along. And then David needed me all the time. Don't you see?" she asked, tears gathering in her eyes. "I just wasn't there enough for Ted. He was so needy, and *I just wasn't there*." She looked so miserable and so alone that again Jack was struck with the need to comfort her, but he resisted the impulse. He did not want her to think he was taking advantage of her. Again the clock chimed, sending its reminder throughout the house. *Don't ask for whom the bell tolls,* Jack thought. *It tolls for thee.* She continued to sip her wine — a lovely statue, her face sculpted and white in the pale glow of the lamp. She looked as if she belonged in the oil paintings adorning the walls, proclaiming another time, another place besides this squalid New England community.

"He told me Yvonne had always understood him, but he knew she was wild, and that her addictions mattered more to her than he did. I probably could have come between them. I might have even been able to save him from himself, but I was so tired." She shielded her eyes with her hands, covering her face. "I just couldn't do it all. To me life was overwhelming. Sometimes I didn't know if I could go on, it was so hard." She listened for a moment, as if trying to gauge David's activity upstairs, then turned to face Jack, her eyes dark in the hollows the previous nights' lack of sleep had created. "So I let him stray because I was too frustrated and too exhausted to help him."

Jack thought of the wild and raucous parties he'd left Felicia at, when he'd returned to his study to write, oddly stimulated by the decadence she'd been enjoying when he left, and he supposed he was partially to blame for the woman's problems, too. It took two to cause estrangement that deep, he realized, and felt sad. He'd never considered it his problem before, but here was this generous woman accepting all the blame for her husband's transgressions.

"I knew what Yvonne was, and I let him go to her. I will never forgive myself for that."

"You weren't jealous?"

Ann Hudson smiled wanly. "I knew he loved me, but all that love was exhausting, too. I keep looking back on that and blaming myself. Just how can love be exhausting? It isn't meant to be. It should be uplifting, it should be joyous. Shouldn't it?"

"Yes," Jack said. "It should be a wild, ecstatic bestowing of spirit on another. The giving should be its own reward, certainly." Yet he, too, had felt worn out by the demands of love, and he wondered why. In a moment of self-understanding, he realized he'd spent a lot of his own life retreating from the responsibility of loving. For him, the needs of women were vast and engulfing, and a man had to protect himself from them or he'd be diminished by all the compromises of self and goals fulfilling those needs would entail. Satisfying any woman meant a loss of freedom he was not willing to relinquish. And so he resisted extending himself lest he lose himself. It all seemed so silly now, but to hear of another person who had made the same mistakes and thus denied herself the rewards of true love, he felt an overpowering sense of kinship that made him feel connected in a way he hadn't felt before, except with Miranda, whom he'd long ago lost, thanks to his own fears of engulfment.

"Ann," Jack said, reaching across the coffee table to place his hand on hers. "You can't blame yourself for not understanding someone as complex as Theodore Hudson." Jack thought of the young boy's memoir and longed to read the rest of it. The child had always felt alone, it seemed. Had his meeting Yvonne staunched the loneliness at all? Or had she merely provided a diversion from his fears? Jack wondered if he would ever know the answer to that question.

"He could be so engaging," Ann Hudson said. "So wonderful and so terrible. Everything would be going along well, and then suddenly, as if for no reason, he'd explode over some trivial incident. Those times I knew he was mentally ill, but I never knew what to do about the anger. It seemed to come out of nowhere, as if it had a life of its own. Without cause, even." She trembled. "The scenes then were beyond belief. I would look into his eyes, and I'd swear that for the instant I was looking into the eyes of the devil. It was not the face of the man I loved."

"And so you grew afraid of him?"

"Yes, I did. I never knew when he'd turn on me. It was all so unpredictable, and then he unleashed the cruelest comments, as if he took pleasure in destroying me. It would take days to get over the experience. I'd slump around the house, lose weight, cry, but it would seem like a nightmare, not something that really happened at all. It wouldn't happen for a while, and then once again, he'd lash out at me over something unimportant, and we'd repeat the same sorry dance."

"It sounds like you were abused," Jack noted.

"And I guess I was, but at the time I thought it must be my fault. Everyone loved Ted. No one else saw that side of him. I wasn't even sure I had the next day when I'd think back about it. I'd ask myself if I'd dreamed it or misunderstood something crucial. I just couldn't believe what I saw was the Ted I loved, the Ted I married. It was like I was hearing and looking into the face of a stranger."

"From what you say, he fits the profile of Borderline Personality Disorder, all right," Jack said. "If I were you, I'd try to move on and to remember his good side. That way you don't have to acknowledge his cruelty."

"Do people like Ted always have a good side?" Ann Hudson asked.

"They often have very seductive personalities; I guess that means people are drawn to them and like them."

"But they don't really have a lot of depth, do they?" Ann Hudson seemed to study Jack's face intently. It was obvious she banked considerably on his wisdom in this area.

"I'd say they deal with the world on superficial terms, at least emotionally. But remember your husband was idealistic. He had grand plans for mankind. Maybe people of extraordinary talents of his sort expend so much energy setting the world right that they have little left to bestow on others. Maybe their desire for connectedness simply isn't that important in the scheme of things." Jack thought about Hudson's compulsive search for self-gratification, and it made sense to him that this was his way of coping with the anxiety provoked by his idealistic strivings. A man who aimed so high surely had his fears of failure and unworthiness. Even a genius wasn't exempt from self-doubt, Jack reflected, feeling once more a tremendous compassion for the man.

"I guess that's why I grew away from him," she said sadly. "I didn't want to, but I did. It seemed I was always walking on eggshells." She stopped. Her eyes opened wide in understanding. "I guess that's at least part of the reason I was always so tired," she concluded.

"You were probably depressed."

"David said that once."

"Did he lash out at David?"

"Never. He had the patience to deal with him. Just not me."

"Maybe he could relate to the boy because he recognized the frightened child in himself. The shamed child, the lonely, misunderstood child." Jack understood that reaction. He'd seen it in others. He'd written about a character like that in his own book. He'd seen a lot of those kind of men, growing up in West Texas, his own father for one.

"Jack," Ann Hudson said suddenly. "Thank you so much for understanding Ted and for believing what I say. I know you'll write a fair book, and I know from reading your novel that you have a good understanding of human motivation. I'm taking your comments to heart, believe me. Now, I must get dinner for David. May I see you tomorrow?"

"Yes, of course," Jack said, rising. "As a matter of fact, I have someone I'd like you to meet." He didn't know he was going to do that, but it suddenly seemed imperative that Ann Hudson and Miranda meet. He had a sense that the two would connect in a meaningful way. He thought of Hudson's erratic treatment of his wife, of his inability to find fulfillment in relationships, of all the misunderstanding that surrounded the man, and he knew that Ann Hudson would benefit from the uncanny insight of Miranda. He longed for her insights himself, he realized, eager to see her at Claire's and to find in her perspective the answers to his own questions. He knew then that it was somehow through Miranda that he'd arrived at the insight into Theodore Hudson that he'd conveyed to the distraught Ann Hudson. It was through her agency that the truth of the man had presented itself at just the right moment today. There was a timing to actions in the natural world that made them work. Jack felt the miracle of today was somehow related to that. She had mysteriously communicated the results of her own knowledge at the precise moment the information was needed, and his own heart had retrieved them – a process so amazing and incomprehensible that he wasn't sure she or anyone else could explain it. He walked out into the thick New Haven dampness, heard the squeak of his shoes on the wet sidewalk, stepped into the car and drove through the streets of the city with a sense of accomplishment.

Chapter Twenty Eight

Jack drove around the downtown block near Claires's several times before parking the car. He still felt confused by the events of today and yesterday. Try as he might, he felt unbalanced, as if he were riding a bicycle over dangerous terrain. In his mind's eye the ghastly vision of Yvonne's final moments rose up to smite him again and again, without respite. He thought of Karen's quiet death, the breaths coming farther and farther apart, the jasmine candles smoldering on the window sill, belying what was going on in that quiet room high in the mountains above Leadville. She had shed her life calmly, clinging to her dignity and faith to the very last. He counted himself lucky that he had witnessed the peace that immediately took possession of her features. He had noted that transformation of her face even then, tormented by his grief and loss. He had supposed the event would teach him something, but then he had forgotten its seeming profundity as soon as the body was transported into town and the funeral arrangements had to be made. He had orchestrated a service which would have pleased her, he was sure, but the whole, wretched ordeal had been difficult; and more than once he had considered getting out of Leadville for his own psychic survival, but he owed Karen, and so he didn't let her down. Her friends had been comforted in that old Presbyterian Church, by the songs she'd selected and the verses Jack recited, favorites of both of theirs.

He supposed that death, however it occurred, was the biggest teacher of all. Once more his thoughts turned to the ugly room at the top of the stairs in the deserted house outside New Haven. It wasn't that he even wanted to know the sordid stories of the people who frequented the place, but he realized the truth of Hudson still hovered on the premises, obscured somehow in those profane walls. He knew he needed to finish the young Hudson's memoir first; then he must once more visit the house in the country. He was sure there were clues hidden there, overlooked by Miranda. It wasn't enough that Ann Hudson accepted her husband's dual nature; for Jack there was more to the story than a personality disorder, but what that could be he couldn't imagine. His mind drifted to Miranda's suspicion that Joline had gone to Las Vegas for an abortion, and that idea aroused his own dark thoughts. If Hudson had violated the girl, then despite Ann Hudson's loyal support of the man, Jack was once again uncertain as to whether he could finish the project.

The truth mattered, for sure, but to reveal the pathology of Hudson was still something he wasn't willing to do in print, even if he could bring himself to tell Ann Hudson the truth. He sensed in her frustration today a marked tendency to forgive the man his depravity in the name of mental illness. Jack knew he couldn't censor the dark acts of Theodore Hudson any more than he could whitewash his own shortcomings. No, if he were to finish the book, he would have to reveal the whole truth, and for him that would be unforgivable as well. He wondered that Miranda hadn't sensed the darkness surrounding the man from the beginning. With a start, he remembered Levy's question of Miranda: *"Are you holding out on me?"* All of a sudden, some things made sense. Miranda must know more than he or Levy. There was something she was keeping to herself, Jack decided. The realization made Jack angry. The idea that she would know about the dark side of Theodore Hudson and put Jack in the position of facing a terrible moral dilemma made him furious. The one trait Miranda and Jack had always shared was a Bible-belted, deep sense of right and wrong. He couldn't believe she would ignore the West Texas Code they had both been raised with, that had guided their lives over a half century. He felt the resentment grow till by the time he parked and walked into the restaurant, he was so angry he couldn't imagine having a civil conversation with the woman.

She had her back to him and was talking earnestly with Joline, whose face was serious and in the shadowed light looked gaunt, as if she were indeed ill. This surprised Jack since he had always noted her plump features, the robust color of her complexion, her clear, fresh expression. He doubted Joline was capable of lying, and that was surprising since she must have survived all those years on the street with a quiet cunning. Yet she seemed to value the truth for its own sake, Jack reminded himself, and Sam Levy seemed to recognize that trait in her as well.

Jack stood at the other end of the restaurant for moments before he approached their table. He couldn't see Miranda's face, but he imagined her vivacious features subdued by the information Joline was imparting. He couldn't hear anything coming from their table but a low rumbling, incomprehensible discourse, which told him its nature was deeply confidential. At last the two women looked up. Miranda's face was deeply flushed while Joline's was pale, and the dark spots around her eyes had deepened.

"I was right," Miranda said without preliminaries. When Jack said nothing in reply, she added quietly, "She did go to Las Vegas for an abortion."

Jack sat down in the extra chair, feeling a deep lethargy settle over him. It all seemed such a waste of effort at the moment to try to plumb the depths of another's life, to try to make it work in print, as if to write were to engage in a deeply contrived effort. Jack wanted to believe in his writing, to feel exalted by the truths he tried to impart, not diminished by them.

Joline said nothing. There were few customers in the restaurant, and all seemed preoccupied with their companions or their reading material. There was no music interrupting the quiet, no audible conversations or laughing. For Jack a palpable sense of expectation hung on the air among the three of them, as if some truth was to be spilled – beyond the disclosure of who sired Joline's baby or whether Hudson was a fraud.

"So did you have the abortion?" Jack asked, no longer comfortable with any knowledge that pertained to Theodore Hudson. He didn't want to know that this young woman who'd survived so much in her sordid life was capable of killing her unborn child.

Slowly Joline shook her head. She looked years older than she had just days ago, and the bright openness of her eyes withheld their customary light. "I couldn't do it," she said, looking down at her pale hands folded on the table. "It may surprise you, Jack, but I kept seeing Ted Hudson in my mind's eye. He would never have condoned such an act. He always preached the sanctity of the human fetus. I couldn't violate his wishes."

"You mean the baby was his?" Jack said contemptuously. He could feel the anger galvanize his entire body and knew if Hudson were there in that room, it was not beyond possibility that he would have killed the man.

Joline stared at Jack with surprise. Her pale features in the dim light suddenly came to life, the sad, depressed expression of moments ago replaced by incredulity and anger.

"How can you even think that?" she demanded, looking back and forth from Miranda to him. "It's enough that Miranda considered it, but you... you....*you*, Jack, should know I would never sleep with Theodore Hudson." With that, Joline rose from her chair and ran out of the restaurant. Jack watched her make her way down the street into the darkness before he turned to Miranda.

"What was that all about?"

"Well, you did insult her," Miranda pointed out. "How did you expect her to react?" There was no trace of anger or annoyance in Miranda's voice, but Jack felt terrible. He had indeed affronted the girl, and he wondered that he'd suspected her of sleeping with Hudson in the first place. He should have recognized a basic morality in the girl. He had to admit it was there.

"It's Levy's, of course," Miranda informed him. "She didn't want to burden him with the news. He wants to get through school before having children, and so does she."

"I should have known that," Jack said, feeling morose. "I wish to God I'd never come to this place. I feel so compromised, so dirty, so dishonest. Honestly, Miranda, I don't know if I can write this book after all."

"I know," she said. "I feel that way sometimes, too." She sipped from a half-empty cup of coffee and looked around the room. "I didn't expect it to go down this way..."

"What way do you mean?"

"Yvonne, you know..."

"Well, what did you know?" Jack remembered once more the earnestness that had marked that evening in Leadville, her impassioned plea for truth and service, and once again he felt betrayed by her naiveté, by her impulsivity or stupidity, he didn't know which.

"I knew about the circumstances under which he died. I knew about the dark mistress. I saw the filth, the squalor, but I *believed in him*." She looked off over Jack's shoulder to the young man serving up food at the counter. Her eyes took in his clean, open face, the white apron over his tee shirt and pants. She seemed to see into the young man's heart as well, his vague hopes and yearnings. Jack waited for her reply, knowing that Miranda had indeed believed in Hudson or she never would have embarked on this journey. That instant he set aside his suspicions and sat back to listen to her explanation, her take on things, which he'd wanted more of for days now. He needed her insight. Somehow this study of Theodore Hudson had derailed him, confusing him to the bitter core. He realized he was not in the proper frame of mind to pursue it further without Miranda's help.

"By now you must know that Analise is dead." She said this quietly, as if testing him.

"I didn't know that. How did you find out?"

"Hudson went to Belgravia years ago. She'd married and lived there, with her two children."

"So how did she die?"

"Cancer. Endometrial. She died young. It was hard on him because he still felt responsible for her. He'd spent years and a lot of money finding her, and then to find out she was dead was a terrible disappointment."

"What happened to her children? Her husband?"

"Hudson left a considerable amount of money for the children – to guarantee their education, but the father wouldn't let them come to America, even though Hudson tried to secure their emigration."

"It was good he did that." Jack studied Miranda's face, the familiar whited complexion and thick hair. Her eyes visibly softened and she reached over and touched his hand.

"Jack, you must believe that I would never lead you on a wild goose chase, nor would I be a party to your compromising your morals. I believe in the man and that what we're doing is important." She touched his lips as if to silence him. He felt the coolness of her fingers, like a balm to his own tortured ego. "Just call all of this an act of faith because that's what it is, isn't it?"

When he didn't reply, searching in his own mind for a sarcastic retort that would put her in her place," she smiled, and the years fell away from her face, reminding him of desert sage and all those discussions of writing back when they were young and not only writing but life itself was merely an act of faith they each indulged in every day. Since then he had become cynical of everything that couldn't be quantified, of anything that smacked of religion or sentimentality. Just give me the facts, he'd been saying for years, and that is what he wanted, nothing that would confuse him further, nothing that would suggest ambiguity or the need for imagination or hope or any excessive emotion. He could feel the deadness inside of him lift somewhat. It was almost as if he could feel it diffuse into a cloud of exhaust surrounding him but ebbing away into the far corners of the restaurant then wafting out the door as people departed. It was as if something heavy and odorous had seeped out of him, leaving him with more energy to carry on. He smiled back at Miranda, once more taken in by her certainty, her clarity of purpose that he had to admit marshaled his own tepid passion toward a higher purpose. He told himself it didn't matter because this time he knew that the experience truly was its own reward. That he and Miranda were in this together, united as they had once been, and that was something. That was the act of faith Miranda alluded to, and it did mean something. It meant a lot.

Jack told Miranda about Ann Hudson's reactions today. Jack still didn't know what to make of the woman, but he did know he cared about her and her son. Whatever happened he wanted the project to turn out to be to her advantage. He felt certain he wouldn't have gone this far if it hadn't have been for her quiet, supportive presence and the love for her husband he sensed beneath her disappointment and anger. That there was such a thing as true love, Jack had always doubted. Love, he had long ago decided, was born of human frailty, a poor substitute for certainty or self-confidence. He hadn't sought it since the debacle of Felicia, and he hadn't noticed its absence either. After Karen's death, he had assumed that quiet grace he'd experienced with her had been the real thing, but he wasn't sure about that. He wasn't sure about anything except that with her, he'd experienced less self-doubt. He'd felt free to express himself to her and others. That in itself had been a new phenomenon, after all. He'd coveted that and then seemingly lost it after Karen died. Now, mired in self-doubt once again, he would have given up if it hadn't been for Miranda's guiding light, her unflagging sense of what was right and true.

"I don't even know the woman," Miranda said of Ann Hudson, "but I still believe in her."

"Why?" Jack asked, stunned by her reaction. "Even after she admitted she knew he was mentally ill, after she admitted she knew about Yvonne?"

"I believe her precisely because she still loved Hudson, despite all his failings."

Jack tried to put his mind around that, but he couldn't. "What else did you find out?"

"More examples of Hudson's generosity. Money he gave sick people, poor people here in New Haven, more things he did for students. He did an awful lot of good in the world."

Jack thought of what Ann Hudson had told him about experimenting with the HIV virus. "He injected himself with HIV, you know."

"I'm not surprised, after what I've heard from associates, students." She took her notebook out of the canvas bag she carried with her and fumbled through it. "It's just so odd after all that negative stuff we heard in the beginning..."

"Did you set Levy straight on Hudson?" Jack asked.

"If you mean disclosing the source of his scholarship funds, yes. Why not? He needs to know the truth."

"How did he react?"

"He accepted it. Joline was here then, and she confirmed it." Miranda wrote something in a margin of her notebook and looked up at Jack. "I did find out Hudson had his detractors, but most of them were in competition with him. For department chair, for the subject matter of their publications, for prestige." She drummed her fingernails on the table impatiently. "All the usual motives."

"Then you think we should just gloss over the man's depravity and call it a day?" When Miranda said nothing, Jack persisted, "Well, do you? Do you?" He could hear the anger and frustration in his own voice, the perplexity, the resigned quality of possible compromise lingering in the air between them like rotting meat.

"No!" she said. "It's just I don't know yet, and until I do, I can't abandon him."

"You know about Yvonne, you know about the place in the country. What else do you need to know? Face it, he was a libertine, a disgusting human being, even if he did have his noble side."

"I'm not convinced he was as decadent as you think," Miranda said, her eyes glazing over like they always did when she accessed some way of thinking he would never understand.

"Did the University cover up the details of his death?" Jack asked.

"It appears so," she said, without pause. "But there were some other details..."

"Such as?" he asked, annoyed at her not telling him about them sooner.

"It wasn't an overdose that killed him," she said.

The rumor had been it was meth. Hudson had been known for using it as well as other drugs.

"It was meth, all right, but the dose was relatively light. It appears what killed him was the interaction of the prednisone he was taking for Addison's Disease and the high dosage of painkillers."

"How so?"

"Cerebral hemorrhage," Miranda said quietly. Tears had gathered in her eyes, and she wiped them away with her napkin. "He must have known he'd die that way. His sister had one, both of his parents, I guess. It was in the family—"

"That does change things a bit," Jack conceded, thinking of the inordinate pressures a man like Hudson faced on a daily basis. The man did so much — traveling, speaking, researching, writing, heading up his huge organization, it was no wonder that he'd die of a cerebral hemorrhage. In a flash, Jack felt contrite. He'd judged the man, and he'd been wrong. Not only had he underestimated the pressures the man dealt with on a daily basis, he'd overlooked the physical pain he endured as well. Jack knew what a baby he was by comparison, gulping aspirin at the mere presence of a headache.

"That doesn't mean he didn't have a dark side," Miranda said, wiping away yet another tear. "I guess he was quite human, if you know what I mean."

Jack thought about that. After all, what did he know? He thought of his own parents and those like them who'd lived out there lives in a one-horse West Texas town, oblivious of what it meant to communicate, to immerse oneself in a book or to pursue a higher education. Parents who wielded iron-handed tyranny over their children and saw that as virtue. Parents who feared teachers because they taught children to think and to question authority. People who died angry, convinced the government had let them down, that their neighbors were out to get them. Those same people believed that peace in the world could be secured only through war.

What did anyone know but the sense their own limited faculties had made of an unfathomable world? The realization of his own fallibility rose in his mind, as lethal as hate or ignorance or murder. He vowed he would never again struggle to grasp anything because too much of what one glimpsed from moment to moment was inscrutable, impervious to understanding, so why did man even try? He felt a curious sense of elation at the thought as if to apprehend that concept let him off the hook in the scheme of things. From now on, he could apply himself to the easy stuff, just the facts, man, as he'd attempted to in the past. He would avoid the arduous path to self-understanding because it was simply not for man to comprehend the eternal verities after all. The game of life had suddenly relaxed its demands, he told himself. He was no longer a prisoner of his rebel will but a tourist at a fancy road show, where the stakes were obvious. You just watched and then you went home and climbed into bed, energy spent, drugged into submission. You didn't have to work at raising your consciousness or discerning the relative merits of spirituality, you just lived, and then you died. If even the life of the great Theodore Hudson was subject to interpretation, then salvation or damnation were mere projections and thus without substance, *shadows*, as Plato would argue. He felt exhausted by the entire conundrum.

"I know what you're thinking," Miranda said, studying him with her all knowing eyes. For once he wanted to slap her for the ease with which knowledge came to her.

"I bet you don't," he said, the bitterness rising in his voice and casting its pall over the nighttime revelers seated at the restaurant tables.

"You must think you got it all wrong about Hudson, but you didn't."

"I feel I did."

"You understood what Yvonne was about. You knew a kind of evil when you saw it. You recognized the threat she posed. What you didn't understand was that she never got to him, not really."

"Then why did he associate with her? Why did he bother with the woman? *Why lower himself?*" He thought of Ann Hudson and David, and his heart still went out to them for the degradation they'd experienced, the lies, the dishonor, the insistent claims on their own righteous hearts. It all seemed so wrong and so unfair that Jack felt as if he would vomit from this cruel awakening.

Miranda's eyes on him were gentle, he noticed, chagrined. She must consider him an awful fool.

"Don't you see, he just wanted to *help* her? He must have thought that sooner or later his goodness would rub off on her, that she'd tire of the boredom and the selfishness her life was about." Miranda made a pretense of studying the handwritten menu above the young waiter serving food at the counter. "You pick and you choose," she said in a trance-like monotone. "Then you answer for those choices, but not in the way you expect."

"Come on," Jack said, impatient. "What is that supposed to mean? Why did Hudson bother with her? It was clear she wasn't going to change."

"But she did," Miranda insisted.

"Are you crazy?" Jack demanded. "How?"

"She reconciled with Joline. She stopped the drugs. What you don't know is that she closed down the house." Miranda fished in her bag and drew out several spiral notebooks, a book of poetry by Dylan Thomas, and a black and white picture of a baby lying on a white bedspread.

"Joline?" Jack asked.

Miranda nodded. "Before Yvonne gave her up."

"Did Yvonne know about Joline's life all those years?" Jack considered the woman a fiend for leaving Joline to her own devices on the streets of New York City, to end up in the countless foster homes Joline had described to Jack.

"She didn't tell Hudson about the baby until three years ago," Miranda said.

"So Hudson found her and made arrangements for her to apply to Yale?"

"Yvonne never knew till recently, but yes, he did that behind the scenes, apparently. Through Joline's counselor at school. Then a year ago he told Yvonne, when Joline joined his lab, and he grew to appreciate and love her."

"Was she Hudson's daughter?"

"No. It was always clear in Yvonne's mind who the father was, and it wasn't Hudson."

"I see," Jack said. "So why did Hudson tell Joline Yvonne was her mother? Didn't he realize how terrible that must have been for Joline, after she'd pulled herself up by the boot straps. It would seem to me the girl didn't need to know that information."

"You see, that's where Hudson was a student of human nature because he simply understood that both of those women needed to know the truth. He'd never known his own parents well, and he realized how much that had cost him. He believed the truth mattered, so he became involved. As it turned out, they both appreciated it."

"But Yvonne still died. That must have been terrible for Joline. So how did that help the situation? The woman must have been dying of AIDS for quite some time. You don't just suddenly get that disease."

"You're right, of course." Miranda thrust one of the notebooks at Jack. "Read for yourself how much the woman loved Joline."

Jack didn't want to read the journal. It was enough for him that Miranda knew the truth, but he didn't want to read the writings of the woman. "No thanks. I'll take your word for it."

"But you must read it," Miranda persisted. "It will break your heart."

So under her tutelage, Jack read the pages she'd marked. He was struck by one entry in particular, and it did wrench his heathen heart. The entry was dated 1962, and the ink was blotched from tears and ran all over the page in thick, murky cursive:

If it were Theodore's, a woman's flowing penmanship had written, I could at least have justified my mistake. But now it looks as if I am damned for my own callous selfishness. I didn't want to bring another into this terrible world, but I have done so, and for that I shall never forgive myself, I thought I loved Jake and he cared for me, but it was all smoke and mirrors. He used me and abused me, but I will not abort the child, no matter that it was a mistake. No, I will have the baby and I will give it up to a good family who will raise it and give it the love neither Ted nor I ever had. If only it were Ted's, I know he would have taken it under his wing, so kind and good is he, but I could never lie to him to gain his support, so I shall not tell him about this terrible thing I have done.

Later pages described how the young Yvonne spent seven months in a Catholic home for unwed mothers in New York City. Afterwards she returned to New Haven and resumed her relationship with Hudson. It was then that she stepped over the line, but he'd stood by her in his own way through the rehab efforts and the illnesses that afflicted her over the years. In thirty years she hadn't told him about the infant she gave up. Only after her diagnosis did she spill the terrible truth after a night of drugging in the house in the country. He'd been astounded, but he'd hired a detective and sought out the girl. According to Yvonne's journal, he'd brought the two together to ease Yvonne's fears of death as much as for anything. According to Yvonne, he'd understood the redemptive power of love. He'd known the relationship would transform Yvonne, and it had. Moreover, according to the journal, Yvonne had chosen the week Joline left New Haven to die. Although she hadn't taken anything to induce her death, she had simply given up.

I can't get out of bed without terrible pain. I have no energy. I simply exist to see Joline, but I don't want her to be here when I die. Ted understands this. He will help me through the ordeal. He realizes that for me now living is worse than dying. He won't help me to go, but he'll stand by me when I ease it along with the painkillers. He's ordered morphine, thank God. I'm such a baby about pain.

Pages later she described the death of Hudson.

I cannot believe he's dead. He was the most decent man I have ever known and now he's gone. Nothing will ever relieve the pain caused by his absence. I think of all the sorrow I caused him, and I know I will pay for that somewhere else, beyond this world, and I deserve to. Only he has stood by me in my aloneness. Only he has understood my alienation from the world. He is the only person who ever loved me. God grant him peace. He so deserves it.

His last cries were for Ann. Ann whom I have hated all these years. And the boy, David. I know I'm unwell in the head as I am in the body, for I have done terrible things to that woman, but now I am sorry, and I beg the Lord to forgive me my jealousy. Please bless Ann Hudson and the boy. Please forgive me...

And finally in larger-than-life letters at the top of one page, she wrote:

God bless Joline. Flesh of my flesh, daughter of my heart and soul...

Jack thought of the beautiful Negress, and although he did not feel the compassion for her he knew all God's suffering children deserved, he did feel pity for her. He read the page with a sense of the woman's new found purpose to gain a relationship with her daughter and her determination to spare Joline the horrible spectacle of her humiliating death. With that, Jack experienced a curious reserve of judgment, as if to withhold his opinion might mean he'd alter it as time went on. We all make mistakes, some of us more terrible ones than others make. We are defined by our mistakes, for sure, but how we deal with them must grant us some mercy, he thought, in a moment of gratitude that said to him there was still time to reverse the mistakes of a lifetime. One had to believe that; one had to cling to that thought as if to let it get away from you was to lose life itself. Yvonne must have thought about all that in her last gasps for breath in that blood-spattered bathroom, watching the life force wreak its mess upon the moldering walls, and yet she'd let go with some self-respect born of the desire to shield her daughter from the grim result of an unseemly life. Joline knew what Yvonne was, but the girl had forgiven her as surely as Ted had. There had indeed been a moment of mercy in that realization before Yvonne yielded up the ghost. After all, there had been Ted and there had been Joline. Someone had seen goodness in her, Yvonne must have realized, as she rose to meet her maker.

Chapter Twenty Nine

"So, you see, the woman wasn't so bad. She was just screwed up, and Hudson knew that and accepted her for what she was." Miranda took the manuscript from Jack and put it back in her bag. Around the restaurant, people were growing noisier. The theater crowd had spilled into the narrow ordering space, and the young man at the counter was busy. Jack noticed Miranda watching him again, and wondered what fascinated her about him.

"I might have fallen for a guy like that, if I hadn't been so crazy about you." She smiled teasingly at Jack, her beautiful mouth presenting a sensuous impression Jack found irresistible.

"What do you see in him?" Jack asked, curious. He had never noticed her stare at another man before, and the whole idea of it intrigued him.

"He's engaging," she noted. "He has a certain true-blue quality about him, which you have to admit is rare nowadays."

"I guess," Jack agreed, although he wondered why that was. When his generation came of age, everyone had seemed to value honesty. Even now, both he and Miranda would comment on that sort of thing: He's a *good man,* or she's a *good person.* He wondered when it had happened that people had stopped praising so-called goodness in others. It seemed the idea of the Golden Rule had disappeared from human discourse, that religion was a taboo subject, that it had somehow become politically incorrect to voice ones objections to abortion, or euthanasia, strident politics or feminism.

"I guess you and I are just old fashioned," Jack suggested. "Maybe we live by obsolete values."

"We certainly fought hard enough against the prevailing ones when we were young," she reminded him.

"Water under the bridge," he said. "We didn't know what we were doing. We didn't know who we were. We just got swept along in a wave of mass hysteria."

"You mean our opposition to the War?"

"That was a lot of it, but also the whole movement to combat social injustice." He thought for a moment. "Yet you have to admit that was a worthy cause."

"Indeed, but I think we messed things up a lot," Miranda said, a definable sadness overtaking her face, as if a shadow passed over her, extinguishing the light in her eyes. "We got good and bad mixed up. We stopped searching—"

"Speak for yourself," Jack said.

She looked at him quizzically, her eyes boring into his without judgment, just a curiosity he hadn't seen in years. Perhaps she hadn't found him interesting after he'd stopped writing and holed up in Leadville with a dying woman. Maybe Don Parrish read the *Kabala* and rode palominos along meandering trails in Hill County against the lush backdrop of a wide, blue Texas sky. Maybe he had a droll sense of humor Miranda appreciated while he, Jack, had no sense of humor. Maybe like the young man at the counter, Don Parrish exuded a simple moral code of acceptance and optimism. Jack saw all these qualities in Miranda herself, but to date he had criticized her for them. He had demanded complexity in his friends and of himself, but it was the sincerity of the kid behind the counter that Miranda admired, and Jack had to agree that those basic moral imperatives of their early upbringing still appealed to him, but they were rarely praised these days, seemingly anachronistic, he thought, with a creeping sense of disillusionment.

"Remember when we used to read Gibran to each other?"

Jack recalled how his own father had thrown out Jack's copy of *The Prophet* because it had lithographs of nude people. "I guess that shows how innocent we were then, considering we haven't read him since."

"I still read him," Miranda said, cocking her head and looking off into space. "He still speaks to me."

"Does Parrish read you poetry?" Jack asked. "Does he like the smell of mesquite and the sound of turtle doves in the morning?" He thought of the way she stole out of their apartment before sunrise and walked for miles alone, her face radiant when she returned. She had always made him coffee before he got up. The thought warmed him with its familiar recall of smells and the cramped, close feeling of intimacy their cozy apartment encouraged. He thought of her lazy nonchalance about housekeeping, the fights they'd had over her mélange of kitsch everywhere. It all seemed so silly now.

"He reads *my* poetry," she said softly. "He thinks I'm very good."

"Does he appreciate poetry in general?" Jack wanted to know that about the man. Parrish had been a thinker, all right, but Jack hadn't considered him an intellectual or a person inclined toward the arts. He'd been surprised to find Miranda considered him a desirable companion, but then Don Parrish had been taken with her from the first, Jack was certain now.

"Don's more concrete, if you want to know the truth. I find that endearing, actually. He's very true-blue."

"And that matters to you, I can tell."

"Yes, it does." Jack recalled the young Miranda, her easy acceptance of everyone. She'd always seen into the hearts of others.

He couldn't argue with that. It had been Karen's goodness that kept him, he knew. And it was still Miranda's genuine lack of artifice and commitment to what was just and true that held his respect after all these years. She was beautiful, all right, but it was her nature with its esoteric strand of curiosity and imagination that still appealed to him. She would be fascinating to any man, he thought, with a vague sense of disappointment.

"You and I have gone our separate ways," she said softly. "I guess I sometimes regret that."

"It had to happen," he said, wistfully.

"Why?"

"We needed to grow and sort things out."

"You did, I didn't."

"Would you have become a faith healer with me at your side, smothering your untamed ways?"

"Probably not," she agreed, looking down at the scarred table with its myriad of carved initials and decades of dirt. "I would never have wanted to leave Texas."

"And I *chose* to leave it," Jack said with such vehemence that he surprised himself. He'd never realized before how much the lazy farm town of his birth had constricted him, pulling at him, arousing a sense of frustration so profound that he fled it as desperately as one did a terrible marriage. He'd left and never looked back, returning for high school reunions and departing as quickly as possible. The old smells, the ruined houses, the dry, unyielding soil depressed him every time.

"Maybe you've made peace with it by now?" She was clearly asking him a question, and he could see a note of hope in her beautiful eyes, but he stopped himself from replying. He owed her the truth and not some disingenuous response.

"I'll have to think about that," he said, returning her candid expression. "I just don't know how I feel."

"When you do, let me know," she said, standing up. She gathered her things together while he rushed to organize his. Around them the restaurant had emptied somewhat, but a few stragglers sipped coffee and talked quietly.

They walked out into the night. The sky had cleared and the air smelled faintly of wet leaves. Jack looked up into the vast array of stars and felt hopeful. There was so much to learn in life, he thought, for once without a trace of regret. Above the neon and the diesel a thousand twinkling stars lit their way to the car. He took Miranda's arm and walked her gently along the rutted pavement. It was as if he could feel her heartbeat as they made their way along the street. Or maybe it was the sound of his own rapture, releasing itself at last.

"I want you to go with me to Ann Hudson's tomorrow," he said as he climbed into the car.

"Sure," she said, as if she had anticipated the invitation.

There was nothing else to talk about this evening, Jack thought, as he drove to the motel. They were talked out, and he was grateful that she didn't expect him to blather on about some insignificant subject to cover his own lack of interest in conversation. His mind drifted from one subject to another, an impressionistic survey of the past weeks, and he didn't even know if that was thinking or ruminating or merely taking in a series of tactile sensations, but the process altered him in ways he couldn't explain. It was as if he could feel a change at the cellular level, as if his body were metabolizing some kind of knowledge he couldn't communicate. His emotions soared, he could feel his heart trembling in joyful anticipation. Something mysterious and transformative was indeed taking hold of him, and it felt good.

They stood before the leaded glass door of the house on Whitney. A cool breeze blew across the open porch, and dried leaves gathered in tiny swirls along the sidewalks up and down the street. Jack thought of that first day, parked across the street when he watched Ann Hudson wheel her handicapped son down the sidewalk under a canopy of branches, the two so complementary in their ways that the scene had touched Jack and enabled him to relate from that very moment to the reserved woman who'd been the wife of Theodore Hudson.

"It is a beautiful old house," Miranda said, touching her hand to the elaborate carpentry. "I once wanted to live in a house like this."

"You never mentioned that to me," Jack said. He rang the doorbell and waited. Above them the birds sang out loudly over the traffic sounds.

"It's every girl's dream, I'm sure." Miranda laughed as if to dismiss that yearning as one that evolved as she grew up. "I wouldn't want it now."

"If you do, I'm sure Don Parrish can buy you one," Jack said, an edge to his voice even he could hear.

"Stop that," she said. "I'm not going to live in Don Parrish's house."

"I thought you were going to marry him and live in Dallas?"

When Miranda said nothing in reply, Jack persisted, a tremulous excitement betraying itself in the quavering of his voice. "I thought you loved him!"

"Maybe I do," she said. She paused, as if for breath, while the birds sang between them, filling the silence. "But I can't marry him."

"Why not?" Jack asked, perplexed. If she loved him, why wouldn't she reach out for the life she'd always wanted, that had eluded her till now? Jack could tell she loved the man by the way her expression softened when she spoke of him, by her ardent defense of him, by the countless times she rushed to call him despite Jack's annoyance at the unnecessary time she was taking up.

Before she could answer him, Ann Hudson stood at the door, her hands outstretched to Miranda. She had on the familiar riding-style jacket and boots, and her hair was swept back by cloisonné combs. Jack had to admit she looked breathtakingly beautiful for a woman her age.

He introduced the two women then Ann Hudson led them back to the family room. "I'll get tea," she said, withdrawing. "Jack, show Miranda Ted's study, if you'd like. I found something she might consider interesting."

Jack dutifully led Miranda into the room that had now changed so dramatically it was hard to identify it as Hudson's. Instead it held pictures of birds, Audubon prints in beautiful walnut frames.

There were certificates of merit from David's school and a poster of Beckham, the English soccer player, on the fireplace where before the likeness of the young Ann Hudson had stood in all her finery, innocent of the sorrow that awaited her.

"It's a beautiful room, isn't it?" Miranda said, touching the rich paneling. The fireplace was burning, and the room smelled of pine. She picked up a leather copy of *Walden* and opened it. Inside it was inscribed *To My Dearest Son David from his father Theodore Hudson. May you learn to appreciate quiet hours alone in nature.* Miranda showed the inscription to Jack then set down the book and looked around. On the desk was a copy of Jack's book, propped up with bronze stallion bookends. Next to it sat a worn leather copy of Turgenev's *Fathers and Sons*, Dostoyevsky's *Crime and Punishment*, and a collection of Russian poetry. Jack opened them; they were marked with red ribbons. Hudson's careful hand had made notes in the margins.

"How nice," Miranda said, peering over Jack's shoulder. Behind them, coming through the door were the soft sounds of Mendelsohn. The music made him ache for Leadville and the quiet of the snug bungalow. He understood why Miranda didn't want to leave Texas. He felt the same way about his place in the mountains. He'd made it a home by living in it through good times and bad, and now a big piece of him remained there. He didn't think he could leave it after so much history had grounded him in that particular place. He looked over at Miranda, her face softened by the firelight, and he hoped they could work something out. It was clear that they had both gone their separate ways, and that was good, he thought. Sensing him looking at her, she smiled up at him, and he knew she felt the same way, that there was no need for them to share their thoughts. These days they thought as one, he realized, like an old married couple. He suppressed a smile and resumed his search of the room.

And then he saw what Ann Hudson must have meant when she said there was something in the study that would interest Miranda. On the hearth beneath the walnut mantle stood a thick photo album. Jack walked over to it and picked it up and carried it to the desk. While Miranda looked on, he slowly thumbed through the glossy pages of Theodore Hudson's life. There were photographs of his youth, with his serious parents, of Yvonne in her childhood, of Ann Hudson at Wellesley, of David as a baby, a toddler, a young man. There were pictures of Hudson speaking at various venues, of his and Yvonne's visits to foreign countries, of Ann wheeling David into various cultural events, of the Hudson house on Whitney, their garden out back, their social engagements. It was a large collection of the memorable moments in the man's life.

Jack was surprised that the collection included both of Hudson's lives, the one with Ann and David, and the one with Yvonne; and yet it affirmed the mutual acceptance of the two women for an unconventional arrangement that had apparently worked, however reproachfully another audience would view it. Jack wondered how the readers of his book would react to the man's unconventional life, to the paradoxes of the man himself. He believed the public would embrace the man nevertheless because of what he stood for — his relentless search for the truth behind physical phenomena and his steadfast efforts to alleviate human suffering. There was no higher goal. People knew that, and they would accept the truth of the man, just as Ann Hudson did. As Jack finally had.

Jack knew that all he had to do was organize the vast amount of information, and the book would tell its own story, without effort. He no longer doubted his ability to dramatize the man's life; he no longer doubted Hudson's claim to fame. More than anything he wanted his book to reflect the very contradictions he'd found so troubling at first. Here was a man whose contributions had changed the world and would continue to do so. Yet here was a man whose character had the same limitations of all men, when you thought about it. Hudson had not allowed his despair to cloud his goals or to camouflage the truth. In that sense, he had been a true hero, and to that purpose Jack would devote his book. And he would do so without compunction. He breathed a sigh of relief. The past had resolved itself.

The three talked all afternoon, and just as Jack had predicted, the two women got along well. Their synergy released itself in a vibrant exchange of communication. Jack found himself simply sitting back and taking it all in. He thought of the young David whose life would be cut short by physical limitations beyond his control, of Joline whose will had propelled her beyond her station in life. He thought of Yvonne and her inability to recognize her value till forgiveness and a belated sense of responsibility enabled her to achieve a sense of purpose in her life. He saw Levy and the frenetic shifting of his eyes, as if he couldn't rely on the world to remain stable from moment to moment, a testimonial to deep seated fear, of Ann Hudson subdued by an overwhelming sense of duty she found hard to deliver. He thought of Miranda and her constant faith in the face of her own suffering and that faith which she witnessed daily in the eyes of her congregation, of Don Parrish and his withered arm and dying idealism. Mostly in his mind's eye he saw the confused eyes of Theodore Hudson whose talents were legendary but who could not endure the discomfort of human intimacy. For him, Jack almost wept. For him, Jack would write his book, and he hoped to hell it would do the man justice.

Jack drove Miranda by the house in the country for the last time. They got out of the car and stood below the concrete stairs, looking up at the naked wood and sparse shingling, at the rotting porch, the blackened, crumbling masonry of the chimney. Eventually the old house would fall down upon itself or be swept away in preparation for a new housing development. The sun shown on the smeared windows and followed anonymous footprints through the mud and grass. Above the scarred front door, white curtains parted the darkness behind the window of Yvonne's room. Miranda took Jack's hand, and they stared at the spot for a long time, remembering that fateful night when a lonely woman succumbed to a horrible death. She hadn't died in vain, instead ransoming as it were a belated grace. What had gone on in that house was now as much history as Yvonne's wasted body or Hudson's Nobel Laureate. Jack was reminded of his own lofty ambitions, quelled by time and failure. Miranda shivered in the cold, and Jack put his arm around her.

"You realize Hudson's visit to me was a plea for forgiveness, don't you?" Miranda's eyes searched his for validation. Her body continued to tremble beneath his arm. In the muffled roar of far off traffic, her voice remained strangely calm and clear.

"I do," Jack said, thinking of his mother and her empty expression when he told her he was leaving Texas for good. She had turned from him and disappeared into the house without a word. He'd thought that strange at the time but had attributed it to her feeling sad about his departure. She hadn't been sad, he realized, only relieved, and he wondered at that now with the birds cawing overhead and the ancient house hemorrhaging its earthly woes. Hudson had died, forsaken in this terrible place, but his legacy would not be forgotten.

He looked down at Miranda. Her eyes were still on him, plumbing the depths, as she always did. They mirrored the gray of the late afternoon, the drabness of the old siding, but they were bordered by the tiny lines of amusement he knew so well. Forgiveness comes in so many forms," she said.

"It does," Jack agreed, thinking of the road leading past the dingy Texas home of his childhood. There had been no trees there, as if the hard ground would not yield the sustenance a single tree required. He'd go back and plant a tree there on the abandoned property – *for her.* He sighed heavily, and Miranda squeezed his hand in reply. "It feels better, doesn't it?" she asked, knowingly.

He nodded and stood there some more, staring at the old house as if it harbored a million secrets that he could fathom, if he just took the time and looked deeply enough. The gray light turned to black, and still the two stood facing the house as the night slowly swallowed the decaying structure and the sky filled with tiny pin pricks of light. The night was cool, and the birds sounded pleasant as Miranda led Jack to the car.

The last image Jack had as he climbed into the car and glanced once more at the neglected expanse of property was of the full moon, a luminescent mandala, bathing the aged structure in a supernatural radiance. Light and dark mingled on the roof and seeped into the nooks and crannies, shadowing the details of the Victorian architecture. Alone except for the trees which provided it some protection from the elements, the house stood tall against the insults of time and circumstance.

Jack started the car and drove toward town. He glanced over at Miranda and thought of their early years as a couple when being together was all that mattered to them. When the heights of joy were long walks along dusty roads or a movie at the local cinema. He yearned for those simple pleasures or at least the capacity to be fulfilled by them. Life had become so complicated that it was hard to recapture the elation of fighting for a just cause or submerging one's own petty desires for the betterment of another or even indulging a capricious lust. As incomprehensible as it was to a generation so full of itself, they had somehow lost their way in going where they had to go. Yet Jack now knew with certainty that it wasn't over till it was over, and he wasn't about to give up. He still had miles to go before he slept. For one brief moment, the image of Theodore Hudson rose in his mind, and he knew he would never again forget what he indeed once knew — before he forgot and the whole, damned miserable struggle began.

Remember Me.........

Printed in the United States
By Bookmasters